Hi, I'm Jonathan - Jon to you. Once from the leafy greens of Limerick, Ireland, I now live in the medieval city of Toledo, Spain, a town steeped in legends and ghost stories. I normally can be found at the local cemetery. But for god's sake, don't sneak up on me, as I'm of a nervous disposition. I have a BA in Literature. I'm a member of the Horror Writer's Association (HWA). I am the author of horror novels *The Squatter* and *Billy's Experiment*. New horrors *Crazy Daisy* and *Hotel Miramar* coming 2023!

The Squatter

by

Jonathan Dunne

Dedication:-

To my daughter Erin, a little girl with a big heart of gold.

1.

Just a few weeks before it happened on live television, Molly Greene was writing the short and not-so-sweet sign on the back of an ill-omened menu specially drawn up for that night's bill of fare. That's how suddenly all of this had come tumbling down. Her financial advisor had called her earlier in the evening, warning her of the implications of keeping the restaurant open one more night. Molly had chosen the last night of the year — tonight — as a make-or-break night. It turned out to be break night. She dabbed her teary eyes and face, then slammed the napkin onto the table in disgust. It looked back up at her with two ominous, grim mascara smudges for eyes and a turned-down lipstick streak for a smile.

Molly huffed a weary chuckle through her tears. 'Me, myself, and I.'

The profound silence in the dim light of the defunct restaurant hit her for the first time as she sat there alone. There was a time when this place was alive with the buzz of chatter, cutlery, and the occasional crash of a plate — always a good sign… busy waiters drop plates. The Michelin star restaurant was a cold shadow of its former self, empty and in darkness, save for the light filtering in from the street outside. Molly sat at her favourite table. On any other night, she'd be sitting at this same table, closest to the cash register, tallying up her generous takings, but not tonight. She'd been stood up. Not by Mike, that would be impossible — he was gone almost three years, but by her government and its absurd red tape. And what about this curfew? Wow, how ridiculous is that?

All these thoughts, along with darker visions, flitted through the synapses of Molly Greene's brain as she wrote the note on the back of the fancy menu while heaving doleful sobs of remorse and regret. It wasn't only that she was forced to close her prestigious restaurant doors, but there was something else she couldn't face right now…something that cut deep. It seemed anyone who had ever mattered had abandoned her wholesale. And the closing of her Michelin star restaurant? Why, that was just the poisoned cherry on this delicious cake of shit, of course.

What's wrong, Mommy? Why are you crying?

Molly flinched and squeezed her eyes shut in a vain attempt to stop the beautiful voice in her head. It was funny how she never saw her little boy like she saw Mike, yet Mike never spoke, whereas Henry did. Well, that's not true either…Mike spoke, but when his lips moved, he spoke in Molly's voice-of-reason. Henry walked right into her head without knocking first. And his little voice came when Molly was at her lowest, to kick her while she was down. The only way she could drown out his voice was to drown herself, in alcohol, so she took a heady gulp of wine from the glass at her table.

She added a full stop to the end of the sign, feeling like the full stop had also just ended Molly's brief, forgettable role on this planet. She stared long and hard into her deep glass of red wine, compliments of the house. They say answers can't be found at the bottom of a wine glass, but the wine sure can block out those unending questions. To stymie another bout of tears, she knocked her drink back in one gulp. The intoxicating heat of the distilled grape juice rose up her chest and neck. What a glorious way to finish 2020. 2018 was dedicated to grieving and trying to get over the car accident. 2019 was pledged to pretending she was getting over the disaster. And 2021? Who knew what lay in store?

Molly went in around the counter and picked up a second bottle of 1981 Bordeaux vintage '81 — one last perk of the job and someone has to drink it. As she went to pour herself another goblet to drown her sorrows, she instead tried to sink herself by pouring the contents of the bottle over her head. Some of the alcohol went down her gullet, but mostly it gushed down her blouse and collected in her soggy bra. Molly Greene looked as if she'd been stabbed, and in a lot of ways, she had.

In the background, Bing Crosby was dreaming about a white Christmas, but that's all Bing was doing — dreaming — in a simmering world where pollution was putting snow into a Snow in a Can. Molly Greene, too, was fantasising about what could've been.

Drenched, she joylessly raised her empty wine bottle, toasting nothing to nobody, before crooning, 'I've been dreaming of a shite Christmas!'

What's wrong, Mommy?

Molly snapped her head around, expecting to see her little boy standing there amongst the tables and chairs. 'Henry,' she slurred, 'what did I tell you about sneaking up on people, hmm?' Her thoughts then turned to her deceased husband, as they so often do in times like this. 'Mike, oh, Mike, what am I going to do, hun?'

Mike was still nowhere and everywhere. She tried to imagine what her late spouse would say. Then again, would Mike offer his wife advice after what happened back in 2018? Would he bear a grudge? Probably not, and that's what made it even worse.

Pulling her coat over her wine-sodden clothes, she collected her things. She then taped the reversed menu onto the door, announcing:

Permanently Closed.

Thank you to all our wonderful customers for making this dream come true. Thank you to our wonderful government for shooting down that dream.

She locked the door behind her for the last time, sullenly muttering, 'Sorry, Mike. Sorry, Henry.' Not only had she let herself down, but she had let them down as well. After all, if it hadn't been for the life insurance money, how else would she have opened a Michelin star restaurant?

Without looking back, Molly staggered across Halpin Street. She took her car fob from her handbag, beeped the BMW open, and sat in. Only now did it hit her how tipsy she was as she searched for the ignition button was. Jesus Christ, how could she be even doing this? After everything she'd been through… after everything she'd put her family through, and that was saying something. And now here she was, a no-good drunk on New Year's Eve.

She slammed the steering wheel before getting out and then banged the door behind her, which landed her on her ass on the street. With zero dignity, she picked herself up and locked the car. The number nine bus would come by in a few minutes. This wasn't the first time Molly Greene had opted for public transport, too liquored up to drive.

As she sat at the bus stop on that freezing night, cold and miserable, just wanting to get home to hold her three girls, Molly made a drunken promise to herself. Would she even remember it in the morning? It didn't matter; it's the thought that counts. Molly promised herself that 2021 would be a year of change.

The bus pulled in. Molly swayed to her feet and fell onto the bus.

Yes, 2021 would be a year of change. Just how much change Molly wasn't to know. Perhaps she wasn't meant to know.

2.

The following Friday morning, New Year's Day, Molly Greene woke to the pointed tip of a mawkish dagger of a hangover held to her temples. Deciding she wasn't ready to face the new year, Molly lulled herself back into a light sleep and—

'Happy New Year, Mommy!' boomed Emma's voice.

'Oh, and you too!' Molly tried to muster up a little enthusiasm as her four-year-old launched herself across the room and crash-landed in her mom's bed. The child flinched as a waft of stale alcoholic breath came from her mom's mouth. 'Your breath stinks, Mommy! Blah!'

Jesus, talk about out of the mouths of babes. Molly felt low, so low. Her breath must be rank. A cold nausea bubbled inside Molly. She was going to puke in front of her child. Molly leaned over the edge of the bed, gagging. But seeing her bloody blouse and bra strewn on the floor, along with everything else she'd left in a pile, was such a shock the empty retching stopped. It was only then she recalled how she had taken an impromptu wine shower, trying to drown herself in her own unsold vintage red.

'Oh, fuck…' she muttered. 'Fuck…fuck…fuck…'

Jesus Christ, everything had become an excuse to drink. Good news? Yes, let's celebrate, why not, chin chin! Bad news? Boo-hoo, let's drown our sorrows, why not, chin chin! She donned her first brave face mask for the day. 'Did you have fun with your sisters and Janice last night?'

The child giggled. 'We played hide and seek. Cora hid behind the curtain in the living room, but just her head. She thought we couldn't see her. Then we had a disco. I was in charge of the cloakroom and finger food.'

Molly couldn't help but laugh. 'Wow! Sounds great. Where are your sisters?'

'Asleep.'

'And Janice?'

'She's asleep too. Louie is awake, though.'

Molly was about to snicker again, but the build-up of pressure brought on an instant migraine. 'So, the babysitter is asleep, but the cockatoo is awake?'

Emma nodded. 'Uh-huh.'

Molly smiled and hugged her youngest daughter. She often wondered if Emma's twin brother would've been anything in character like Emma. They were born twins, so he would have that same owlish look. Molly had created an imaginary composite of his face. Her instinct told her Henry wouldn't have been anything like his twin sister; Emma's big character made up for losing her twin, Molly liked to think. Maybe she was fooling herself.

They rested in Molly's bed for another half hour. Molly tried to savour the moment, but as she caressed her daughter's silky blonde hair, she wondered what the fuck she was going to do with the rest of her life, and it was still only 1 January.

A knock on her bedroom door broke her from the stream of desperation. 'It's open.'

Janice popped her head around the door. 'Happy New Year!'

Molly put on another brave face — one of many masks she wore daily. 'Happy New Year, Jan.' She struggled to find any enthusiasm, sinking into her drawn apathy. 'Were the girls good for you?'

Janice smiled at Emma. 'They're always good for me.'

Emma smiled and snuggled up to her mom.

'Thanks, Jan. When are you going to accept payment from me? It's unfair to rely on you every time I have to work…' That's okay because there is no work anymore…

'Psh,' Janice waved away Molly's suggestion. 'I told you I love spending time with the girls. Anyway, you already pay me to be a waitress. Coffee?'

Shit. 'Sorry?'

'Do you want a coffee?'

'Oh, that would be heaven. Strong, Jan, make it black.' She answered in a resigned tone. 'I've got some…news,' she added with hesitation.

Janice nodded, then flashed a concerned look at the bundle of smelly clothes on the floor by the bed. 'I don't like that word: news.' She kept staring at the pile of crimson, crumpled clothes.

'It's not blood before you ask.'

Janice smiled wanly. 'I wasn't going to ask.'

This answer unnerved Molly, as if Janice wasn't counting out anything anymore.

'Breakfast?' Janice asked Emma. 'How about those chocolate monster thingys?'

8

'Yummy!' rejoiced Emma, leaping out of the bed and followed Janice downstairs.

Molly lay there for a moment, appreciating the good friend she'd found in Janice, who had become a shoulder to cry and lean on. Janice lived just down the street. But after the accident, she had practically become a live-in nanny at the Greene's place. Molly had hired Janice to be a waitress at the restaurant, but she'd become so much more. Janice hadn't worked at the restaurant the previous night. Molly would have to deliver the bad news this morning.

She hauled herself out of bed, still not ready to look at the day in the face. The stinking pile of clothes was dumped directly into the washing machine in the utility room. She showered and cleaned herself up, donned a little masking make-up while thinking about the Beatles' 'Eleanor Rigby' and how she kept her face in a jar by the door.

Downstairs, Molly met her other two daughters, Mina and Cora. They were in their pyjamas, curled up on the sofa, playing Minecraft.

'Happy new year!' Molly smiled a rictus grin.

It didn't matter, though. All she got back was a droning, 'Happy New Year…' because the girls were too engrossed in mining gemstones and adding extensions to their virtual pads. Louie, the cockatoo, however, gave Molly a wondrous morning greeting with his daily, ''Allo…'Allo…'Allo!' from the perch in his spacious cage in the kitchen's corner. His raised golden crest was like a folding and unfolding Spanish abanico. The Greenes had adopted the bird a month after the accident — the accident being year zero in Molly's life, divided into before and after. One night, Janice and Molly enjoyed a harmless drunken giggle when Janice suggested a cockatoo had replaced Mike. Molly saw the funny side of it, but she was struggling.

Janice shoved a steaming mug of coffee in front of Molly. 'There, drink that. I'll join you, but then I must be off. Things to do, you know yourself.'

'Um, Jan, we need to talk.'

Janice stiffened as she sipped her coffee. 'Oh?'

'I've been putting it off for a few weeks…months. The latest lockdown is the final nail in the coffin — my coffin.'

Janice put her mug down and sighed. 'I was waiting for this. The restaurant, right?'

Molly nodded. 'My financial advisor told me one more night of losses would shut the place. I thought by getting Pedro,' Pedro being Molly's Michelin star chef, 'to draw up a special New Year's Eve menu, that might draw the punters. But the government has scuppered my plans with their absurd rules and regulations. Special menus need special ingredients. I have to shut the place down to cut my losses. I have no choice but to close Molly's. This pandemic has been detrimental to the hostelry business.' She swore into her mug of coffee. 'Just when we were starting to take off. Christ! I'm so sorry, Jan.' As an afterthought, she added, 'I'm going to pay you for your babysitting services. Maybe it'll go some way to making up for your lost waitress wages.'

'Don't be silly. I love the girls; they're my friends.'

Tears came to Molly's eyes. 'You'd be a better mom than I ever will be.'

'Well, now you're being silly.'

What Janice didn't know — what nobody would ever know — was that little Henry would have been with them here on New Year's Day, right now, if Molly hadn't fucked up on a grand scale. Molly Greene was taking that secret to her grave. Mike and Henry had already taken the same secret to theirs.

Janice racked her brain for ways in which Molly could keep the restaurant on standby, but Molly shot down every proposal. Janice suggested crowdfunding on Patreon, and Molly responded by snorting laughter into her mug.

'So, what's your plan?'

Molly shook her head despondently. 'I'm not sure, but I know this: I need to find a job to keep this roof over our heads. This mortgage is going to cripple me. Or I need to sell up, that's another option.' She paused. 'Thank Christ I was renting the restaurant premises. I had plans to buy it, y'know? Touchwood I didn't.' Molly tapped the leg of the table. 'I've got some savings to tide me over.' She looked around the kitchen, ,wishing Mike would saunter through the kitchen door to help her. She could see them both, right now, waltzing around the kitchen to Eugen Doga's haunting 'Gramophone'. As she watched that lovely couple dance around the kitchen island, she said, 'I think I want to sell up.'

'You do?'

Molly nodded. 'This place is full of ghosts.'

'Well, it just so happens that I know a couple looking for a house in this neighbourhood. I'll let them know, shall I?'

'Hmm? Yeah, why not.'

'You sure? I don't want to tell these people your house is for sale only for you to change your mind.'

Molly considered her friend. 'The more I think about it, the more sure I am.' She paused before opining, 'This could be a sign, Janice.' She gazed into her mug of black coffee. 'This isn't working. I need hair o' the dog right now.'

Janice wasn't as fast to grab the half bottle of wine on the counter as she had been with Molly's coffee. 'You won't find answers at the bottom of a glass.'

'Who said anything about a glass?' asked Molly as she got up from the table and chugged from the bottle. She wiped wine from her lips, casting a sidelong glance across the kitchen, just to make sure the waltzing couple was still there. They weren't. They were never there when Molly was drinking.

Janice stayed quiet for a moment, her lips pursed as if determined not to say anything, and stared off into space, but she just couldn't hold it in any longer. 'It's the first of January and it's better to start the year off on the right foot, even if that meant hobbling at the beginning. 'That's your real problem right there,' snapped Janice. 'I promised myself I wouldn't mention it, but someone has to say something, Moll. You've got a drinking problem.'

Janice's outburst shocked Molly. She drew up

12

defensively. 'No, I don't. Look…' She made a point of finishing the bottle of wine, then slammed it onto the counter so hard that Emma, who had been engrossed in her chocolate monster thingy cereal, startled, which sent the contents of her spoon up her nose and down her pyjama top. She gawped at her mom as her bottom lip curled downwards, not knowing whether or not to cry.

Reaching for a towel, Molly apologised. 'Oh, I'm sorry, baby!' She kissed her head and started cleaning her child's face.

Janice wasn't done yet. 'I'm giving you a friendly warning. Make 2021 the getting-your-shit-together year.' Janice shut her mouth, but just couldn't keep in the rest of the words screaming to get out. 'And you know something else, Moll?'

'You're going to tell me anyway,' Molly back answered as she wiped down Emma's pyjamas.

'I'm glad the business folded. I'm happy for you!'

'And what the f… does that mean?'

'That restaurant was dragging you down.'

This was the last thing Molly thought she would say. 'Janice, we were in the newspapers. Food critics loved our food. We were making good money.'

'Yes, true, but at a price you could never pay back.'

Molly took umbrage at her remarks. 'Look, I've got a bastard of a hangover, Jan. No mind games, please.'

'Christ! Really? A hangover? What other proof do you need? How can you be so oblivious, Molly?'

By now, Cora and Mina were shooting surreptitious glances over the back of the sofa in the living room towards the kitchen.

'The restaurant was turning you into an alcoholic. Has turned you into an alcoholic. You were drinking more wine than your guests were.' She flashed air commas. '"A little tipple here" and "a little tipple there". You ended up drinking the cooking sherry! You could've been crepes flambé if someone held a match up to you!'

Molly felt the tremble of laughter coming on, but swallowed it.

'We were concerned for you, Moll. Y'know, we were going to stage an intervention.'

Molly's brain wasn't able to keep up with these vicious pearls of revelation. 'We? Intervention? Who is we?'

'Us, the staff, even your precious Michelin-quality chef, Pedro, was in on our little secret. Every minute you turned your back to have "a little tipple" we were devising a plan on how to intervene. We know what you've been through and it's a delicate subject, but, Christ, someone had to do something! I think you would've lost the business without a lockdown. Every pandemic has a silver lining.'

'Jesus, what's wrong with everyone?' cried fifteen-year-old Mina, eyes stuck on the TV screen.

'Nothing, love,' Molly assured her. 'We're just… talking.'

Cora rebutted with her familiar dry wit. 'Thank God we all don't talk like that.'

Molly told her girls to go back to their mining and killing sheep, or whatever it was they were doing.

'And I know you won't want to hear this,' continued a fired-up Janice, 'but when…' she lowered her voice, '…was the last time you sat down with them,' she gestured to the girls, 'and asked them how their day was? They grow up so fast, Molly. You're going to miss out on their childhoods. A mom needs to be there…'

Molly's tone turned venomous. 'Don't you dare! You just waltz in here every now and again, and think you can judge? We can take up this convo again when you're a mom and you see the reality…' She regretted it the very moment the toxic words left her lips. Janice couldn't have kids of her own. 'I'm sorry. That wasn't called for.'

Janice acknowledged her apology. 'I'm sorry too. I crossed the line. But I still think you need to face whatever it is you're running from, Molly. I love you to bits, you know that, but you need to get this out of your system once and for all. Leave it back in fucking two thousand and twenty.'

'Mommy,' Emma interrupted, pointing at Janice, 'Janice said fucking.' The four-year-old made air commas around the swearword, which made them laugh, especially because Emma had been using air commas around everything.

'Yes, I know Emma. But you don't need to repeat it.'

Janice apologised to the child. 'I'm sorry, you're right, Em.' Janice slapped the back of her hand and

Emma giggled, which helped the anger in the kitchen dissipate.

Emma left the table and galloped off towards the living room, leaving the two women in silence at the kitchen table.

'Jan, I've decided. I'm going to sell up. It's not too late to restart this year. Kill two birds with one stone, financial and mental reasons are why I should no longer be in this house. Going to kill all kinds of birds…' she called across at Louie, 'So, watch yourself!'

The cockatoo squawked back at her and they shared a cautious laugh.

In that moment of weakness, Molly wanted to tell her friend she was feeling doubly sad and regretful about the closing of the business because she had opened Molly's with the pay-out she received from her husband's life insurance policy. Not only had she opened her dream restaurant with blood money, but she'd been integral in the shedding of that blood. Molly Greene had let Mike down twice, once in life and now in death. But what she really wanted to tell her best friend was how little Henry just kept on waltzing in without being invited. Of course, it was a figment of her imagination, but her dead child always popped up when least expected and she was a nervous wreck because of it, Molly had never gotten over the car accident, but Molly refused to allow her grief to metastasise into a downward spiral of depression. The restaurant, funnily enough, had kept her afloat.

Janice pointed at the empty wine bottle on the

counter. 'Promise me you'll make that your last drink. It's still not too late to make your new year's resolution.' Not waiting for Molly to promise it would be her last drink, Janice knocked back the dregs of her coffee and got up. 'Now,' she said in that merry way of hers, 'I'm glad we've had this little heart-to-heart. I'll love you and leave you. I've got an empty fridge that needs to be filled, blahdy bah blah.' Janice collected her things, said a curt goodbye to the girls, then kissed Molly's head on the way out. 'Sorry for the tough love,' she whispered.

Outside the front door, Janice burst into lamenting tears. An overwhelming sense of loss consumed her for no apparent reason.

That afternoon, the Greenes went for a brisk walk along Sandycove beach on the Dublin coastline, to blow away the cobwebs of 2020 and to take in a lungful of fresh air for the coming 2021. The icy wind cut through them, but they were together. Molly looked at her girls, really looked at them for the first time in what seemed like a lifetime, as they danced, cart-wheeled, and giggled. After all, they'd been through, they deserved a good mom, but Molly didn't deserve them. It was odd, but even though the Greene's livelihood was shut down, Molly was experiencing a deep and great sense of freedom on Sandycove beach; a catharsis as the waves rolled in and out. Thinking about the near future was daunting, yet there was an overriding sense of galloping into the unknown; an electric adventure that carried some sense of hope. Her heated chat with Janice had done her the world of good. Janice always said that one could change their whole life in the blink of an eye, just by adopting a positive attitude. That had sounded like self-help bullshit to Molly, who needed no help, but as she gazed out to sea, she realised Janice was right. The crashing waves entranced Molly. She thought about a lot of things while Cora and Emma laughed their heads off and happily dragged seaweed along the shore while Mina scrawled their initials in the sand: MG...CG...EG...MG. But Molly's dreamy smile faltered as she realised two names were missing: another MG and HG. The rushing tide came in over their initials. When the current receded, it was as if the Greene family (what was left of it) had never existed.

3.

Molly Greene popped the homemade lasagne dinner into the oven around 6pm that Friday evening. Cora and Emma were in the living room. Molly wasn't sure what they were up to, but she could hear them laughing and that was good enough for her. Mina was upstairs in her bedroom where she spent most of her time these days, chatting with friends online. With the pandemic restrictions, face-to-face contact was becoming less and less a reality and the reality was becoming virtual. Molly had always hated social media. The amount of time her daughter wasted on the phone, gawping at yawning pigs on TikTok, annoyed her no end.

While the lasagne baked and the girls were doing their own thing, Molly decided it was time to fetch the plastic folder from the wardrobe upstairs. It was something she had been putting off.

She laid all her affairs out in front of her on the kitchen table, work contracts, policies, insurances, and the house mortgage. She quickly concluded she could make a clean break if — and it was a big IF — she could sell her house. The sale of the house plus her own savings would set them up in another life until she found other work. As she sat there looking over the paperwork, that niggle of languid fear bristled inside Molly. No matter which way she added, multiplied, subtracted, or divided, the same answer always came up. The numbers told her she had to move, considering the high living cost in the capital, and nobody was hiring in the hostelry sector now.

By the time the lasagne was ready to be served, Molly Greene knew what she had to do. There wouldn't be any estate agent open until Monday, but she needed to feel like she was moving forward (despite being secretly afraid she'd only talk herself out of it if she actually stopped to think). She quickly googled real estate agencies in her area and called the first one on the list. Her call went directly to the agency's voice messaging service and an operator quickly collected her contact details and told her the information would be passed along to an estate agent. She felt the compulsion to explain why she was selling up, but she hung up before making an ass of herself — Molly tended not to know when to stop talking when leaving a voice message.

'Good!' She clapped imaginary dust off the palms of her hands as she felt more weight lift from her shoulders. She didn't get that sinking feeling of regret once she put the phone down. The trickle of fear she'd experienced moments ago had been replaced by exhilaration. Happy that things were moving forward, Molly called the girls for dinner.

Only five minutes into dinner, Molly's phone buzzed on the table.

Mina snapped, 'Don't answer it.'

Molly flashed a I'm-the-mom-in-this-house smile of condescension at her eldest daughter. 'Hi, Janice.'

'Hey,' Mina complained, 'why are you allowed to

use the phone at the dinner table and I'm not?'

Molly gestured her daughter to shut up and eat up. The fifteen-year-old was about to continue her little protest, but the words dried up in her mouth when her mom dropped her fork of lasagne in a mild state of shock.

All eyes were on Molly now…

'You can't be serious?' Molly asked, 'When?'

The daughters watched their mother's face continue to beam even brighter with more unheard words. Her smile was infectious and rubbed off on the girls. They all began to smile at each other, not knowing why they were smiling.

Molly continued. 'What? No, no, I'm not going to change my mind. This is another sign.' Molly peeped at the girls with a twinkle in her eye. She thanked Janice and hung up. Her amazement was palpable. She stared at her phone for a few seconds in stunned amazement. 'I've just sold the house…'

Cora, thinking she was missing something, turned to her elder sister for her reaction. Mina seemed as confused as Cora was. Emma turned back to the job of separating her lasagne into layers.

'Hello? Did anyone just hear what I said?'

Cora answered, 'This is a joke, right?'

Mina snapped, 'Mom, tell us this is a joke, please. I'm starting to sweat over here.'

It was about now when Molly realised she'd fucked up. She should have told the girls earlier. They had every right to know about her drastic plan to sell up. She had run with the idea and never bothered considering how they might feel. 'It's not a joke.'

Cora protested, 'But we have all our friends here!'

'But you can make friends anywhere,' Molly answered, feeling disingenuous.

Mina, visibly shaken, chimed in. 'You're wrong, Mom. Just because we're kids do you think our friendships aren't as important as adult friendships? That we can pick up friends as we go along and drop them as if they never meant anything to us? Wrong! I think you need to have a little drink.' She regretted saying it before the words left her lips. She wasn't brave enough and was too proud to say sorry, but Molly knew Mina regretted her words just by her awkward body language.

'I think you need to have a little respect for your mother!' Molly back answered. This wasn't going the way she had envisioned. 'Look, I admit I made a mistake in not telling you about my plans, but I need you to think of me for once in your lives. This is very exciting. You just don't know it yet.'

'Oh, could you get any more con…con…?'

Cora prompted her older sister, 'Condescending?'

Molly cleared her throat. 'Now that we're all here, I suppose that it's better if I tell you.'

Cora sarcastically muttered under her breath, 'Better late than never.'

'I'm closing the restaurant…rather, the government is closing my restaurant.'

Mina looked around with a suspicious air. 'What do you mean?'

'The government restrictions have been crippling

our business, and we had to shut our doors last night.' Molly shook her head in disbelief, hearing herself say those words. 'Girls, we're going on an adventure.'

Cora's eyes widened in hope. 'An adventure?'

'What kind of adventure?' Mina was more skeptical.

'Maybe we're going to begin a new life somewhere else. Well, there's no maybe. We are going to begin a new life somewhere else.'

Mina was having none of it. 'Count me out — I've got Sophia's virtual birthday party on Wednesday evening.' She got up from the table. 'I've lost my appetite.'

Molly ordered, 'Sit down. We need to talk.'

Mina did as she was asked, but not without voicing her opinion. 'You need to talk, but you don't listen.'

Cora appeared to be on the fence about this mysterious adventure. 'Where are we going, exactly?'

'I don't know,' answered Molly, 'and that's why it's an adventure. But I know we need to get out of this house.'

Mina suggested, 'We could move down the street. That way, we still have our friends.'

Molly sighed, realising the battle she had in her hands. 'Mina, I don't think you're getting the point.'

'Explain it then.'

'I need to get away from this house…too many memories. It's too painful.' She took a deep breath and let it out. 'I can't let go of your dad and brother.' Molly refrained from telling her girls how she heard Henry every now and again and saw Mike.

The sisters exchanged glances and lowered their heads in tacit agreement.

'I can see more clearly now that I don't have a business anymore. I see I've been missing out on you guys. This is a sign.'

'You keep saying that, but signs are what you make of them.'

Mina's wisdom impressed Molly.

Cora looked about the kitchen as if she was seeing it for the first time. 'But this is our home.'

For this to work, Molly needed Mina on board. She needed to put this in terms her eldest daughter would understand. 'Mina, you're right, I don't listen…but I need to be the mom and think about what my family needs. And right now, we're up shit creek without a paddle. I'm not working anymore and we cannot afford to live in this house…in this city.'

'What's a shit creek?' asked Cora.

Mina glared at her younger sister. 'It's a torrent of shit, Cora, you don't want to be caught in…kind of like what we're in now. And before you go asking, a paddle is a—'

Cora barked back, 'I know what a paddle is. I'm not stupid!'

'Oh no? You look stupid!'

At this juncture, Emma burst out in peals of laughter, spraying her general area with lasagne, apparently finding her sister's comment highly amusing.

'Just get another job, Mom,' Cora opined.

'It's not that simple, Cora. Look, I know this is

difficult for you to understand now, but you will in the future. I was using the job as an excuse to stay away from home…away from you guys, and that's very, very wrong.' Molly decided her girls deserved the truth. 'I was also staying away from the house because I didn't want to be reminded of your brother and your dad. The place is full of ghosts.'

Emma peered over her shoulder sheepishly.

Molly couldn't help but laugh. 'Not real ghosts, I mean the memories.'

'What about my friends?'

Molly was kind of hoping they would forget about that. 'I know, Mina. I feel your pain.'

'No, you don't.'

'Yes, I do. I moved away from my friends when I was your age because my dad worked in the army and we moved around a lot and video calls didn't exist then. You only speak to your friends online these days anyway, so it's going to be no different wherever you are in the world. That's the beauty of the Internet. And don't forget you'll make new friends at school.'

'Don't go there, Mom.'

'You'll have two sets of friends: your new schoolmates and your online buddies. I don't care if you're online with your friends all evening just as long as you get your homework and your chores done.' Molly might come to regret that one, but she was clutching at straws.

Mina wasn't giving much away, but her silence was enough to go on for now. If Mina could just accept the situation, then Cora also would. Molly

25

wasn't worried about Emma or Louie the cockatoo.

'I just need you to trust me, guys. I want to get away from the past.'

'You cannot escape your past,' answered Mina matter-of-factly. 'Surely you know that?'

'I don't want to escape my past; I have beautiful memories too. But I do want to put distance between me and my past.'

'I trust you, Mom.'

Molly, surprised by Cora's sudden change of heart, leapt up from the table and smothered her daughter in a hug. 'Thanks for understanding, sweetie.' She turned to Mina. 'Trust me?'

Without looking at her mom, Mina nodded. 'Okay, on one condition.'

'And that is?'

'If it doesn't work out, we come back.'

'Deal.' Molly shook her daughter's hand as Mina added the caveat. 'Three months.'

Molly snapped her hand away. 'We won't know anything in three months. Six months?'

Following a long pause, Mina shook on it. 'Deal.'

Molly was over the moon. 'Yahoo!' She swallowed the two of them in a hug.

Emma jumped in to join them. Whenever hugs were going around, Emma was always there. The four-year-old then asked with a face of sincerity, 'What about Louie?'

'Let's ask him, shall we?' Molly called across to the cockatoo. 'Louie, you want to go on an adventure?'

The cockatoo looked through his bars, rose his head crest, and squawked a series of warbling clicks and caws.

Molly declared, 'We'll take that as a yes!'

Emma and Cora clapped their hands with excitement and whooped for joy, though the bird could equally have been issuing a dire warning to the Greenes.

4.

During the rest of dinner, the Greenes discussed the prospect of their new lives. Molly kept up the adventure element, afraid that a lull would give the girls too much time to think. Mina was still on the fence about it. That was clear. Cora, however, was already making plans, imagining how she would decorate her new bedroom.

Once dinner was over, Molly left the girls to their own devices. They all went upstairs, where Mina filmed a make-up tutorial for Instagram, using her sisters and Louie as guinea pigs. Using a cockatoo as a guinea pig with eyeliner and blush guaranteed at least a million extra views.

Downstairs, Molly did something she thought she'd never do again: look at the online job sites. She focused on two of the main employment web pages. Her first impression was one of shock when seeing how few restaurant manager positions were available. The government restrictions had been responsible for permanently closing 18,000 bars and restaurants across the country. How discouraging! She was about to give up hope when she spotted something of interest. A family-run restaurant called Wilma's was looking for a manager, though it looked and sounded like a very run-of-the-mill eating establishment. Yes, it was a step down in prestige and salary, but Molly didn't mind too much if other factors made up for it. She checked the location…

'Old Castle? Hmm, never heard of it,' she muttered to herself.

A quick Google search revealed that Old Castle was right across the country, down in the southwest in Limerick County. It was a small town with a population of just 6,900 inhabitants. Curiosity piqued, she looked at a few images and was pleasantly surprised to see that it was a picturesque country borough with a majestic Norman castle and a statue of a knight on horseback standing on the castle grounds overlooking the town square. Wanting to see more, Google Maps gave her a virtual tour through the streets of Old Castle. She smiled to herself, as quite by accident, she passed by Wilma's. The little restaurant was located right in the town square and Molly felt this magical feeling of wonder come over her. She could see herself there, busying herself around the tables, greeting guests, peering out at the main square every now and again to see life go by. In her mind's eye, it was a perfect world of quaintness, where everybody's big wide grin was in full view, where face masks only existed in the operating theatre.

Growing excited, she wanted nothing more than to apply for the job. She wrote a short but sweet letter of introduction and attached her resume.

But an unexpected uneasiness rose in her just as she was about to press the Send button. She gazed about the kitchen with the inexplicable sensation she was being watched. Every kitchen appliance was staring at her. The hairs bristled on the nape of her neck and her flesh prickled into goosebumps. A wave of acute loneliness and insecurity squirmed inside her. Even though the girls were in hysterics upstairs, they seemed very far away now. Was she doing the right thing by applying for this job in a town she didn't even know existed until five minutes ago? She thought about calling Janice and asking her opinion, but this was something she had to do alone. She wasn't going to listen to her friend, anyway.

There's no harm in applying for the position.

Molly looked up from the table to see Mike standing against the countertop with a comforting smile on his face, though his features were oddly static. And, as usual, he had spoken in Molly's voice. She smiled back, looked at her MacBook screen, then sought Mike who was no longer there. Of course, he wasn't. The advice-giving hallucinations always came in the form of Mike. Molly would imagine what Mike would say, or more accurately, what she'd like to hear him say. Whenever she saw him, Mike never opened his mouth, but just stood there with a knowing smile. He always spoke in Molly's voice while Molly wasn't looking, like now.

'You're right, Mike.' Molly hit the Send button. The moment her resume was sent, she considered the remote option of saying yes if she was offered the job.

She'd need accommodation for her family. Again, adopting a no-harm-in-looking approach, Molly opened the first national real estate website she found. For filters, she added: Old Castle, House, For sale,

Four bedrooms.

On the page were eighty-five properties. Molly scrolled down through them, looking at the pictures as her first filter. One by one, she discarded every property. Not a single listing was adequate. Probably eighty of the eighty-five needed refurbishing, and the remaining five either had no heating or some other major repair. Not even 200,000 euros would get her decent accommodation, even out in the sticks where Old Castle was located. Rather than trying another page that would spit out the same results, Molly went to the Google search engine and typed: House for sale, Old Castle, Limerick County.

It was no surprise when the same websites appeared. But something caught her eye. It wasn't an official real estate page, but an online notice board advertising everything from second-hand clothes for sale to lost dogs. But Molly's keywords had brought up something new. Skimming over the advert, she checked the date. If it was to be trusted, the advertisement was refreshed only hours ago. She read the quirky notice with the eye-catching title.

"Good Home looking for a Good Home"

Stately Victorian farmhouse set in the beautiful unspoilt landscape of Old Castle in West Limerick County.

The property comprises six bedrooms, four toilets, two bathrooms, a kitchen, two dining

**rooms, utility room, basement. Central
heating. Three working fireplaces.**

Strictly families only

**Price on application and subject to special
conditions. Call Richard…**

'Strictly families only?' Molly found a few oddities in the advertisement but overlooked them while she perused the attached pictures. True, the house looked its great age and dilapidated, but the potential, oh, the potential. The house seemed to have everything, not needing any immediate repairs. Yes, life would be a little rough and ready for a while, but they could rough it until she could find the funds to do some repairs. Molly's imagination was running away with possibilities. It was almost too good to be true… Wait, it probably was too good to be true. She needed to keep her feet on the ground. Molly read over the strange wording on her MacBook screen a couple of times more. She was getting that sinking impression it was a hoax. But what if it wasn't?

There was only one thing to do. She picked up her phone and keyed in the number. As she listened to the ringing, she wondered who would answer. You can tell a lot about a person just by the way they speak. Her eyes flitted over that strictly families only clause again. What the hell was that all about? Would whoever she was about to call consider a single mom with children as 'family'? Perhaps he or she was a zealot with strange ideas on family values and morals. Molly could do without living in the vicinity of that kind of individual. No matter how many times she tightened the elastic band on that family mask to keep up appearances, the plush red velvet theatre curtains inevitably rot and fall away to reveal two missing members of the Greenes. Mike and H—

'Hello?'

A man's voice brought Molly back to the present. She cleared her throat, finding herself more nervous than excited. 'Um, hello, am I speaking to Richard?'

'Yes, Richard Prendergast.'

Judging by his steady, well-spoken, and reserved voice, Molly put Richard Prendergast in the conservative fifty-five to sixty-five age category and from a solid background. But Molly was to discover, over the next couple of weeks, that there's a lot more hiding in a voice than is revealed.

'My name is Molly Greene. I'm calling about the house…the farmhouse for sale?' Molly thought about her voice, and it sounded as if it was coming from someone else. She wondered if she was crazy to be even contemplating a move so drastic? A creaky old farmhouse in a provincial town? Not for a second had she considered what Mina and Cora would say to this succinct piece of information.

'Yes, what would you like to know?'

Don't do it, Moll…

'Well, I've got a few questions. But I think we can

save ourselves a lot of time and effort if you could cut to the chase and tell me the price of the house. I'm already assuming I can't afford it, so…'

'Well, first off, Mrs Greene—'

'Um, Miss Greene. Molly, call me Molly.'

There was a slight pause. 'Miss Greene, would you be bringing your family? I think that's the real issue here before we speak about the, um, conditions.'

'More than the price? I doubt it. But, yes, I'm a single mother with three daughters.' Molly was feeling like she was in a job interview, and with it came a slight pulse of fear. In a sudden sense of desperation, she considered telling Richard Prendergast how, once upon a time, she had a complete family until one night, a drunk, not unlike her, wandered into oncoming traffic. The End.

'Ah, wonderful,' answered Richard Prendergast, a tad overly ecstatic.

'It is?'

'Oh, yes. Single mom, eh?' His cadence changed. 'Three daughters?' He asked this question as if he was pondering what it could be like to have three daughters. 'Impressive, very impressive.' It was as if Molly had won a purple heart medal in combat.

'Oh, add a cockatoo to that.' There was a pause down the line. Molly cringed, thinking it was the moment for a little light comedy. 'Sorry, it's just a joke.'

'Oh?'

Molly enlightened Prendergast. 'We have a pet cockatoo named Louie. Superfluous information, I'm

34

blabbing on again.'

Don't do it, Moll…

'Three girls and a cockatoo will be perfect to breathe some life back into that old farmhouse. Are they hard work, Miss Greene?'

'No, we just clean out his cage every couple of days. He'll sing, 'Gone Fishin' ' if you give him a small banana…'

'No, the children, I mean.'

'Oh, sorry!' Molly laughed it off awkwardly. 'I suppose I do have a few extra grey hairs on my head, but they're worth it.'

Prendergast laughed dryly. 'Do you have children?'

The individual on the other end of the line stalled and Molly was aware of the uncomfortable silence. 'Um, no…no, I don't.'

In the brief hiatus between both 'no's', Molly felt Prendergast was about to add or clarify something that never came.

'So, would you like to speak about the conditions of the sale, um, Molly?'

Yes, I passed the first test, thought Molly. I'm officially part of a family: f-a-m-i-l-y. But for some reason, Molly wasn't sure if she wanted to know anymore. She was getting this inexplicable unnerving vibe over the phone; something about Prendergast rubbed her the wrong way. It had been so long since any man rubbed her any day, but she was long enough in the tooth to know an odd vibe when she felt one. 'Go on,' she said in a resigned manner. 'Hit me with it.'

'The house is free.'

Don't do it, Moll… Why don't you listen to me, dammit!

Molly heard the voice. She'd already heard it twice since dialling but had overridden it because it was Mike and Mike was Molly. She knew if she turned around right now, he'd be standing at the kitchen door with that knowing, eternal rictus grin on his face. A Mike cut-out. 'Sorry, I didn't catch that. Free? As in *free* free?'

Prendergast tittered. 'The farmhouse is free, but it comes with a price.'

In a week from now, Molly Greene would think back to this very moment…this very line oily Prendergast had just uttered so easily over the phone, and by then, it would have a very different meaning to what she supposed he meant. 'Heating? Electricity? Is that what you mean? But wait, are you actually telling me the house is free? As in free-of-charge? Or free of mould or something?' Molly was on sensory overload.

There was another uncomfortable silence just then. Molly figured Prendergast had put the phone down. Or maybe someone or something had distracted him. 'Hello?'

'Sorry, yes, I'm here. Yes, the house is free, though I admit there is a spot of mould above the shower in one of the bedroom bathrooms.'

Molly giggled like she was ten years old. 'Are you f… serious?'

'Yes, but it's just a little spot, six inches in diameter perhaps. I'm sure a spray of ammonia or bleach or something should—'

'No, the house…mould doesn't bother me.'

It would, though; mould would bother Molly.

'Miss Greene, Molly, the house is free right now for the right family. But let's wait a while and see if the place…grows on you.'

Molly didn't question if she was the "right person" because she was sold on the free house part of the deal and it seemed as if she was already in, judging by Prendergast's rhetoric. 'I understand the house is free, but it comes with a price. Everyone has bills to pay. Unless it's falling down and needs repair, I'm not up for that…neither is my bank account.'

Could this really be happening? Molly was strapped for cash right now and suddenly she's on the phone being told that a great old farmhouse was free, FREE, if she wanted it. Hello? Mould? Helloooo! Molly couldn't contain herself. 'C'mon, this is too good to be true.'

*It is too good to be true…*came Mike's voice in her ear. *Listen to yourself.*

'Exactly, you don't exist. I am listening to myself!'

'Sorry?'

Molly was mortified. Since when had she begun to talk back to Mike? 'Sorry, I, um, my four-year-old is here, and she's distracting me.'

Another dry laugh came down the line.

'Where's the catch?' Molly probed. 'If there's something hidden, I'd like to know before going down there to have a look at the house.'

'Well, yes. We do have one stipulation. The house must stay in the Prendergast family. If you aren't suited for the house, we will part company. I will reclaim the house and you will find alternative accommodation. You have my word you will not pay a penny while you are at the house. I don't presently have children and I'm the last of the Prendergasts… though on a technicality, I'm not. I don't want the house, but it's in my care until the suitable candidates take it off my hands. The house will become yours when the time is right.'

If you aren't suited for the house? Did he just say that? He did, I'm sure of it. Shouldn't it be the other way around? Another odd line Molly would recall at a later date was the one about presently not having children. What did that mean? Did he have children yesterday? Or maybe it's tomorrow when his children will miraculously appear? She didn't give it any further thought. Money — money — was on Molly's agenda. 'But I thought you said it was free?' She was feeling like she'd been duped. That horrible nauseous feeling of knowing you have just been scammed or going through one in real-time. 'Maybe I'm jumping the gun here, Richard, but when will the house be ours?' Molly couldn't believe she was even asking this question. The gall of her to even ask when she's already being provided free accommodation. This was an amazing strike of good luck! 'Sorry, I know I'm being cheeky, but I need to know where I stand. I'll be moving my entire family down there and…'

'I understand. The house will be yours when the time is right.'

'And when will that be?'

'That depends on many factors.'

Molly found the whole thing very odd, maybe even suspicious. 'So, once again, the house is free? As in no money will pass hands?'

That dry, almost condescending laugh came again. 'There's nothing free in life, Miss Greene, Molly. Even the air we breathe is on loan. You've seen climate change?'

It was the way he spoke which Molly found disconcerting. He wasn't telling her everything. She knew that. But what could be so terrible in the face of receiving a free farmhouse? C'mon, nobody's kidding anybody here. The place is a mansion. There was nothing to mull over. She'd have second thoughts if it was a shitty little flat on a bad street. 'Climate change is a major concern, but right now my concern is having a roof over my head.'

'The farmhouse will be yours. In return, we ask that you bring the old place back to life. What that place needs is the warmth of a family…to hear the giggle of children in its many rooms. A good home for a good home.'

Molly was now beginning to understand the wording of the unusual advertisement title on the screen in front of her now. Her excitement grew again. 'I don't want any trouble after we move in.'

'To put your mind at ease, I live close by should you ever need me.' He concluded by saying, 'You won't have any trouble with me, Miss Greene.'

And here was yet another line Molly would recollect in just a few weeks from this moment. But, by then, it would be too late. If Molly had listened to what the man wasn't saying, she would've picked up on the subtlety of what he was saying. But on this evening, not for a moment did Molly think he was only guaranteeing she wouldn't have any trouble from him specifically.

'I just want to clarify that the farmhouse is quite secluded, Miss Greene. I can guarantee peace and tranquillity, but I cannot guarantee happiness. That comes from within.'

What a peculiar thing to say, thought Molly. 'Peace and tranquillity sound like music to my ears. My family and I have been through quite a lot in the last couple of years and I need to reconnect with my daughters.'

'Well, then this was supposed to be,' Prendergast assured her. 'It was written in the stars.'

Molly was sold. 'I'd like to visit the house tomorrow if that's okay? Around midday? I'll bring a friend. She's a building surveyor who knows about this stuff,' Molly lied, just to call Prendergast's bluff. If he had anything to hide about the structure of the house, then now was the time to unhide it.

'Perfect, Miss Greene. Bring as many experts as you want. They will all tell you the same thing: you'd be a fool to pass up on this once-in-a-lifetime opportunity.'

Molly felt like she was a contestant in a game

show. 'Okay! See you tomorrow!'

Just as Molly was thinking the call had been easier than she thought it would be…

'Miss Greene?'

Molly was about to hang up. 'Yeah?'

'I have a filtering process.'

This took a second to sink in. 'O-kay?' *WTF?*

'You have only told me your name. Where are you from and have you done anything in the past I should know about?'

'I'm from Dublin. But I'm not sure what you mean when you ask if I have "…done anything in the past"?' Molly laughed nervously. 'Prison time, you mean?'

Prendergast huffed a tired chuckle. 'No, I mean work-wise? What have you done with your life?'

'Oh, um, I used to own a restaurant…Michelin star. I had to shut it down because of what we are living at the moment.'

'Uh-huh. Yes, Covid hasn't done any favours for anyone, especially someone in your sector.'

This sudden last-minute interrogation was bugging Molly. 'Sorry, why did you say you need this information?'

'I just want to run a little background check on the candidate to whom I might be handing over the house. Small price to pay for a big house. I'm sure you understand.'

'Yes, okay. I understand.' Molly hung up. As she did, a foreboding sliver of undiluted dread froze her to the spot. She put it down to nerves and daunting

41

new beginnings.

She called Janice. 'Hi. Got any plans tomorrow?'

'Nope,' Janice answered without hesitation.

'Want to go for a drive?'

'Sure. Where?'

Molly explained the odd occurrence and amazing good fortune that had occurred.

'Are you sure this is legit?' asked Janice. 'It sounds off. I mean, it's weird, Moll. A background check? Free house? I'm thinking those might be a couple of red flags.'

'We won't know until tomorrow. Oh, by the way, do you know anything about surveying buildings?'

'What?'

At this juncture, Molly heard an intercepting call on the line. 'Forget it. I'll call you back.' She answered the incoming call.

'Molly Greene?'

It surprised her to hear a soothing woman's voice on the phone. Molly placed the speaker at around sixty years of age. 'Yes, I'm Molly.'

'Molly, you applied for a position at my restaurant recently.'

Molly did a double-take. 'Recently? It was just a few minutes ago.'

'Well, your resume is very impressive. I won't beat around the bush. I need a manager at Wilma's A.S.A.P and it looks like you might fit the bill. I'm going with my hunch and that's that. If you're willing to go on a hunch, I'd like to offer you the position.'

She was stunned. Could this New Year's Day get

any weirder? It really did look now as if her luck gods in the sky were beaming down on her, all in unanimous agreement that Molly Greene deserves a few bolts of luck. Molly liked her already. 'Don't you want to do an interview or something?'

'Would you feel better if we did? I didn't want to be dragging you across the country for an interview. And, besides, we both know you're over-qualified for this position. I'd consider it an insult to interview you. Rather, you should be interviewing me!' She cackled a hearty laugh down the line. 'We serve low dining, not exactly Michelin quality — maybe Dunlop!' Wilma joked again.

'I admire you,' Molly gushed, 'staying afloat in the current atmosphere.'

'The secret to staying afloat, dearie, is to serve cheap food for everyone and anyone. I'm proud of the shite I serve,' she joked, taking Molly by surprise with her wicked tongue. 'Serve shite and you'll be right!' Wilma rhymed off.

Molly chuckled. 'I'll be in Old Castle tomorrow, as a matter of fact. We could have an interview?' As she spoke, Molly found this whole thing running far too smooth, to the point of spooky.

'Oh, isn't that a stroke 'o luck, hmm? What brings you down this side of the country?'

Molly was on the point of telling Wilma about the farmhouse, but she decided she didn't want people knowing her business until she had everything in place. 'Oh, a friend and I are just going on a tour of the Wild Atlantic Way and Old Castle is on the route.'

'Well, if you're in the vicinity, why not pop in for some lunch or a coffee and we can have an informal chat and I can show you around the place? I'm not big on formalities.'

'Sounds perfect, Wilma,' Molly agreed and hung up the phone.

*

While Molly Greene was on the phone with her prospective new boss, Ricard Prendergast was sitting at his desk, referencing and cross-referencing a one Molly Greene. It wasn't difficult to find her online. Everything checked out with what she'd told him. Google, the ultimate witness, confirmed it. She was the owner and manager of the now defunct Molly's Michelin-star restaurant. Even had its own Wikipedia page. She was also the same Molly Greene whose husband and son had been taken prematurely in a horrific car accident a couple of years ago. Molly Greene was the perfect guinea pig.

5.

On Monday morning, Molly Greene dropped off the kids at school and drove down the country in a south-westerly direction with Janice. Molly's parents had agreed to pick up the kids after school and take them to their place for the afternoon. The kids had a good relationship with their grandparents, even though the pandemic had sharply curbed their visits. For now, Molly had told none of this to her parents. They were aware her business was on the rocks and worried about their daughter as any parent would. It was only a matter of hours before they'd find out about her closing the business. By then, Molly hoped to have some semblance of direction in her life and maybe today was the beginning of Molly's transformation. Considering all of this had happened within hours, she wasn't doing that bad.

Molly and Janice spoke about a lot of things on that four-hour drive to Old Castle. Molly did most of the talking, relaying how her life had been before the car accident. Janice knew Molly post-accident and hadn't been privy to her life pre-accident. Molly painted a happy picture of their lives and went into great detail about what kind of people Mike and her son were. It was the first time since the accident that Molly felt ready to talk about her old life. She could do this because she was excited about the future. This new year, 2021, was going to be her year, she was certain of that. She left out the bit about why Mike and Henry had even been out on that ill-fated Valentine's night.

Molly and Janice arrived in Old Castle at 1pm, four hours from when Molly had dropped off the kids at school. They parked in the town square in the shadow of the Norman castle. Molly smiled when she saw Wilma's restaurant across the street, fitting snugly between a butcher shop and a pub. To be fair, the term restaurant should be used loosely; it was more of a family-run cafe.

The women separated with Molly going into Wilma's while Janice took a walk around town. A quaint bell tinkled as Molly stepped inside. Wilma was a large, jolly woman wearing a hippy tiered dress and sandals. Her impressive head of long silver-white hair gave away her age. She was delighted to give Molly a brief tour of the place. Immediately Molly knew she'd come home smelling of fries and not oysters with white truffles. The place wasn't imaginative, but the staff seemed friendly, and Wilma was a dynamo of energy despite her advancing years. She was a no-bullshit old soul who had been dishing out fish n' chips and meat pies longer than she cared to remember. Though played down her restaurant, it was clear she was very proud of her establishment and wanted things done, 'The Wilma Way'.

The conversation went as Molly had envisioned, then things took a turn when Wilma changed the topic. 'So, you're coming down from Dublin for this job?' Her perplexed face said it all.

Molly nodded, wishing to leave it there. 'That's right.'

'Uh-huh?'

She would not rest, and Molly could see that. 'We needed a change.'

'Why Old Castle, do you mind me asking?'

Why? Molly didn't know why. 'Old Castle chose me…'

Wilma nodded, not seeming entirely convinced. 'Oh, come on now. We both know that's bunkum, Molly.'

Molly went on to explain she'd never heard of Old Castle until yesterday, but felt as if this town had chosen her. 'I know it sounds cheesy, but I'm starting to believe it. I found your job offer online. That was the reason. Then, well, that got me looking at other opportunities in Old Castle…like a new home.'

'Yes, you have a family. Figured as much. I'll have a snoop around. Nothing happens in this town without me knowing.' She tapped the side of her nose and Molly believed what Wilma didn't know about this town wasn't worth knowing. 'I'll see if there are any nice properties available in the area. I'm a good friend of the local real estate agent here in town.'

'Well, we are going to look at a place today. I think I have found the deal of a lifetime,' Molly told her with great excitement.

'Oh? Where?' Wilma asked, with a certain level of caution slipping into her cadence. 'I might know it.'

Molly hesitated. She wanted to keep her business to herself, but Wilma knew the area. Molly didn't have the experience and knowledge of a local who knew the truth and not something sugar-coated on the Internet. 'It's a place outside of town. I spoke to the owner yesterday. We're going to meet him this afternoon.'

Wilma was intrigued. 'Oh? Do you mind if I ask who?'

'Prendergast is his surname.' Molly witnessed Wilma turn as ashen as her hair. 'Richard Prendergast?'

'Yes, do you know him?'

'I know of him.'

This cold abruptness told Molly everything she needed to know. 'You don't seem convinced?'

'Oh, Molly, please tell me you're not moving into the farmhouse?' The jolly Wilma who had greeted Molly was gone now.

'Well, I got a deal I can't refuse.'

'And what was this deal?' Wilma probed with great suspicion, sidling up next to Molly.

So, Molly told Wilma how the phone exchange had gone down on New year's Day. As she recounted the conversation, Wilma came over all strange. Molly thought the woman was going to faint. She guided her to a table and sat her down. Molly sat down next to her. 'What's wrong?'

It was as if the woman had just had a near-death experience. 'You can't stay at that house, Molly. You can stay anywhere else, in a dog kennel should you have the inclination, but not that place, dear Jesus in Heaven.' Wilma shook her head in desperation.

'That's no place for children, Molly.' She warned with pleading eyes.

And this is why Molly should've kept her big mouth shut and stuck to her plan of telling nobody anything until it was done and dusted. 'Oh, it's a little rough around the edges, but we can adapt. I'd be a fool to pass up this opportunity. Wilma, the restaurant ruined me. My money is tied up in my house. Thankfully, I was all up to date with my expenses at the restaurant despite haemorrhaging money towards the end. I need to sell my house in Dublin just to survive, but I think I might have found a buyer. Please tell me how I can turn down an offer like free accommodation in that enormous house?'

'That's not the issue, Molly.'

'So, what's the issue?'

Wilma grew even more awkward. 'The house has a history.'

. 'We all have a history.'

'Not this kind of history. You're not the first family to move into that house. Every family, a certain kind of family, that ever stayed at that place never lasted more than days, a week tops.'

Molly snorted laughter. 'I'm starting to feel like I'm starring in a thriller.'

Wilma wasn't entertaining Molly. 'This isn't a film, Molly.' She paused for thought. 'Things aren't right out there at the farmhouse.'

'But what does that mean?'

'I can't say anymore, Molly.' She smiled apologetically. 'It's just something we don't talk about. The farmhouse is something we've all grown up with here in Old Castle and people have just gotten used to it. Generations have come and gone, and we have learned to pretend it doesn't exist. Just be content in knowing that things have happened out at that place that defy explanation.' Wilma catches Molly's attention. 'We don't like to draw attention to the place, so we keep it to ourselves and any… misfortune is dealt with appropriately.'

'Misfortune?'

'How can I put this without startling you? People become accident-prone after moving into the farmhouse. We've all noticed people move in during the day and move out during the night…and always in a real hurry. Bad energy.'

Molly's skin prickled, imagining those anonymous people leaving the farmhouse during the night. Just then, she spotted a small tray of rough gemstones by the cash register at the front door and the swirling tendrils of blue smoke spiralling from a lit incense stick. *Wilma was a spiritual person who believed good luck comes pre-installed in gemstones and carcinogenic incense sticks cleanse the air of negative energy.* She was stereotyping, of course she was. Still, whatever Wilma said should be taken with a pinch of salt as to not delude herself. 'I don't believe in good and bad energy,' Molly said with conviction. 'Life can be a fickle friend. She can turn her back on you whenever she pleases. There is no such thing as luck. We're either in the right place at the right time or the wrong place at the wrong time.'

Since the accident, Molly had shut down many possibilities she would've once entertained. She was at the right place at the right time when she'd first seen Wilma's job offer and the quirky advertisement for the farmhouse. As opposed to Mike and Henry, who had been in the wrong place at the wrong time… thanks to her.

'I'm just giving you a friendly warning. There's bad energy in that house.'

Molly was irritated. The more Wilma warned her about the place, the more she wanted to fly in the face of adversity. Nobody was going to make her mind up for her; she'd been through too much for that. There was nothing that could scare her, especially bad energy, in an old house. Jesus, she'd been living with bad energy in a new house for the last couple of years.

She thanked Wilma for her advice and told her she would take on board what she'd said, and she left it at that. Wilma invited Molly and Janice to have lunch at her restaurant, '…on the house' but Molly needed to clear her head. She'd had enough 'Resident Evil' for one day. Molly made up an excuse and said her goodbyes.

'Listen to what I've told you and you'll have no worries.'

'So, when do you want me to start?'

Wilma laughed and apologised. 'Sorry, forgive me. I got so heated on the farmhouse topic that I forgot the reason we were speaking in the first place. I'll call you in about three to four weeks from now. How does that sound?'

'If you need a week or two extra to sort out your stuff, then we'll survive. All good things are worth waiting for!'

They left it at that and Molly said goodbye.

She met up with Janice and they went for a walk. Old Castle was a picturesque town with a murky river running through it. People seemed friendly and the atmosphere was one of welcome. Strangers on the street saluted Molly and Janice as they walked by. Being city dwellers, they found this human touch a nice thing and put it down to small-town courtesy. The more Molly saw, the more she felt at home in Old Castle. She felt she could live the rest of her life right here. They found a souvenir shop, which they thought was hilarious in this backwater. Molly couldn't resist buying a cute little instrument called a kalimba or thumb piano for each of the girls. To make it extra special, the instruments had 'Old Castle' printed on the side. The women found this even more laughable. Then they bought a couple of sandwiches with coffees-to-go and went for a stroll through the town park known as 'The Demesne'. As they ambled, Molly relayed Wilma's friendly warning to Janice.

In hindsight, she regretted mentioning it because Janice would use this later.

'You think there's something to what she's saying?'

'No, I don't. And you want to know something else? I don't care. I can deal with anything after what

I've been through.'

Janice couldn't disagree with that. 'There's no harm in looking, I suppose.'

They left town and headed west, following the directions Richard Prendergast had given Molly. But they didn't need the second half of the coordinates as they both saw the farmhouse looming in the distance, down in a valley, appearing through gaps in a thick spruce forest that hid it from the outside world. Molly almost crashed the car when she saw the true size of the place.

They pulled up at a gate. Beyond the gate was a laneway that led to the farmhouse in the dale below, nothing fancy, no long sweeping avenues. The gate was more the type found on a farm to keep cattle from wandering. It surprised Molly to see another house, inside the gate and off to the left. It was a much more modest affair, yet quaint. It was almost like a miniature version of the farmhouse. The lane went by this house and disappeared down into a steep wooded hillside. But it was the suited, tall, gaunt man standing at the gate with a preoccupied gaze that garnered all their attention. His salt and peppered hair was brushed back tight from the forehead. It gleamed with gel of some description and he wore it rather long, growing it down to the collar of his shirt. Veins undulated in his temples. His eyes were set far back in his head, resulting in a gloomy stare.

Molly greeted him from within the car with a smile and a wave, telling Janice, 'That must be him… Prendergast.'

Janice smiled too, and worthy of a ventriloquist, uttered through taut lips, 'He doesn't look too friendly.'

The individual nodded a dour salute. Molly whirred down her window. 'Richard?'

The man nodded. 'Welcome home,' he said from behind his face mask.

The women exchanged a fleeting glance of amusement before getting out of the car. They pulled on their face masks and introduced themselves and fist-bumped rather than handshakes. Prendergast told them he lived at the house known as the Gatehouse. He seemed to be in a hurry to get on with the tour, opening the gate and padlocking it once Molly had driven through. He got into an old gas-guzzling Jaguar and they followed the Jag down the hill. Molly guided her BMW around the few, but deep, potholes.

On the short drive down the lane, Janice mentioned, 'This guy is the dragon at the gate.' But Molly was too engrossed in the beautiful surroundings and the spruce trees lining the winding lane.

Both women gasped a 'Wow!' when they drove into the expansive front yard of the farmhouse, which was immense, grey, and looming, and what seemed to be one-too-many windows looking down on them.

'This is where you want to live?' asked Janice with raised eyebrows. 'No, wait, this is where you want your girls to live? Oh, Mina's going to just love this place.'

'I hear you, but I'm the boss in this family and

what I say goes. If it doesn't work out, then I'll put my hand up and take the fall, but what I see is a lot of potential.'

'For what?'

Prendergast called, 'Are you coming?' from the front door of the house. 'Or have you seen enough already?' The women were sure they saw the hint of a smile on Prendergast's face.

'Oh, so he does sarcasm, too? You two would get on like a house on fire.'

Janice asked, 'What potential?'

'I'll tell you later.'

They crossed the front yard to meet up with Prendergast. Halfway across the yard, Molly muttered to Janice from the corner of her mouth, 'I'm getting a weird déjà vu right now.'

Janice turned to her. 'Do you know this place?'

Molly shook her head, perplexed. 'Nope. Only from the online pictures.'

Prendergast gestured at the surrounding property. 'All the land you can see from here belongs to the property.' It was difficult to see anything with the encroaching woods, which was going to swallow the house and all belonging to it very soon.

Prendergast unlocked the front door with one of many old iron keys. They waited for him to go inside, but he wasn't budging. He was backing away. 'This is an open house,' he informed them. 'You can't get a feel for a place when there's somebody looking over your shoulder.'

Janice had one eye on Prendergast and the other on

the hallway of the house. Molly saw she clearly didn't trust him and waited until he had walked, rather trotted, across the front yard before she stepped inside. Prendergast appeared to be in a real hurry to get back to his car and the whole thing seemed to be a distraction for him, giving the women the distinct impression he would prefer to be anywhere else besides here. The women also noticed how he flicked the central locking when he sat in the Jag. 'Well, that's curious,' Janice whispered to Molly. 'I was quite certain he was a predator.'

That same sense of déjà vu she'd gotten crossing the front yard swept over Molly as she walked across the threshold. The place was cold and fusty and smelt like antique furniture. The house itself felt like a character that wanted to tell its 200-and-something-year old-story. They walked through the bowels of the house, from the first floor up to the third-floor attic which had been converted into a bedroom. Molly could imagine Mina claiming this room as it was the largest and the coolest room in the house. Her spirits were given a boost when she saw the interior of the farmhouse was in surprisingly good nick, a little rough around the edges, but definitely liveable. The place had some mould issues, especially upstairs in the en-suite bathroom belonging to the last bedroom along the hallway where they were inspecting. Despite the mildewy walls, Molly could see herself having this bedroom, especially as it had the en-suite plus the bonus of a fireplace which, judging by its state, hadn't seen a fire for a century or more. 'My

God, Jan, can you imagine having an open fire on a winter's night in your own bedroom? It doesn't get any cosier than that. I'm jotting myself down for this room.' But it was more than the fireplace and the en-suite bathroom. She felt at home in this room; it was familiar for Molly.

'What's that smell?' asked Janice.

'Mould?'

'Well, yeah, but there's something else.' Janice walked around the bedroom. Following her nose, she was drawn to the open fireplace. She got down on her haunches and sniffed at the opening. 'Call me crazy but I'm smelling oranges or lemons or something from this fireplace…mouldy citrus. There's something else I can't put my finger on, but I know I've smelt it before.'

'Hmm, interesting. Thank you, Holmes.'

'You're welcome, Watson.'

Something else they found a little odd during their brief tour of the farmhouse were the locks on the outside of the bathroom doors, as well as on the inside. Molly wondered if it was just her who found this unusual, but she could tell from her friend's puzzled expression that Janice was wondering the same thing.

'So, Sherlock,' jested Molly, 'can you explain this mystery with the bathroom door locks?'

'Fuck knows, my dear Watson. I've got one or two possible answers…but none you'll be wanting to hear any time soon.'

'Hmm, the plot thickens.'

The women didn't have time to joke around or come to any logical conclusion because Richard Prendergast was calling from the front yard. 'How is it going in there? Will you be longer?'

They went back outside where Molly told Prendergast she needed to talk it over with her advisor.

Janice and Molly retired to Molly's car. They sat for a moment, taking everything in.

'It's decadent, don't you think?'

'That's one way of putting it,' Janice answered, sounding unconvinced. 'Decadent is romantic. This,' looking about with an upturned lip '…is not romantic. Look, it's got charm. That's as far as I'll go. I just don't find the place welcoming. There's a couple of odd things in there.'

'But the place is in good condition,' said Molly.

'It's in better condition than I thought it would be,' Janice answered. 'Moll, I know we were goofing around in there, but why would someone need a lock on the outside of a bathroom door? The only logical conclusion is to lock someone in. And, another thing, did you notice how nervous the guy is? He didn't want to be in that house. Didn't that Wilma woman say there was something not right with the house?'

'Jan, he's eccentric. Wilma is a new-age hippy, and they can say anything. There are no credible witnesses here today. I can't pass up this opportunity. It's free, Jan, free! Maybe I should show you my bank account and that'll help convince you. Look, there's another reason I want to move in here.'

58

'This should be good…'

'The farmhouse could be an amazing restaurant.'

Janice considered her friend, wondering if she was pulling her leg. 'You're serious?'

'I've never been more serious in my life. Secluded and exclusive. It's got Michelin written all over it. Have you seen all that land? You saw what we paid and charged for fresh produce…and double that if it's eco-friendly. Imagine cutting out the middle-man?'

Janice was caught for words. Hopeless desperation grew on her face as she realised she had already lost her best friend. 'You've made up your mind. It doesn't matter what I say. You just brought me along to keep you company. You're here already, growing micro-greens for your Michelin star. One day you're going to discover why this place has locks on the outside of the bathroom doors and you'll be standing there with a couple of lettuce heads to defend yourself.'

Molly broke down in nervous laughter. She leaned across and kissed Janice on the head. 'Janice, write a novel while you're looking for a new job — crime caper. I'd buy it, just to see what crazy shit's going on in your head.' She got out of the BMW.

*

Janice watched her friend cross the front yard with a spring in her step. Only when she was right next to the Jaguar did Prendergast open his window, just enough to speak through. Janice had keen eyesight and she could see his doors remained locked. Jesus, he was frightened by them…or maybe he was afraid of catching Covid. The elderly were more prone to its effects. But he wasn't in that age category. She heard muffled words pass between them before they fist-bumped. 'Oh, Molly,' Janice said softly to herself. She was going to miss her best friend. She was going to miss them all.

Molly crossed back to the car with a big grin on her face. Half her face was hidden behind a face mask, but Janice knew by looking at her.

*

In silence, they drove back up the lane to the road. Janice cast occasional glances at stoic Molly who was remaining tight-lipped for now. Prendergast parked up his Jaguar outside the Gatehouse, unlocked the gate, and waved them through.

It wasn't until they were on the road back to Dublin when Molly burst out in tune with, 'It's ooo-fficial! We're moving in once we've got everything sorted.'

Janice was regretting finding a buyer for Molly's house. What she regretted more was telling Molly she had found a buyer for her house. Still, she was a good friend and good friends help each other, even if…

'I didn't notice a gate at the farmhouse.'

'Hmm?' asked Molly. 'There is a gate, a big one with a padlock. How could you have missed it?'

'I saw a gate by Prendergast's place, but there isn't any to the farmhouse. That gate you're referring to is intended for both houses.'

'Better again. My neighbour will be "the dragon at the gate" as you so lovingly called him — I was listening to you. He'll protect us from the outside world. I think I need some of that right now. Just to heal, Jan, y'know? Just be a recluse for a little while.'

Janice was thinking it was easy to be a recluse at the farmhouse, but she wasn't sure much healing would go on. 'I hear you.'

Further up the M7 motorway, Janice added, 'You know that means Prendergast can come and go to the farmhouse whenever he wants and permission every time you come and go from the house? In a way, you are his prisoner. He'll know where you are at all times…'

Molly shook her head and tittered. 'Like I said, Jan, write that comedy caper.'

'Maybe I will.'

'You know,' Molly reflected, 'I should think about a school for the girls. Would you mind to Google a school?'

'"Google a school!"' Janice snorted with laughter. 'Oh, my good Christ, I've heard it all now!'

They shared a real gut-buster of laughter just then.

Janice would remember this moment. If only she had known it was to be their last laugh together.

*

It was quite easy to find schools in Old Castle because there was only one which functioned as a primary and secondary school. The population was so low Old Castle didn't need another school.

'Do you want me to call the number?'

Molly nodded. 'Switch on Bluetooth.'

Janice rang the number. The dial tone filled the

BMW just once before a man's voice answered. 'Saint Molua's, hello?'

Molly filled him in on the situation. The chirpy man told Molly they prefer to have new students begin at the start of the term. 'Strict...not strict policy,' he said with a shy chuckle. Molly did some quick mental calculations. She informed the secretary she didn't think she could make it for the start of the term date, which was the second week of January, but with a little luck, they could start around the third or fourth week of January.

'I can't confirm now, but I don't see any problem. Student-to-teacher ratio is lower than it has ever been here in Old Castle. Everybody's getting out while they still can.' He laughed down the line, leaving Molly and Janice throwing amused glances each other's way. 'If there's an issue, I'll call you. Go ahead with your plans and please call me if there's any change...or if you change your mind. It wouldn't be the first time,' he finished on an ominous tone.

During a quiet part of the return journey, Molly thought about the previous night. Before she'd gone to bed, Mike had appeared at the kitchen table in his usual car accident attire, but without a drop of blood. 'Are you doing the right thing?'

She wasn't sure if he'd been referring to the symbolic glass of wine she'd helped herself to (the last one in this house and any house was the excuse to herself) or the fact that she was moving her family to an uncertain future.

As she drove, Molly Greene asked herself why her

deceased infant son never appears. Because it's too painful. Mike is painful too, but he offers advice and makes her question herself. He is her moral compass. But Henry? Henry was just a little boy whose life was taken far too young and taken because of Molly. Her mind had blocked out Henry, only letting him filter through in daylight hours when everything was happy, safe, and familiar. Henry never made a sound when night drew in around her, when her fears and anxieties came crawling from the woodwork of her being. And if little Henry ever threatened to peep around a corner, Molly drank him right the fuck back from where he'd come from. Another reason her Henry never appeared was that as a child, and she couldn't voice a child's thoughts like she could her husband's.

And just like that, Molly Greene was about to step into the next phase of her life. And she was taking her living family with her.

6.

A mere two weeks later, Molly Greene sold her house to friends of Janice, who were looking for something in the neighbourhood, quick and painless. Molly was delighted with Janice and bought her a Brown Thomas voucher as a thank-you. Having the sale of the house allowed her to breathe a little and have some money towards essentials like water and electricity. Janice, on the other hand, wasn't as enthusiastic and had told her she regretted ever mentioning it since the day they visited the farmhouse. Not that Molly was leaving her old life, in a way, yes, but where she was going was the real problem. She was taking the girls to that creepy place in the woods with an even creepier landlord — if that's what he was — living on the same property. That was the real issue. But Molly's mind was made up and Janice had to respect that. Janice commented, 'People have to make their own mistakes in life to learn about life. That's what I believe,' she told Molly.

Moving day came just another week after that. It was a Wednesday when Molly closed the door on the house for the last time. Everything had happened quickly and smoothly — so smoothly Molly was waiting for something to go wrong. It felt strange to throw the spare key through the letterbox. The moving company she had hired to take everything had already left and would be at the farmhouse sometime this evening. Molly didn't drive away slowly. If anything, she revved up. Not wanting to make anything of it, she held her silence. The girls were already in travel mode with their eyes on their tablet screens and their ears plugged in. It amazed Molly how they could be so, well, cold. Maybe that's not the right word. It didn't seem to faze them that they would never see their childhood house again and Molly felt a little lousy for taking them away from everything they knew. Maybe it was their way of coping. Whatever it was, she was secretly relieved a tear-fest had been avoided. But this wasn't about the kids; this was about Molly. She needed to put distance between herself and the ghosts that had haunted her since the accident. As she turned the bend on her old life, she glimpsed Mike in her rear-view mirror, waving them off from the front door with a rictus grin stretched across his face. He was waving because she wanted him to wave. Her heart fluttered and tears came to her eyes when she saw, standing next to Mike, a strangely still little boy. It was Henry. She was seeing him for the first and probably last time since the accident. He was waving just like his dad because Molly made him wave like his dad. Slow, deliberate, and otherworldly. He was there because it was the last chance for Molly to make him be there, to see him wave them goodbye and for her to say goodbye.

Janice was supposed to come and say bon voyage, but she didn't turn up, which peeved Molly a little.

On the four-hour drive across the country, from

east to southwest, Mina gave her mom the silent treatment.

Once they were within a kilometre or two of the farmhouse, Molly told her daughters to keep an eye out for the house down in the valley. Through gaps in the spruce forest, they saw the large, looming building. Cora was in awe of the mysterious place while Mina threw her eyes to the heavens, as if wondering what she had done to deserve this.

When they arrived at the road gate, Molly called Richard Prendergast. He didn't answer but appeared from the front door of the Gatehouse looking identical to the day Molly had met him, with the same grey suit and burgundy shirt and tie. His glistening salt and peppered hair was combed back tight against his head. But this time, Richard Prendergast was carrying a bottle of wine and it was distracting Molly. He walked up to the BMW and greeted everyone. 'Welcome home,' he said in that warm way of his and with that same odd greeting he'd given to Molly and Janice the first time they met. She didn't fully understand it then either. But in time, Molly Greene would begin to comprehend why she had come home and why she was welcomed.

'A little celebration,' remarked Prendergast as he handed Molly the bottle of wine.

'Oh, wow, thank you!' My name is Molly Greene and I'm a recovering alcoholic...

'A homecoming gift,' said Richard Prendergast.

Molly found this a little odd, but a lot of things

Prendergast said were just that — a little odd. Housewarming gift would've made more sense, she thought. She forgot his strange words when she looked at the label on the bottle of wine and almost fainted to see the date 1898. 'But this… this wine is…' she started, but he cut her off.

'Compliments of the house, Molly.'

Molly had some knowledge of wine and the bottle she was holding in her hands could easily be worth thousands. She took the bottle graciously and didn't mention she wineboarded herself in a Bordeaux vintage on New Year's Eve. How far she'd come in so little time. In just that brief moment of clarity, she felt good; proud of herself. She decided this rare bottle of wine would be left in the kitchen as a constant reminder of the new Molly — that indestructible Molly. But even more incentive than the new Molly was the old Molly. And, if push came to shove, she'd sell the goddamn thing for a ridiculous price.

Prendergast produced a bunch of keys on a keyring and explained what each key's purpose was, all quite rudimentary. Molly beamed with pride and excitement as he handed over the keys to her. 'I have a good feeling about this,' he smiled.

Molly rejoiced with a wide grin on her face, 'Me too.'

'I think you'll find your true purpose in the house. Anything that has gone before will seem…trivial.'

She wasn't sure what he meant by that, but she nodded and smiled. Having a Michelin star restaurant in Dublin City had been a roller-coaster of a ride, anything but trivial.

He unlocked the gate to let Molly through, then closed it in so abruptly behind her that Molly thought he was going to smash the gate on her rear bumper.

'You know where I am if you need anything,' he called. He also informed Molly the truck had already gone down with her things about twenty minutes before her.

Molly thanked him. She thought about asking him for a spare key for the gate, but she just wanted to get down to the farmhouse and settle in. She had plenty of time to sort out loose ends.

'I want to invite you up to the Gatehouse for dinner.'

This was the last thing Molly expected. 'Oh, really?' She was suspicious. Prendergast had another thing coming if he thought this was going to be that kind of agreement. She had been given a large country house and she should have known he would want something in return. She wasn't willing to become Prendergast's live-in lover, or in this case, locked-in lover. She was starting to sound like Janice.

'And,' Prendergast was quick to add, 'bring the girls, by all means.'

'Oh?' Molly repeated, taking back everything she'd mentally said.

'Though they might be bored, as I no longer have children.' He paused before clearing his throat and pouncing with, 'How does Friday evening at seven suit you?'

Molly was never any good at thinking on the spot.

'Well, um…' She didn't feel comfortable about the idea, even if her kids were invited, plus she didn't want to agree to something that could become a habit. But she was curious about his children, him having passed a few odd remarks. What does "I no longer have children" mean exactly? She felt that same evasiveness on the phone the first night she spoke with him when it came to the topic of his children. Molly graciously accepted his offer.

'Great! Do you like Italian food?'

'Everyone likes Italian food.'

'And your girls?'

'Sure!'

'Then lasagne it is!'

Molly thanked Richard Prendergast for his hospitality and drove off.

As they rounded the bend in the lane, the landscape opened up, revealing the 225-year-old farmhouse in all its bucolic, intense splendour.

'It's scary!' protested Cora.

Mina back-answered, 'It's pathetic, that's what it is! I'm going home!'

'You are home, Mina,' interjected Cora, rubbing salt in her sister's wounds as they pulled into the front yard. The workers already had Molly's belongings moved from the truck to the front porch of the house. Her mere few possessions looked a little sad…or to coin one of Mina's phrases: pathetic. All her worldly possessions were right here in the corner of the front porch.

Mina refused to get out of the car. Cora got out of

the car and stared up at the ominous building. 'Why this house, Mom? Out of all the houses, why this one?' She asked in disparaging tones.

'Because this is a listed building of cultural importance. It is a time capsule. Oh, and did I mention it's free?' She winked.

'At least you did one thing right,' Mina snapped.

Molly turned to Mina. 'And that is?'

'You didn't pay for it — it's a dump. No wonder it was free.'

Molly showed her right palm to Mina. 'Speak to the hand because the mom ain't listening.' Cora snickered at this. 'You're in one of your moods, sweetie. Come back to me when you get over yourself. In the meantime, I've got to move some furniture.' Molly turned to the furniture removal guys. 'Everything okay?'

One of the motley group, pulling hard on a cigarette, muttered from the side of his mouth. 'Everything would have been just dandy if your security guard hadn't interrogated us.'

'What do you mean?'

'He held us up for a good 15 minutes,' said another of the group, 'demanding to see paperwork. He even checked off the furniture and compared it with the inventory list.'

Molly found this unusual and more than a little creepy. 'Okay, that's being a tad overprotective. I'm going to speak to him.' Just because Prendergast owned the house didn't give him permission to go through her things and Gestapo-question her visitors.

If that's the kind of deal he thought this was, then he had another thing coming and Molly was going to nip this in the bud before it festered.

Molly unlocked the front door. The disgruntled removal company hauled their things inside: tables, chairs, mattresses, bed frames, cardboard boxes. Molly orchestrated the distribution of everything with meticulous precision. Cora and Emma chipped in by taking their few possessions into the farmhouse. The only possessions Emma brought were her Barbie and Creepy Baby, one of those real-life babies that looked just too real to be real. Molly's reaction to the thing was, 'No offence, Jan, but it's creepy as fuck' when Janice had given it to Emma for her birthday. They had shared a good laugh at that. It was the only toy Emma had ever shown interest in, besides her ratty-haired Barbie.

'Cora,' Molly called, 'how about collecting up your rocks and taking them to your new bedroom?'

'They're minerals, Mom. How many times do I have to tell you?' Cora gathered up her framed pictures, music posters, and her extensive mineral collection, associated literature, and gemstone paraphernalia.

Mina begrudgingly took her things inside, everything that was ever worth anything stuffed into her backpack.

Molly showed the girls their bedrooms. She wasn't sure if that was even legal, nor did she care, as she wouldn't be lighting a fire in any bedroom. The Victorians might have done it, but not Molly Greene.

On the sly, Cora protested that Emma's room was a little larger than hers, so Molly obliged and switched them. Emma didn't seem to care either way. To win her over, Molly gave Mina the top attic room. The attic room had a bay window that projected outwards from the main front wall of the farmhouse. It was the largest room by far, occupying the entire upper floor of the house. It was almost like a self-serving apartment annexed from the rest of the house. Mina was at the age where she needed her independence and if she closed her door, she would never know there was a house full of 'embarrassing' people below her, which was just perfect for her video chats.

*

Mina seized the moment and sat on the bay windowsill to call her friends for a group chat. She curled up like a cat on the sill cushion and, for the next half an hour, ranted and complained about the musty old farmhouse, her crazy mom who didn't care about her feelings, and how she was determined not to make friends at her new school. But she admitted, 'I do like this room. It's got a lotta character and the icing on the cake: I don't hear Cora or Emma screaming.'

As she spoke, she absently gazed through her bay window. From this vantage point, she had a partial view of the private lane leading down from the road at the top of the hill. As the January dusk drew in, Mina was sure she saw a figure standing still in the middle of the lane. She was almost positive an individual was watching the farmhouse, but the figure could easily have been looking the other way. It was too dark to tell…

*

After Molly hung the message blackboard and the wall clock in the kitchen, she, Cora, and Emma got together and designated the room at the end of the hallway by the kitchen door with a shabby old Chester armchair as a playroom and hangout for the girls. Cora took to it like ducks to water, hauling in stuff they had brought from Dublin and making it their own.

While the girls were playing in the playroom, Molly got back to the kitchen and put everything in its place. The kitchen was the only room she vaguely saw as home. To make it even homier, she switched on her Bluetooth speaker and played Eugen Doga's 'Gramophone' from her phone. She waltzed around the kitchen to the tune, placing cutlery and crockery in various drawers. There was a time when she waltzed with Mike to this very same tune, but in a different kitchen and a different life. They might share a bottle of wine or two — Molly would have the second bottle after Mike went to bed.

Molly suddenly remembered she had left Prendergast's 'homecoming' bottle of wine in the car. She went to the key-holder hanging by the backdoor (which led from the kitchen) and grabbed the fob, then switched on the porch light and went outside.

It was only five in the evening, but it was virtually night. The evening was still, silent, and freezing. The aroma of pine coming from the spruce trees

73

surrounding the farmhouse filled Molly's nostrils as she stood there on the front porch. Moths came to flutter and whirligig around the porch light, which Molly noticed now was cracked. The night fliers blindly collided and smashed into the bulb casing, stunning themselves and falling to Molly's feet. She'd read once that nocturnal insects are attracted to night light because the creatures confuse it for the glimmer of the moon. The artificial light draws them in and jams their gravitational system. Molly stared at the bugs zipping around the porch light. The more she stared, the more entranced she became. A noise somewhere off in the woods broke her from her daze.

Molly was about to leave the front porch and cross the gloomy front yard to the BMW, but for some inexplicable reason, profound fear stopped her from leaving the safety of the porch. The safety of the porch? The mother-of-three became aware of her surroundings. She furtively eyed the spruce trees and the darkness below their single sweeping canopy. To her dismay, Molly realised anybody could be out there right now, looking out at her from the cover of darkness. Insecurity overwhelmed her. She jerked and swivelled around to get back inside, hair raised, skin tingling.

'Cop the fuck on!' Molly admonished herself. 'You're a city girl out in the country! This is what the country does! It freaks us out…the peace, tranquillity, and silence.' It was the silence more than anything that Molly found unnerving, something she thought she'd never experience.

Pulling on her brave face mask, Molly pressed the BMW's key. The car chirped as the head and taillights lit up the front yard. Feeling a little more confident, she tiptoed across to the car and pulled the wine bottle from the passenger seat. She tried to fool herself by walking nonchalantly back to the front door…but halfway across, Molly bolted and fumbled to open the door, slipped inside, and locked the back door. Looking through the kitchen window above the sink, she pressed the fob again to lock the BMW. 'Get a grip!' There was nothing out there but owls, foxes, bats, badgers and anything else lurking behind those spruce trees with trunks easily wide enough to conceal the most obese of stalkers — 'Stop!' Molly felt foolish. She had frightened herself. Not one thing outside her head had presented her any reason for alarm except that noise somewhere out in the periphery of the woods that had broken her from her strange trance while she looked at the kamikaze moths and midges death-dive the broken porch light. The 'homecoming' bottle of Spanish wine was placed on the counter with a jitter in her hands. She replayed 'Gramophone' and hummed along with the haunting music while, outside, winter evening drew down the curtains of darkness. She sighed with relief, realising how uptight she was. Molly sat herself down at the kitchen table to compose herself. She glanced at the bottle of wine on the counter. To test herself, she placed the bottle of wine on the table in front of her, accompanied by a wine glass and a bottle opener. She sat there, staring at the bottle, willing it to pour her a

75

drink. 'What are you doing?' She asked herself. 'I thought you'd gotten over this?'

She needed a task, fast, anything to get her mind off that fancy bottle of wine whispering sweet nothings in her ear. Molly threw herself at the kitchen cupboards and started sorting everything in an obsessed feverishness, clattering pots and pans, loud enough to block out the dulcet tones coming from the wine bottle. She would beat this. The farmhouse would be her cold turkey on many levels.

As the wall clock counted down six electronic chimes, Molly Greene was overcome with a sense of inner peace and bliss she hadn't felt in, well, a long time. Light and hope consumed her. And it had all come at 6pm sharp.

The girls were playing and giggling in their new playroom and Mina, oh poor Mina, was upstairs chatting with her friends. God only knew what she was saying to her BFFs back in the capital. That was the only thing Molly felt bad about, but she'd make friends at her new school in Old Castle, Molly was sure of it. And until that happened, Mina would be at a loose end.

*

Meanwhile, upstairs, Mina was lying in her bed. The sloping ceiling came right down to the headrest of the bed. Some would find it claustrophobic, but Mina secretly loved it. Not that she'd tell her mom, not yet. She had finished her online chat and was writing a fanfiction story for Wattpad while listening to Tom Odell on her headphones when a muffled thud brought her out of her story and 'Another Love' in her ears. Looking about the bedroom, she half expected to see Emma appear from one corner. Only she could hear her younger sister downstairs with Cora. Her headphones drowned out all external noise, but she'd heard a bang come from somewhere close in the room. She lay there in bed, poised, listening. When no other sound was heard, she switched on her music and got back to her fanfic. The moment she did, another distinct thud came from what seemed to be all around her.

'What the…?'

Mina whipped the headphones from her head and listened out. The 15-year-old could hear her sisters downstairs and her mom making an unholy commotion with pots and pans in the kitchen. But the bang was closer; she'd felt the vibration of the impact on her headrest. A prickle of fear fluttered inside her. She tried to pay no attention, convincing herself she was fine by getting back into her Wattpad story, but she left the headphones off this time. No sooner had she begun to type when a thump, right above her head, startled her. Mina let out an involuntary screaming whimper. The sudden bang had alarmed her, but what scared her even more was that the roof was just above her head. There was no attic — she was in the attic. What could have made that noise? Her fingers froze above the keyboard and she stared up at the lowest corner of the ceiling to her left. There was something on the roof, either birds or rats. She would prefer mice, mice are cute, but mice don't make a clatter like this. Rats do, though. She concluded that rats had a nest inside the roof. She hated rats with a passion, but at least rats are normal. That conclusion appeased Mina, and she immersed herself back in her story.

Until the drumming came, very faint, but it was there, next to her head, an abstract tapping that might've had a pattern to it. Tap dancing rats? Holy fuck. She put her ear to the wall and could hear a rhythmic knocking from inside. Three taps…pause… three taps…pause. Her bed was jammed into the corner of the attic room. Outside was the gable end of the house…on the third floor. The noises she was hearing were coming from impossible places now. She then recalled how Cora and herself would tap out goodnight in Morse code on their Dublin bedroom walls from their beds at night before sleeping. Those taps seemed to be coming from just inside the wall, but the sound was being carried through the brick from somewhere below in the house. Mina would bet any money her little sister was down there right now, idly hammering on the wall. It wouldn't be the first time. But she needed to know that her little sister was pounding on the wall.

Trying not to freak out, Mina leapt out of bed and abseiled down the two flights of stairs. She found her sisters sitting in the old Chester in the playroom, looking at something on Cora's tablet. They looked too cosy to have been making any racket during the last ten minutes.

With a horrible sinking feeling, she asked. 'Did you or Emma just bang on the walls? Please tell me you did?' But she already knew their answer, judging by their sudden surprise at seeing her in the doorway.

Cora shook her head. 'Just looking at funny dog videos.'

Mina went to the kitchen. It looked as if a bomb had landed on the kitchen counter, targeting pots, pans, frying pans, and every other piled-high cookware. 'Were you tapping or hammering something just now?'

Molly was struck by the alarm on her daughter's face. For a second, she had to remember what she'd just been doing. 'Yes, I was hammering an old nail that had come out of the back of the cupboard.'

Mina left out one long, exasperated sigh of relief. 'Oh my god, that explains it. I could hear that all the way up in my bedroom, like right above my head in the ceiling. I almost shit myself.'

'Old house,' Molly suggested.

It was a suggestion Molly Greene would come to rely on more and more over the coming days.

Mina went back upstairs to her bedroom and continued writing her short story, Billy's Experiment, on her laptop, but she didn't pull on her headphones. She hadn't the two lines written when the distant tapping started up again in her left ear. She laid her laptop on the bed and pressed her ear against the wall. The tapping stopped, and in its place, Mina heard scratching. Wow, sound really carries in this h…

The scratching came loud in her ear, from just

inside the wall. She could virtually see the fingernails scraping the wall from the inside. A shiver of horror rippled through her frame. She spasmed from the bed before stumbling down the first small staircase leading from her attic room down to the second-floor landing. She crashed into her mom at the bottom of the stairs.

'Jesus!' yelled Molly. 'What—'

Mina, pale and breathless, snapped, 'And now?'

'Now what?'

Mina noticed the small suitcase in her mom's hand. 'Where were you just now?'

'Getting one of the suitcases. I'm just going to put away some clothes, Mina. Somebody's got to do it… hint, hint.'

Mina asked with wild, stark eyes, 'And before that?'

'Um, I was putting the tea towels away. What's wrong with you, Mina?'

A distressed look came over the young lady. Angry crimson rose up her neck and into her face. 'I'm hearing strange sounds in the ceiling above my bed.'

Once again, Molly used the 'It's an old house, Mina,' excuse. 'These old houses creak and groan, especially at night when the temperature is going down. Don't forget these houses have a lot of wood and wood never truly dies.' She made up that last piece of succinct information, but she was impressed with her little white lie; anything for some peace.

'Wood doesn't make scratching noises.'

'True, but you know what does? Rats. I'll speak to

Mr Prendergast — Richard. Maybe he has rat poison or a trap or something.'

Mina recoiled at the image of a writhing nest of rats just above her head. She thought about mentioning how she'd seen someone watching the house from the lane, but she just wanted to get back to her fanfic and forget all of this. She turned and went back upstairs to her bedroom. On the stairs, she muttered, 'When will you give up this craziness and take us home?'

'I heard that, missy!' Her mom called back up the stairs.

*

Molly smiled to herself as she went to her bedroom and put away the clothes she had packed in the suitcase.

Ten minutes later, she left her bedroom to go downstairs and check on the girls when she caught sight of Mina standing halfway up her stairway at the point where the stairs make a sharp right. She appeared to be sitting down and Molly could only see her upper body and a little of her head at the bend on the staircase. The light was poor in that middle section of stairs, being illuminated between the light thrown from the second-floor landing and Mina's room upstairs.

'You're not still standing there, are you? I heard what you said. Like Cora told you earlier, we are already at home so, please, try to make this easy on me. I promised you all we would quit this place if it doesn't work out.' She wasn't lying. Molly had promised this, and she would honour her word. Her children would always come first. But this was about to take on a whole new meaning.

The 15-year-old was remaining so uncharacteristically quiet and still that it disquieted Molly.

'Mina, are you okay?'

'Yeah?' Mina called from upstairs. 'I'm writing.'

Her voice was too far away. Mina was upstairs. Molly's heart fluttered in her chest and pulsed in her temples. Dumbstruck and slack-jawed, she watched that impossibly still silhouette standing where Mina's stairs dog-elbowed upwards on a hard right angle.

'Mom, forgot to tell you, I saw someone up the lane.'

'Oh?' Molly hadn't processed one word of her daughter's sentence, still transfixed on the staircase. Frozen to the spot, she couldn't even bring herself to blink in case she missed something. The more she looked at the shadow, the more she was convinced she was looking at something else. Molly was screaming inside, wanting nothing more than to turn away and pretend she hadn't seen a thing.

'Mom, what's that smell?'

Molly couldn't find the energy to answer.

'Like oranges or something? Christmassy smell. Are you cooking?'

That lingering aroma Molly had smelt the first time with Janice came wafting around the second-floor landing. The silhouette was so statuesque Molly thought all she was looking at was the banister (torso) and orb finial (head) of the ornate staircase matrix in the shadows. The nervous bubble of relief laughter was just beginning to come fizzing up at full throttle when the black mass shifted on the stairs. An anaemic emotionless face gazed down at Molly from the dimness. She slapped her hand to her mouth, not sure if she had screamed or not. Gooseflesh bristled along the nape of Molly's neck, back, and arms. It stared down at her, rendering Molly paralytic.

'Mom?'

'Yeah?' Molly realised she was whispering. 'Yeah, Mina?'

It was a child. At least, that's how it presented itself to Molly, yet there was a disquieting elderly quality to the face. The look reminded her of how Henry had looked when he was born. That first picture Mike had taken of his son was only minutes after Henry had come from Molly's insides. Henry was wearing one of those little woolly hospital hats to keep his bald head warm. From that moment until he lost that newborn wrinkled look, Molly used to call him her 'li'l ol' man.' But the ears that got the most of her attention. Whatever this was, peering down at her from beyond the balustrade, crouched, sickly, unblinking, had large ears that stood out in relation to the rest of the head.

'Mom? You there?'

'Uh huh,' Molly answered absently. She was trying to internalise what she was witnessing on the stairs. Her skin tingled. So intense it was like an electric shock running through her.

'Mom,' called Mina again, 'remember I told you I saw somebody on the lane? I think it was Prendergast.'

'Who?'

An argument erupted downstairs between Emma and Cora. Molly turned to ask what was wrong. When she turned back, whatever had been on the stairs was gone.

'There's only one Prendergast, Mom.'

'Hmm?'

'Mom, what's wrong with you? You sound like you're drugged or something.'

Trying to pull herself together, Molly answered, 'He owns all the property around here, so he's within his rights to walk his own land.' She desperately wanted to tell someone about what she just saw, but the last thing she was going to do was tell Mina or especially Cora.

'I thought this was our house?'

Molly didn't want to get into the odd arrangement she had with Prendergast.

Emma and Cora came thundering up the stairs looking for Molly to settle a dispute. Something about Emma's Creepy Baby going missing for the third time in an hour. She was blaming Cora, and Cora was blaming her sister for being so absentminded. Emma started crying, and nothing was worse than Emma's screams. Molly took a deep breath and glanced over her shoulder at the staircase before going down to the playroom. The creepy doll was stuffed into Emma's dollhouse. Molly considered Creepy Baby as it had become lovingly known as. The ragged thing was half bald with a lazy right eye. The doll had been stripped of her clothes long ago. That got Molly thinking about the dollhouse. It was strange to see it here in a different context. She had grown so used to seeing it back in their Dublin house that she no longer saw it. But now she was reminded how Mike had made this dollhouse for Cora for Christmas, their last Christmas together.

Another argument solved, Molly got back to the kitchen, her mind on fire with all sorts of possibilities. What had she seen on Mina's staircase? Molly gazed at that lush bottle of wine on the kitchen counter by the hob, begging to be drunk. She cursed Richard Prendergast for even bringing it. A tipple, just to take the edge off from what she had seen. Mike would understand. She went to uncork the bottle, but Mike's voice didn't come from behind her as it normally did to question what she was doing. Her moral compass had abandoned her. No, he hadn't abandoned her — this is what Molly wanted and Mike wanted what she wanted. Mike hadn't followed Molly to the farmhouse because they had said their goodbyes in the rear-view mirror of Molly's BMW…

A muffled thud of something falling sounded somewhere over the kitchen. She checked to see where the girls were. Cora and Emma hadn't moved from the playroom, although another screaming match had erupted. Something about Creepy Baby playing hide-and-seek, not that Molly really cared. The noise couldn't have come from Mina's room either, her bedroom being on the third floor. By process of elimination, that left the middle floor: their bedrooms.

Her head still reeling from the vision on Mina's stairs, Molly braved the elements and went back upstairs. Mina was already up there.

Halfway up the main staircase, that sweet, cloying perfume bloomed in her nostrils. It was the smell of overly ripe fruit, citrusy and oddly familiar. Curiosity getting the better of her, Molly continued upstairs. At the top of the stairs, she turned left towards the girls' bedrooms. She glanced into Cora's bedroom. It still had a couple of boxes of clothes waiting to be put away, but nothing indicative of the bang she'd heard. Her mineral collection was strewn all over her bed, from low grade ruby and emerald to pink and smoke quartz, but nothing on the floor. Whatever had contacted the floor, she was sure of it.

'Cora,' Molly called, 'please put your rocks away.'

Downstairs, Cora yelled back, 'They're minerals, Mom! By the way, Creepy Baby's gone again…'

'Cora, just deal with it, please. I'm busy.'

It rocked Molly to see how Cora had already placed the framed pictures of her dad in the most prominent positions of the bedroom. As always, when Molly discovered Mike's things or pictures of him, it sucked all her energy. It felt strange to see Mike here on Cora's shelves, in a house that wasn't her home, not yet. The more she looked at the photographs, the more she felt Mike was becoming a man she once knew. Mike was becoming a very familiar stranger.

With a heavy heart, Molly walked further down the hallway to Emma's bedroom, which was also laden with cardboard boxes waiting to be put away. Nothing seemed out of place, except for that stale citrus aroma, stronger in this room with an atmosphere Molly couldn't put her finger on. If asked, she might describe it as that feeling one gets when they know someone else is in the house as opposed to being alone.

She was about to walk away when she noticed Creepy Baby on the ground at the foot of the bed. Molly frowned in confusion. She had just found the scabby thing in the dollhouse downstairs. The girls hadn't been up here in the last five minutes. Yet here it was, in all its disturbing glory.

'Mommy…'

Molly startled. 'Oh, you fucker!' she spat. Had Creepy Baby just spoken? The doll hadn't uttered a word for months since Emma had the inspired idea of taking it into the bath with her. Falling on its head might've jolted it out of its short-circuited muteness. But how had it gotten up here to speak to Molly in the first place?

She knelt down to pick it up. As she got back to her feet, the mother-of-three caught a glimpse of beneath Emma's bed. She was standing by the time she realised there was something under there, hunkered down. At first, she had thought it was an old overcoat…until it moved.

Stifling her scream, adrenaline flowing, Molly bolted from the room but stalled halfway down the hallway. Summoning up every inch of courage, she reversed back to her youngest daughter's doorway, heart pulsing louder and louder in her temples. She stalled at the door. A hot flush of fear rose up her neck and face like a heat rash.

'Mommy?'

Hearing that again sent Molly over the edge. Fainting nausea washed through her.

'Mina? Muh-Mina? Can you…'

The last thing she remembered before blacking out was dropping to the floor by the bed. No, that's not entirely true — the last thing Molly Greene remembered before losing consciousness was what she saw crouching under Emma's bed.

7.

Molly Greene woke to three anguished angels looking down at her.

'She's awake!'

'Yeah, okay, Cora! We can all see that. There's no need to scream.'

Then it was Emma's turn to ask Mina to stop shouting.

Molly smiled, happy she was back in her homely chaos.

Cora asked, 'What happened?'

'That's what I want to know…' answered Molly.

Mina filled her mom in. 'I came down from upstairs and I found you here on the ground. I didn't know what to do, so I called Cora and Emma. I think you were only out seconds because one minute you were calling me and the next minute you weren't. I came down to see what was wrong, and I found you here.'

From her left peripheral vision, Molly could see the black gap which was the area beneath Emma's bed. She couldn't, nor wouldn't, bring herself to turn her head and look under there, just to see if anything was still lurking. Molly desperately wanted to tell everyone what she had seen, or what she thought she'd seen, but how could she speak about this in front of the girls? 'There's something under Emma's bed!' is what she wanted to scream, but she took one look at cute little Emma and knew she couldn't. Little by little, her consciousness came trickling back, and now she could see her youngest daughter was holding Creepy Baby in her clutches. Emma smothered her mom in a hug. 'You found her again! Thank you! Thank you!'

Molly smiled, but she eyed the doll. 'Em?'

'Yeah?'

'Does your baby talk?'

Emma shook her head. 'Don't think so.'

'Cora, when was the last time you saw Creepy Baby talk?'

Cora laughed to herself. 'Oh? Lemme see, that would be right before Emma washed her hair in the bath. Her last words were, "Help! I've got wires 'n batteries n' shit inside meeeeeuh…"' Cora imitated a dying robot.

Emma found this to be hilarious, and even Mina giggled.

Molly would have found this funny but, firstly, she was lying on the ground after having fainted, and secondly, she was sure she heard Creepy Baby call her 'Mommy'.

The children helped Molly get to her feet. Mina guided her to Emma's bed, but Molly wouldn't sit on the bed.

'What's wrong?' asked Mina.

'Nothing.'

'Sit on the bed,' Cora encouraged her mom. 'You need to rest.'

'No, no. I'm fine. Stress of moving… Nothing else.'

The three girls eyed Molly with vague suspicion.

Molly asked Mina to go downstairs and make her a hot and sweet cup of Barry's tea to get her back to normality. She told Cora to go and help Mina. Cora obliged with a smile, as was her gentle way. Once the girls had gone downstairs, Molly asked Emma for Creepy Baby. Emma handed over her baby doll with an air of inquisitiveness. Her blooming smile showed she was happy her mom was giving her baby so much attention. But she became horrified the second her mom violently pumped her baby's chest to make it talk.

'C'mon, talk now!' grunted Molly.

But Emma didn't like how her mom spoke to her baby now. 'Stop, Mommy. She doesn't like it.'

'Talk now you little fucker!' Molly beat the rubber baby on the wall, just to hear the thing chirp would suffice. 'I know you can talk!'

Emma's bottom lip drooped before letting out a long heart-felt raucous bawl.

Hearing her child wail like this shadowed everything she'd seen in this house over the last few hours. What had gotten into her? For a second there, she'd forgotten her daughter was standing next to her. 'Oh, I'm so, sooo sorry!' She handed Crecpy Baby back to Emma. 'I just wanted to see if I could make her talk, that's all. I know you loved when she spoke. I was too rough, I'm sorry.' She empathised with the child, imagining what Emma saw through her eyes. It was traumatic, just as if someone came along and started trouncing Emma in front of Molly. She felt terrible. Molly gave Emma a hug. In turn, the child gave her baby a tight embrace while her mom checked under her bed, of all places. Emma giggled, presuming a game of hide-and-seek was on the cards. The second Molly got to her feet, Emma made a dive and ducked under the bed.

Molly snapped, 'Emma! Come out!' before thinking.

Her daughter popped her head out from under the bed. Her impish smile faded when she saw her mom's concerned expression. This was no game.

Molly paused. 'There could be...spiders under there, Em.'

On hearing the keyword spiders, Emma's eyes flared.

Molly couldn't help but smile at the irony. Spiders would be the least of Emma's problems if she had seen what her mom had thought she'd seen.

Emma made to army-crawl out from under the bed when...

Molly's smile dropped from her face when she saw the instantaneous distress growing on her child's face. 'What's wrong, Em?'

'I can't...I can't...' Emma's face reddened in angry streaks. 'Mommy?' Her voice was controlled, but the next words out of her mouth would come in a scream and Molly just knew it from worldly experience. 'I'm stuck!'

Molly panicked, witnessing the sudden alarm on her daughter's face. 'Don't worry, Em. I'll get you out. Stop moving! You'll hurt yourself. You're just stuck, that's all.'

But the child was panicking, flailing blindly under the bed.

Molly knelt and tugged at Emma's upper arms, but that was only making things worse.

'Ow! You're hurting me!'

Molly was growing more frantic by the second. 'Sorry! I'm just trying to get you out!' She kept her voice in check. Emma would panic even more if she heard the panic in her mom's voice. 'What part of you is stuck, Em?' She couldn't understand it. Emma had dived under there with an inch of clearance between her spine and the bed frame just a second ago. Molly jumped to her feet and, with a heave, lifted the lower-left corner of the bed. More than enough for Emma to escape. But the child didn't budge. 'My foot's stuck, Mommy!' Emma bawled, thrashing around.

Mina called up the stairs. 'Your tea's ready, Mom.'

'What's wrong with Em?' Cora questioned, coming up the stairs towards them.

Oh, Jesus! Oh, Jesus Christ in Heaven! Molly screamed inside her head. There was nothing under the bed where Emma could get her foot stuck! Consumed by undiluted horror and dread, Molly eased the bed frame onto Emma's little footstool, which levered the bed frame upwards six inches on one side. Molly dropped to her hands and knees to wedge her daughter out…

Emma couldn't see her lower half-hidden beneath the bed and thank Christ, she couldn't because what Molly witnessed in that moment changed how she looked at the world. Who would've ever thought that what lurked in the shadows beneath Emma's bed — her safe haven — would change how the world looked at Molly?

The pungent stench of rotten citrus was overpowering down here underneath the bed. And now she could identify that other hidden ingredient: cloves. That smell was a very mouldy orange stuck with dozens of cloves. With the odour came a whiff of memories. Molly's mother had shown Molly the homemade hack. Stick cloves in an orange and it will perfume the room for a week, filling her bedroom with Christmassy fragrance until the orange turned mouldy and stale. Molly recalled disgust and fascination as a child, watching the carpet of green mould slowly swallow the orange. Her mom asked her to throw it out. Molly did as she was asked, but kept the dirty secret in the garden shed. The garden shed smell of her childhood was the same fragrance she was smelling now under her daughter's bed.

From the shadows beneath Emma's bed protruded a pallid arm spider-webbed with blue varicose veins and a fist that vice-gripped onto her child's struggling left leg. The most horrendous realisation of all was that Molly was sure it was the arm of a child. Molly caught hold of Emma, not caring how much she hurt her arms, pulling them out of their sockets if she had to.

'Ooow!' Emma protested. 'You're hurting me. Let go!'

For a strange moment, Molly wasn't sure if her daughter was speaking to her or the hand clutched

94

around her ankle.

Primordial maternal instinct, deep inside the chasm of Molly Greene, kicked in. Fury, profound and frightening, burnt bright inside her. 'Let go!' She bellowed, pommelling herself backward onto the heels of her palms. In bug-eyed fear, Molly saw the hand in the gloom release her child's ankle. Molly leaned over and hauled Emma from beneath the bed, pulling her with such force that she skidded with the girl across the floor, wide and free of the bed. She held the hyperventilating child in her arms and told her everything was going to be okay. During the whole ordeal, Emma hadn't let go of Creepy Baby. It broke Molly's heart to see how important the ugly rubber doll was to Emma. It was her comfort thing. God, she was still just a baby.

It was only then that Molly noticed Cora standing in the doorway, looking hypnotised. 'What happened?'

'She got her foot stuck under the leg of the bed,' Molly lied. 'She's okay now. Show over.'

Cora just stood there for a second, taking stock of the situation, eyes flitting back and forth. The oddity of her mom's excuse hung in the air, and Molly saw that doubt flicker in Cora's eyes.

Cora knelt down and hugged both her mom and sister. 'You saved Creepy Baby! Yeah!' she rejoiced, and this snapped Emma out of her blank-stared shock. She nodded and laughed through her tears.

Nerves shot, Molly suggested, 'Let's go down for that cup of tea.' *You need wine…a lot.*

Molly went back downstairs to find the fresh brew of tea Mina had placed right next to the bottle of wine. *Almost like a dare,* thought Molly. Emma seemed to have already forgotten her ordeal and went off to the playroom with Cora. But from this moment on, Emma would suffer from claustrophobia, and she would never know what the trigger had been.

As Molly absently sipped her tea, she watched the moths circling the cracked porch light. She went over what had just happened in Emma's bedroom. Her mental retelling stopped and looped around the moment Molly had barked at whatever the fuck was hiding under her child's bed. The anger and rage she had felt at that moment left her worried. It was as if she hadn't known herself. Where had that reaction come from? Who was that Molly? The more she thought about it (and she didn't want to think about it) the more she came to the unnerving conclusion that it had been something building up in her a long time. In a peculiar way, Molly had been killing time until the evening when she would have to show her thunder at the thing keeping her child hostage under her bed. But where was the source of this River of Rage? High in the lofty peaks of Guilt Mountain, where Molly kept her anger in a cave called Henry.

How could this be happening? Is this even happening? Molly looked about the kitchen suspiciously, realising the farmhouse hadn't been quite vacant when they'd moved in. She struggled to get her head around what was happening. She had never entertained the idea of…she couldn't even bring herself to think the G-word, let alone say it aloud. What would people think? Had she overlooked the small print of this verbal contract between herself and P—

Her phone rang on the table, startling the bejesus out of her.

'Hello?'

Speak of the devil…

'Hi, Molly. This is Richard Prendergast. I just wanted to know if you're settling in, okay?'

Molly burst out in hysterical laughter. 'Settling in? That's one way of putting it. I've got questions for you.'

There was a pause on the line. 'Are we still on for lasagne at my place on Friday? You can ask all the questions you want then.'

Molly didn't think she could wait until Friday. Then again, she hardly even knew what today was. 'When, sorry?'

'We already spoke about it. The day after tomorrow, Friday.'

'Um, yes, I think it should be fine.' She thanked Richard Prendergast but wasn't quite sure if she should put the phone down because there was a pause on the line.

'It's an old house, Molly.'

'Oh, you're still there?'

'It's an old house, and like us all, it creaks and groans as the years pile up.'

Molly wasn't sure where this was coming from. 'Oh?'

'The beams in the house are a couple of hundred years old. They swell and shrink. Don't be alarmed if it sounds as if there are people walking around in the attic.'

Molly laughed uneasily. 'Well, I'll think it's Mina. She chose the attic room.'

'Molly?'

'Yes?'

'You might feel claustrophobic energy in the farmhouse. Or you might feel disorientated. This has happened to me on several occasions when I lived there. But don't be put off by this. Some floors are not level and I know one or two walls on the second-floor tilt ever so slightly. The combination of creeks and groans, off-kilter floors, and crooked walls can have a strange, disorientating effect on the mind. Still, it's free, and isn't that what counts, hmm?'

Was Prendergast trying to excuse the presence in the house by inventing some lines from a horror film? It sure sounded like it. Before Molly had time to process Prendergast's words, he bid her a curt farewell. She needed to know who or what she had seen on Mina's staircase and what had grabbed Emma under her bed? Jesus Christ, was she for real?

Louie, the cockatoo, started flapping in his cage, startling an already on edge Molly who was already on edge. The bird squawked and thrashed about its large dome cage propped on a stand in the corner by the kitchen door.

Molly had never seen the cockatoo so agitated. 'Lou, I've neglected you. Is that it? I'm so sorry, I've been busy with the move and I ignored you.' Molly went to the cage and opened the door, then waited for the cockatoo to sidestep outside his cage, as was his custom. The bird loved to have free rein in the kitchen back in the Dublin house. But Louie wouldn't budge and this, too, was a first for Molly. The bird backed up on his perch and cowered there at the furthest point from the open door, craning his neck and flexing his crest. He eyed Molly and, no matter how much she tried coaxing the exotic bird, he would not leave the safety of his cage.

That Wednesday night, their first night at the farmhouse, the Greene family slept soundly in their beds, except Emma, who refused to sleep in her bed. She slept with her mom, and Molly was more than happy to have her by her side. It took Molly a long time to drop off to sleep that night, but eventually, her youngest daughter's deep-sleep breathing had an ASMR effect on her, lullabying her into a comatose slumber…until she bolted upright. She gazed at her sleeping daughter lying next to her in the beams of luminescence coming from the overhead moon outside the window.

'Em?' Molly nudged her sleeping daughter. 'Em, are you awake?'

Emma turned around to her mother with an I-am-awake-now disgruntled look of disgust.

'Em, can you remember what Creepy Baby used to say?'

The child was too tired to answer, and Molly felt

bad for waking her, but she had this sinking feeling in the pit of her stomach. 'I'll give you money to buy anything you want in the shop if you tell me what words Creepy Baby used to say before you took her for her bath.'

'I love you.'

'Em, I love you too, but I need you to remember what the doll, I mean Creepy Baby, used to say?'

The four-year-old repeated what she said the first time. 'I love you.' Her eyes rolled up under her eyelids and she fell hopelessly back to sleep.

'I love you, Emma, but I need…' The rest of Molly Greene's sentence dried up in her throat when she realised her daughter wasn't telling her she loved her but was simply telling her what Creepy Baby used to say before she was short-circuited in the bath: I love you. Molly remembered now: give her chest a little squeeze and 'I love you…' would come forth in glorious monotone. Unless the rubber doll had a selection of choice one-liners, Molly had heard Creepy Baby utter a new word: 'Mommy'.

8.

The Greenes spent most of Thursday unpacking and tidying things away, trying to make the farmhouse feel like home. Cora and Emma seemed to be settling in quite readily despite the previous evening's horror, which hadn't left Molly's thoughts, but she was determined not to let it get the better of her. Molly had a purpose here, she could feel it, and had felt it the first day she'd visited the farmhouse. Thinking back, she couldn't remember if she'd said that to Janice. She could sure remember feeling it in the front yard.

Meanwhile, Mina was in denial of the fact that the farmhouse was their new home, forever holding out for life back in the suburbs of the capital city.

Molly placed the Home Sweet Home mat at the front door. It didn't feel like home, not yet, and it wasn't all that sweet. She was ill at ease, no great surprise there considering what she'd witnessed. Or had she? None of the girls had seen or heard anything out of the ordinary, thank God. If they had, they'd already be on the road to nowhere. Molly had been under a lot of strain lately and going cold turkey wasn't helping. Wow, she just realised hallucinations are part of cold turkey. Does that extend to alcoholism too? Whether she'd imagined the thing or not, she had one thing clear, there was something missing and she knew what it was: Mike. He hadn't made an appearance yet and, before the move, he'd been appearing five or six times a day to give her advice with that cookie-cutter cutout vibe he always had. Another way of looking at it was Molly was healing. She needed to cut herself free to heal. Still, she was hardly at the farmhouse for 24 hours. Was it any wonder it didn't feel like home?

Molly wanted to call Wilma just to confirm everything. She was starting next Monday, and she hadn't called Molly since they spoke on that first visit. Wilma was cutting it a little fine. Sitting at the kitchen table, Molly couldn't recall if she said she'd call Wilma or vice versa. She took the initiative and called, but no one answered. She'd get back to her in her own time. Wilma was a busy woman. There was a logical explanation, of course, there was.

That evening, as Molly prepared dinner, a rush of fuzzy optimism and well-being consumed her when the clock struck six battery-operated chimes. She was listening to Eugen Doga's 'Gramophone' at the time and turned up the volume to hum along with the waltz, remembering how they used to waltz around the kitchen to this very tune. She got to her feet and danced with a little side-step and a sweep of her toes, breaking into a slow-motion, dreamlike waltz and twirling around the kitchen. The waltzing music echoed around the farmhouse, even faintly audible outside, as the gnawing wind soughed and whistled through the spruce needles.

As Molly breezed by the window above the sink, she caught a blissful glimpse of herself in the glass and smiled back. With the reflection of the light in the kitchen bouncing off the window, she didn't see the stalking silhouette standing outside the kitchen window. She was too taken by her waltz with the ghost of a memory.

A sickly sweet fragrance of rotting citrus wafted into the kitchen, almost visible it was so thick and ropey, and brought her waltz to an abrupt end. Molly switched off the music. As she did, her attention was drawn to the ceiling, of all places. A spot on the ceiling, more or less directly above the kitchen table, pulled her interest. She could've sworn she heard the shuffle of dancing feet for a fraction of a second. It was almost like musical chairs, but the feet kept waltzing for a millisecond after the music stopped, enough to catch Molly's attention…and catch the phantom dancer.

'Girls?' She wasn't sure who was up there. No answer came back. 'Girls, who is hungry?' Not for the first time, Molly asked an inane question to disguise the real question — the real question being who the fuck was doing the waltz upstairs if everyone is downstairs? Molly Greene's skin bristled as energy filled the house.

'I'm starving,' called Cora.

'Me too!' came Emma's voice.

Cora answered back, 'She's always hungry. I think she's got worms!'

And Mina? 'Mina, you hungry?' Mina didn't respond, so Molly walked to the doorway and yelled upstairs, 'Mina, dinner's ready in ten.'

'Okay!' came Mina's barely audible voice, too far away to be on the second floor. 'I'll be down in twenty minutes. I'm on a video call.'

Who was Molly kidding? She wasn't the waltzing type anyway, not really. Not to be intimidated in her own home, Molly tramped upstairs. She checked every room, but there was nothing there — which was the problem. She went back downstairs to the kitchen.

Cora and Emma were standing by the cockatoo's cage.

'Mom,' Cora started, 'can I give Lou a tour of the house before dinner? He's been in his cage since we got here and I thought he could do with a fly around.'

'Okay, but you clean up the poops. If I find one, I'll pluck him.'

Cora laughed and opened the door latch. She put her hand through the opening to caress Louie's golden yellow crest, something the exotic bird loved to have done to him. But not this time...

It was Cora's sudden yelp that shocked Molly, making her drop a bottle of soy sauce onto the floor where it smashed into smithereens. She cursed as Cora howled in agony, holding her left hand to her chest. 'What happened?!'

'Lou bit me!' Cora managed to blurt out between doleful sobs.

Molly was dumbfounded to hear this. She looked at the bird and back at her daughter. 'Are you sure?' It was a stupid question, but she had to make sure.

'No, Mom! I bit myself!' At least Cora's sarcasm was still intact.

Molly looked at the wound and winced. The bird had sunk its formidable beak into the chunky flesh between the thumb and forefinger of her left hand. 'Jesus Christ, I think that's going to need stitches.' Molly panicked, realising she didn't have a family doctor! She had overlooked the prospect of family doctors and hospitals which are fundamental when it comes to having children. She pulled up Google on her phone and searched for the nearest family doctor. She couldn't understand why Google Maps was telling her that a GP's surgery was just a minute's drive from the farmhouse. She zoomed in to see it was signalling the Gatehouse. Flummoxed, Molly called Richard Prendergast.

He answered on the first ring. Molly informed him what had just happened, and Google Maps was directing her to his house.

'Um,' he hesitated, 'okay, bring her to the house. I'll meet you there now. I'm just out for a walk.'

'Okay, but shouldn't I be taking her to a doctor?'

Prendergast hung up on her. Molly called Mina down from the attic. She filled her in on what happened and told her to watch Emma. She grabbed the car key from the key holder by the backdoor, pulled a jacket over Cora's shoulders, jumped in the car, and spun out of the front yard for the Gatehouse. It had begun to rain and was coming down in great sheets. The BMW's windshield wipers thumped back and forth on full throttle, but they couldn't keep the windscreen from flooding. Molly had to squint to see the lane ahead.

A minute later, they were parking up in front of Richard Prendergast's place. He was there to meet them, dressed from head to toe in an ankle-length black raincoat. 'I was out for a walk.'

In the moment's chaos, Molly questioned what he was doing out on a horrible night like this.

'Come inside,' he beckoned them. 'You're going to get soaked out here.'

Molly stalled. 'We need a doctor or a hospital. I don't think this is the best time for coffee! Where's the nearest hospital?'

Prendergast ignored Molly, turning his attention to Molly's daughter. 'And what might your name be?'

'Cora.'

'Cora, let me see the wound.'

She lifted her trembling hand to Prendergast. He studied the lesion through the raindrops. 'Follow me.' Prendergast went inside. Cora followed, but Molly hung back. 'But why…?' Neither of them paying any attention to her. She had no other choice but to follow on.

Prendergast took them down the hallway of the Gatehouse. On both sides of the dim Paisley wallpapered walls, they sailed by a dozen or so framed photographs of a woman and a boy, from posing in the snow and on balmy beaches. At Richard's striding heels, Molly only briefly saw the framed photographs as she was more taken with the condition of the Gatehouse; to say it was missing a woman's touch was an understatement. And she was wondering what was going on.

At the end of the hallway, they turned right into a sparsely furnished room, but it had enough furniture to spark Molly's interest. Against the back wall was a substantial desk. Behind it was a swivel chair upholstered in emerald, green leather. High on the far wall, a locked cabinet housed bottles, jars, and vials. But it was the examination bed against the opposite wall that really piqued Molly's curiosity. By the time Prendergast produced a vintage brown leather valise from beneath the walnut desk and unclasped it, Molly had deduced Google Maps was correct: Prendergast was a GP. Inside the leather bag, Cora and Molly saw more medication. Richard looked through the clinking bottles and jars before producing a vial and a syringe.

'Cora, this is a tetanus shot.'

'Are you…?'

'Yes, I'm a physician…GP…family doctor. I took early retirement, but I'm still a licensed family doctor. I keep meaning to update Google. Now, ready, Cora?'

Cora winced in pain. 'Yeah.'

Prendergast injected Cora into the upper right arm. She didn't flinch.

'There's my little champ!' congratulated Molly, then asked her friendly neighbour if Cora needed stitches.

'These bites carry a high risk of infection and stitching the wound might increase the chance of it getting infected. It should be left alone — open air is the best cure in this case. I'm going to give you some painkillers, Cora.' He took a jar of pills from the medicine cabinet which Molly noticed was locked, then handed them to Molly. 'Take one every eight hours, only if you really can't manage the pain. Painkillers are too easy to swallow and make the pain magically disappear, but your body is much better off without the chemicals.' Richard led them to the front door. 'And be careful with that cockatiel!'

'Cockatoo,' Cora corrected him with a giggle. 'Thanks for helping me.'

Richard seemed taken aback by Cora's sincerity. 'It was my pleasure, really. It felt good to be a physician again.'

As the trio receded down the hallway, Molly was struck once again by the framed pictures which lined both sides of the hallway. She couldn't help but wonder who these people were. Prendergast had given her the impression he didn't have a family, though his wording was a little off.

Richard Prendergast bid them goodnight, and they sprinted across to the BMW to get out of the rain. Molly desperately wanted to share her disturbing experience with him, but not in front of Cora.

'Are we still on for that lasagne?' she called from the window of her BMW.

'It's made already!' he called back through the rain from the front door. 'It's in the fridge, ready to pop into the oven.'

Molly was impressed. 'Wow! Not even a bought one?' She laughed and thanked him once again for his free consultation.

Molly and Cora left. As they drove back to the

farmhouse, Molly's head was filled with unanswered questions.

'Mom?'

'Yeah?'

'Why did Louie bite me?'

'I don't know, sweetheart. Maybe it's the change of the environment. I'm sure he will come around soon and, before you know it, he'll be sitting up on your shoulder, nibbling at your ear.'

Cora tittered at the thought of this, but Molly wasn't so sure. Louie was a different cockatoo than the one in Dublin.

The BMW's headlights washed across the front yard. Through the pouring rain, they could see the silhouette of Emma waving at them from the lace curtain of the living room, then skedaddle out of view. Cora laughed despite her pain. 'She's so cute! She wrecks my head, but I still love her.'

Molly agreed with a warm smile. 'She can be a major head-wrecker when she wants to be.'

They went inside.

'Everything okay, Mina? Turns out Richard Prendergast is a doctor.'

'I got an injection!' Cora sounded proud as she skipped down the hallway towards the living room with her mom. 'It doesn't hurt now, but Richard said it would hurt a little tomorrow. I didn't get stitches because…'

They walked into the living room to find Mina and Emma snuggled up on the newly positioned sofa, watching TV. Emma had her eyes closed while Mina was shushing them to keep their loud voices down because Emma had fallen asleep.

'Oh,' Cora announced, 'Emma's asleep, hmm, o-kay. Then she won't want any ice cream,' using the trigger word. Cora knew there was no ice cream in the fridge — they hardly had milk.

Mina screwed up her face, as if wondering what had got into her sister. 'You sure Louie didn't give you a disease?' she whispered. 'Emma's asleep. Keep your voice down.' She turned to her mom. 'Can I go back upstairs and continue my video call?'

By now, Emma should have sprung up with a roguish grin on her face and bulled her way to the empty fridge freezer.

'What?' Something didn't add up.

Molly began to smell faint traces of cloves and citrus…

'What's that smell?' Mina asked her mom. 'Are you cooking oranges or something?'

And there it was, someone else confirming what she thought had only existed in the garden shed of her imagination.

Cora sniffed at the air. 'I don't smell anything.' She looked back at Emma before she left the living room. 'Okay, Em, you've passed the test. Great performance! You should be an actress in Hollywood…you'd find work easy cos you wouldn't need any make-up to play a monster or something scary.'

The strength went from Molly's legs and she flopped onto the sofa next to Mina.

'What's wrong?'

'Nothing, just tired,' lied Molly, finding that telling untruths was coming second nature to her at the farmhouse. Then again, she'd lived with the mother-of-all-lies for the last few years. Things were changing at the farmhouse. Not only had Mina confirmed what she was smelling in the house, but Cora had just waved at Emma…only it wasn't her little sister. If Emma was asleep on the sofa, then who had they seen waving out at them? The sooner she had that lasagne dinner with Richard Prendergast, the sooner she would have answers.

'He was great with Cora.'

'Who?'

'Richard Prendergast. Maybe it's good to have him around after all. It's always handy to have a retired doctor on the grounds.'

'I don't know,' reflected Mina. 'There's just something about him I can't put my finger on. I told you I saw him watching the farmhouse.'

'Who would you prefer watching your house: Richard Prendergast or a stranger?'

Mina thought about that. 'Hmm, interesting predicament. I don't know which is worse…which is better. Good question, Mom.'

It might be just her imagination, but Molly was thinking her daughter might actually be coming around. The old Mina was filtering back, little by little.

Molly was still thinking about what they'd seen from *the* front yard and if it was possible the lace curtain had shifted in a draught and its many folds appeared as if someone was waving? A trick of the light in the car's headlights? Now that she thought about it, it had been difficult to discern if the waving silhouette was behind or in front of the lace curtain. There was no way she could convince herself it had been an optical illusion. If that was the case, Cora hadn't imagined it too.

'Starting school next Monday. Excited?' Molly made a mental note to call Wilma tomorrow morning.

'Don't want to talk about it,' answered Mina, shutting Molly down.

'You'll be fine.' *Is Cora fine upstairs on her own right now?*

Mina grew pensive. 'Mom, can I ask you a question?'

The sincerity in her daughter's voice threw Molly a little. 'Yeah?'

'There's something odd about this house.'

Molly sat up. 'Oh, yeah?'

Mina nodded. 'I'm not saying it because I don't want to be here. It's actually quite a cool place…my friends think it's the bomb.'

'What?'

'The bomb.'

'Is that good or bad?'

'It's good,' she reassured her mom. 'But I'm hearing strange sounds in the fireplace.'

'Where?'

'The fireplace in my bedroom.'

'What sounds?' Not that Molly really wanted to

112

know.

'I don't know…kind of rustling or something. Just muffled sounds. And I've noticed they only start up in the evening.'

'That'll be birds nesting in the chimney.' Another easy lie. 'I've heard the same thing in my fireplace.' That wasn't a lie.

'And you know something else?'

'Yeah?' asked Molly.

'I think all of these fireplaces in our bedrooms are connected.'

Molly didn't like where her daughter was going with this. 'Why would you say that?'

'I can hear voices in the fireplace. I think it's you or Cora talking…or maybe it's coming from Emma's bedroom. The voices are too far away. All I hear is like a humming, but I cannot pick out words.'

'Call me up next time you hear something. Everything's got a logical explanation.' Molly's whole body bristled. She glanced at the substantial fireplace in the living room, how its cavernous inside faded into the dark.

'And there's something else…'

Molly gestured her eldest daughter to go on.

'I've felt a cold hand on my face while I slept.'

Molly gulped. A cold sweat beaded on her forehead. 'Just a dream…' Wow, she was losing count of the lies.

'I mean, I know I'm just dreaming.'

A wave of relief passed through Molly.

'But the dreams are so, well,' she searched the air

for a suitable adjective, 'vivid. I mean, I could actually feel that hand on my cheek, like I'm doing it now.' Mina held her right palm to her right cheek. 'But the hand was like a dead fish slapped to my face.' She concluded. 'My dreams are so vivid here.' The 15-year-old almost sounded proud.

Cora appeared in the hallway. 'So, how 'bout that dinner?'

Molly startled. 'Jesus! I forgot dinner! I was in the middle of getting it when you were bitten. I was wondering why I felt peckish. Anyone want a sandwich?'

'I cleaned up the mess on the floor, by the way. The place smelt like a Chinese restaurant.'

Something else Molly had forgotten about. 'Oh my God, thank you! We left in such a hurry…'

Cora and Mina joined their mom for a cold beef and pickle sandwich at the kitchen table. Molly was just telling them she needed to go into town to do some shopping when a distinct shuffle sounded on the ceiling above their heads, at the same point where Molly had heard the movement earlier in the evening. Their sandwiches poised at their lips, mother and daughters gawked upwards in unison. It would've been a comical moment, except there was nobody upstairs. And just to make sure, Molly got up from the table and checked on the child from the doorway. She had a clear view of the sofa against the back wall to the right. Emma was snug as a bug in a rug, but that didn't help her situation. They remained frozen, waiting, peering upwards. A minute or two later, they

114

shrugged it off and went back to eating their delicious cold beef and pickle sandwiches. In the middle of their chewing, a slow, agonising drag crossed the ceiling above their heads.

Cora leapt from her chair into her mom's lap. The concern on her sister's face seemed to petrify her even more.

Mina whispered in a low voice, 'What the fuck was that?'

'Mina, language,' scolded Molly. 'We're living next to the woods, guys. All kinds of things prowl around this place at night, foxes, badgers, wolves, bears…'

'Bears?' exclaimed Cora. 'Wolves? I prefer the creepy noises! And bears don't live in a house, Mom… unless this is Goldilocks and the Three Bears.' When Cora was nervous, she didn't know when to shut up.

'Well, I was just joking about the bears and wolves.' Molly tried making light of the situation but was only making it worse. Could it be she was getting used to the strange sights and sounds of the farmhouse? And even more blasé about lying?

'Mom, what was that?'

'Mina, we're surrounded by trees,' she gestured to the window above the kitchen sink, 'the place has to be teeming with wildlife. Bet it was a fox. I saw one yesterday when we got here. Caught it running across the front yard when we pulled in.' She was stretching, and she knew it.

*

The new mother of the house gazed right at him through the window. The eye contact had only lasted a millisecond, but long enough to tell him he still had a heart. She had done the same earlier during her impromptu waltz about the kitchen. How beautiful she looked. She had even smiled at him through the glass that time.

*

'Really?' Cora asked. 'Foxes? I love foxes.' A cloud of doubt floated across her face. 'Upstairs?'

Mina interrupted, 'That's another fairy-tale right there, Mom. Don't go there.'

The sudden series of knocks on the ceiling put the fox, bear, and wolf theories to bed, unfortunately.

With wide startled eyes, Cora observed, 'I know foxes are clever…but Morse code?'

Molly appreciated being a witness to the girls who were learning about themselves tonight. Cora discovered she fell back on humour when she's terrified and added Chatty Cathy to that growing list. Mina, on the other hand, reacted to the terrifying situation by forgetting how to breathe. And Molly? She lied.

The colour drained from Molly's face when the knocking turned into animalistic scratching and scraping. She could lie till the cows come home, but she couldn't disguise the terror in her face. 'It's an animal,' Molly assured them in hushed tones. 'I don't know what kind of animal, but we are out in the country and these are country sounds. You have grown up in the city and all of this is new for you.'

Molly only half-believed what she was telling her daughters. She, too, was a city girl and all of this was new to her, including Morse-coding foxes, house-dwelling bears and wolves. What would Mike do? Finding inner strength, she got up from the table in a huff. This has got to stop! 'This has a logical explanation and I'm going to find out what the hell it is. Until that happens, our minds are going to play games with us.'

But the minute she got up from her chair, the farmhouse fell silent.

Despite protests from Mina and Cora, Molly went upstairs and found nothing out of place. What she did notice was that faint aromatic lace of citrus and cloves lingering on the air.

That night, Mina, Cora, and Emma slept with their mother. At the rate she was going, Molly would be sleeping on the rug next to the bed tomorrow night.

Molly was sandwiched between her daughters, listening to their deep breathing in stereo surround sound, unable to sleep. She wondered if she had made a mistake in coming here. No, she wasn't wondering — she knew she had been mistaken in thinking she could live here at the farmhouse. At least, live here happily. Maybe she should have listened to Janice when she'd had the chance. Molly found great comfort in listening to her daughters' deep breathing all around her. It was beautiful and hypnotic.

She fell asleep, even if it was temporary.

After 3am something woke Molly. She was disorientated as she surfaced from sleep, thinking she was still back in Dublin. It took her a second to get her bearings. She listened out for what had woken her. She lay there for a few moments before sleep began to catch up with her. Just as she was going under, the knocking came in loud and clear. It was coming from the outside wall by the opposite bedroom window.

Curious and determined to put her daughters' minds to rest, Molly carefully climbed out of bed between the sleeping bodies in a game of nocturnal Tangle Twister, crossed the chilly bedroom, and hoisted up the window. It squealed in its frame. The fresh, windy night welcomed her when she popped her head out and discovered what the terrifying tapping was: a branch. That good ol' much-loved mommy 'n' daddy home favourite to calm a sensitive child's night terrors: it's just a branch blowing in the wind, sweetie, nothing to be scared of.

The branch in question was that of a leaning spruce tree slapping and scraping on the eaves of the house. Molly giggled into the night, the relief so liberating. She made another mental note to ask Richard Prendergast if he had a saw. The branch could be back if she leaned out the window. Or maybe Richard would do it for her if she batted her eyelids? No, bad idea. Go back to sleep, Molly.

But Molly Greene didn't want to go back to sleep. She just had to wake her girls and let them know. She crept back to the bed and called their names gently in their ears. They didn't take kindly to being roused from their sleep, especially Mina, but when Molly explained to the two older girls, they'd heard nothing more than a tree branch, they softened and even went back to their own beds, content in knowing the truth. 'There's always a logical explanation,' Molly whispered to them as they smiled wearily and dragged themselves to Cora's bed. Mina didn't have the energy to walk upstairs. Molly kept her youngest daughter in her bed for now. It was simple bliss to jump into bed and have the luxury of stretching. With this novelty, sleep hijacked Molly quickly and before long she was dreaming a vivid dream where she was knocking on the Gatehouse front door. Prendergast answered with a wide smile and dilated pupils. He looked stoned. Molly asked him if he would mind cutting the jutting branch knocking on the house eaves in the wind. She did that subliminal thing with her hair that men noticed — she'd seen the move on the National Geographic. But Prendergast's face grew dark and thunderous. He told Molly if she had sex with him right then and every day for the next month, he wouldn't go near the farmhouse. Molly asked if she could be his wife and he could become the girl's adoptive father — their new father. He declined the attractive offer, telling Molly she was the mother, and her place is, and always has been, the farmhouse. Besides, he had a family, sort of, but he wouldn't go into any more details. What he could do for Molly was give her the loan of his saw. In this dream world, Prendergast was already standing in his doorway with the rusty saw. He handed it to Molly, and they shared a kiss, nothing passionate, just a token that long-married couples give each other to let them know they still exist. That night, Molly was leaning out of her bedroom window on the second floor. She was halfway through cutting the annoying spruce branch when she felt a pair of hands caress her buttocks from behind before a tremendous force launched her clean out through the window and down to the yard below where a loud crack…

Molly snapped awake as her body broke in her dream. The digital read-out on the clock on the bedside locker told her only an hour had passed since she'd fallen back to sleep. She presumed what had woken her was the same spruce branch knocking in the wind, but then she heard Louie squawking downstairs. ''Allo!…Allo!…'Allo!' his helium monotone voice rang out. She stiffened. Her eyes widened and her heart thumped a little faster in her chest. The only reason the bird reamed off his party piece greeting is that someone had just walked into the kitchen. The cockatoo was a creature of habit and Molly knew this. It had been part of the Greene's daily morning routine:

'Morning, Louie…'

''Allo!…'Allo!…'Allo!'

She couldn't sleep now. Cursing to herself and subconsciously trying to make little of the bird's sudden outburst, she ventured on down. *What does a girl have to do to get a night's sleep in this place?* she pondered as she padded down the stairs. As she passed Cora's bedroom, she peeped inside, happy to see the two of them sleeping soundly. At least the bird hadn't woken them.

She went downstairs and gawped at the kitchen doorway, wanting nothing more than to turn on her heels and bound back upstairs. But Molly had been thrown into the big ring of life and had become one of life's fighters. She knew she would regret not finding out why the cockatoo had decided to utter his morning greeting at four in the morning.

But sometimes, in life, there are things meant to be left unknown. Molly Greene, of all people, should have known this.

Taking a deep breath and forgetting to exhale, Molly walked determinedly into the kitchen, almost having fully convinced herself she hadn't heard anything out of the ordinary. She played dumb and pretended she hadn't heard the cockatoo greet nobody in the middle of the night.

Bang on cue, the bird greeted Molly with his, ''Allo!…'Allo!…'Allo!'

Molly answered, 'Hi, Louie. You're up early.' Her eyes swept furtively over the kitchen. Everything was as she'd left it…almost everything. She wouldn't have seen it only she'd just remembered she needed to call Wilma ASAP and find out when she was supposed to start at the 'restaurant'. She'd backed up to write 'Wilma' on the chalkboard when she saw it…

The stick of chalk fell from her fingers when she saw the image of Louie on the message board. She froze, sensing something or someone so close behind her she could practically feel their presence brush up against her T-shirt and sweatpants. Molly had never suffered a stroke, but she assumed the numbing paralysis she was experiencing right in that moment came close. There was pressure in the kitchen. She could feel it, tangible. And, yes, sniffing at the air, she found minute traces of rotting oranges. Molly Greene backed up to the kitchen table, slid onto a chair, and swivelled herself around to stare at the chalk illustration in all its creepy glory. Maybe one of her girls had done it. That was the only logical explanation. Mina didn't draw it and that was for sure; Mina had little talent for drawing, it just wasn't her thing. Then she thought of Cora. Could her ten-year-old have drawn this? It was true, Cora had a few artistic bones in her body. Possibly she might've done this, but there was something alien about the bird, alien to Molly. Cora hadn't drawn this either. That left Emma, and that simply wasn't an option. Molly wondered if she should question the children in the morning, but that might rouse suspicion, and they were already on tenterhooks since that impromptu ceiling extravaganza. She didn't need to ask the girls because they hadn't done this. She got up from the table, wiped the board clean, and went back to bed. It just didn't happen, did…not…happen. Goodnight!

9.

On Friday morning, Molly Greene got up a little earlier than the others to make pancakes. While she was mixing the batter, she recalled the accomplished drawing of the cockatoo on the message board. She glanced across at the chalkboard and her whisking came to a stop when she saw an even more accomplished cockatoo than the one she had wiped out. Accomplished or not, Molly wiped the board clean for the second time. She was tired of lying to her children and none of them would've believed she had drawn the wonderful chalk illustration. For once, Molly couldn't blame the talented foxes, wolves, and bears that lurked in the woods around the farmhouse.

But it wasn't the message board garnering her attention; it was the blanket of snow covering the countryside. The flurry of snowflakes had fallen during the early morning, leaving the place looking like a Christmas postcard. The spruce woods stood stark white and in profound insulating silence. Molly couldn't contain herself with excitement and was like a child again as she woke her own children to tell them. It was Emma's first-time seeing snow and Molly would forever hold on to the look on her daughter's face when she drew back the curtain to the expanse of whiteness outside. And with the beauty came the darkness as Molly found herself thinking about Henry and how he might react to the snow. Cora, too, was excited to see the snow. She could just about remember when she'd last made a snow angel in the park after coming out of school six years ago in Dublin. Molly tread lightly when it came to waking Mina, but she sat up with an expression of wonderment that took Molly back 11 years to when Mina was Emma's age now, that face of open joy.

The Greene family convened in the kitchen and munched on pancakes.

Molly suggested, 'How about we go for a walk in the woods? How cool would that be in the snow? This is our third day and we haven't had a chance to explore much of the surrounding area.' She couldn't believe only three days had passed, not even three days.

Emma cheered and started gobbling down her pancakes with raspberry jam. Her reaction was so hilarious Mina and Cora almost choked on their mouthfuls of pancake. Emma was the first to finish breakfast and slide away from the table.

At some moment, between clearing away the breakfast things and tracking down their hats, scarves, and coats, Molly happened to glance at Emma, and what she saw stopped her dead in her tracks. The four-year-old was standing on the step she used in the downstairs toilet to reach the sink. She had taken the step to the message board, and hoisted herself up and was drawing something. Molly watched from a distance, not saying anything. The other girls were too interested in what attire they would wear for the stroll in the snow to notice anything. Molly's mouth fell open as she watched her daughter draw the same image she had wiped off the board last night. It was a carbon copy of the drawing of Louie, the cockatoo. But what was puzzling her, and frankly disturbing, was how Emma drew the picture. She was silent and focused, her hands and arms working in careful unison, forming smooth arcs that seemed far too precise for Hurricane Emma. It seemed as if Emma had been drawing all her life, how she executed the chalk lines and curves in complete silence. It gave Molly the hair-prickling creeps. Molly stood there, slack-jawed, as if an unseen pair of hands were guiding Emma's hands. And the most disturbing of all: Emma was using her left hand. She was right-handed.

Tired of being the only one to witness these eccentricities of the farmhouse and a desire to know if she was overthinking things, Molly beckoned her daughters. 'Mina, Cora,' she spoke softly. The girls wandered over. Molly nodded in Emma's direction. She saw how both girls reacted in the same way with odd fascination. Molly was relieved. She whispered, 'So, it's not just me?'

Cora replied, 'Um, since when can Emma draw?'

Mina observed how her little sister drew the exotic bird as if she'd been doing it all her life. 'Am I fucking seeing things?'

'Mina, language,' Molly answered, not taking her eyes off the message board.

'And since when is Emma left-handed?'

Molly answered, 'I'm asking myself the same question.'

As the four-year-old was putting the final touches on the bird's crest, Mina spoke up. 'Em, I didn't realise you were so good at drawing.'

The child didn't acknowledge her older sister.

'Emma,' asked Cora, 'who taught you how to draw like that?'

No answer.

'Maybe she saw a YouTube video?' opined Mina. 'Em, could you teach me how to draw something?'

Emma continued with the delicate shading of the bird's head crest by rubbing the chalk on its long side to achieve a softer shading effect.

'Okay, now that's creepy,' declared Cora.

Molly was feeling nervous about the tenebrous situation. 'Emma…Emma?'

'Why won't she answer us?'

'Mina,' Molly snapped, 'I don't know.'

The four-year-old's mind was far away, absorbed in her creation, unaware of her surroundings.

Mina, seeing the growing dismay on her mom's face, barked, 'Em!'

The child stopped, arm still raised to the chalkboard. The four-year-old slowly turned around to her family, stared at her sisters and mom with a wide-eyed grin none of them had ever seen before. The maniacal expression was so uncharacteristic of Emma that Cora cringed upon seeing the strained smile on her sister's face and she sidled up to her mom for safety. Her reaction was instantaneous. 'Mom, what's wrong with her?'

Meanwhile, Mina just stood there, biting her upper

lip, arms folded defensively. She was older and tougher than Cora, or so she thought, until she, too, pushed up against her mom for safety. 'Mom, what the fuck?'

Molly whispered, 'W.T.F will do, remember?'

Before their eyes, Emma put the final touches on the illustration and jumped off the footstool. 'Can we build a snowman?' she asked, as if nothing out of the ordinary had just happened.

Cora let out a long wail of a sigh and deflated into a floppy heap on the ground at her mom's feet. Mina walked off, fists clenched and ready to thump something or someone, before coming back. 'Em, who showed you how to draw like that?' Mina needed answers.

Emma just shrugged with an air of innocence that would fool anyone. Molly and the girls had their suspicions. You just never knew with Emma. She was a cunning child and a real terror when it came to things disappearing around the house. Back in their old place, Emma used to hide the TV remote control every week. Everyone searching high up and low down until Emma would miraculously announce, 'I know where it is!' and produce the missing device. Even more wondrous, she would always know where to find the device when Molly offered Monopoly money to the first person who found it. And she didn't limit her talents to only the remote control; Molly's phone, Mina's teeth retainer, and Cora's mineral collection would also go missing.

By the time they were outside in the front yard throwing snowballs, the girls had forgotten all about Emma's strangely creative turn. They built a snowman by the front door. Molly filmed them on her phone, knowing she was capturing gold for the future. Emma looked cute as a button in her winter get-up. Mina went inside and reappeared a minute later, holding a carrot to her nose. Molly was ecstatic to see her eldest daughter enjoying the snow as much as her four-year-old sister. Mina gave the carrot to Emma who had the honour of giving their snowman a nose while Cora went foraging for stones beneath the drift of snow to give the snowman a mouth. Molly then made a little dedication to their new house, filming it and giving background on how the Greenes had ended up at a 200-year-old farmhouse on the opposite side of the country.

But, as Molly suspected, it wasn't long before Emma was crying over her frozen, wet, numb hands. They went inside to warm up a little, made a quick change of clothing, and headed back outside for a walk. The family went by the edge of the spruce woods, sometimes going further into the copses where space allowed. The canopy was dense and granted no light to penetrate, leaving everything in perpetual darkness. The thick blanket of brown needles crunched beneath their feet. Apart from that only sound, the silence of the countryside was intense. Molly couldn't recall ever feeling so happy at that moment, walking through the snow in the countryside with her children. She looked back at their footprints in the snow and smiled. But, as always, two sets of footprints weren't present.

On the way back to the house, Cora noticed fresh, large footsteps in the snow that didn't belong to any of them. 'Look,' she pointed out, 'these are our feet.' She pointed them out in order of size, starting with Emma. Then she pointed to a set of prints in the snow which Molly would've overlooked if they hadn't been shown to her. With growing perplexity, Molly realised Cora was right: there was an extra set of footprints intermingled with their own. Every few meters, an extra larger footprint not matching any of theirs was discernible in the snow. It was clear the owner of the feet chose their exact path.

'Whoever owns those footprints was trying to camouflage their footprints in ours.' Mina further suggested, 'Why else would they walk in our tracks?'

'Because it's easier?' Cora asked.

Molly failed to entertain the possibility the owner of those footprints was trying to go unnoticed by camouflaging their steps in theirs. If that was the case, these treads could only belong to one man: Richard Prendergast. Unless he allowed hunters onto the land. Molly wasn't sure, but she thought it might be hunting season now. Maybe Richard had given permission to hunt his land. If not, they could be poachers. She scanned the surrounding trees and fields. The glare of the sun bouncing off the snow was blinding. But there was nobody else out there besides them at that moment. Molly indicated to everyone to be quiet. They listened out while Emma looked at them in astonishment, wondering why everyone was suddenly playing statues. 'It could be anyone,' she concluded.

They walked ahead. A few meters on, the footprints went off at an angle towards the main road…in the direction of the Gatehouse.

Having enough mystery for one morning, Molly decided to take a deep breath and enjoy what was left of their walk in the countryside. 'Okay, guys, listen up. I'm done thinking for today.' She closed her eyes for a second, and a second was all it took to reach a Zen-like state, listening to the crunch of snow, the sun on her face, the gentle sough of the cold wind through the t—

'I told you creepy Prendergast was a stalker, Mom,' interjected Mina, shattering Molly's state of Zen to kingdom come. *Oh, well, it was nice while it lasted.* She repeated, 'It could be anyone.'

Mina wasn't sold. 'Enjoy your lasagne this evening, Mom.'

For the rest of the day, the girls were exploring outside, throwing snowballs, and having a good time. Molly peered through the window above the kitchen sink now and again to see them playing in the expansive backyard. It brought joy to her heart to see the three of them bonding. Seeing something like this made the move worthwhile and beat school hands down.

Later that Friday evening, Molly rounded up Cora

and Emma to go to Richard Prendergast's house while Mina stayed back to do a 'live'.

'A what?'

'It's when…oh, forget it. I'm doing a video call with my BFFs. More to the point, why are you even going for dinner with *Bendergast*?'

Molly laughed. 'Mina, don't call him that. You saw him on the lane. Big deal.'

'He was following us on our walk this morning.'

'Did you see him?'

'Well, no, but who else would it be?'

Molly didn't want to entertain Mina any longer on the subject. But her daughter staying in the house alone preoccupied her, even though she didn't want to admit to herself that she didn't trust…Mina? No, she didn't trust the house. 'Could you do your live thing from the Gatehouse? I don't want you to be alone.'

'Why? I'm old enough to take care of myself.' Mina smiled her winning smile. 'Louie will take care of me.'

'Hmm, he's not exactly a Rottweiler.'

'Look, it's fine, Mom. Only lunatics would be down here at night,' Mina pointed out.

'That's what I'm afraid of.' *It isn't what's lurking outside the house, but what's lurking inside it…*

'C'mon, mom.'

The more Molly thought about it, the more she realised this might be an opportunity to let Mina settle in a little better. Let her bond with the place. She deserved a little free rein. 'Okay,' she acquiesced, 'but have your phone charged, got it? Call me for any reason.'

'Oh, yeah?' Mina mocked. 'I'll be calling you, but you'll have your phone on silent.'

Molly fetched her phone from her back pocket and flashed a sarcastic smile. She took her phone off mute and cleared her throat for comic effect. 'Call me.'

The girls wrapped themselves up in their woollies. As Molly did, she thought it was a little strange bringing them. She wasn't sure of the purpose of this evening's lasagne dinner at the Gatehouse. Maybe she should've jokingly called Janice to babysit. But Janice would've probably offered to travel across the country to babysit the girls. That's Janice. Molly would be starting at Wilma's restaurant soon and she'd need to find a local babysitter, anyway. Maybe Richard Prendergast knew someone.

'Have fun!' called Mina from the hallway. 'Don't do anything I wouldn't do!'

Molly looked back over her shoulder as she grabbed a pair of face masks hanging from the coat perch. 'It's strictly plutonic,' she smiled, handing one mask to Cora and strapping another one to herself. Apparently, Emma was too young to catch Covid.

'It's platonic, mom.' Cora corrected her.

Instead of taking the car, Molly decided they would walk. There was a nip in the air, but a bright sky full of stars was on display when they set out on the lane. The snow was thawing. They passed by the snowman they'd built earlier. His face had melted in the afternoon sun and now his smile was down-turned and sad, so sad that Molly cut him a new grin and straightened up his drooping carrot nose. It was only a ten-minute walk to Richards's place, but it took them double that time because Emma stopped every few footsteps to study something on the ground or in a tree, anything to slow them down. Molly's patience finally wore out, and she picked the child up and carried her. As they walked, Molly became preoccupied with the infinite darkness radiating from the woods. It was pitch black in there and, from the corner of her eyes, she was beginning to see shadows moving around through the blackness. Next to her, Cora sang a song about a yellow submarine to keep her nerves at bay. But instead of a yellow submarine, she sang about a big ol' creepy house. 'We're all livin' in a big ole' creepy house…big ol' creepy house….big ol' creepy house…'

By the time they were halfway up the lane, Molly was regretting coming on foot. She was sure something or someone was moving along with them from the edge of the woods. She'd even heard the crunch of melting snow.

Cora quipped, 'It could be a bear, Mom.'

The light emanating from the Gatehouse provided much relief.

'Mom?'

'Yeah?'

'Can we ask Richard to give us a lift back?'

Molly chortled. 'Yeah, maybe it's a good idea.'

Richard Prendergast, looking dapper as always in his tweed suit and slick hair, greeted them with an easy smile.

Just then, Molly remembered her strangely erotic dream featuring sexual favours and a rusty saw, ending with someone fondling her ass before shoving her out the bedroom window while she cut the branch that was knocking on the side of the house.

He beckoned them inside and told them to leave their coats on the coat perch by the door. As Molly hung her coat, she got a clear view down the hallway where she had walked just last night with Cora. She sensed on a subconscious level, she sensed something different about the place, but in the flurry of the moment, her mind was consumed by other pressing concerns like Emma, who had thought that taking her coat off over her head without undoing the buttons was a good idea. After prying Emma's head free of her duffel coat, Richard brought them to the living room. He invited Molly to sit down and told the children they could have a snoop around the old piano in the far corner of the room. Everything about the place spelt wealth, pomp, and circumstance, but relegated to a bygone era.

Prendergast was the ideal host, smiled on cue, and did all the right things. But there was something not right about him and Molly had sensed it the very second they walked inside the front door of the Gatehouse. Her interest was first triggered when Emma made to shake his hand — an adult thing Emma liked to do to get laughs. But Prendergast became awkward and waved nervously at her with a big wide grin that didn't meet his eyes. Emma, being a child, didn't pick up on the subtlety of body language, so she kept her hand extended and made Prendergast squirm. For a finish, he pretended to have forgotten something and walked off. He had also done everything possible to avoid any physical contact with Cora and Molly. He was keeping his distance from them. She experienced an unsettling flutter of adrenaline. Then again, Molly had forgotten they were in the middle of a worldwide pandemic with strict social distancing.

Richard asked, 'Are we missing one?'

Molly's heart skipped a beat. *We'll always be missing one.* 'Oh, you mean Mina. Yeah, she's busy with friends.'

Richard's face changed just then. How, she wasn't sure, but it changed. 'At the farmhouse?'

'No. She's on a video call. She misses her buddies back in Dublin. She's,' flashing air commas, '"doing a live."'

'And what's a…'

'Don't ask me.'

'Well, she's always welcome, any time of the day…or night.'

*

Meanwhile, Mina had started up a live on Instagram in her attic bedroom with three of her best friends and now ex-classmates. The conversation started up on the topic of the bitch in the class, Clara, and how she was smoking flavoured e-cigarettes since getting back from the Christmas holidays and selling the flavours to any of the other wannabes. After clearing up all the gossip, Mina offered them a virtual tour of the farmhouse. The girls liked the idea, so Mina left her bedroom and took them on the house tour. Before she left her room, she panned onto the fireplace and told the girls how sound travelled through the chimney flue. 'Voices come out of the fireplace.'

The girls found this to be very intriguing.

'I can hear Mom and the girls speaking from other rooms,' she said proudly, knowing this was cool. And the girls agreed. 'Though I can't hear what they're saying, but I hear talking. Probably better off. You guys know what Emma can come out with sometimes.'

They laughed.

As Mina was descending the staircase, recording live, she heard Louie squawking his morning greeting from the kitchen. ''Allo!…'Allo!…'Allo!'

The girls laughed on hearing the bird in the background, calling 'Louie!' in unison.

One friend called, 'My favourite cockatoo!'

Mina laughed along, but she was confused by the bird's sudden untimely greeting. 'Oh my God, that's so weird,' she commented with her camera pointing down the stairs as she continued to descend. 'I've never heard Louie say that at night. In that aspect, he's more of a cock instead of a cockatoo.' Mina giggled crazily, realising what she'd just said. That started everyone else off. The cockatoo insisted on continuing its morning welcome. Mina was bewildered. 'But do you know what's even weirder? He only speaks when he sees someone.'

The laughter subsided into an uneasy silence. The girls in Dublin were glued to their screens now as they went downstairs with Mina, seeing what she was seeing.

''Allo!…'Allo!…'Allo!' squawked Louie again.

Along with Mina, the girls stalled on the lower staircase landing. The girls began chattering in low hushed tones between themselves. Mina thought she heard something from the kitchen. She silenced her phone and listened. There was no other sound save for the cockatoo fluttering about in his cage. He seemed agitated.

She unsilenced her phone in time to hear one of the girls egging Mina on, 'C'mon, what are you waiting for?'

Mina didn't want to look like a chicken in front of her besties, yet she couldn't deny the tightening ball of nerves in her solar plexus. Warily, she walked down the hallway and into the kitchen. As she scanned the room, she also panned the camera around for her online friends. There was nothing out of the ordinary, but the cockatoo was acting all erratic, hopping around his cage, bouncing on the spot.

'C'mon, Louie.' Mina opened the door, but the bird moved as far back as possible, squawking incessantly.

Her friends were delighted to see the bird. 'The cockatoo is cuckoo!' joked another girl.

Mina laughed along half-heartedly. Louie had become a friend, and she didn't like what she was seeing now. The bird was in distress.

'What's wrong, Lou? Why don't you want to show off your crest to the girls? You love doing that.'

The others giggled.

'Let's wait a minute,' she suggested. 'He might have some pre-show jitters.'

Mina left the cage door open and sat herself down at the kitchen table. She continued to talk about their move to the countryside and the creepy Prendergast guy who was having lasagne with her mom and her sisters right now, and how she had seen him spy on the farmhouse. Oh, and how could she forget the extra set of mysterious footprints in the snow this morning?

One of the friends quipped, 'I thought the countryside was supposed to be boring?'

'Me too,' Mina agreed.

The bird calmed down and came out to play though without his normal gusto. He perched on Mina's shoulder and nibbled her ear to a round of online applause and hoorays. Her friends, back in Dublin, were in laughing hysterics when the exotic bird raised its crest for a selfie…a million views guaranteed right there for her Instagram account. If these golden moments kept up, Mina would need to monetise her account.

'Are you alone?'

Nobody heard Mina's friend, Sinead, ask the question while the others fawned over Louie.

Sinead asked again, louder this time. 'Hey, Mina, didn't you say the rest of your family was gone somewhere for dinner?'

'Yeah, why?'

'There's someone else in the house, Mina.'

'What do you mean?'

'Someone passed by the camera.'

Sinead had been the only one to see this, judging by the reactions of the other two friends.

'While you were doing the selfie…someone passed by the doorway to the hall.'

A prickly silence loomed in the farmhouse and that same uncomfortable feeling permeated the girls' bedroom 235 kilometres away in the Dublin outskirts.

'Look, Sinead,' Mina snapped, 'I don't like practical jokes. You're there with the girls and I'm here on my own in this big old house.'

'I'm not joking, Mina! I've just seen someone pass by the kitchen door behind you…in the hallway. But fast…like blink-of-an-eye fast.'

'Well, I saw nothing,' said another girl, Fiona. 'Then again,' she took off her glasses and waved them around, 'I'm half blind with these Coke bottles.'

The girls huffed a nervous laugh that dried up all too soon…

The sudden blinding scream from her phone caused Mina to drop it to the kitchen floor, cracking the screen. They continued to bawl and cry up at her. Mina picked up the phone. 'What?!'

Sinead was crying inconsolable sobs while Fiona and the other girl were screaming at her to shut the fuck up while also trying to tell Mina…

'A-A fuh-face just peered around the corner of the doorway, Mina! It looked like a child… A boy…'

'It was a little person!' cried Fiona.

'A what? Who?' Mina ran numb, too terrified to turn around, but she could see the view behind her, in her phone screen. She hadn't seen anything because she had been too occupied with taking the selfie.

The cockatoo was squawking his morning salute again, which only served to increase the manic chaos.

'A midget!' called the third girl.

'O-kay so that so un-PC, Deirdre!' retorted Fiona. 'That's like a slur! It's called dwarfism, hell-o! What year is this??'

Deirdre screamed back. 'Who gives a fuck?!'

Sinead added, 'Wait, so, dwarf is okay to say? No offence, but that's "Lord of the Rings" shit right there…'

Mina flipped. 'Shut the fuck up, everyone!'

Heavy silence prevailed in the farmhouse kitchen and in Sinead's bedroom in Dublin.

'What…did…you…see?'

Now Fiona had joined the blubbering ranks.

'Get out of there!' Sinead said in a low grave whisper. 'You're not alone, Mina.'

Deirdre said, 'There was something wrong with the face…it was old or something. A child with an old devious face.'

Mina's whole body broke out in goosebumps.

'Is nobody going to mention the ears?' asked Deirdre between sobs. 'Mina, it had big…BIG…ears. Remember, Chops?' Deirdre was referring to one boy in their group of friends at school who had tragically cupped ears. 'Well, think Chops on steroids.'

Mina had heard enough. It was the mention of the ears that had finished this little masquerade. 'Okay, okay, I see what's happening here. You had me going there for a minute.' She placed the cockatoo on the roof of his cage and left the kitchen, walked up and down the hallway, and even peered into the playroom. 'See, there's nothing here.' On a subconscious level, she was already getting the whiff of mouldy oranges.

She panned around for the others' benefit. She plopped herself onto the beanbag in the playroom. Laughing, she said, 'You three morons thought it would be funny to scare me. Am I right?'

Fiona was about to say something, but Mina cut her off. 'So, how about we get on with the farmhouse tour?' Mina took them back to the kitchen. 'The coolest thing in here are the old beams.' She panned upwards to show them the numerous beams traversing the ceiling. As she crossed the kitchen, Deirdre screamed: 'What the fuck is that?'

'There! Next to the fridge!' Fiona pointed at her screen. 'You just walked by it.'

Mina backed up to the fridge and looked with her own eyes, not through her phone screen. 'There's nothing there, guys.' She turned the phone screen to the fridge tucked into the corner of the kitchen, which one of them had referred to. 'Satisfied? Enough is en —' She didn't hear the rest of her own words with the screams coming from her phone.

'There's something there, Mina!' Fiona shrieked.

Deirdre roared. 'Can't you see it?'

'It's right in front of you!' cried Sinead. 'How can

you not see it?!'

Mina flipped her phone camera around and looked through her phone to see what they were seeing. A helpless whimper escaped her…

A hunched undulating mass, like a heap of black blankets with something moving beneath them, huddled against the lower half of the fridge. Mina flinched, screamed, and dropped the phone for the second time. She reached down to pick it up, not taking her eyes off the fridge. And the fridge was all she could see — the shadow figure was only present on the phone screen. She ended the call and zoomed in on it with trembling hands. Something looked up at her from the rippling dark anomaly on her screen. She was sure of it. The dim whites of eyes, rather, her brain picked out a pair of eyes in that squatting thing. The shape rose. Mina fell back against the kitchen table but steadied herself when the thing only reached as far as her chest, taking on the ethereal silhouette of a shrivelled, sickly adult or child.

Mina realised she was sobbing. With shaking hands, she dialled her mom's number. The thing was motionless, standing there. She couldn't make out a clear face in the shadow, but she could feel its stare. When she diverted her eyes away from her phone screen to look at where the thing was standing, but nothing was visible to the naked eye. Again, she looked through her screen and it manifested there, stooping and amorphous. It was so still Mina wondered if, in fact, she was just looking at some form of energy emitting from the fridge or a heat signature of some kind. But every few seconds, the thing would shift into a different position with unnatural jerky movements that reminded Mina of an animal shuffling in the undergrowth.

Squeezing every inch of willpower, Mina called her Molly. 'For fuck's sake! Pick up for once in your life!' As she listened to it ring out, she cursed Molly. When had she ever picked up the phone when she needed to? She couldn't think of one occasion when Molly answered her call, not one. They'd just had a conversation about it for the love of Jesus! She switched on the camera again and lowered her phone. It was still there, hunkered down, immovable as any piece of furniture, as if it was playing Hide-and-Seek. Mina slapped her right hand to her mouth to stop the scream as a wicked face, morphing and melting, looked right at her with a mischievous grin.

In the background, Louie broke out in another round of disorientated, crazed greetings. That sickly sweet fragrance clung thick in the air, making Mina nauseous and ready to throw up. She became faint. Unable to take any more, she screamed a ragged cry before bounding by the fridge and through the kitchen entrance. Her flesh prickled as she was sure she heard a cackle of laughter as she screamed her way through a pocket of chilly air. She slipped and skidded her way through the kitchen and grabbed the car key from the hook in the key holder by the back door, relieved the others had walked to the Gatehouse.

It was freezing outside. A fresh flurry of snow was falling. Mina had been bugging her mom to give her a

143

driving lesson around the yard, reversing, parking, U-turns. Now was a good a time as any to get that first driving lesson. She bounded across the front yard to the BMW. Her mind was on overdrive to the point of blanking out, struggling to focus. She jumped in, catching her leg in the door as she slammed it. A cry of pain escaped her mouth as she winced and put the car into D for drive, then floored the BMW. The car's rear end spun wildly on the snow as the tyres tried to find a bite. Mina felt she was moving in slow motion while the BMW's engine screamed into high gear. She knew whatever she'd seen — they'd seen — in the farmhouse could easily have gotten to the car by now. Mina craned her neck around to get sight of anything in the front yard or on the front porch, but there was nothing.

The BMW found traction and Mina barrelled forward. The back end of the car fishtailed out of the front yard and up the lane she went. Adrenaline had taken over, rendering Mina nothing but a jittering jelly of nerves and it was her nerves that were in the driving seat now. Her foot trembled on the accelerator. The BMW's headlights panned left and right as the back wheels of the car reeled up the lane while Mina tried to keep the vehicle centred. The spruce woods zoomed by on her right, nothing but a dizzying blur of flashing green in her headlights. She could barely see ahead, not because of the out-of-control BMW, but because of the flood of gushing tears washing out everything in front of her.

10.

At the Gatehouse, Molly hadn't felt the vibration of her phone, or even heard it, because she was too involved in a conversation with Richard Prendergast. Plus, the girls were going apeshit on the keys of the old piano in the corner of the living room, which didn't seem to faze Prendergast. In fact, the more racket they made, the happier it seemed to make him. Molly had apologised twice already, but Richard insisted on listening to their charmingly insane music.

'Only the sweet innocence of childhood could make this music. Let's appreciate their senseless yet timeless performance while we have it.'

For a second, Molly thought he was being ironic. She was gearing up for a laugh, but his stoic expression remained unaltered. Instead, Richard sipped on his port wine and watched Molly's daughters with a reminiscing amusement, smiling lips poised at his glass. His answer had astounded her. Only a scarred soul could have come out with such a profound observation.

Curious, Molly wanted to find out more about this Richard Prendergast, whom she found mystifying. He had a story to tell. She could see it in the wrinkles and furrows of his worn face, just as complete strangers would know Molly had a story to tell. She hadn't forgotten the framed pictures of the boy and glamorous woman lining the hallway and couldn't hold it in. 'Are you married? Kids?' She made it sound as if she was asking in innocence.

'Um, you're my guest, so how about we talk a little more about you first?'

Molly shrugged. 'Okay. I suppose you want to know why a single mom with three daughters is living in your farmhouse?'

'I know why you're living in the farmhouse.'

She frowned. 'You do?'

He nodded. 'Because it was meant to be.'

Molly chuckled. 'Everything is meant to be.'

He smiled. 'I suppose we all need a little yin and yang in our lives.'

Molly didn't even know what he meant by that.

'I received over 10,000 applications for the farmhouse.'

'And you chose us?'

'Yes.'

'Why? I'm grateful. Don't get me wrong.' Now, Molly! *Now's the moment to ask him if the farmhouse had been fully vacant when you had moved in…*

'Because the Greene family tick all the right boxes. Now, tell me about you, Molly?' Prendergast cut the conversation short.

Molly decided to play along for now. She would have her moment later; she could be a patient woman when she wanted. Her life story spilled out as she went on to tell her host all about herself, not all, but just enough. The reason why she was a single mom was included, and, during the conversation, there were times when Molly felt as if she was being gently interrogated. She hadn't spoken to many people about

146

losing her husband and son in the car accident. But those who had heard her story for the first time all shared that same expression of shock and sadness. Yet Richard didn't flinch. Molly had never been the type to seek pity from others, but she was hoping for more of a reaction from her new neighbour. She felt as if she'd left something out. Perhaps the numbing horror she'd felt when she received the news, or perhaps the gut-wrenching, harrowing moments when she went into Henry's bedroom, finding his toys where he'd left them. But no line, no matter how gory or dramatic, made any impression on Richard Prendergast.

In fact, later that evening, the idea would cross Molly's mind that he already knew about the hypnotising horror in her life; she was just confirming what he already knew. After all, he told Molly he would run a background check on her. He had probably already read about the car accident that had ruined her life. Everybody has secrets, so he wouldn't have read that Mike shouldn't even have been on the road that night because Molly had gotten blind drunk at a going-away party at work and had forgotten to collect her eldest daughter at the local shopping centre.

Molly went on to tell Richard about opening her own Michelin star restaurant in a posh area of Dublin, but skipped over the succinct detail of how she funded the restaurant with Mike's life (death which she'd caused) insurance payout. She finished with a little ditty because it was that or stifle the tears. *'Then*

147

along came a Covid spider, sat down beside her, and frightened her customers away.'

Richard flashed a consolatory smile.

'In retrospect, I now know I would have left Dublin anyway. The closure of my restaurant was just a catalyst.' Molly finished by saying, 'So, you can see why it was a blessing in disguise when I saw the online advertisement for the farmhouse.'

'Like I said, it was meant to be.'

Richard Prendergast was eluding two topics: his family and the strangeness in the farmhouse. He had made no allusion to the latter. And he was clearly reticent about speaking of his family.

'I think there's something you're not telling me, am I right? I clearly remember asking you the first time we met if there was anything hidden in this deal. Anything I should know about…be concerned about?'

Prendergast remained expressionless. His silence spoke volumes.

'Okay, why are we really here?'

'You tell me.'

'No, you don't get to turn this on me. My intentions were clear to you from the beginning. I understood when you said "a price to pay" you meant roughing it and getting an old house up and running with some family love. "The house is free, but it comes with a price." Isn't that what you said to me? What is this price you've been keeping from me?'

Prendergast studied her for what seemed a lifetime before taking a deep breath and asking, 'Have you noticed anything unusual about the farmhouse?'

Molly didn't have to think about it. She'd already seen and heard many things she couldn't explain. She was about to mention the list of absurdities that always began around six in the evening when it dawned on her they may be speaking about two completely different things.

Deciding they weren't on the same page, she went on playing dumb instead. 'In what way?'

'You will find the farmhouse has its own special kind of reality. An old building becomes a character by absorbing the energy of those who once called it home.'

'Richard, how about we stop beating around the bush? You need to tell me why I'm here.'

Headlights suddenly filled the living room, arching across the chimney breast and bookshelves, followed by the sound of a car skidding to a stop, then the crash of metal…

They were already on their feet, running down the hallway to the front door. Molly was fleetingly disorientated and was sure some driver had lost control of their vehicle as they passed the Gatehouse on the country road and had crashed into the gate.

Molly was flabbergasted to see a car had crashed into the gate alright, but from their side of the gate before hearing the crash. And not only that, but it was her BMW's snout stuck in the bars of the steel gate and none other than her own Mina at the steering wheel!

'Jesus Christ, Mina!' In complete lack of comprehension, she stared wide-eyed at the BMW.

'You don't even know how to drive!'

With a spooky calmness, Richard asked Mina if she was hurt. Mina assured both of them she was fine. Molly quickly clocked the damage to the snout of her car. Bad news for her pocket, but reassured the gate would protect them from the outside world.

'Let's go inside,' suggested Richard.

Molly noticed he was casting furtive glances around his front yard. It looked as if Richard didn't want to be seen…or didn't want his guests to be seen.

They went inside to the living room and Richard sat Mina on the sofa. She was hyperventilating, struggling to catch her breath.

'Give her some room,' Richard suggested.

Knowing he was a doctor, Molly gladly stood back. By now, Mina was in the full throttle of a panic attack.

'Mina, tell me two things you see here in this living room.'

This question seemed to confuse Mina.

'Mina, two things?' Richard gestured around the living room. 'Have a look…'

'Um, the boat,' Mina pointed to the model of a blue and red large wooden sailing yacht on the windowsill.

'Very good. What else?'

Mina looked around the room with wide eyes. 'The piano?'

'There's no wrong answer, Mina. Good. Now, two things you can hear right now?'

Mina listened out. 'The clock…' The black and

gold trim antique grandfather clock stood to attention in the corner of the room, tick-tocking sombrely, marking down the seconds no matter the beauty and chaos going on in the world.

'Uh-huh, what else?'

As Mina tilted her head to listen, Molly wondered what her daughter would say. 'I hear my sisters.'

Richard smiled and stood back. 'How do you feel now?'

'Wow, she's not hyperventilating anymore!' exclaimed Molly. 'Where did you learn to do that?'

Mina managed a smile. 'Better, thanks.'

'Wow, where did you learn to do that?' asked Molly again. 'I'm impressed!'

Every now and again, Mina suffered from panic attacks and shortness of breath. Molly would use this simple technique in the future if the situation ever arose…and it would.

'I've had to use it in the past.' Richard Prendergast wasn't willing to expand on that.

'There's someone in the house!'

Molly thought her daughter was fooling around and asked her to get serious. 'Mina, is this another one of your little dramas?'

'There's someone else in the fucking farmhouse, mom!'

The piano playing stopped as Cora and Emma were stunned in silence to find their hysterical sister in the living room…and swearing, although that was nothing new.

Molly looked at Richard, but Richard didn't seem

concerned about a stranger in the farmhouse. In fact, Richard's smooth calmness exuded tranquillity. Maybe it was the fact he is — was — a doctor and such things don't faze him?

Mina saw Richard's nonplussed reaction and pleaded with both of them, 'I'm not imagining it!'

'Mina,' answered Molly, 'nobody is disagreeing with you.'

She threw Richard a dirty look. 'He doesn't believe me.'

'Oh, I believe you.'

Mina looked at him with undeniable hope. 'You do?'

'Oh, yes, I believe you believe what you saw.'

Mina rolled her eyes. 'It's not the same.' She turned back to her mom. 'The girls online saw it too! They saw it first…on my phone camera. I…I…' Her mind was racing again.

'Relax, Mina,' soothed Richard. 'You're here now with us and everything's fine.'

'I was giving them a virtual tour of the house when they saw something behind me while I was taking a selfie with Louie.'

Richard repeated, '"A selfie with Louie?"'

'Look, that's not important. What is important is that they saw someone pass by the door behind me, then we saw someone or something in front of the fridge. I thought they were trying to spoof me and I was getting angry because there was nothing there, but when I looked at my phone screen I…I could see it too, crouching down by the fridge.'

Molly could almost see what her daughter had seen just by looking at her teary wide eyes flitting back and forth as she recalled the event, pure dread on her face, nostrils running snot without her knowing. Molly found this the most distressing — Mina was at the age where she was concerned about how she looked. Everything had to be just perfect. It just told her whatever Mina had seen was real and was consuming her mind. Molly handed her a balled-up tissue from her pocket.

Mina accepted it graciously and wiped her nose. 'It was trying to hide or something…it was completely still. As if it was pretending not to be there, but I could see it!' She was panicking again.

Molly's blood ran cold. She'd witnessed the same phenomena on the stairs.

Richard suggested taking deep breaths.

Realising Cora and Emma were standing next to them, Molly asked Cora, 'Take Emma exploring the house…' with pleading eyes. 'I don't want Emma seeing her sister in such a state.' Molly gestured to Richard.

Richard did pause before agreeing, making the situation a tad uncomfortable.

Cora wasn't stupid. She'd seen and heard enough to know something weird was going on at the farmhouse and Molly knew this. It had nothing to do with Emma seeing her distressed sister. With reluctance, she took Emma's hand and went for a walk as her mom had asked. The sisters went down the hallway.

Meanwhile, in the kitchen, Molly asked, 'Do you think your mind was playing tricks on you?'

Mina stared at her mom with raised eyebrows. 'If you think four minds playing the same trick at the same time is possible, then yes, it's possible.'

'Okay, okay, I had to ask because I…because' she flashed an awkward glance at Richard, 'I had to make sure. Because I…'

Whatever way Richard Prendergast looked at Molly, she knew at that moment, through the power of telepathy (or perhaps it was that brief biting stare) to shut her goddamn mouth and never mention what she was about to mention. His haunting words whispered in Molly's ears, The farmhouse is free, but it comes with a price…Christ Almighty, this hadn't anything to do with leaky pipes or a fresh coat of paint. How could this even be possible? Without saying it, Richard Prendergast just confirmed something else was occupying the farmhouse. A squatter was living with them and he had let them move in.

Molly had been on the verge of confirming to her daughter that she, too, had seen odd things at the farmhouse. She was sick and tired of making up silly little excuses and lies. Perhaps it would be best to tell Mina that her sister, Cora, had also seen something, only she hadn't realised. Thank goodness. Seeing the confounded terror on her daughter's face both saddened and frightened her. She deserved to know the truth. She felt guilty. But there was fear rising inside her and it overrode everything else. Why didn't she listen to Janice when she had the chance? Because she was impatient and she was in a rush to get away from her old life, that's why. Molly, more than many other people, knew there was nothing free in life. Everything needed to be paid back at checkout time.

Mina continued. 'Wait, I'm remembering there was something else… a smell of fruit…stale fruit.'

Richard Prendergast interjected, 'I would be very interested to see this video, Mina. May I?'

Mina was about to replay her live video call when she stopped and reddened. 'Shit, I didn't record it.' Disbelief filled her face.

'Hmm,' went Richard. 'Then it's your word against ours.'

Molly turned on Richard with venom in her eyes. 'It's not really her word against ours, Richard. I believe she saw something. Nobody is against anyone here.' Molly flashed her mom a thank-you smile. 'But,' Molly added, 'I also believe there's a logical explanation.' *There is no logical explanation to what you saw…an anaemic hand coming out of the darkness beneath your daughter's bed and grabbing her ankle doesn't have a logical explanation…*

It was something Mike might say, but it was her conscience speaking directly to her. If it had been back in the old house, Mike would have said this in Molly's voice.

Richard nodded approvingly. 'Absolutely, Mina. Everything in this world has an explanation.'

He was lying and Molly knew it. And she'd started

155

it by mentioning that what she saw has a logical explanation. There she was, lying again.

Mina whispered, 'It looked like a child, Mom.'

Molly stared incredulously at her daughter. 'A what?'

If Mina had been more observant at that moment, she would've seen the flicker of familiarity in her mom's eyes. 'It had the form of a child…only it didn't at the same time. I thought I saw a face — eyes — in that creepy shadow by the fridge. I think it was a boy. I don't know why I thought that. It just felt like a boy. The girls say they saw a face peeping at me, but it was the face of an old man.'

Molly shivered all over and drew her hand to her mouth in some attempt to stifle her tears. She was overcome with a dizzying wave of melancholy and sadness. She'd had that same impression when she'd seen something on the staircase.

Richard Prendergast took this as his cue to jump in. 'Your mom has been telling me you've been finding it difficult to adapt to your new house. You miss your friends a lot. You want to go back to them, isn't that right?'

Mina knew what Prendergast was up to. 'Look, I see where you're going with this. What you say is true, I do miss my old life. But that doesn't alter the fact that there was something else in the kitchen of the farmhouse. I didn't make it up to get out of the place, if that's what you're thinking. That's not how I roll, c'mon.' She looked at her mom. 'Even Louie knew there was something up, mom. I was upstairs when I heard his morning call. He never speaks at night.'

Molly had witnessed the same thing. Her eldest daughter was merely confirming everything she already knew.

'So, you're relying on a cockatoo as a witness?' Prendergast snickered. 'I don't think that will hold up in court, Mina.'

Molly was tiring of Richard's dismissals. 'Hey, listen. You don't know us very well. So, y'know, don't get all judgey and condescending.'

'I'm just trying to reason with the girl.'

'Well, you're not going about it the right way. Sarcasm doesn't help anyone.' Molly got up. 'Let's go home.'

'I'm not going back into that house, mom. None of us should be in that place and it was a mistake to come here. I told you that, but you didn't listen as usual.'

Oh, fuck, here we go. Molly knew this would come sooner or later. She had to do some quick thinking. 'Mina, maybe Richard is right? You said you only saw this…thing through the lens of your phone? These things malfunction all the time.' It ate her up inside, knowing she was lying to her daughter.

'Not you too?' Mina exclaimed. 'We all saw the same thing, Mom! Why are you taking his side?'

'I'm not taking his side. I'm just trying to look at this logically. You all saw the same thing because you were all looking through the same screen.'

'She's right, Mina. None of you saw anything with

your own eyes.'

Mina threw another dirty look Richard's way.

Molly paused. She debated whether she would say her next words, though she felt the situation warranted it. 'I never told you this, but I cannot tell you how many times I thought I saw signs around the house after your dad and brother died. Little clues that they still might be with us in some way, watching, listening. But nothing ever happened.'

'Mom, sorry, but that's creepy.'

'How can it be creepy if it's your dad and brother?'

'I couldn't have put it better myself,' interjected Richard. 'Never underestimate the power of the mind,' Richard chimed in. 'Seeing is believing…you believe in what you saw, but what was it that you really saw?'

Molly wanted to thump Prendergast just then. But for the sake of everything, she kept her clenched fists by her side. Why didn't she just own up to the fact that there was something in the house? If she had been in her right state of mind, surely, she would've taken her daughter's side and told Prendergast where to shove his goddamn farmhouse. But Molly had to think about the bigger picture…it was free accommodation when she didn't have a job yet. And when the house became hers, she was going to transform it into a triple Michelin star restaurant for the high-class and above. For now, the pros outweighed the cons.

'Lecture over?' asked Mina. Self-doubt sunk in and the fight seemed to leave Mina. She looked about, all confused. Had she imagined the whole thing? If she had imagined it, then so did her friends. But it was true, at the end of the day all they had seen was an anomaly on the phone screen and, perhaps, their overactive imaginations came up with the rest.

'C'mon,' suggested Molly, putting her arm around her daughter, 'let's go home and I'll get you nice and cosy with a hot water bottle and a hot cocoa. How about that?'

Reluctantly, Mina agreed. 'But what about Louie? He started saying hello to someone who wasn't there?' She wasn't prepared to give up the fight just yet.

'I think we have to remind ourselves that Louie is a bird, Mina.'

Molly flashed eye-daggers at Richard. 'She knows Louie's a bird. But I get your point,' she conceded. She turned to her daughter. 'Richard is trying to say…'

'I know what he's trying to say. You're both treating me like I'm an idiot.'

Molly felt rotten. She called out for Cora and Emma. 'Girls, we're going.'

*

Cora and Emma had been playing a pointless game of hide-and-seek with less hiding and even less seeking. The only hiding options were the featureless hallway and Richard's defunct surgery. There were another three rooms along the hallway, but Cora discovered them to be locked.

Cora found Emma standing halfway down the

hallway, picking at the drab wallpaper. And speaking of the walls, hadn't there been pictures all along here when she'd come to treat her cockatoo bite? If Cora looked along the walls from just the right angle where the hallway light shone, she could see the dark outlines where the photographs used to hang. 'Em, what are you doing? Stop that.'

But Emma continued to pick at the wall. 'I want to hide in here,' said Emma.

'What do you mean?' Interest piqued, Cora joined her sister and was amazed, or rather confused, by what she was looking at. There, embedded in the right-hand wall of the hallway, was the outline of a door that had been wallpapered over.

'Girls, let's go!'

*

They walked outside to the fresh wave of powdery snow. Molly took one look at the car and cringed. Then she looked at the perfect gate.

Richard handed Molly a key.

'What's this for?'

He gestured to the gate. 'Next time you'll be able to unlock it,' he said to Mina with a vague grin before closing the door.

Molly examined the damage to the front of the car. 'Christ, how much is this going to cost me?'

Mina apologised. 'Your insurance will pay for it.'

With a laugh, Molly said, 'Yes, but they will more than make up for it when it comes around to the time of renewing my policy. Insurance companies are the Mafia, Mina.'

The girls sat in the BMW. Before Molly got in, she turned to Richard and, in clipped tones, warned, 'We need to talk.'

On the ride down the lane, Cora broke the silence. 'Mom?'

'What?' Molly wasn't in the mood for Cora right now.

'There was something really strange in the hallway.'

Molly found Cora in her rear-view mirror. 'What do you mean?'

'Well, the first thing was that all the pictures that were there last night were gone.'

'You're right!' exclaimed Molly. 'That's what was missing! I was trying to figure out what was different.'

'And there's a hidden room.' Cora was incredibly nonchalant about her statement.

'A what?' Mina's eyes widened.

'I found it!' added Emma.

'The wallpaper is covering a doorway.'

Emma rejoiced. 'I found it!'

Cora continued. 'I found Emma trying to peel off the wallpaper. She said she wanted to hide in that room cos we were playing a rubbish game of hide-and-seek. That's when I saw, like, the shape of the door.'

'Are you sure?'

'It's there. Have a look next time you're up there.'

This succinct detail just added to the strangeness of, well, everything.

Cora nodded dramatically. 'Remember, there are two rooms on the right side of the hallway? There's one locked room and, further down, there's the study, or whatever you call it, where Richard gave me the injection. There's a door opposite the surgery that is locked. If you look to the side of the wall, you think there's just one door, but really there's another door opposite the locked door next to the surgery.' Cora giggled. 'That sounds complicated. What I'm trying to say is that there are four doors, two on either side of the hallway.'

They pulled into the front yard of the farmhouse. In the passenger seat, Mina spasmed and yelped, 'What's that?!' as the car's headlights washed over something standing in the yard.

Molly glanced at her terror-struck daughter. 'Mina, it's the snowman.'

In the back seat, Cora laughed out of turn, quickly sobering up when she saw her sister was a jittering nervous wreck.

'Sorry, I thought it was…something else.'

'You don't have to be sorry for anything, love. C'mon, let's get that hot cocoa.'

Molly saw the front door wide open and scolded her daughter. 'You left the front door open? Anyone could have walked in, Mina!'

'It was already inside, Mom.'

That line shook Molly.

They got out of the BMW and crossed the blanket of snow to the front porch.

As she walked by the snowman, Cora did a

double-take on his face. 'Wait?'

Molly turned to see the snowman's face had been altered while they'd been gone. With burgeoning dread, she saw how his stone smile which she'd fixed on leaving the farmhouse was now a stone-cold grimace, eerily unsettling in the moonlight.

Thankfully, Mina had already gone inside; she'd had enough drama for one night. And Molly, thinking on the spot, told Cora she had done it as a joke, adding, '… which sort of backfired,' and made a point of creating the smile for a second time that evening. *And the lies keep coming…*

Looking over her shoulder at the lone snowman, Molly hurried Emma and Cora inside, using the freezing night as an excuse to get inside the house.

Yes, get inside where the real trouble lies in wait…

That Friday night, Molly tucked her girls into bed. Cora and Emma had been playing doctors and nurses in Emma's room and Cora had fallen asleep in Emma's bed with Emma. They looked so cosy there together, but they wouldn't have enough room in Emma's bed, so Molly had carried Cora, all floppy and drowsy, down the hallway to her bed. Molly then tucked in Emma and, as per the nightly routine, plugged in her light in the socket next to her bed. Looking at the warm amber light transported Molly back to the house in Dublin. If Molly just focused on that cosy light, and nothing else, she could've sworn she was back in her old house, gazing into that same cosy child's light that staved off all night terrors…all

163

night terrors except the real ones.

*

Mina, meanwhile, had opted to sleep with her mom, something she hadn't done for years. Her experience had left her mentally drained but, by the time bedtime had come around, she had more or less convinced herself she had imagined the whole thing. Not understanding what she had seen, Mina had googled the possibilities of what she — they — might have seen. Google had led her from one strange phenomenon to the next, culminating in the oddest article about fridges and how they have gas inside — it's what keeps the fridge cold…something Mina had never thought about. But sometimes this gas can leak. Maybe that's what they saw, then worked themselves up into a hysteria. She didn't want her friends to be talking about what happened this evening because it was embarrassing. Embarrassing? Yes, at 15 years old everything is embarrassing.

She texted her friends about her findings and was happy they bought it…until Fiona texted back:

The face we all saw spying on you from the kitchen door wasn't fridge gas.

11.

During Friday night and Saturday morning, the muffled cries of a child awoke Molly. As she surfaced from the depths of slumber, she was mistaken in thinking that Mina, lying next to her, had whimpered in her sleep. But she was sound to the world, breathing deeply. The house was in utter silence until the low, doleful sobs started again. Molly, to her dismay, realised it was Emma. She couldn't remember the last time she'd heard her daughter crying at night.

The flashlight on her phone aided her as she slipped out of the bed and walked down the hallway to Emma's bedroom. She didn't like the idea of wandering around the farmhouse at night alone, now that she knew she wasn't alone, but her daughter's plea overrode all fear.

Emma was sitting up in bed when Molly got to her bedroom, tears rolling down her cheeks, squinting into Molly's bright LED light. 'Em, what's wrong?'

As she sat on the bed next to her daughter, she was surprised to see Emma's night light on her pillow.

'Someone plugged out my night light. I woke, and it was all dark.'

Molly stole a nervous glance about the bedroom. 'But what's it doing here?'

Emma shrugged. 'Don't know, mom. I just woke, and it was there.'

'Why did you wake up?'

'Because the night light wasn't on.'

This made little sense. 'But you were asleep, Em. You wouldn't have known it wasn't plugged in unless you woke first to find out it wasn't plugged in. See what I'm saying?'

'So, whoever plugged out my light woke me to tell me?'

A gentle tide of fear came lapping at Molly's insides. 'Uh-huh.' She had made a point of plugging in the light herself.

'Anyway, don't worry, I'll plug it back in. You need to get back to sleep, 'kay?'

Emma agreed, flopping onto her pillow and falling back to sleep in seconds as if her pillow had released a waft of sleeping gas. Molly felt jealous on seeing how easy it was for her daughter to nod off with the click of a finger, whereas she spent many hours tossing and turning, thinking about everything and nothing.

As she reached down to plug the light in, she froze. A gentle ripple of childish laughter could be heard. Where had it come from? It seemed to come from beneath…

Molly jumped to her feet, remembering her last experience in this corner of Emma's bedroom by the fireplace. Every hair on her body stood on end like she'd just walked into a force field of static electricity. The gentle low luminescence coming from the light cast a warm glow on the floor, but it didn't reach beneath the bed. But she couldn't just leave the room knowing her daughter was asleep, utterly defenceless. Summoning up every fibre of her being, Molly eased herself onto her knees and angled her phone light into the darkness beneath her sleeping daughter. For a second, she thought she saw something move, but was sure it was only an optical illusion of the light moving shadows. As she swept her phone from left to right, that same innocent titter of laughter left her in a dumbfounded paralysis. That childish laugh had come from above the bed, not below it.

'Oh, Jesus!' Molly flashed her phone light in her daughter's face and watched her giggling to herself as she slept, happily lost in some nocturnal dream. She took a deep breath of relief and collapsed into a crumpled heap next to Emma and curled up by her side, hugging her like it was their last night on Earth together.

A few minutes later, Molly slipped out of Emma's bed and was about to leave the room when she heard that giggle again. She jerked, flicked on the light switch, and scanned the room. She shone her phone light on Emma. The child's face was serene, free of worry…until she started speaking in absurd non-sequiturs: 'No, she won't…Nothing will happen here…No, you go…No, you're not…She loves us. You stay…No, it's not. It's your home.'

As Molly listened in on the gibberish, it took on a more sinister meaning with a disturbing sense to it. It sounded as if Emma was in conversation with someone else inside her sleep, only Molly was privy to this side of the conversation. Then again, children become strange versions of themselves when they talk in their sleep; possessed and speaking the absurd gibberish dialect of Sleeplandia. Especially when in the grips of fever. Molly was no stranger to this. All her kids — all — had those horrible fevers that always creep up at night.

With great hesitation, Molly switched off Emma's light and waited at her door. Waited for what, she didn't know.

Satisfied (forcing herself to believe), Molly turned to head back to her bedroom. No sooner had she turned from the door when a child whimpered and sobbed from inside Emma's room. But it wasn't Emma. It sounded like a little boy whimpering. She could not believe what she was hearing; could not understand it. The blood and energy drained from Molly's being. Her legs wobbled and buckled at the knees as a dizzy spell overcame her. She reached out to the wall to steady herself. Once the wave of nausea passed, she was seized by a taut knot of fear before her motherly instinct kicked in and overrode everything else except Emma's safety. She bounded across the room, grabbed Emma. As she exited the bedroom, she clearly and distinctly heard a voice behind her:

'Mommy, please.'

The ethereal cry of help stopped Molly in the hallway with Emma in her arms.

'Mommy?' came the second call that sounded more like a plea.

'Oh, Jesus,' Molly whispered. 'Oh, Jesus...Oh,

Jesus…' over and over again. Not only was there a child's voice coming from her daughter's bedroom when there was nobody in it, but there was something deeply disturbing about the cadence of speech which Molly found — or assumed she found — vaguely familiar. And with that strange familiarity came the sudden sensation of being alone; acute loneliness and a pining for home where she thought she already was. With that loneliness came the oddest sense of déjà vu. Molly found herself stalling; torn between getting her child away from this bedroom, but a deep desire to go back into the room to the other weeping child. The more she listened to that weeping, the dreamier she felt.

Molly carried Emma in her arms to her bedroom and laid her on the bed next to Mina. Great, there goes my bed again, she considered in the madness of the moment. She listened out to hear nothing but a pervading silence, heavy in the farmhouse. In a dreamlike trance, Molly left her sleeping daughters and returned to Emma's bedroom. As she padded barefoot down the hallway, she continued to feel as if she was in a hallucination, watching her dislocated self from behind as the fantasy version of herself walked to Emma's bedroom and there was nothing the real Molly could do about it but go along for the ride.

She lay down in Emma's bed and waited.

12.

The Saturday morning sun coming through the window woke Molly Greene. Disorientated, she wondered what she was doing in her daughter's bed until she remembered everything from the night before. She thought it had been an elaborate dream, but the fact she was in Emma's bed said otherwise. Jesus Christ and all the saints, how could this be happening? The feelings Molly experienced as she lay in Emma's bed were an eclectic mix of dread and horror, with an underlying and unmistakable feeling of excitement and the strangest sense of fullness and feeling complete. Why? She had no idea, but the surreal notion they were sharing their house with a squatter of the nonliving kind made Molly content; filling a void somehow. To think—and Molly was struggling with this—that a spirit lingered in the farmhouse was difficult to digest and, ironically, life-affirming.

As per tradition, Louie, the cockatoo, stretched his neck and squawked, "'Allo!… 'Allo!… 'Allo!' as Molly entered the kitchen, feeling as if she hadn't slept. Needing a little peace and tranquillity before the kids came downstairs, and the chaos began, she prepared her pancakes and have her breakfast quietly. She also needed to assimilate what had happened last night. The whole thing seemed surreal, and the only one who would verify any of this craziness was Richard Prendergast. Nibbling on her pancakes and honey, she slowly began to piece the puzzle together, starting at the beginning, the very beginning, when she had first called Richard Prendergast. The odd stipulations and strange remarks were now beginning to make sense. "The farmhouse is free, but it comes with a price" was making troubling sense. Christ, what had she got herself into? She lost her appetite and struggled to finish her mug of coffee. It was still too early to ring Prendergast, she decided after checking her watch. Though, under the circumstances, she didn't think this was any time for courtesy.

While she pensively sipped her coffee, she noticed Louie's cage door was open. It had been closed last night. She was sure of it. Her nightly routine included checking the front and back door of the house and Louie's door, just in case one of the girls might've left it open. It was open now. She'd have to have a word with the girls. But the bird was still in his cage. This had happened on more than one occasion up in Dublin and the cockatoo had an all-night party while the Greenes slept soundly. The following morning, the pantry had been raided and Molly was finding cockatoo poop for weeks after. But not here; the bird remained as far from the open door as possible, crest half raised, in its day of mourning.

'What's wrong, Louie?' She waited for the bird to answer. 'If you could only speak.'

The bird answered, 'Allo! 'Allo! 'Allo!'

Molly huffed a tired chuckle. 'Oh, apologies, you can talk.' Molly picked up her phone and, absentmindedly, began swiping through the photos she took yesterday while the girls were building the snowman. The proud mother-of-three's smile melted and was replaced by a curious squint. Molly looked at the picture on her screen again, up close this time. There was something in the background, so minimal she had missed it the first time. Not sure if it was a matrix thrown by the spruce trees on the edge of the woods, Molly went to fetch her reading glasses perched on the overhead fan above the cooker. She donned them and hovered back to her chair at the kitchen table, then gawked at her phone screen once again. The lenses of her glasses discarded any play of branches and shadow…

Molly's body went limp. Her mug of coffee loosened in her grip and spilled onto her slippers and the stone floor. She was only vaguely aware of the hot coffee seeping through the fabric of her slippers to the toes of her right foot as the blurry blob now had a defined face and had taken on the distinct features of a child, a boy, peering inquisitively from behind the trunk of a tree. The child was the insipid colour of china, probably why Molly hadn't spotted the image at first glance, having little difference between the child's facial colour and the snow. The child was somewhat translucent, with an odd blurriness to his extremities, as if the infant was moving quickly when the shot had been taken. To Molly, it was as if the lone infant had been carelessly photoshopped into the picture. Was this Mina's idea of a joke? She was handy at editing images for her TikTok channel, but this felt all wrong. Further lending to Molly's notion

172

— wish — this was a trick of technology and the child was placed incorrectly into the picture, hovering an inch or two above the floor of pine needles…only now she knew in her heart and soul this was no Photoshop fail…

Fuck! was all Molly could think.

Her eyes flitted about the kitchen, like a sniper looking for any movement. She glanced at Louie in her sweep of the kitchen.

In time, the cockatoo would become the Greene's canary in a coal mine.

With increasing dread and claustrophobia, Molly studied the picture in her phone gallery. This was the first hard evidence they weren't alone at the farmhouse. They were sharing their house with a spirit, a squatter from the other side, and it was a boy. As this sunk in, Molly was filled with a bolt of everlasting hope and happiness, a sensation her life was complete. She had experienced the same heart-racing optimism in Emma's bed last night. Molly found infinite comfort and unending hope in knowing spirits, ghosts, do exist. Why? The answer was hazy. For now, just out of reach.

The girls came down for their pancakes. The atmosphere was jovial, and everyone was in good fettle, except for Mina, who was moody and pensive. Hardly surprising, considering what she had gone through last evening. Molly felt sorry for her daughter. She didn't like to see her suffer like this, especially when she could make things right by telling her she had indeed seen a supernatural phenomenon…um, no, on second thought, probably not such a good idea.

When they had finished breakfast, Cora pulled on her warm clothes and went outside to play in the snow while Mina petulantly traipsed back upstairs and closed her door. Molly followed Mina up as far as the first set of stairs and called, 'Mina, everything okay?' Stupid question, but she didn't know what else to say.

'The girls aren't talking to me.'

'Why?'

'Their parents have decided that I'm a bad influence.'

Molly repeated her question.

'Don't know. After the live yesterday, the girls were so distraught their parents agreed that I'm trying to corrupt their minds.'

Molly didn't have an answer. She turned back, unsure how to make this right. Downstairs at the kitchen table, she sat down to think out the best line of action. Emma was still sitting there, which was a little out of character. Emma found it difficult to sit still anywhere except when eating and she was the first to whirlwind away from the table once she'd finished eating.

'What's wrong, Mama? You look sad. Don't be sad.'

Molly couldn't help smiling and swept up Emma in her arms. 'Nothing to worry your little head about, darling.' As she held her daughter in her arms, she briefly wondered where on Earth she'd heard Mama?

174

Probably picked it up on a YouTube video or something. It was funny to hear her say it.

Emma put her arms around Molly's neck and squeezed her in a hug. At that moment, Molly was the happiest she had been in a long time, just to feel that meaningful, honest embrace from her four-year-old meant so, so much. It was everything she could ever ask for. It was priceless…

Priceless until Molly felt the blood rise in her cheeks as her windpipe narrowed. 'Em?…Emma?'

Frightening Molly just as much was the sound of panic in her own voice. Before she knew what was happening, the child's hug had turned into a python's hug, constricting the life from her.

Emma's vice-like cuddle squeezed in around her throat, tighter and harder until black stars wormed and undulated before Molly's eyes. She was passing out. Before she grew too weak, she tried to angle her arms back far enough to wedge her hands in between her chest and Emma's chest, but the child was a tight, sinewy knot locked onto her. Her legs had fastened onto her backside and she wasn't letting go. Molly fell back against the table.

'Emma!' wheezed Molly. 'Let…muh-me…go! Juh-Jesus!'

She tried calling out for Cora or Mina to pull the child off her, but the moment she opened her mouth to scream, Emma squeezed down even more with unnatural strength, adding pressure to her chest and pushing the air out of her lungs. Then, in her ear, Molly felt her daughter's soft warm breath as she uttered the devastating words, 'Why don't you love me, Mama? Can't you see me? You see the others? What's wrong with me? You can love me too, Mama!'

These chilling statements paralysed Molly as she succumbed to the lack of oxygen. 'I…see…you,' she said between gagging breaths.

The moment she uttered those three words, Emma went limp in her arms, like a marionette without its puppet master. Molly's knees went from under her, dropping hard onto the stone floor. Emma came down on top of her. Molly gasped for air, never feeling more alive now that she was dying, and she was dying. She felt it; that living thing, the elixir of life, leave her. Molly regained her composure. Emma lay on top of her and bawled her eyes out while wondering what both of them were doing on the kitchen floor.

'What happened, Em?'

'I don't remember.'

'You don't remember anything?'

Emma looked about the kitchen for an answer. 'I just remember I saw you, here at the table, then… then…'

'Yeah?'

A darkness washed across Emma's face. 'Then I felt strange.'

'In what way, Em? Strange in what way?'

'Don't know, just weird. Like that time they put me to sleep before they took out my app…appix…'

'Appendix?'

The child nodded. 'When they sprayed that stuff in

176

my face to put me to sleep before the operation. I tried to keep my eyes open, but I couldn't.'

From the mouths of babes, thought Molly with a shiver. *Right, that's it! I'm calling Prendergast. This is getting way out of hand…*

Cora came bounding into the kitchen from the backyard, blowing hot air into her cupped hands, unaware of what had just preceded her. She was too taken with her frozen fingers and toes to notice the flush on her mom's face or the garish redness on her neck.

'Cora, do you mind taking Emma under your wing for a while? I just need to call Richard and ask him a few things about the house.'

Once the girls had scattered, Molly got on her phone and called Prendergast.

He answered on the first dial. 'Molly?'

'Okay, so I think you've got some explaining to do.'

Richard didn't have to second-guess what Molly was harking at. 'I think I know what this is about.'

'Can you come by? Like right now? I'm scared, Richard. Things…inexplicable things are happening in this house and I need to know I'm not going crazy thinking that I'm the only one.'

'How about you come here?'

'Why is it always me who has to go to you? I think you owe me an explanation.' Something dawned on Molly. 'Wow, you are afraid of this house, aren't you? That's what all of this is about. Not once have you stepped inside this house. "You can't get a feel for a

177

place when there's somebody looking over your shoulder" were your exact words when we first came to look at the house, I believe.' Molly looked about her for any unwanted eavesdroppers. 'You know that my daughter tried to choke me just now? I'm tired of lying to my children.'

'You're just holding information from them. You are protecting them like any good parent would. That's not lying.'

'Hmm,' Molly wasn't so sure. 'That's lying to some people. And I'm holding information from them because you held back information from me. Look, we're going off point here. Meet me halfway down the lane if you won't come to the farmhouse. I know this sounds childish, but I refuse to go to the Gatehouse.' Molly recalled what Cora had said to her about this mysterious hidden door in the hallway of the Gatehouse. 'Look, wait, this is ridiculous. I'll come to you, but you come to me next time.'

'When can I expect you?'

'Now.'

13.

Molly brought Emma with her to the Gatehouse with her and left the others behind. Cora and Mina were too involved in some TikTok videos to be concerned with going anywhere. Molly debated whether or not to leave them, but she refused to go down that road. And Mina needed some cheering-up time with her sister, anyway.

As Molly drove up the lane towards the Gatehouse, she decided there and then that she had been through far too much in this life to be intimidated by anything or anyone from the afterlife.

The backyard of the Gatehouse was freely accessible from the lane, so Molly pulled in. Prendergast appeared at his back door. Molly greeted him and walked through to the living room. As she passed down the hallway, she scanned the walls for this hidden door. And in that brief moment, as she passed through, she was sure she caught sight of the vague outline of the doorframe beneath the paisley wallpaper which left much to be desired. It could also have been just a trick of the light.

'Coffee?'

'Coffee?' snapped Molly. 'What I need is a stiff whisky. Anything with alcohol in it! Do you have any Listerine on-hand?' she joked hysterically. 'Before we talk, I need to use your bathroom?'

'Sorry?'

'Yes, coffee, thanks. I know I've just left the farmhouse, but I think Em has a kidney infection.'

She cringed.

'I've got medication for that if you wish.'

'Oh? Um, I'll wait a day or two to see if it clears.'

He paused before answering, 'Sure,' with hesitation. 'Down the hallway. You can't miss it.'

Molly took herself and Emma down the hallway towards the toilet. Halfway down the hallway, Emma called, 'There it is! The secret door!'

On cue, Molly almost died of mortification. Prendergast had to have heard her. 'That's our secret,' she whispered, ''kay, Em?'

The girl nodded with an impish grin. 'Shh!' Emma slowed to take a closer look at the point where she had—

'Did you find it?'

Molly startled. She turned on her heels to see Prendergast standing there at the other end of the hallway, eyeing them.

She reddened up. 'Um, yes!' She flashed a meek smile and continued to the bathroom. As she closed the door, she took a quick peek down the hallway to see Prendergast standing there, and it gave her unending creeps. Now that they were in the toilet, Molly wasn't sure what to do, but they needed to kill time. A minute passed by, no more, when a sharp rap came on the door. 'Everything okay in there?'

Molly was lost for words. 'Um, yes?' Why wouldn't it be? Was it normal for a grown man to come knocking on the toilet door? If she had been three or four years old, she might understand, yes. Maybe the child needed help, but a grown woman?

No, sorry, not normal; just another abnormality to tag on to the creeping list, out here in the sticks where everything stands slightly out of kilter with the rest of the country. 'Just, um, tidying myself up.' She cringed with embarrassment.

Prendergast's footsteps receded down the hallway.

Molly leapt out of the bathroom into the hallway with Emma. As they walked back down the hallway, Molly glimpsed the hidden room as she passed. Yep, it was definitely there, wallpapered over from the outside world, preserving whatever was inside. But right now, Molly didn't care what was inside. She just wanted to get the truth from Prendergast, the small print.

'Okay, enlighten me.' Molly refused to take any more bullshit. 'Tell me everything you should've told me on the first day.'

'I was desperate, and you were in the right place at the right time. You and your family were the perfect candidates.'

Molly answered back, 'And why is that?'

'Many reasons.'

'Let's start with the first one.'

Prendergast paused to think. 'You're having financial trouble.'

'Who says?'

'You, Molly. It was what you didn't say. I provided you with a free house. And you jumped at the chance even though you kept your guard up.' He stalled; the smile gone from his face now. 'Apologies for my bluntness, but you are a broken family. I know this

181

because I come from a broken family, and no amount of make-up, lipstick, and sunny smiles can conceal the truth. We both know where our minds wander at night when the doors are closed and we're on our own.'

Prendergast's words chilled Molly right through. More numbing was how he delivered what was essentially the truth. 'Do we look like a broken family? Do you even know the definition of a broken family?'

'I think we both know I'm referring to a family with parts missing.'

Molly came to her defence. 'Excuse me, but who do you think you are? You know nothing about us.'

Richard Prendergast began to spout off Molly Greene's life in one long monologue, as if reading her life bio from Wikipedia. Not once, during his spewing of Molly's memoir, did he look at her, but gazed dreamily at Emma. He finished up his spiel. 'Ah, what I wouldn't give to be a young boy again, without a care in the world. But nothing is ever perfect, Molly. You know why? When we are young, we don't realise we are young. When we are old, we realise we are old. True freedom we had as children only exists in memory.'

In dogged defiance, she asked, 'What difference does that make?'

'Oh, but it makes a world of difference, Molly.'

'Please tell me what's going on.'

'An experiment.'

Molly did a double-take on that. 'An experiment?'

'Yes.'

'And who are we? The guinea pigs?'

'Mommy, I want one!'

'Not now, Emma!' Molly thought back to the online advertisement. 'If my memory serves me correctly, your advertisement read something like a good home looking for a good home. There was no mention of an experiment. And I don't recall any mention of guinea pigs.' To deal with this bombshell, Molly snapped into her sarcasm mode. It was a laugh or cry situation.

'My offer still stands. You and your family have free accommodation. When the time comes, all things being equal, you can have the house, but should things not work out,' he paused, 'then, as I've already said, the farmhouse will come back to my family.'

Molly didn't want to ask, but she needed to know. 'Who else is living at the farmhouse?'

He paused. 'Something walks alone at the farmhouse, yes. A spirit trapped in the confines of the house. There have been many sightings of a child… but others say it's not a child.'

Molly was starting to believe this was all just a vivid dream and, any moment now, she would wake up and breathe a deep sigh of relief. 'It's a boy, Richard. We have all seen him to one degree or another. And you know something else? I think he's lonely. When I'm around this…energy, I feel nothing but intense sadness.'

Richard Prendergast studied Molly as she spoke. He hung on every word. 'You see, you're already on its side.'

'I'm not on anyone's side.'

'Listen to yourself. That's what it wants you to think. We've had umpteen families pass through the house, some for only two days, some lasting weeks. The spirit is looking for the right family.'

'A broken family?' Molly prompted.

'Broken families have cracks to slip in and out of. A broken family is more open to…hmm, how can I put it? External factors. A family, such as yours, is susceptible to certain things, whether that is good or bad. Emotionally, you have been through the wringer. You and the girls have experienced horrors other families should never have to experience. What I'm trying to say, Molly Greene, is that you — you — have built up a resilience. You are the rat immune to the poison.'

'So, wait, I'm a lab rat and a guinea pig? Wow!' she joked, but immune? This struck a chord with her, though she wasn't sure why. She wasn't sure of anything anymore. The meaning of his words left her clueless. She knew she should be raging because Prendergast had duped her and her family. But she wasn't. Crazy as it seemed, she didn't mind the idea of being a guinea pig in some social morbid experiment. Why? Because she was immune and broken. Being a lab experiment sounded kind of fitting.

Prendergast played along with Molly's morbid sense of irony. 'You are whatever animal you choose to identify with.'

'I'm definitely a rat.'

A vague hint of a smile appeared on Prendergast's lips.

'Is it dangerous, whatever is in the farmhouse?'

'Hmm?' Prendergast was away in a world of his own, gazing at Molly's daughter. 'Sorry, I was just remembering.' He cleared his throat. 'My extended family and I believe the child who walks alone is a festering wound which has turned the house septic. We are looking for the anti…septic.'

Under normal circumstances, Molly might've laughed her ass off at this play-on-words, but the atmosphere in the Gatehouse was far too intense. 'I saw pictures on the wall when we took Cora to your surgery. But now they're all gone. And I know there is an extra hidden room in the Gatehouse.'

Prendergast turned on her with darkness in his eyes. 'That is none of your concern. I have already told you I am from a broken family. Once upon a time, my family and I used to live at the farmhouse. But certain circumstances, which I prefer not to talk about, ended me up with me alone at the Gatehouse without my wife and son. Never tread on rotten boards.'

Molly didn't know what that meant. Perhaps it was something along the lines of not talking about something you know nothing about. She had wrongly assumed he had been referring to his childhood family, parents, and siblings, not his present family… wherever they were. She decided not to push the matter. Prendergast wasn't messing around, and she could see, somewhere deep in his eyes, the man was hurting. He carried an intolerable burden. 'I'm not going to apologise, considering you brought us here under false pretences.'

'Let's get one thing clear: I didn't bring anyone here under false pretences. You brought yourself here. And I stand by my word — you can have the house if it chooses you.'

She gulped down the last of her cold coffee and made to leave, having just had the most surreal conversation of her life. 'Emma, let's go.'

'Sooner or later, you are going to hear stories about me in Old Castle. I assure you that none of them are true.' He finished by saying, 'Old Castle is full of gossipmongers who have nothing else to do with their time besides meddle in other's lives because they don't have a life of their own.'

He accompanied them to the front door. Before they left, he told Molly, 'You will know if you are the chosen one.'

Molly couldn't help but laugh. 'Now that's a line from a movie! How will I know if I am the chosen one?' She asked, playing along with Prendergast.

'You'll know.' Before he closed the front door, he issued a last few words to Molly. 'You're free to leave at any moment you choose.'

Standing at the entrance to the Gatehouse, Molly knew in her heart and soul this was a turning point. And she thought it came as a bit of a surprise to Prendergast when she answered defiantly, 'I'm not going anywhere. The farmhouse is my home. This was meant to be. There is nothing in life or the afterlife that can scare me now. You see, Richard, I've been sort of living with the afterlife for the last few years. A chunk of me broke off and died with my son and husband that night. Ever since the car accident, I feel dislocated, dislodged, unhinged, undone, constant déjà vu. Sometimes I hear an echo where I shouldn't.'

Even Molly couldn't believe her manifest. This was cathartic because it was the first time she had spoken to a virtual stranger about how she felt. But even though it was an immense relief to tell someone, other than Janice, how she really felt, pride was getting in the way of reality. If Molly had been truthful with herself, she would've admitted free accommodation was the motivating factor at this precarious point in her life. 'I accept your experiment. I'll be your lab rat…or guinea pig.'

'Mom, I prefer a guinea pig…'

That Saturday night, everyone was in their beds asleep. Molly was sitting at the kitchen table gazing out the back window at the moths flitting and dancing around the broken porch light. Her morning encounter with Prendergast this morning was but a freakish memory now. She would triumph in this house and she didn't care who or what else was squatting in the farmhouse.

The farmhouse was quiet tonight — too quiet — and Molly pondered whether this was all plain madness. She felt as if she was living in a dream where anything was possible, including sharing her

187

house with a spirit in the afterlife, who also shared the same house. Yes, the same could be said for her old house back in Dublin, but that was just Molly, herself, and her. In this dreamworld such absurdities are taken for granted, but Molly did have a meeting with a grown man just this morning and, in that meeting, she was told that she and her family were a nest of lab rats in a social experiment, light emphasis on the social aspect of the experiment.

But what worried her more was not living in a dream but in the real world where she had to work and earn an income for her kids. Why hadn't Wilma called her? She would have to go and speak to her directly. Molly had already planned to do this, but other matters from Dreamworld had got in the way. She was trying to work out how she could cut down on expenses. She was never more grateful to have free accommodation, and she felt she'd done the right thing. The farmhouse was her saving grace, and she would conquer it, by God. She looked about for Mike to tell her as much, but Mike had gone because Mike had been a figment of her imagination. At least, she thought so.

She found herself glancing at the symbolic bottle of Spanish wine on the kitchen counter. It was the perfect moment right now to have a little tipple and God knew she deserved one. She made her way over to the counter and located the Mickey Mouse bottle opener they'd bought at Disneyland Paris only weeks before the accident. She took the bottle of alcohol and looked at the date on the label again. As she did, she noticed the bottle jiggle in her jittery hand. *Oh, God, just one drop. Wine is all over the bible, she thought. That must make it next to godliness, right? It represents the blood of Christ. What harm can there be in a little blood of Chr——*

The atmosphere in the kitchen changed. She swung on her heels, poised, breath held. Every hair stood on Molly's body as an electric charge filled the kitchen. Molly considered her mind was playing games with her when Louie started up in his cage, bouncing on his perch, emitting shrill caws. He was her canary in a mine.

'Louie, shh! You'll wake the girls!'

Too late, someone was already coming down the stairs. She had first dismissed the footfalls as the farmhouse settling down for the night, but now the creaks were pronounced and there was something furtive about them. She tried to discern which one of her girls it was. Mina thundered up and down the stairs, but these footfalls were slow, steady, calculating. That eliminated Mina. It wasn't Emma because the four-year-old's little legs and feet moved quickly. That left Cora…but there was something off about the rhythm of her footfalls if it was Cora.

Terrified, Molly stood there with her back against the kitchen counter, wine bottle in one hand and the Mickey Mouse bottle opener in the other, while her heart pulsed in her chest and temples…

Mina glided into the kitchen, looking through her mom with large dark pupils, an unmistakable sadness in her stony face.

'Mina?'

Her daughter didn't answer her, didn't even acknowledge her mom. Molly's flesh crept as her eldest daughter just stood there. 'What's wrong?'

Mina was sleepwalking. It was the first time she had ever seen Mina sleepwalking — it was her first time seeing anyone sleepwalking. Her daughter padded barefoot around the kitchen, searching for something. Molly didn't know what to do, but she'd heard somewhere it was a bad idea to wake a person who was sleepwalking. Mina stalled, her back to her mom, then padded backward and turned to Molly and looked right through her.

Following her line of vision, Molly peered over her shoulder and through the window to the back porch. She wasn't sure if her daughter was looking through her or the window. A flicker of recognition passed over Mina's face before she started uttering gibberish. Nonsensical utterances that gave Molly the creeps. Her child was only sleepwalking, but it was still unnerving.

'Why me?' Mina asked. 'Oh, no…no…no…I'm just the puppet. *I've got no strings…*' she began to sing, then giggled heinously. Her eyes focused directly on the bottle of wine in her mom's trembling hand. She reached out for the bottle and Molly, slack-jawed and dumbfounded, handed it over to her daughter. Mina took the bottle, looked blankly at it — through it — in the same way she had looked at her mom just now, and put it back on the counter where it had been keeping an eye on Molly since they'd arrived. With a slow turn of her head, her eldest daughter gazed through Molly with an utter lack of comprehension as she left the kitchen. Molly followed her daughter through the kitchen door and watched Mina drag her feet down the hallway and up the stairs. Jesus Christ, Mina was dragging her feet, something she never did. It seemed as if a fifteen-year-old who merely looked like a daughter had entered the house. Mina ascended the stairs, stopped halfway up, and turned to look back at her with that same expressionless face before continuing to the next level.

Troubled, Molly sat back down at the kitchen table and eyed the wine bottle. She went over what had just occurred in her head and questioned if Mina had been sleepwalking.

It was just after one in the morning when Molly heard the gentle sobs. She got out of bed and crossed the hallway; Emma's bedroom was closest to Molly's. Halfway across the hallway, Molly heard them again and froze. The weeping wasn't coming from Emma's room. She then considered that maybe the pitiful crying was coming from Cora's room. It didn't sound like Cora, but she also knew children were capable of making the strangest whimpers at night. She tread down the hallway to Cora's room. Even before arriving at the doorway, she knew it wasn't Cora. And it wasn't coming from Mina's bedroom upstairs. She listened out and homed in on the intermittent cries of lament.

To Molly's stunned shock, the weeping was seeping from somewhere between Emma's and Cora's bedrooms, inside the wall between the doorframes. Molly convulsed and stepped back. With her back against the opposite wall, she held her breath, afraid the sound of her breathing might cloud her senses. She listened to the weeping seeping from the wall. There, from somewhere inside, were the distant moans of a child. She wasn't sure if it was a boy or a girl — did it really matter? — but the pining sobs were heart-breaking. And for a delusional, nightmarish moment, Molly Greene thought she might've been listening to Henry, her son. Her lost son. A strange image of a forlorn child crouching just inside the wall, surrounded by rock and wood, rose in her mind's eye. She drew her hands to her mouth to muffle her own cry, forcing herself to get her breathing under control. She approached the wall and pressed her ear to the blank space between the doorframes of her daughters' bedrooms. Coming from very far inside the farmhouse infrastructure, she was sure she could hear the child muttering sadly to him or herself, nothing discernible. But she was unable to decipher what the child was mumbling, reminding her Mina had said the same thing about their voices travelling in the chimney system...only now she knew it wasn't their voices. The voice, the crying, transported Molly back four decades to a long, long summer when she and her cousin fashioned a simple walkie-talkie with a length of chord and two empty tin cans. The strange echoing voice she'd just heard inside the wall reminded her of her cousin's magical telephonic voice coming through the hollow tin can held to her right ear. There was silence before an agonising wail, more animal than human, came at Molly from just inside the plaster. Paralysing fear screamed inside her. She wanted to run, but the shock scrambled her senses.

The sound was moving inside the wall now until the farmhouse and its melancholic foundations wept. The haunting moans were emanating from further down the hallway, at the top of the stairs, where a quirky alcove was set into the wall with a time-worn wooden seat. Cora loved to sit here.

Molly went to the alcove and sat, dread oozing from every pore of her being, yet oddly calm as if this was meant to be; it was only a matter of time before they would meet again. The moment she sat on the bench, the crying ceased. She whispered into the darkness. 'What is it, little one?'

A wave of freezing, static electricity plumed on her left side. Her body bristled as something freezing, and oh so light, brushed across her hand, a subliminal stroke of a feather tip. Molly shuddered and did everything in her power not to flinch and scream. Instead, she bit down on her tongue and could taste the gritty coppery warmness of blood fill her mouth. She felt what she thought was a hand gently place itself on the back of her right hand. Tears streaking down her cheeks, her stomach muscles ached as she kept her sobbing to herself. The tears didn't spout from shock, but infinite sadness. She took a deep breath and opened her hand…then jumped off that cliff into a free-falling world she never knew existed…

The slight weight of a small hand rested in her palm. She did everything she could to not convulse. She folded her fingers but the little hand oozed between her digits like mercury.

And then it was gone, leaving Molly Greene sitting there in dumb silence, wondering how she had ever come to be sitting in the alcove.

14.

It was Monday morning, and the kids were starting in their new school. It was Emma's first time at any school and she had that advantage over her sisters. Mina and Emma, like any average fifteen- and ten-year-old girls starting at a new school, were jittery balls of nerves and wondered if they would 'fit in'.

Molly felt for the poor creatures. She wanted to soak up every minute of Emma's big day, but she couldn't get over what had happened late Saturday night, Sunday morning. It haunted and consumed her to the point that she couldn't engage and everything else seemed like a distraction.

The 15-minute drive was a silent and tense one, save for Emma's occasional slide into *Old McDonald had a Farm*. When Molly pulled up at the school building, she noticed the weird glances from the other parents standing around the main gates. Even some children seemed very preoccupied with the novelty Greene family. Molly was sure she even spotted one or two teachers gawking through the window blinds. Maybe it was because these backwater locals weren't used to seeing human beings. Was she being paranoid? Everyone was wearing the obligatory Covid face mask, which sadly normalised the situation, telling Molly Old Castle wasn't some village in a lost dimension. On the downside, those face masks only highlighted the ogling eyes that looked away when Molly met their anonymous stares. What the fuck was going on here? She suspected some backwardness, but the stares were vindictive, not inquisitive.

Molly had other things to worry about, however. There would always be hicks in places like Old Castle, forever, because that's just the way things are. Having wished her three daughters a good day, she drove to the centre of town and parked up in the square by the stone cross, and made her way to the front door of Wilma's. The Closed sign on the door didn't deter her from knocking. She knocked. A second later, Wilma came trundling into view and opened the door. 'Sorry, dear. We're not open for another hour.'

Wilma's reaction took her by surprise. 'Um, I'm Molly Greene. We met a few weeks ago.' She pulled down her face mask for a moment for Wilma to recognise her. 'I'm your new restaurant manager?' Molly reminded her. Even before she finished speaking, she knew something was wrong.

Wilma stalled and looked at Molly as if it was the first time she'd ever heard of her. 'Ah, yes, sorry. My memory isn't what it used to be, dearie.'

Molly was getting negative vibes as Wilma distanced herself. 'Um, I'm a little busy now.' She gestured inside the restaurant to a young man who saluted Molly. Void of enthusiasm, Molly waved back.

'It won't take long,' Molly interjected. 'I just want to finalise my begin date and work out a few details… kids. I thought we would've spoken before now,' Molly hinted Wilma might have been in touch.

Wilma eyed her uneasily while glancing over her shoulder towards the town square. 'Hmm,' she nodded.

With a slight huff, Wilma invited Molly into the restaurant and told her to take a seat at a table. Wilma then took the man into the kitchen where an uncomfortable (for Molly) hushed conversation took place. Molly thought he was delivering food or perhaps repairing one of the kitchen appliances. But it soon became apparent who the man was and why he was here. Molly couldn't believe what she was hearing. Her heart began to race.

A few minutes later, the neat young man appeared from the kitchen, nodded a curt goodbye to Molly, and vacated the restaurant in a real hurry.

Wilma stood there, looking all embarrassed and apologetic. 'I owe you an explanation. But first, let me get us both a coffee.'

Molly didn't answer. All she could think about was her dwindling bank balance and the three kids who depend on her. The house was free, and she was determined to make it hers in this strange social experiment. But what about electricity, pay-per-view TV, water, internet, and everything else? A flutter of panic rose inside her.

Wilma returned to the table with two mugs of steaming coffee and apple tart with a dollop of fresh cream. 'We need to talk,' started Wilma. 'Tell me how everything is going on up there at the farmhouse?'

It surprised Molly to know Wilma knew where she was living. She was aware she'd mentioned it in their last meeting, but had confirmed nothing. 'Oh, fine. It's an old place with a lot of character.' *That's an understatement.* 'Rough around the edges. But I moved in because of the potential of the place.'

'Oh, it's got potential all right.'

Molly wasn't sure if Wilma was being sarcastic or if there was a hidden meaning in her answer. 'How did you know where we lived?'

Wilma chuckled to herself. 'There's nothing nobody knows in a place like Old Castle. And you can imagine someone in my line of work hears and knows everything that happens in this town. You moving into that house was a big deal here. It's the talk of the town!' She giggled and her whole frame shook.

'It's no big deal. People move into old houses all the time.'

Wilma considered her. 'But not old houses like that one, dearie.'

Molly was suspecting the reason Wilma hadn't called her was because of the farmhouse. With a hint of defiance, she answered, 'I need some money to do up the place a little. Can we talk about my job?'

'Ah, yes.' Wilma took a drink from her mug of coffee. 'I'm afraid there have been, um, changes.'

'I've gathered that.'

'I'm sorry you saw that. Tom has been chosen to be our new manager.' Wilma spoke as if Molly had just seen a grizzly sight. 'It was just bad timing.'

'No, Wilma,' Molly back answered, 'bad timing is when a person is promised a job and that person moves their entire life to that job, only to be told there was never any job in the first place.' Molly was struggling to keep her cool. She couldn't see over the expenses and bills mounting in her mind's eye.

'Molly, I can't let you work here. I would love to, but recent…things have come to light and I couldn't have it on my conscience. Not only that, but your presence here would have a negative effect on my business and God knows that's the last thing we all need right now.'

Molly felt like a street beggar who had just wandered into Wilma's to bum from her feasting clients. She couldn't believe what she was hearing.

Wilma shifted. 'I shouldn't even have you in here right now.'

The conversation had taken a sinister twist.

'Please, at least, do me the honour of an explanation?' Molly was crying inside now, but she needed to hold face.

Wilma grew wary, casting a sheepish glance around her restaurant even though there was nobody there. 'It's better you know now rather than later when you've settled into the farmhouse. There's still time to get out, Molly.'

'What are you talking about?'

'The farmhouse has a murky past, dearie.'

'That doesn't bother me. We all have a past. I have a real murky past.' She huffed a chuckle because it was true. Molly was on the verge of telling Wilma her life story but decides against it; she doesn't deserve it. 'What's the problem with the house?'

'It's not a problem with the house; it's what's in the house.'

This line would stay with Molly.

'And what's in the house?'

'You tell me,' answered Wilma, holding Molly's stare.

As on many other occasions, Molly Greene decided playing dumb was the best strategy. 'Besides mice in the roof?'

'There's something in the roof, but it's not mice, and count yourself lucky if there are mice. I bet you haven't seen one mouse?'

Molly shrugged her shoulders. 'Not sure.' She hadn't.

'I bet you haven't seen one animal around that place.'

She hadn't. It was true, not even a rabbit or a bird in the unending woods around the house. Always complete silence, and she could hear it even now. She had thought the silence was the peace and tranquillity of the countryside when, in fact, something more sinister was at play. The only animal she saw was Louie, if he could be called an animal, and he had been agitated since they'd moved in.

Wilma went on. 'Something happened there a long time ago, and the place hasn't been right since. Now, I love a good mystery. Who doesn't? I'm even partial to a Stephen King book every now and again, but whatever is out there at that house makes Mr King look like a kiddie ride at Disneyland.'

Molly laughed it off. 'The only evil in that place is

when my teenage daughter misses her friends. You don't want to be around her.'

Wilma chuckled. 'Families move in every now and again but move out days later. You're not the first family, Molly. And God strike me down for even saying it, you won't be the last.'

'Superstitious hocus pocus,' replied Molly. 'I don't have time for such nonsense. I've got three daughters — that's reality right there.'

'Then, for the love of Jesus, get out of that place, Molly. I've got cheap digs above this place. Why don't you and your girls move here while you get your life in order? It'll be a tighter fit than the farmhouse, but it'll be a safer fit. And, who knows, I don't know if this kid is going to live up to his managerial resume if you get my meaning. It could turn out to be a very cosy live-in position for you and the girls, Molly. School just around the corner. Nothing to be sniffed at.'

'I have my life in order, Wilma.'

'Didn't Prendergast tell you what happened?'

Molly shook her head.

'I suppose he forgot to tell you his wife and child disappeared off the face of the planet five years back?'

Molly's jaw dropped. A flush of red rose up her neck and cheeks.

'Hmm, thought not. And I suppose he forgot to tell you about the police enquiry that went on for a year and a bit? Hmm? Overlooked to tell you he had been at the centre of a murder investigation, only the law could never find enough evidence to pin it on him? Did he tell you that, Molly? Nobody knows if he did it or not. Prendergast has a lot of acreage out there, plenty of space to bury unwanted items.'

Molly was collapsing inside, but she wasn't going to give Wilma the satisfaction of watching her crumble. 'If scare tactics is your thing, then it's not working.'

'I'm only filling in the blanks, dearie. What I do know is this: Old Castle's foundation is now built on smoke and mirrors.' Wilma smiled and sipped her coffee. 'We try to keep a lid on things. We don't want any bad publicity in Old Castle. Imagine what damage that would do to local businesses. Whenever there's a little episode out there at the farmhouse, our local police force, aka Mike Furlong, makes sure it stays in Old Castle. Hmm,' she smiled a wry smile. 'What happens in Old Castle stays in Old Castle. That should be our town logo.' She chuckled, then with grand airs, she announced: 'What happens in Old Castle, stays in Old Castle…' Wilma went on. 'People in Old Castle have been living with this macabre secret all our lives. We've become, what's the word, immune? Reality has become legend, and legend has become myth. I know what you're thinking, Molly: hicks in the sticks, right?' Wilma nodded. 'And you're still telling me you haven't noticed anything odd about the place?'

'No.' Molly wasn't going to give her the satisfaction.

Wilma didn't look convinced. 'Uh-huh.' She

paused. 'They call it the squatter.'

Molly found this of great interest. She was sure she had used the same description herself without anyone ever mentioning it or had she heard it somewhere?

Wilma was shaking her head.

'What?'

She pointed at Molly with a stubby finger. 'You're the squatter. Never forget that.' She took a deep breath and flashed a consolatory smile. 'Anyway, dearie, I'm not here to sell you anything. Time will tell.' Her easy smile made Molly uneasy. 'And if you do change your mind, like I said, I rent a small apartment upstairs. It's empty at the moment. It's a squeeze for of a family of four, but it would buy you some time until you found more appropriate accommodation.'

Molly finished her mug of coffee and apple tart. 'Thank you, but I'm going to take my chances.'

'There's no work here in Old Castle, Molly. You shouldn't have come down here.'

'You shouldn't have offered me a job. If you hadn't offered me the job, I wouldn't have come down here.'

'There's something broken in that house.'

A broken family for a broken house... Molly was gutted, yet obstinate. 'I'm determined to make this work,' she remarked as she got up to leave.

'And I truly hope it works out for you, Molly. But, please, for the love of God, consider what I've told you here today. You watch that Richard Prendergast.

That man is not liked around town. He used to have a medical practice, but he was boycotted. He was forced to close his practice.'

Molly flashed a wane smile and shut the door behind her, knowing in her heart and soul. She would never work at Wilma's. She was better than that, and this was yet another sign that bigger things were waiting for the Greenes.

As she crossed the street, a hysterical fit of laughter seized Molly. She was never meant to have worked at Wilma's. It was the house's way of getting her to Old Castle — the farmhouse. That's where Molly would triumph. She sat in her car, laughing her head off. It was only then when she spotted Wilma watching her from the restaurant window. She flinched, all embarrassed, but the more Wilma stared at her, the more she needed to set free that crazy laugh bubble inside her. Like back at school again, failing to hold in a gut-buster of a giggle, Molly broke down in an unadulterated fit of raucous laughter until she went blue in the face. She slammed on her steering wheel with the hilarity of it all. Meanwhile, Wilma kept on staring. Her body appeared to go limp behind the restaurant glass as she watched Molly sink into the realms of possessive laughter.

Driving back to the farmhouse, Molly was more determined than ever. She was saddened, yet had garnered an extra fondness for the house with the worst reputation in Old Castle. It was kind of cool. She was going to prove to everyone that they're wrong. Yes, this was her mission and challenge. The farmhouse would either make or break Molly and she would break in the taming of the beast if need be. Brave inner thoughts worthy of any mindless Hollywood blockbuster, but reality isn't so fun when reality kicks in. The only beast around here were the idle minds and busy tongues of the country yokels. The farmhouse would be their victory, a broken house for a broken family.

An hour later, Molly was online, filtering through the non-existent local jobs in the hostelry sector, when she received a call from Janice. 'Hey, Jan!'

'What's with the silent treatment, girl?'

'Sorry, I've just been getting busy settled in…and settled out.' She paused and tried her best to hold it together. At Wilma's, she'd erected a tough exterior, but now the sad reality was taking hold. 'The job fell through.'

'What? You can't be serious!'

Her voice jittered. 'I can and I am.'

Janice swore down the phone.

'Exactly,' answered Molly.

'What happened?'

Molly was about to tell Janice the reason Wilma had reneged on her word, but she thought it was best to keep it to herself for now. 'It's complicated. Punchline is that I don't have a job BUT I *do* have a free house.' At this point of the conversation, Molly felt a sudden chill creep up on her from behind and was sure she heard shuffling around in the hallway. She swivelled around in her chair and got up to check. There was nothing out of place. She walked back to the kitchen table and sat down to pick up her phone… only her phone wasn't where she'd just put it down. Once again, she heard movement in the hallway and, this time, grew wary as she crossed the kitchen and peeped around the corner of the door. Molly was sure she could hear the tiny voice of Janice coming from the receiver of her phone, but couldn't pinpoint where it was coming from exactly. She froze when she got back to the kitchen to find her phone where she'd left it. Molly listened out, but all she could hear was the distant voice of her friend calling out her name. She picked up the phone. 'Sorry…'

'Jesus, what was that?'

'Emma took the phone.' Molly, on tenterhooks, lied. 'Sorry about that.'

Janice roared with laughter. 'Ha! I knew it was her!'

'What?'

'The Emma giggle — I'd know it anywhere.'

Molly felt sick.

'She still does that, huh?'

'Yep. Anyway, Jan, I've got to collect the kids. Their first day at school. Who knows what kind of reception I'm going to get? Talk later.'

'Okay,' answered Janice. 'Molly?'

'Yeah?'

'Is everything okay?'

'Yeah. And you?'

'You don't sound okay, Moll. There's something up, I know it. Why don't you come home?'

Molly wanted more than anything to tell Janice about the presence in the house, but she decided it wasn't a wise move. She needed more time to deal with this. 'Thanks, Jan, but I'm going to stick it out in the sticks.'

'Well, let me come visit you. How about that?'

'Yes, that would be nice. I'll text you when we're up and running. We're still trying to find our feet here.' But at that moment, Molly pondered if there might ever be a good time for Janice to call.

'Okay, Moll. I still think you're crazy, 'kay?'

'That's okay, Jan. We established that a long time ago,' Molly tittered. She was about to hang up when she heard Janice's voice yell from the receiver. 'Yeah?'

'I almost forgot the reason I rang.'

'Oh, so you weren't checking up on me?'

'Well, yes and no. What's up with the photos you sent me?'

Molly frowned. 'What photos?'

'Hmm, I think a little Emma elf might've been busy with your phone again while you weren't looking,' she said in a naughty tone. 'She must've sent thirty or forty pictures from all around the house. She's dangerous with that phone. Imagine she sends the wrong pic to the wrong person?'

'Well,' Molly laughed, 'my phone is quite innocent these days.'

They shared a laugh.

'Okay, so, tell me. What did she send you?'

'Some of them are a little creepy.'

'Creepy?'

'I'll just send them to you. Have a look for yourself.'

'Do that. Okay, this time I'm going. Talk later. Send me those pics!'

Molly put the phone down and fearfully looked around the kitchen. Whatever was in the house was looking at her 24/7 like a security guard staring at a surveillance camera. But it only manifests when the sun went down. That's when it liked to come out and play. As Molly prepped the kids' lunch, every few seconds casting a nervous glance over her shoulder, her phone dinged several times over to announce Janice's photos. She popped the lamb stew into the casserole dish and switched on the oven, then tapped on Janice's texts to see a string of images. Even from a quick glance, she could tell Emma had been the culprit. She flicked through the photos with a wide grin on her face. It was funny to see the world through her little girl's eyes. The photos were blurry and most of them were an inconsequential erratic pot-pourri taken in the kitchen, hallway, and the playroom. She laughed and shook her head through 19 of the photos, but the smile dropped from her face as she arrived at the last picture: number 20. If she had not been sitting down, she would have fainted. Horror sweating from every pore of her being, she stared at the grainy image of herself sleeping in her bed.

Molly googled an app which would take a picture of anyone who messed with her phone. She found a free one with good reviews, so she downloaded it and waited for something to bite.

Unable to stay in the kitchen any longer, or even the farmhouse, Molly Greene put the oven on the timer and went outside to her car, where she sat for an hour, contemplating the brooding house. What nested within its walls?

15.

At 1.45 that Monday afternoon, Molly Greene left to collect the kids from school. She watched the farmhouse watch her in her rear-view mirror as she receded up the lane. A tremble enveloped her as she recalled her sleeping face in the photograph; the last self-portrait Molly would ever desire to see.

After school pickup, Molly didn't have any time to think about the mounting oddness in the farmhouse because her girls were full of stories about their first day at school. Emma was over the moon with the whole affair. Cora, too, enjoyed her first day, though still treading lightly. Molly was over the moon to hear Cora had already made a friend, Theresa. They'd eaten their lunch together in the schoolyard. All was working out (mostly) great in Molly's head until Cora mentioned, 'Oh, and you know what Theresa said? She said her mom and dad don't want her speaking with me.'

Molly felt herself wither inside. 'Why?' But she knew why…

'Because we're living at the farmhouse where bad things happen.'

Molly was fit to hit someone. She tried to control her surge of anger. 'What would they know? Have you had bad things happen to you?'

Cora shook her head.

'Cora, you listen to your mom. There's nothing bad in this house.' And, for once in her life, she felt

210

she wasn't lying. But what she held back was that there was something good in the house; something neglected and looking for a little love and attention in a sterile world. And Molly was filled with a warm fullness just then, happiness beyond happiness, such a feeling of completion and if she were to die right now, she would be happy in knowing she had attained something special. 'The problem in this town is that people don't mind their own business and you know what happens in those places?'

Cora shook her head again.

'They talk between themselves and come up with their own truths — half-truths. Rumours.'

Mina was sitting in the passenger seat next to her. If Mina's face was the weather, it would be raining right now, with gloomy thunderheads lurking on the horizon.

'And you, Mina? How was your day?' Molly asked cheerfully, though she knew Mina's day hadn't gone smoothly, just as she assumed it wouldn't.

'I'm getting the silent treatment.'

'Oh?' asked Molly, feigning surprise.

'Nobody wants to talk to me.'

'Mina, why are you always the victim? Hmm? Have you considered that it might be you giving your classmates the silent treatment?'

Around 5.30 that evening, Molly prepared a potato and leek puree for dinner. As she was peeling the potatoes, her mind was on other things, like the pictures Janice had sent her. She'd thought Emma had

211

been hiding her phone. As Eugen Doga's 'Gramophone' played in the background, Molly noticed a knocking coming from another location. She turned down the volume and waited. The knock came again, a single knock on the back door — the wrong door for anyone to be knocking at. Molly was no expert on door-knocking, but a single knock was just off-putting…on a back door?

Mina called from somewhere upstairs. 'I think there's someone knocking on the door, Mom.'

A loud knock, aggressive this time, made her shriek and frog-leap backward to the table. She stared at the back door and tried not to imagine what was behind it. Gliding up to the door to listen, and listened, she wished she had one of those fisheye things.

Thud!

The knock came again, even heavier than before. What surprised her — disturbed her — was the knock had come from the lower half of the door, as if a child had just knocked, yet the decided force behind the knocks said otherwise.

Deciding she was the boss…ghost…mother… everything of this house, Molly twisted the knob and swung the door out wide. An icy draught of wind crept in around her ankles, but nothing else crept in. She buttoned up her cardigan and stepped outside. The wind whistled through the trees. There was nobody out here, but that didn't come as any surprise. A wide smile graced Molly's lips. The child who walked alone was playing with her, looking for a little attention. 'Peekaboo!' Molly called out into the night. 'I can see you!' It was all just a game. 'I've just made potato and leek puree…or you might prefer eek! puree,' she joked to nobody. 'Why don't you join us for dinner? Don't be a stranger.' The biting wind got the best of her. 'Brrr! It's freezing out here.'

*

He was standing just inside the tree line when the woman exited the back door of the house and called, "Peekaboo! I can see you!" He almost stepped out from behind the tree just then, but there was something about the way the woman had spoken in every direction, not only his. She had seen him, he was sure of it, but she couldn't pinpoint his exact location. It was only a matter of time before she'd catch him in the act. Maybe he should use a different lookout point?

*

That Monday night was the quietest night at the farmhouse…save for the knocking branch right outside her window. Molly Greene had learned to decipher between natural and unnatural sounds and what she was listening to at that moment was the leaning spruce tree by the gable end of the house. Smaller branches scratched and scraped off the wall. Sooner or later, she would have to cut that damn branch if she wanted to get any sleep, not that sleep was ever guaranteed at the farmhouse. Restless, she lay in bed going over the latest events: the photo of her sleeping self. As she ran over everything in her mind, the branch knocked on the wall…knock…

213

knock…knock…

'Fuck!' she swore and flung back the blankets, making yet another mental note to go to the local chemist and buy organic sleeping pills — organic. She crossed the bedroom and opened out the window, needing to see just how much of that annoying branch needed to be cut back. Even before she opened the window, something struck her as odd: there was no wind. In fact, the night was dead still, but maybe dead still wasn't the correct wording, as something frightening caught Molly's attention. She would never get used to how her body reacted to something it couldn't understand…creeping flesh, blurred vision as she struggled to focus on what she was really looking at…impending sense of dread even though she knew the leftover spirit in the house was a gentle soul.

There was something crouching amongst the branches of the spruce, some 30 feet off the ground. For a moment, it looked like a black bin liner had been swept up there in the wind and stuck in the needles. If the moon hadn't been shining so brightly tonight, Molly wouldn't have seen the stationary silhouette perched in the tree. A cadaverous face, hidden in the shadows of the branches, thrown by the moonbeams, stared across at her, seemingly photoshopped into the tree. The distance between the ground and the first branches of the tree was easily 20 feet. No child could get to the first set of branches without a ladder, rope, or even nails nailed into the tree. Molly guessed this child was similar in age to

214

Emma, judging by the height more than anything. It was difficult to put an age on the face from this distance. The face wasn't clear enough to discern an age — if spirits even have an age other than the age they died at. Despite the fact that the face of the wraith wasn't clear, Molly could see its ears, which seemed too large for its — his? — head.

They stared at each other across the void. She wasn't even positive the child was there until the apparition stirred. Like an optical illusion, the child leaned on the branch, extending to Molly's window with the heel of his boot, and began to heave his weight on the branch, down…up, making whatever Molly was looking at very real and tactile. The child had an unnerving way of moving, similar to a wobbly animatronic mechanism while remaining motionless between movements. It was as if someone else was guiding the ghoulish automaton by remote control.

The branch dipped and rose, rocking higher and lower as the child leaned back and forth until the branch knocked gently on the eaves of the house. Gobsmacked, she heard what she'd been listening to all this time in her bedroom at night. Had it been the child who walked alone? She had assumed all along it was the wind, but now she had to rethink everything. Whatever this was, it liked to dwell and jump in and out of the realms of possibilities and coincidences.

The funereal child shifted again before scrambling further up into the tree at a disturbing rate, animalistic in nature. Molly craned her neck to get a view of the top of the tree from her bedroom window, but the tree was too high and too near for her to see the top.

Molly ran downstairs and outside. When she gazed up into the tree, but there was nothing up there. She stepped back a few feet and peered into the lofty reaches of the large spruce. The moon shone right through the branches and nothing was there that shouldn't be there. Whatever had been perched there was gone. Molly trembled with a strange mix of fear and ethereal dread. She didn't know how to process this; her mortal senses were at odds with this immortal being. But she was sure it was playing mind games with her. Even more troubling was how it played literal mind games with her, as if the thing in the tree had secret access to the deep synapses of her brain. She was sure of something else: she was a mother, and she knew when a child was trying to get her attention. What had been up that tree just now was once a child and Molly Greene had immense pity for it.

16.

The following Tuesday morning, Louie greeted the four women of the farmhouse as normal with his 'Allo! 'Allo! 'Allo!'

Over breakfast, Mina came out with, 'I've got a new friend. Her name's Christine.'

Molly couldn't fathom it. 'Serious?'

'Yep.'

'Great! Why didn't you tell me yesterday?'

Mina shrugged. 'Forgot.'

If only Mina knew how preoccupied Molly was with her, even if she seemed more concerned with the house and its extra occupant. This was the way forward: happy children, happy parents. Off the cuff, Molly suggested. 'Why don't you invite her over this weekend?' No sooner had she said it when she got cold feet. She didn't want the responsibility of someone else's child when she couldn't guarantee the safety of her own, and that notion frightened her out of her wits whilst sitting at the kitchen table surrounded by her children. *What's wrong with me?* She would've loved to get a little guidance from Mike just then.

'Well, that's the thing. I invited her over, but she freaked out. She told me she might not wake up in the morning.'

'Did you wake up this morning?' Molly slammed her butter knife onto the table, startling the girls. 'Y'know what? I'm sick and tired of this small-town attitude. You tell your friend Christina there's nothing wrong with this house.'

'Christine,' interjected Mina, taken aback by her mom's sudden outburst.

'It might've had some bad luck in the past,' continued Molly, 'but we're here to turn that around. We're not just any guinea pigs…'

Emma chimed in between mouthfuls of cereal, 'Can I get a guinea-pig, Mom? Pleeeease?'

'We are the guinea pigs, sweetie. Now, eat up, we'll be late for school.'

Now, both Cora and Mina glanced at each other across the table, just to verify they had both heard the same thing.

'Guinea pig?' Cora lip-synched to Mina, who just shook her head in bewilderment.

'And you know something else?' Molly added, 'If Christine doesn't want to come, then you dare her to come.'

'What?'

Something clicked in Molly's ever-so-slightly adrift and floating-out-to-sea reasoning. She could use this to her advantage. After all, Old Castle tongues liked to wag, so why not use them against themselves? This anonymous Christine would be her lit match to the fire. She would spread the word through Old Castle that the farmhouse was harmless. To turn this around, Molly knew she needed the locals on her side. 'Let her stay Saturday night.'

'Her parents won't let her come.'

'Let me speak to them. Get me her mom's number.'

On the spot, Mina sent a text to Christine who was never offline. Seconds later, 'I forwarded you her mom's number.'

'Wow, that was fast. I remember when people used to make phone calls.' As she said it, Molly's phone chimed.

'Carrier pigeon, you mean,' joked Mina.

It was lovely to see her caustic sense of humour come back. 'I'm not that old!'

They all laughed. Even Louie got in on the act by squawking approval.

'I'll call her mom later.'

They finished up breakfast and the morning chaos ensued as everyone ran around getting ready for school.

The Greenes, mainly Molly, were greeted at school by even more biting stares than the previous Monday. Molly didn't care because she was sailing on a higher plain now.

When she got back to the farmhouse, she sat in her car, gazing at the brooding building, and wondering what came next in this ghoulish experiment where a listed building and her home was the prize.

She took her phone from her handbag and dialled. 'Hello, this is Mina's mom. Am I speaking to Christine's mom?'

'The new girl?'

'Um, yes, Mina. And my name's Molly.'

'I know who you are.'

Judging by the tone, she regretted knowing who Mina's mom was.

The woman on the phone confirmed Christine had mentioned a new girl at school but refrained from using the friend term. She seemed preoccupied.

'If you're busy, I can call you back any time? How does that suit you?'

'How 'bout you never call me back? How does that suit you?'

The woman's sudden rudeness startled Molly. She was close to hanging up or asking the woman if she was having a bad day. Thinking about her daughter, she forged ahead, pretending she hadn't heard a word, or playing dumb, as she liked to do. 'Mina would like to invite Christine to stay this weekend. Saturday night? Friday night if Saturday doesn't suit.'

'Please, don't suggest any night. I've already spoken to Christine about this. Your daughter is more than welcome to stay the night with us, but my daughter won't be going anywhere near that house, and I don't care if you're Mother Teresa. That's my final offer, Mrs Greene—'

'Miss…'

'Miss Greene, I work for the town hall and I petitioned to have that place knocked to the ground, but the mayor — the mayor — responded by saying it would bring bad luck on the town. That will tell you how seriously we take the farmyard.'

'It's a listed building. It cannot be knocked. And it's a farmhouse. There's a difference.'

'We are the local planning authority, Miss Greene. We call the shots.'

'I don't know what you're talking about. It's a

private residence.'

'For now…'

Molly wasn't picking up on this oblique threat. 'And what does that mean?'

'It means time heals all wounds.'

Molly uttered, 'Jesus Christ,' under her breath. 'And what does *that* mean?'

'It is only a matter of time before that building is abandoned. Why the Prendergast family would hold on to it for so many years is beyond us. But mark my words, the farmhouse *will* be abandoned sooner or later, and I'll be there with my demolition papers. That place has brought nothing but misery to this town.'

Molly couldn't believe the arrogance of this woman. She couldn't take this small-minded bigotry any longer. 'I never thought I'd say this, but I agree with you: the house is haunted. But my hand on my heart, whatever is in that house has no bad intentions…a little love is all it needs.' Molly was fervid on the topic. Did she regret saying it? No.

Christine's mom laughed down the line. 'Oh, don't we all!' Her remark was hilarious, apparently. She composed herself. 'If I get my way, I'll have that place razed to the ground.'

Molly was both astonished and a little gutted. She didn't care if this woman was her daughter's friend's mom. 'Who died and crowned you queen of Old Castle?'

Christine's mom responded by hanging up.

'Rude,' Molly called to her phone before grabbing

her handbag and going inside.

The ominous energy descended the moment she stepped inside. She realised she'd felt this energy from the first day but had put it down to the character of the old building, but now she knew it was coming from a deeper level. To help ease the tension, Molly called out to the cockatoo. 'Hey, Louie! I'm back.'

The bird squawked back.

'Yeah,' Molly answered. 'Just dropped the girls off at school. Now, I'm going to get myself a hot mug of tea and sit down for half an hour to look for a job.' The sound of her own voice soothed her. She got her cup of tea and took herself to the kitchen table, where she opened her MacBook for some serious job-searching.

She called out, 'Look, I know you're somewhere nearby…watching me. I can feel you watching me.' She was on the verge of saying: I want you to know that you don't scare me, I don't scare easily. Even ghosts don't scare me. But Molly decided it was best to speak to the presence in the house as if it wasn't one, because the child who walked alone — the squatter — didn't know it was a ghost. She didn't want to scare the ghost. Molly determined she was going to speak to it as she would to a child. 'Don't be afraid,' she said in a raised voice, and took a sip of her tea. 'I'm Molly Greene. You can call me Molly. I used to be somebody, but now I'm nobody. I've had my fair share of bad luck…until I came here, and I found my purpose in life.' She decided not to get into the accident. 'I don't want you to be afraid. This farmhouse is big enough for us all to live under one roof. But do me a favour, don't sneak up on me. It makes me nervous. Just make your presence known because I'm not too fond of all this creeping around — it's not how we roll. Just putting it out there. No more peekaboo, got it? Now, if you don't mind, I'll get back to finding a job.'

If anyone could see her now, they would probably have her committed. She giggled a little to herself and waited for an answer or a sign that never materialised. Not that she was surprised because whatever was in the house preferred the element of surprise. Molly felt at ease with herself. This was the way forward; she was certain of it. Molly would treat the lost child as one of her own. She laughed to herself, wondering what the paperwork and red tape were like to adopt the ghost of a child.

Around 6pm that Tuesday evening, as the first of the moths began to flutter around the cracked porch light, an overpowering sense of happiness filled Molly Greene. She wasn't sure why, but she was beginning to understand a pattern. Thinking back through the few evenings she'd been here, this warm sense of being at one with herself consumed her, almost like a catharsis, and always around 6 in the evening.

Cora and Mina were busy doing their homework upstairs while Emma was handing out paperwork to her imaginary classmates sitting in the playroom. My, how she loved school, which was a blessing for

Molly. She naturally took to it which was one headache less.

Molly noticed she was running low on food. Her ex-chef had taught her how to use spices in her cuisine. She'd come to love those from the Mediterranean and she was out of thyme and had zero oregano. She turned to the chalkboard to add spices to the growing shopping list when she stopped dead, chalk held to the board. Her face screwed up at the chalk drawing on the board. She had been walking by it all day and hadn't noticed it, which begged the question: when had it been drawn? One thing she knew, it wasn't there when they left for school this morning.

The accomplished chalk drawing of the farmhouse displayed (and this is where Molly did a double take) five, yes, five people building a snowman. Her skin prickled with the acceptance that Emma hadn't been drawing that picture of Louie while they had all watched her do it. She had been under the influence of whatever was in the house. Molly refused to use the word, but her child had been *possessed* and there was no other way to say it. To think four-year-old Emma had been under the influence of the spirit who lingered in these walls was frankly terrifying. Molly recalled how her daughter hadn't been herself at that moment, the way she looked over her shoulder at them…through them. This spirit, this lone walker, had possessed her child. That was crossing the line.

In a raised voice, Molly Greene announced, 'Okay, I am asking you to leave my children out of this.'

Molly wasn't sure how to speak to the presence. She didn't want to go in all Hollywood gung ho, holding a bible and a cross. This thing in the house was once a child, died as a child, and still thought it was a child, she reminded herself. 'Please leave my children alone. In time…my own time…I will introduce you to my three daughters. But not now. They have a new life to be dealing with. Call it a hunch, but I'm thinking you might be too much for them to take on board right now. As the old saying goes: you can look, but you can't touch.' She hung back on her next words for quite some time. 'I will be your mother if that's what you want. I know you're looking for a little love, me too! As they say, a little love makes the world go 'round…'

They also say: be careful what you wish for.

'Mom?' called Cora from the second floor. 'Who are you talking to?'

'Shit,' Molly profaned, realising she'd spoken too loudly. 'I'm, erm, writing a story!' Molly called back. 'Yeah, I've got an idea for a thriller, no blood. Well, maybe just a drop. I'm just trying to figure out how it should be worded.' *Wow, that was a whopper!* But now that she thought about it, she was jobless and had time to write a novel…even a good one that might sell a few copies and keep her kids in gigabytes or whatever the internet is measured in these days.

According to Molly Greene's Sony Dream Machine cube clock (a throwback from the nineties), the voices began at 2.33 am. A conversation coming from her bedroom fireplace woke Molly. Intrigued by this phenomenon, she climbed out of bed and stuck her head into the substantial hearth. There was a house party going on in the fireplace. The cadence of speech contained all the rises, drops, and pauses of any lively conversation, and it was terrifying. Mina had commented she'd heard voices coming from her fireplace and had assumed it was other members of the family speaking in various rooms and their voices carried through the flue system. Molly could confirm now it wasn't, not that she was in any rush to tell Mina. She tried to block out every other sound of the house and concentrate solely on the fireplace conversation, but it was just out of earshot. Then the conversation stopped. Her heart thumping, Molly went back to bed and stared at the ceiling, wondering if she would ever have another full night's sleep again. It confounded Molly how the farmhouse had another life to the one she saw, bustling with nocturnal happenings. Molly gazed across the bedroom to the fireplace in the shadows, waiting for it to speak. It remained silent.

At 4:45 am, incessant chattering woke Molly. It sounded as if people were outside in the front yard talking, with blatant disrespect for the people trying to sleep inside. The voices in the distance were reminiscent of her old house in Dublin and how she would hear late-night passers-by on the street outside. Determined to go back to sleep and let the other side of this house get on with its nocturnal business, Molly stuck her head under a pillow and waited for sleep to take her…and waited…then waited some more. She considered how what would have frightened the living shit out of her just a couple of days ago had now become second nature to her now, here at the farmhouse.

'Fuck's sake!' she spat and followed the voices which took her downstairs. The sound of the talking loomed closer as she descended. At the bottom of the staircase, she stalled and listened to the conversation coming from the kitchen. The door was closed, yet she was fully sure she hadn't closed it before going up to bed. She had no reason to close it. The kitchen door held framed frosted glass and she could see vague shapes and outlines through the glass. Her skin crept as she harkened to the childish voice. It was the squatter, the lonely spirit they shared this house with. She shook her head in disbelief as she listened to that echoing voice coming from not only the other side of her kitchen door, but from the other side. It was one of many surreal moments Molly would take to her early grave. Maybe not her grave — her shrine, perhaps…

With exhilaration and numbing fear, Molly could hardly contain herself. This was the first time she listened to her illegitimate ghost child's voice. It conjured up memories of hearing her daughters call her 'Mama' for the first time.

But as Molly listened, it became evident the child was conversing with a silent partner…the other half of this two-way conversation was inaudible to Molly, yet the child was responding to a second nocturnal stranger. The child whispered feverishly. Molly felt ill. She was in a bad dream…the surreal psychological horror type that stays with its captive audience (the dreamer) for days after. The more she heard, the more she realised this wasn't a chat, but a chant. The ghostly presence in Molly's kitchen was repeating some kind of phrase over and over again at sickeningly high speed, too fast and muffled for Molly's ears.

As if starring in a bad comedy, Molly suddenly felt her nose itch and tried to block a sneeze that came snorting down her nostrils…

The delirious whispering stopped.

Silence.

With bated breath, Molly watched the darkness through the frosted glass with unblinking eyes. A blurred white face appeared up against the frosted glass and stared out at Molly with black gaps for eyes. Molly slapped her hand to her mouth to smother the scream that came out in a stifled cry. She swivelled on her heels and stumbled up the steps, whimpering words even lost on herself. When she got to the top of the landing, she found Mina standing in her doorway with a head of tousled hair and she was rubbing her eyes.

'You look as if you've seen a ghost. What's wrong?'

'Cats…' The lying Molly surprised the mommy Molly with her ingenuity and callousness.

'Huh?'

'Bloody tom cats outside,' she fabricated, 'whining and screaming. It's horrible. They sound like crying babies.'

Mina shook her head. 'Okay, Mom, whatever.' She turned and went back to bed.

With both relief and bridled panic, Molly's whole body went limp just then. Fighting not to run, she quick-stepped down the hallway and ducked into her bedroom. She leapt into bed and bawled into her pillow until her stomach muscles ached. Once the wave of panic subsided, Molly quieted. The house was still. She could feel when the farmhouse was asleep and awake. The farmhouse was sleeping now. But how could she possibly do the same now? More gooseflesh bristled through her as she pictured that ivory face and two dark holes where beautiful eyes should've existed. It had been down there in the complete darkness, speaking, whispering, chanting. *Does that mean there's more than one?* Molly asked herself. She needed to speak to Prendergast. Putting her daughters in danger was not a part of this experiment. Then again, she had already offered up her children as willing guinea pigs, willing because they weren't aware they were in an experiment. This was more upsetting than anything.

17.

Wednesday started like any other chaotic morning at the farmhouse, but Wednesday wouldn't end like any other Wednesday. Today, as they say, would be a game-changer.

As was routine, Molly got dressed and called the girls for school. Things began differently the moment they got down to the kitchen. Louie was more excited than usual, squawking and warbling, gulping and clicking, but the cockatoo didn't emit its trademark morning greeting: 'Allo 'Allo 'Allo! which they found odd, having become so used to it. This was to be the first of many peculiar occurrences that marked this Wednesday as a turning point in this ghoulish social experiment. Instead, the bird said something else as the Greenes busied themselves around the kitchen, sorting textbooks and making lunches…

'Peekaboo, Mommy!'

Everyone dropped what they were doing and turned to look at the bird. With wide astonished eyes, Mina asked, 'What did he just say?' Cora answered, 'I think he said "Peekaboo, Mommy."'

'Peekaboo, Mommy!' it squawked. *'Peekaboo, Mommy! Bawk! Bawk! Peekaboo, Mommy!'*

They all stared at the dancing cockatoo.

Emma chanted, 'Peekaboo, Mommy!' to a constant giggle around the kitchen.

It was a surreal and miraculous moment for everyone. The bird speaks!

Mina turned to Cora. 'Who taught Louie that line?'

'Don't look at me. Peekaboo, Mommy? I don't think so.'

Mina and Cora looked to their mom for answers. Molly's reaction alone was enough to tell the girls she, too, had nothing to do with the bird's new repertoire. The fact Emma was marching around the kitchen, chanting her new favourite phrase, was also an indicator she hadn't taught the cockatoo the new phrase either.

On the clock, the organised chaos of the school morning took over and the cockatoo's miraculous words were side-lined for another moment.

On the drive to school, something was perturbing Molly. It was something about the way Emma had been chanting Louie's new phrase: *Peekaboo, Mommy!* Over and over again. And by the time they had pulled up at the school building, Molly had figured out where she'd listened to that chant before, only sped up a hundred times faster to inhuman levels. And here comes the creepy icing on the moulding cake: *it* had taught Louie the expression. And what about the bloody cherry on the creepy icing? The bird! The child who walks alone had been speaking to Louie last night. That's why Molly hadn't perceived any answers coming back. It had been repeating her expression to the cockatoo.

That was all very well, but Molly had distinctly discerned two voices come through her fireplace.

It was only on the drive back to the farmhouse when it dawned on Molly that she'd used that 'Peekaboo, Mommy' expression just yesterday morning when she sat down to do some job-searching. The shock was so great Molly's hands trembled on the steering wheel of the BMW. Fearing she might go off the road, she pulled into the next gateway to steady herself. As she sat there in a stranger's driveway, she realised the squatter had heard every word she had half-jokingly said.'Jesus Christ…' Molly uttered over and over again, shakily pulling away from the gateway.

*

About the same time Molly Greene made an unscheduled stop in a stranger's gateway, Cora was just beginning her first biology class in her new school. Mrs Noonan had arrived late to class. 'You must be Cora Greene.'

Cora nodded and smiled meekly.

'Pleased to meet you, Cora.' She turned to the class. 'Everyone, say hi to Cora.'

The children droned in unison, 'Hi, Cora!'

Cora smiled back, mortified. Just when she thought she was going to get away with any more embarrassment, Mrs Noonan asked, 'How's life in the farmhouse, Cora?'

'It's different,' awkwardly, she answered.

Her answer was met with a round of approving nods, including Mrs Noonan, who smiled a smile that didn't reach her eyes. 'Oh, it's different all right. And what do you mean by that?'

All eyes were on Cora now.

Red-faced, Cora wasn't sure what to say. 'I mean, it's good…'

'What's good about it, Cora?'

Mrs Noonan's tone of voice was beginning to change now, and Cora could feel the sudden tension in the classroom air. The question was strange. It sounded like it had double meaning or one of those questions…she couldn't remember…it begins with an R. Her mom had told her a few times; a question which doesn't require an answer. Being an honest child, she chose to answer the question directly. 'Um, it's got lots of rooms?'

'Uh-huh…' Mrs Noonan was apparently fishing for a specific answer.

Cora didn't know what else to say. 'Um, there's a lot of space outside? And we have our very own little forest.'

In mocking tones, Mrs Noonan declared, 'How quaint!'

'Not really.'

The other kids laughed, which didn't appear to go down well with Mrs Noonan.

'It's quite a spooky place at night.'

'Are the woods the only spooky place at night, dear, hmm?'

Cora racked her brain. 'I think so.'

Mrs Noonan wasn't happy with Cora's answer. Call I could see this but she wasn't being deliberately evasive. 'What about inside the farmhouse? Is that a spooky place?'

Again, Cora clammed up. 'Well, it's old. It makes lots of noises at night.'

The other kids flashed cautious glances at each

other.

'But Mom says old houses are like old people — they creak and groan.'

More surreptitious giggles.

Cora was expecting at least a smile from Mrs. Noonan, but all she got was unamused iciness. 'Cora, do you know the farmhouse has brought nothing but misery to this town? Do you know that?'

Cora clearly hadn't a clue what Mrs Noonan was talking about.

'Anyone who has ever moved into that place has had nothing but bad luck.'

Cora noticed how Mrs Noonan's neck, specifically the small section visible between the top of her turtleneck and chin, had reddened. It was the only area of bare skin not coated in a layer of makeup. It was an angry, scary red, bright as a warning Stop! traffic light. 'It's just a house.'

Cora was sure Mrs. Noonan's nostrils flared inside her face mask. 'It's *not* just a house, Cora. So, let me ask you the question that I — and the rest of the class — want you to answer. What's it like living with the infamous squatter?'

The lull in the classroom was palpable. Fifteen disbelieving, slack-jawed children gawped at Mrs Noonan with saucer eyes. Half of the kids in this class were even afraid to utter the squatter word for fear of summoning evil to their homes, and brazen Mrs Noonan had just come out with it. Some of the children appeared to be on the point of crying. Brendan 'Beatbox' Branagh looked as if he'd just soiled himself. Number one and number two, both barrels.

Paula James at the front middle desk raised her hand.

'Yes, Paula? Enlighten us.'

'Miss, I don't think you should mention…it. You'll bring bad luck to our class.'

Paula James spoke in comical mechanic fashion, as if she had been coached on this since she was old enough to stand. It had been something drilled into her from an early age and the result had no more effect than Siri reading a night-time lullaby to a baby.

Mrs Noonan was very quick to inform Paula that she was engaging in '…small-town superstition,' adding, 'One must come in contact with the squatter to become infected. And God knows we have enough with this Covid 19 pandemic.' She said it like she was reading the news. 'Simply speaking about the malicious entity in the farmhouse won't do you any harm, Paula.' She looked at the others. 'Is that clear? One must have contact — physical contact — with the squatter to contract its lurid disease. One must be within its reach to catch its rotten cold.'

The kids turned from Mrs Noonan to ogle Cora. Jenny Liston, sitting at the same table as Cora, made a point of shoving out to the end of her desk, getting as much air between her and Cora as possible.

Cora picked up on this and hung her head in shame.

Mrs Noonan asked, 'You don't know about the squatter, do you?'

Cora shook her head despondently.

'Firstly, do you know what a squatter is?'

Again, humiliated Cora shook her head in silence.

Paula James shoved her hand up again.

'Paula?'

'Miss, a squatter is a person living in a property without permission.' Again, in delicious monotone, Paula gave the distinct impression that everything she had learned in life was learned off by heart which she could later spew out to impress. Paula James was a real-life zombie from a real-life zombie family, and Mrs Noonan knew this.

'Very good, Paula, good-for-nothings is what they are. Shove 'em all into a barrel and kick the barrel off the side of a cliff is what I would do, but I didn't open my mouth.' Turning back to Cora. 'But you have a special squatter in your house, isn't that right, Cora?' Mrs Noonan lavished in her self-importance, no more than a glorified bully in this redneck town.

'I don't know.'

The class was completely silent now, all eyes on Cora.

'Did your mommy tell you to say that when people asked?'

'No, I just don't know what you're talking about.'

Someone over to the left sniggered.

On cue, Mrs Noonan's nostrils flared. The redneck's red neck was the same colour as a baboon's behind and it was distracting. 'Look, Cora, you're fooling nobody here. We all know about the farmhouse and the uninvited guest lingering in its

236

dank walls.'

Cora interjected, 'Well, there is one other besides us…I forgot.'

Everyone sat up. Audible gulps clicked around the stuffy classroom. Even Mrs Noonan's face changed in some way behind her mask. 'And who or what is that?' Once she'd asked the question she looked like she regretted asking it, as if what Cora was about to say would damn them all for eternity.

'Louie,' Cora answered.

The teacher repeated the name for the benefit of the class. 'Louie? Hmm, not a very scary name.'

'Louie isn't scary. He's just a cockatoo…although he bites.'

Norma Kelly, sitting at the back of the class, laughed so hard she rip-farted, practically blowing a hole in her chair. That was enough to send the whole class into unadulterated peals of laughter, falling around the floor.

'Silence!' screamed Mrs Noonan from inside her face mask. She glared at Cora. Those eyes, heightened by the lack of the rest of her face, stared into Cora's very soul. There would be a price to pay the price for having made Norma Kelly fart with such gusto. 'The farmhouse is haunted. Did you know that, Cora?'

Once again, the classroom fell into silence, Norma Kelly's ripper but a distant memory now.

A lot like Paula James, Cora then made the mistake of simply regurgitating her mom's words. '"Small-town nonsense," that's exactly what Mom says.' Cora was feeling braver by the second and decided to give a little love back. 'Mom says people in Old Castle are…' she tried to think of choice words such as inbreeds and gossipmongers, but they wouldn't come to her, "…backward and have nothing else to do but talk about other people's lives because they don't have lives of their own."'

'Oh, did she now? It doesn't surprise me. Any mother who would willingly bring her family into a place like that only thinks of one person. Can anyone tell me who that one person is?'

Paula James shot her hand skywards, but Mrs Noonan ignored her. 'I'll tell you, shall I? Herself. Cora's mom was thinking of herself. But, then again, maybe that's only my little backward mind?'

Cora was really beginning to despise Mrs Noonan. Jenny Liston, sitting next to Cora (though as far away as possible) appeared surprised to see tears well up in her classmate's eyes and roll down her cheeks into her school-issued face mask. She tore a piece of paper out from her copybook, scribbled something, then discreetly passed it in front of Cora.

Cora's eyes dropped to the message:

She's a bitch. Nobody ever loved her. Mom told me she goes to a sykiatrist.

Cora smiled inside her face mask as Mrs Noonan continued her tirade. 'Cora Greene, ever heard the expression: there's no smoke without fire?'

Cora nodded. 'It means—'

238

Mrs Noonan turned to the class. 'Class, can anyone tell me what that expression means?'

A sea of blank faces stared back at the teacher.

'Well, in this case, it means the people in Old Castle, us, the small-mind gossipers, are gossiping for a good reason. Every fire starts with smoke. The fire is spreading, Cora, not rumours. Hence, no smoke without fire. And the day you see smoke come from those chimneys is the day you run, Cora.'

Interrogation over, Mrs Noonan sniffed defiantly and turned to the board where she proceeded to explain human reproduction.

*

At 3pm that afternoon, Molly went to school to pick up the girls. Cora wasn't her chirpy self when she sat in the car. Molly asked her what the matter was, but Cora was in one of her silent moods, which are more damaging than screaming moods.

'I know something's wrong, Cora. Please, tell me.'

'Nothing, Mom. Let's just go home, please.'

Molly boldly folded her arms. 'I'm not driving this car until you tell me.'

Passing parents and children stared at the fancy BMW with the Dublin number plate while trying to get a glimpse of the farmhouse freaks inside.

Hesitantly, Cora went into how Mrs. Noonan, the science teacher, interrogated her in front of the whole class. Molly saw red as her daughter elaborated on how they were sharing their house with an evil entity called (here, Cora paused to remember the squatter) which spread bad luck to anyone who comes in

239

contact with it, like, "…a rotten cold."'

'Okay,' Molly snapped, 'Mina, you're in charge here. Listen to music. Play a fairy-tale for Emma on your phone, please.' Molly went to get out of the car. 'Mommy's going to sort more shit out.'

Fearfully, Cora asked, 'Where are you going?'

'I'm going to pay Mrs Noonan a little visit.'

'Please don't. That'll only make it worse.'

'What do you mean? No teacher speaks to a child like that. This is 2021, Cora. Fair enough, maybe it's 1921 in Old Castle.'

Mina pleaded with her mom. 'She's right. Just let it slide.'

Molly was fit to hit someone. Who did that bitch think she was to embarrass her daughter on her first week at her new school?! Any week at any school! No way! Not on Molly's watch. But, let's face it, the real issue here was that she had been trying to keep this from her daughter, but now Cora, and the others in the car, were beginning to learn the truth — if living in a haunted house can ever be considered the truth. For that, Molly hated herself just then.

Reluctantly, she sat back into the car and made to pull away from the kerb…before slamming on the steering wheel. 'No, Cora! You're not going to be treated like that!'

Cora began to cry. 'Please, don't.'

'I'm hungry!' protested Emma.

Mina came to her sister's defence. 'Just to let you know there are no other schools in Old Castle, Mom.'

'I'm just going to reason with her, guys. I promise.

240

You can't let people walk all over you, Cora. I'm going to speak to her…as a friend.' She didn't believe it.

'I'm hungry!' Emma yelled again.

Cora fished inside her backpack. 'Here, she can have my sandwiches. I lost my appetite.'

Molly couldn't fathom what she was hearing. Cora had the best appetite in the house. The child was too nervous to eat because of that teacher and Molly knew that. Jesus Christ, this broke Molly's heart. Whatever chance there had been of her just shutting her mouth and driving off vanished in that moment.

'Mina: fairy-tales…phone…Emma. Cora: sit tight.'

Inside the school, she introduced herself to the male secretary, a clean-shaven individual in his late thirties. 'Molly? As in Molly Greene?' asked the secretary with great interest.

Molly smiled back. 'Yes, I know. My reputation precedes me. I'm looking for Mrs Noonan?' She flashed a glance at her watch to give the impression she was in a hurry.

'She's preparing tomorrow's class. You'll catch her if you hurry. What is it concerning?'

'She terrorised my daughter in class today and I want to know why.'

The man inside the glass nodded knowingly. 'She can be an old dragon,' the secretary whispered from behind the glass.

'Dragons don't exist,' Molly answered.

'This one does, and she spits fire.'

Molly found her anger dissipating from her as the secretary made her laugh. It was such a pleasant surprise to meet somebody who hadn't already condemned her and her family to Hell without ever meeting them.

'You'll find her at the end of the hallway, last class on the right. You know you have arrived at the correct classroom when you begin to smell smoke. I'm Gerry, by the way.'

Molly thanked Gerry and walked down the hallway.

'Is it true?'

She turned back. 'Sorry?'

'Is it true what they say about the farmhouse?'

'And what do they say?'

'That it's "haunted".'

'Do I look like a woman who would live in a haunted house?'

Gerry considered Molly. 'Yes.'

Molly chortled and walked off with the distinct impression that Gerry had been flirting with her, just a little, maybe.

She arrived at the last classroom on the right. Through the glass panes, she could see Cora's science teacher, but there was no smoke, not yet. Not exactly what she had in mind, maybe more sophisticated than what she had assumed which threw her a little. Just by looking at the woman, Molly instinctively knew Mrs Noonan wasn't your typical sticks hick.

She tapped on the door and popped her head inside. 'Mrs. Noonan?'

'Yes?'

Molly was met by a glamorous woman in her late fifties, not looking like she'd been a teacher all her life, but maybe a mid-life career change. Mrs Noonan wore a stylish beige rib-knitted turtleneck, knee-length tartan skirt, and expensive leather boots. She had probably turned heads when she was younger. She probably turned a few now, too.

'Hello, I am Molly, Cora's mom. I was wondering if I could have a word?'

Mrs Noonan looked as if she'd been waiting for this. 'You can arrange a tutorial through the secretary. Speak with Gerry in the office.'

'If it's all the same with you, I prefer to get this off my chest now and we can start afresh. I want to talk about an incident that happened this morning. Cora is quite upset, and she is normally a happy-go-lucky child.'

Mrs Noonan still hadn't the decency to look at Molly, too concentrated on dividing photocopies into neat piles. 'Again, you can ask for a tutorial. We all have to go through the channels, Molly, no special treatment here.' She was pressing all the wrong buttons.

'I want to know what happened this morning? Cora's in a state. I have no problem in taking this to the ministry of education.' She lied. Of course, she lied.

Mrs Noonan said, 'I asked her about life at the farmhouse.'

'You did more than that if Cora's version of events

is anything to go by. She's quite tough. She's been through her fair share. I don't know if you're aware of our past…' Molly found herself yearning to tell her story, and she hated herself for it, using the tragedy — her sob story — to look for pity and a little leeway. She was better than this, and she knew it.

'The children must be aware of the dangers of the house.'

'Oh, here we go…' Molly argued. 'There is no danger.'

Mrs Noonan sighed, shook her head resignedly, and turned from Molly to busy herself with her paperwork.

Molly, understanding she'd just blown any chance of a civilised conversation, made to leave. 'I'll book a tutorial with Gerry and maybe you can—'

'Molly, take a seat.'

'Hmm? Oh, okay.' Molly was taken aback with Mrs. Noonan's sudden softness.

'Why don't you sit there,' she gestured Molly to a desk at the back. 'That's Cora's seat.'

Molly was aware that the girls were waiting in the car, but this, she felt, was important. Mina could hold the fort for a few extra minutes. She sat on the chair which was too small for her. It was odd to think of her own daughter sitting here, living a separate independent life Molly would never truly know.

'My intention today was not to frighten the child. Cora is a sweetheart. I've only known her a few minutes, but I can already see her enormous potential. It's a privilege to have a student of Cora's stature in my class. And please accept my apology for being so hard on the girl. There was no excuse.' She hesitated. 'It hit a raw nerve…literally.'

Wow, Molly wasn't expecting this…why did—

Molly's phone rang in her handbag. For once, she didn't have it on silent mode, but she took it out to silence it. This was one conversation that would not be interrupted by a phone call. In that brief moment, she saw it was Mina. She hung up. 'Sorry, it's my daughter. Whatever it is can wait.'

'Answer it.'

'No, no. She probably wants me to hurry on because she's hungry.'

Mrs Noonan flashed a curt smile. 'I'll cut to the chase, Molly. Ninety-nine per cent of this town spreads unfounded rumours, but one per cent have real stories about that farmhouse. I'm in the one per cent and I'm telling you there's something evil in that house.'

'With all due respect, I think that's bullshit.'

Mrs Noonan pulled down the neckline of her turtleneck. 'Is this bullshit?'

*

On the street outside, a group of kids had gathered around the Greene's BMW, staring in at Mina and Cora who did their best to look anywhere else except at the group of girls standing outside the car. Not just any kids; if delinquents existed at the school in Old Castle, then this would be them. One of the girls, Clara, was in Mina's class. She handed out e-cigarettes to each of her cronies and offered a multitude of flavours at a competitive price. They smoked and stared, then stared some more, intimidating Mina and Cora. Fortunately, Emma seemed more taken with Hansel and Gretel on Mina's phone. Then Clara and her mindless mob decided to take it a step further and sit on the crushed bonnet of the car.

Cora muttered, 'Call her again,' while trying not to look panicked.

'I'm calling, but she never answers!' hissed Mina, afraid to make eye contact.

Clara came up to Mina's window and tapped. 'You should go back to where you came from.'

The other girl added, 'You're going to wake up the squatter and then we all pay the price.'

'What are you talking about?' Mina answered.

'That place is haunted,' warned the third girl. 'Tell your mommy to take you back to wherever you came from. Things are different here.'

Having heard enough, Mina rose the volume on the radio. Mother Mother's 'Hayloft' drowned out their words of warning, which wasn't a good idea. Three angry faces exploded at them through the glass. The higher Mina rose the volume, the angrier they got until Clara thumped the back window behind Cora's head. The three began fisting the BMW's windows in unison, thumping louder and louder. With each wallop, they chanted, 'Go! Go! Go!' The growing din in the car was terrifying.

In defiance, Mina rose the volume to the max but even Mother Mother couldn't drown out the interrogating racket. To add to the cacophony, Emma realised what was happening around her was far scarier than Hansel and Gretel.

Mina called her Mom again. 'She just hung up on me! The only time she's ever answered her phone, and she hangs up on me!'

*

Molly was taken aback by the scar running along Mrs Noonan's neck, just above her left collarbone.

'A long time ago,' the teacher laughed to herself, 'in another lifetime, an ex-boyfriend and I were out there at the house for a dare. It was unoccupied at the time, between families, and it was possible to get into the farmhouse through the back kitchen door.'

Molly could see that same door right now in her mind's eye.

'The place was a wreck in those days. It's a long story, so I'll cut to the chase. My parents paid for an abortion for me. I was eighteen. Abortion was illegal in Ireland in those days, so my parents shipped me off to England to have it, without ever consulting me and how I felt. Anyway, my then-boyfriend didn't know this until I told him after the fact, even though I had promised my family and myself that I would never, under any circumstances, tell him.'

Molly started to feel very uncomfortable…

'But for some reason, a beautiful carefree feeling came down over me as we stood there in the kitchen.'

The hairs prickled on the nape of Molly's neck. 'What time of the day was this? Can you remember?'

Mrs Noonan flashed a knowing glance at Molly.

'Hmm, you have noticed the same thing, haven't you?'

'Just asking.'

'Molly, we're talking about forty years ago. I don't know what I had for breakfast this morning, but I can tell you that feeling of flying started around six o'clock in the evening.'

Molly tried to hide her amazement. She had experienced this very same feeling of floating on more than one evening.

'That beautiful feeling of elation that came over me…' Molly could see the living memory of that awareness in her eyes now, '…told me to never ever have secrets because secrets are exciting when they're fresh but begin to rot when they pass their sell-by date. In that moment, standing in the cold kitchen of the derelict farmhouse, I felt it was unfair not to tell Tom about the baby — the foetus. Oops, big mistake. I'll never forget the odd feeling that came into the kitchen the second I told him.'

Molly's phone screen lit up the inside of her handbag, but it was on silent.

'This is going to sound like a cliché, Molly, but something joined us that evening in the kitchen. Tom turned into someone else, his face…his face even changed. Before I knew what had happened, he stabbed me with his penknife and ran off, leaving me there to bleed out on the rotten linoleum floor, which is why I like to joke about that moment and how it touched a nerve with me.' She didn't have to point it out; Molly had already picked up on it. This wasn't going how Molly had envisioned it. 'Jesus Christ.'

'Between conscious and unconscious, as I lay there on the cold kitchen floor like a stuck pig, I heard voices.'

Molly's skin prickled. 'Voices?'

'Whispering. As God is my witness, Molly, I heard whispering and a conversation right there next to me. But even though it was right there next to me, I couldn't make out a single word.' She became lost in that moment. 'The more I think about it, the more I'm convinced it was a foreign language.' She studied Molly gravely. 'But I did pick one word out of the semiconscious mumbo-jumbo.'

Molly flinched a little when her back bristled. 'Which was?' Molly wasn't sure she even wanted to know what was said.

'"Mama…" is what was said. "Mama"'

Molly felt her face redden and tears come to her eyes. It was how Mrs Noonan had said it. She could feel the desperation in those words.

The teacher came down and sat beside Molly at Cora's desk and put an arm around her. 'It was a long time ago. I've got over it, but it has left its mark in more ways than one.' This was the one moment where Mrs Noonan sort of lied: she had never stopped visiting her psychiatrist in the city, not that Molly was to know that.

Molly hid her face in her hands and cried.

'I'm fine, Molly. I'm okay now. And I want you to be fine too…and your lovely girls.'

Molly wasn't crying for Mrs Noonan; she was

crying for the lonely child of the farmhouse who had been abandoned. Mama? No child should ever suffer, in this or the next life. Molly hadn't believed there was a next life until just a few days ago.

Molly got up. 'I understand what you're saying, but your ex-boyfriend did that to you, not the house.'

'No, Molly, the house did that to me. Better said, something in the house did that to me through Tom. The minute I admitted to the abortion, something woke in that house, then it woke inside Tom. You're cohabiting with this ancient thing in its lair.'

Molly kept her opinion to herself, but this was a clear case of being in the wrong place at the wrong time. The farmhouse was this cursed town's scapegoat. She began to understand the hatred locals held for it. It was the cancer of the town. 'I appreciate you telling me your story, Mrs. Noonan. It can't be easy. The kids are waiting in the car.'

'Oh, it's no story.'

Molly left the classroom and walked back along the hallway to the main entrance. As she walked by the secretary's hatch, Gerry called, 'I'm writing a book about the farmhouse. What's the weirdest thing you've seen?'

Molly backed up. 'My cockatoo saying stuff nobody taught him. How's that for weird?'

'That's weird,' Gerry agreed. 'But anything juicier?'

'Hmm,' Molly played along. 'I don't know where to start. I've already witnessed enough strange things to fill your book ten times over.'

Gerry was visibly impressed. 'Maybe we could have a coffee sometime and you can share your experiences I can use for the book?' Gerry peeped over his shoulder. 'We like to keep that house a secret here in Old Castle,' he said in hushed tones. 'I don't want to ruffle any feathers, so I'm going to write the book as a novel based on a true story. Just invent new names but use factual accounts. I've been researching the place for a year now.'

'Hmm,' Molly smiled coyly, 'okay, you've got a deal, but on one condition.'

'Oh, I don't like conditions,' Gerry quipped. 'What is it?'

'We go fifty-fifty on any royalties,' she half-joked. 'I need the money.' She was saddened a little when she realised she really did need the money.

'Wow, fifty-fifty? Who's writing the book, me or you?'

Molly fired back, 'Who's got the unique first-hand experience?' She left through the main doors.

Outside, Gerry caught up with her. 'Here's my number for that coffee. Fifty-fifty, I accept.'

Molly smiled and thanked him. That was when she heard the crazy blowing of a car horn and was flabbergasted to see it was coming from her car. She was just in time to witness three girls pounding on the windscreen of the BMW. Molly ran across the street, screaming, 'What is wrong?!' For a second, she thought they were trapped in the car.

The group of girls scampered off.

When she got to the car, she found the girls, all of

three of them, in an awful state.

'Where were you?!' yelled Mina. 'I was calling you! You never answer your phone!'

'I was speaking with Cora's teacher. I was sorting out shit!'

Cora shouted, 'You should've been here backing us up!'

Emma added, 'I'm hungry!'

'I was already in the school backing you up, Cora! How was I supposed to know what was happening out here? I can't be everywhere at once! Don't be victims! Stand up for yourselves!'

'That's easy for you to say,' Mina answered back.

'Who are those little bitches, anyway? I'm going to rip their heads off!' Molly got in and slammed the door before driving off. 'Give me names and I will go to their parents.'

Mina snapped, 'No! If you say anything to those girls or their parents, we may as well just leave this town. Our lives won't be worth living.'

Molly remembered the terror the bullies had instilled in her and her friends at school and understood perfectly. She agreed to do nothing for now and this placated the girls. But what didn't placate them was what the bullies had said? Molly saw that Cora was mulling something over in her mind. Sure enough, halfway home, she said, 'They said the house is haunted. Not only haunted but haunted by something evil.'

Molly answered back, 'Well, they're wrong. There's nothing evil in that house, except Emma

252

when she's hungry.'

Molly's joke lightened the atmosphere, but Cora remained silent, staring at the road ahead. Despite her funny joke, Cora couldn't shake the feeling there was something hidden in her mom's answer. 'What do you mean "There's nothing evil?" That sounds too much like there's something in the house but it's not evil.'

'Well, you understood wrong. Believe what you see. What do you see in that house?'

'Mould?'

'What else?'

'A mom, three girls, and a cockatoo.'

'Exactly, you don't need to see any more than that.'

Cora answered, 'Okay,' and left it at that.

Mina said nothing but listened intently.

Molly thought about Gerry, that coffee, and those royalties. The closer they drew to the farmhouse the more convinced she became that earning royalties was a possibility. How much? She had no idea, but right now, anything was better than nothing. People love a good ghost story. By the time they were pulling into the front yard, the seed of an idea was forming in Molly's head, but for the time being, it remained below ground.

That peekaboo Wednesday had been a turning point, but it wasn't over yet. After dinner, while Emma was playing in the playroom and Cora was upstairs doing her homework, Mina came to her mom with something on her mind.

'Mom?'

Molly was at the kitchen table, filtering through inane job positions too far from the farmhouse. 'Yeah?'

'I want you to be honest with me.'

Molly looked up at her daughter. 'What's wrong?'

Mina was pensive. 'Just a few things don't add up. Or maybe they add up, but not adding up right.'

Molly had a feeling this was coming. She had seen it in her daughter's face on the drive home from school. 'Mina, I'll be as honest as I can, but sometimes, parents have to tell white lies to their kids because it's needed. Which sounds better? You're going to the doctor to get a needle in your arm or you're going to the doctor to get your booster?'

'Those bitches terrorising us in the car, they're telling the truth, weren't they?'

It was time to be honest with Mina. She deserved that much. 'Yes and no.'

Mina raised her eyebrows.

'This is going to be a lot to process. I'm still trying to get my head around it.'

She sat back, startled her mom was speaking in this way. She clearly hadn't come here to hear this. Molly figured she had come to hear something along the lines of: *Mina, don't listen to those morons. Couldn't you see at least two of them were mentally deficient?*

'Yes,' Molly started, 'we are not alone in this house. That's absurd, I know. I have seen it with my own eyes on more than one occasion, and you have

254

too: on your phone. Even your friends back in Dublin have seen it. Cora has seen it that night it — he — waved out at us from the living room while you were watching TV with Emma sleeping next to you. And,' she added, 'you've heard him, or maybe them, in the fireplace. Those voices you heard weren't any of us. I've heard the same thing from my fireplace in the middle of the night.' Molly went on to tell Mina about seeing the child standing in the branches of the spruce tree outside her bedroom window and the horrific moment he had looked at her through the frosted glass of the kitchen door. By the time she had finished, Molly surprised herself by changing the pronoun from 'it' to 'he'.

Mina grew pale as Molly spoke. Her jaw dropped, little by little, until she had an almost comical gormless expression on her face. Her eyes flitted back and forth nervously as she relived those seemingly normal moments while lying on the sofa with her little sister. She recalled a sudden chill in the room and an unexplained change in the atmosphere. Then came that odd aroma of mildewed oranges and cloves that passed right beneath her nostrils. She shivered as she recollected the voices coming from her fireplace. It was true, she thought she'd heard a male voice in there, somewhere.

Molly regretted being so graphic. She hadn't meant to come out with it like this, in one projectile vomit, but she couldn't hold herself back, such was the pressure of telling someone on her side like her own flesh and blood. She felt the immense relief as those bubbling, troubling thoughts drained from her body like an exorcism.

Mina was silent.

'Mina, say something.'

'You lied to me.'

'When I asked you to say something, I didn't mean —'

'You lied to us.'

'I did it to protect you, Mina.'

'Bullshit.' Mina shook her head adamantly. 'You were protecting yourself.'

Christ, maybe she's right…

'That thing I saw while doing a live with the girls in Dublin, I thought it was fridge gas! I'm such an idiot for believing you!'

'Don't say that, Mina.'

Mina looked about with a sheepish turn. 'Why are we even here??' Mina bolted from the kitchen and went upstairs.

This Wednesday was to be another turning point for both Mina and Molly, mother and daughter. It was to be the day when Mina realised her mom wasn't the indisputable pillar of wisdom and knowledge she had always thought her to be. And it was to be the day when Molly realised her daughter was growing up and could see the truth for herself. This was a bitter pill to swallow, more so because it had come about due to Molly's stupid lies.

Molly followed her daughter upstairs and knocked on her door.

'What?' yelled Mina. 'Wait, is that the ghost or is

256

it Mom?' Mina chided.

'It's the ghost, sorry, I mean your mom.'

'NOT funny.'

'Can we talk?'

There was a second there when Molly thought her daughter wasn't going to open her door. When she did, she sat on Mina's bed. 'There's more…'

'How could there be more?' Mina asked with incredulity.

'Good more.'

'This better be good!'

'Look, it's just a harmless little boy looking for someone to notice him.'

'Are you for real right now? I mean, how do you even know?' Mina slapped her hands over her face and dragged her fingers down over her eyes. 'Please, am I dreaming right now? What the fuck is going on here?'

'Mina, foul language isn't going to get you—'

'Mom, a fuck here and a fuck there is *nothing* compared to what we're dealing with!'

'Look, I've held its hand. That's how I know it's just a boy who is looking for something…maybe a mother.' Molly drew the line at telling her daughter she'd already offered to be the child's mother or mother figure.

Mina gawped at her mom as if waiting for her to start laughing and tell her it's all a joke, but her face didn't change.

'All you need to know is there's no badness in this house and you tell whoever says the opposite they're

257

wrong. It's a child, a boy, and I don't think he knows he's dead.'

'Okay, that's it.' Mina pulled her backpack out from her wardrobe and started flinging everything and anything into it. 'I'm packing.'

'Oh, that's lovely. Going on holiday?'

'No. Just leaving.'

'Where to?'

'Anywhere but here.'

'How did I know you were going to say that? Molly was expecting this drama from Mina, so she had her arsenal of trigger words ready. 'Mina, you're old enough — and bold enough — to think like an adult. So, I want you to think very carefully about what I'm going to tell you.'

'Mom, nothing you say now is going to make any difference.'

'Firstly, you're not going on any holiday because I'm broke. I am b-r-o-k-e broke. I was promised a job in Old Castle, but that fell through due to, um, the short-sightedness of the local community that is the backward superstitious peasants. I need to find another job fast. Do you see the precarious situation we are in?'

Mina stopped shoving underwear into her backpack.

'The good news to this little drama is that this house is free.'

'Free as in…free?'

'A-ha! Thought that might catch your attention. Let's delve further, shall we?' Molly smiled. 'Not only is it free, but the house will be ours if we get through a…' *choose your words wisely,* '…trial period. Just like you would in a job. If we like the house,' *and if it likes us,* 'we can live here for the rest of our lives. A lifetime of free accommodation, Mina! Do you realise the money we'd save? All that moola could go for your stuff.'

'What stuff?'

'Exactly! All kinds of stuff you've always wanted.' Molly was beginning to feel like a second car saleswoman, but with a conscience. 'Not only that,' she growing excited now, 'I've got some amazing plans for this place.'

'Back to you again, I see.'

'Mina, all I'm asking for is that six months we originally shook hands on. You made a promise, remember?' And this was Molly's trigger word: promise. 'I'm relying on you to help our family get through this. I told you because I think you're mature enough to handle this.' Molly wasn't so sure about this if she was being honest with herself. 'I need someone I can rely on. You know how to handle Cora, leave Emma up to me. If anyone can convince Cora it's you.' She finished by giving one final ultimatum. 'Everyone thinks we're going to lose. Let's prove them wrong together. This house is going to be ours and I'm going to convert the place into a restaurant where world leaders are going to dine.' She clapped. 'Watch this space. We're going to be rolling in it, Mina. You're going to have a bling-bling car and a horse made out of diamonds…'

'I just want a mom.'

Mina's comment was a sword to the heart.

'Just kidding! I'd love a horse made out of diamonds!'

'Mina, don't do that to me!'

'And how about this bling-bling car?'

Molly threw eyes heavenwards. 'How about a few driving lessons first?' Then she cleared her throat for effect.

Mina considered her mom with a defeated expression and, one by one, began to stuff her underwear back in her drawers.

Molly smiled. 'You should fold those.'

'I'm not folding anything people don't see.'

'For now…'

'Yuck, mom! So inappropriate!'

'New town…new boys, la-dee-daa…'

'I'm fifteen, Mom…'

'When I was your age, I was—'

'Okay, talk later. Six months, then I'm moving in with Janice.'

Mina and Molly shook hands before hugging each other.

If only Mina had known how much truth there was in that, she wouldn't have opened her mouth. But it wouldn't be six months.

Victorious, Molly left the attic bedroom. At the bottom of Mina's stairs, Molly heard her daughter call out, 'I'm scared, but living with a ghost is kind of cool! That easily makes me the coolest girl in the class.'

Molly didn't mention how Mina had taken the wine bottle from her hand as she was about to uncork it. She conveniently overlooked the succinct fact that Mina wasn't a sleepwalker, but she couldn't rule out possession, just as Emma wasn't a gifted artist and didn't try to strangle her own mother. She was trying to find a reason or a pattern for this love-hate behaviour and, until then, some things were just better left unsaid.

*

Upstairs, Mina almost blurted out, 'How many sisters have a ghost for a brother?' It cut just too close to the bone. She cringed and felt she should cry but couldn't find the water in the well. It had been so long now; she'd begun to think of Henry as a little kid she once met in a previous lifetime.

18.

Molly Greene, exhausted and troubled, decided she needed some time away from the farmhouse. After dropping off the girls at school that Thursday morning, she went for a walk in Old Castle's vast park known as the Demesne. Hundreds of rooks in treetop rookeries made a racket above her while she silently walked alone and in solemn silence. It got her thinking about all the trees surrounding the farmhouse and not one bird in them. Molly was worried. Highest on her worry list was her dwindling funds. Thank Christ for the free house…not that it was free in every sense of the word. But, at this stage, Molly Greene was coming around to the idea that she would've preferred paying a simple and cheap monthly rent instead of paying with her soul. Walking through the fallen leaves, she couldn't help but feel that there was something right in front of her face, but she couldn't see it. She thought by coming for a walk here she might tease it out, but Molly knew from experience that the more she tried to figure something out, the more she couldn't see it. These types of answers always come in a bolt of lightning. It was definitely there. The seed of something was there. It would come to her. She just needed to be patient.

During that Thursday morning amble, with the advantage of the cold light of day, Molly questioned whether the presence in the house had her best interests at heart or if its motives were more sinister. She knew one thing for sure and that was Janice would tell her to get out of that house if she knew what was going on. And she'd be right.

So, what was stopping her?

Firstly, pride. Molly wanted to prove to herself that she could do this. She'd been living in the shadow of the deaths of her husband and son far too long and she needed to get out of that shadow that followed her wherever she went. She needed to find a place where shadows don't go, where shadow goes to die. And then it came to her, where she would find this place. She needed to go where there was no light; darkness kills all shadows. She needed to become the darkness. *What better place for her metamorphosis than the farmhouse?* She thought to herself as a couple of power jogging women passed by, staring her down. Not that she gave two flying fucks anymore.

The second reason why she wanted to stay at the farmhouse was a financial reason. She couldn't afford to move anywhere else with her current job (jobless) situation, so all other reasons were sort of moot.

Thirdly, and it was this factor Molly couldn't understand, there was something else keeping her at the farmhouse that was nothing to do with pride or dwindling finances. But this is what she couldn't figure out on this damp Thursday morning. She needed to speak to someone, and a process of elimination pointed to Gerry McAuliffe, the school secretary. He was probably working now, but she could send him a message and fix a time and place for that coffee. She took her phone from her handbag, remembering she had installed an app on her phone

263

that takes pictures of the person who tries to unlock a phone or messes around with the passcode. She typed in the passcode and went to her gallery. Her heart sank. She had been hoping to see Emma's mischievous face caught in the camera lens, but the picture was clear enough to tell her none of her children…the living ones, at least…had taken her phone. The camera had caught a trailing blur of a child's pallid face. Yet, looking deep inside the blurred image, Molly could make out an old, contorted face too, as if she had double vision. Too horrified to look at the image any longer, she closed the app. The moment she closed the app she was filled with an acute sense of being adrift. She felt alienated from her girls, especially Emma.

Then she noticed she had an extra video in her gallery. She clicked on it and watched the horror unfold.

This time, instead of a series of pictures, he had made a video. Molly watched her kitchen on her phone screen, the camera shaky and erratic. Then she zoomed out into the hallway with the squatter and up the stairs to the first floor with sickeningly abnormal speed. It was so fast Molly grew nauseous just looking at her phone screen. Watching what the squatter was watching in that moment was fascinating…until she — *they* — glided into Emma's bedroom. She lost her breath as listened to her daughter's breathing through her phone's speaker. The camera then left that room, and with blinking speed, stopped outside Cora's bedroom. Here, too,

Molly listened to Cora sleeping soundly, and she was grateful for small mercies. Despite the stomach-churning speed, the lone walker, the squatter, didn't make a noise. It was utter silence on the phone's speaker except for her daughters' deep breathing. Then, the thing moved again, and a millisecond later, she was looking at her grainy self in the video. More gooseflesh bristled. The phone left her room and travelled with that same freakish velocity, went upstairs to Mina's bedroom where sleeping Mina was filmed for two minutes, right up close to her face, before turning and zooming down two flights of stairs to the kitchen. If nothing else, it was a window into the world of the dead child who haunted these walls. As she watched through his eyes, she felt a great sadness for the spirit. The loneliness must be intense, like finding oneself on the other side of the moon with no way home yet still be able to see planet Earth with every rotation of the sun. It was while filming in the kitchen that Molly heard the strange and distant giggle of the child behind the camera. Then the phone floated across the kitchen, catching Louie in the shot. The bird rose its crest, bobbed and weaved, but didn't open its beak.

Molly forgot to breathe with what came next. The phone shuddered into the wall by the fridge, then crawled vertically. She saw her own kitchen from an angle she'd never seen before and hoped she'd never see again as the camera rose upwards towards the ceiling, then crossed onto it with a sickly fluid motion, traversing the ceiling upside down, before scampering down the opposite wall by the cockatoo's cage. Louie cackled, cawed, and made an unholy racket in his cage. How Molly hadn't heard the bird while she'd been sleeping was mystifying.

Just before the video finished, Molly heard that haunting giggle.

She sat on the park bench, looking around to see if anybody else had observed what she'd just witnessed on her phone. Away from her phone screen, it was a normal and dreary Thursday morning. Molly was living in two worlds down here in Old Castle.

She took a shortcut back through the park, then got into her car by the school and drove off…not noticing anything different about the BMW until she got out of the car in her front yard and saw the red graffiti spray paint spanning the left side of the BMW, from the front left wing to the rear brake light: GET OUT! it read in angry red strokes, dripping down the side of her car, reminding her of blood, which was probably the perpetrator's objective. She turned to Google for advice, quickly finding out that hairspray can remove fresh spray paint. Though she didn't have hair spray, Mina did, so she fetched it, and spent the rest of the morning cleaning and rubbing down the side of her BMW. As she rubbed feverishly, she also worked herself up into a frenzy. Had the artist (using the term lightly) intended the GET OUT to mean vacate the farmhouse or Old Castle? Molly drew the conclusion it meant both, not that it bothered her in the slightest.

The job of cleaning her BMW took just over three

hours. The only good thing to have come from this was that Molly had got in a wonderful workout of stretching, squatting, pulling and dragging. Her legs and stomach muscles ached by the time 1pm rolled around.

Before she went to school for the kids, Molly made a quick Plan B lunch: pasta and bacon tacos. While the pasta boiled and the tacos fried, Molly went online to check the job pages once again. No new positions had been updated, surprise, surprise, and not one reply from the several mediocre positions she applied for, from manning the breakfast area in the local hotel to helming a factory canteen. The human resources departments knew she was clearly overqualified for the positions available. This is what Molly assumed the problem to be, but the more she thought about it, the more she warmed to the idea that she wasn't being ostracised because of her impressive professional resume, but her name. It was who she was and what she represented. There could be no confusion whether she was the same Molly Greene who had moved into the farmhouse with her family… They had every detail about her in those attached CVs. It was the mindset of the town of Old Castle, and it had started with Wilma's change of heart when she found out who manage her restaurant (glorified café). Molly Greene working at their premises made for bad publicity.

With a deep sigh, she looked at her MacBook again and trawled through the job announcements. Then, quite by accident, as is so often the case when surfing the internet, one thing leads to another, and Molly comes across an interesting job prospect. An unnamed theme park in Dublin was looking to hire actors for their new haunted house attraction. Molly was desperate but not that desperate, however the job offer brought a smile to her face as she could imagine herself hiding in the darkness and jumping out to spook suspecting tourists, camouflaged in ghastly face paint…

She threw her head back and laughed. 'One visit to my house and every haunted house attraction in the country would close down…I'd put them all to shame. Want to see the real thing? Roll up! Roll up!' Molly cheered before falling silent…

…then that heavenly lightning bolt was summoned from the skies.

She was right! The best ideas came when we are least expected them. The excitement growing inside her was almost like an electrical current. Trying not to get too excited, she closed down the job pages and opened the Google search engine, where she typed: HAUNTED HOUSE GHOST TOURS.

A hundred different tours popped up in front of her. It didn't take long to see that they were tacky. But what grabbed her attention were the crazy entrance fees those tacky attractions were commanding. Her face flushed with excitement at the prospect. With a thrilling flurry, a hundred different ghoulish ideas came zinging around in her head. She didn't have to build any attraction park…she was living in her own very haunted house attraction and it was real! She didn't need fog machines or animatronics. The farmhouse was the MOTHER of all haunted houses!

Bursting with excitement, Molly Greene called her friend Janice, who answered on the second dial tone. 'Well, hello stranger! Where have you been? Any news?'

'Any news? Hmm? Let me see?' And so Molly told her everything, from start to finish, almost everything. As Molly relayed her story, she could feel the silence building on Janice's side.

Her first reaction was to ask Molly if she was, 'nuts? You've only been gone a few days! Brilliant but nuts!' Janice went on to tell Molly she wanted to go down there and see for herself. 'I've always wanted, and not wanted, to witness paranormal activity. Have you thought about how your spooky business is going to affect the locals?'

'Since when does a businesswoman pay any attention to what others say?'

'Okay, okay. I'm just concerned. I mean, are we even having this conversation?'

'It's real. I never thought I'd say this, but I have the ghost of a child, a boy, living in my house. I can't even believe this is happening, Jan. We've held hands!'

Janice didn't say anything for quite a while. 'Are you sure you're okay?'

Molly read between the lines. That seemingly innocent question was a loaded one. 'Oh, Jan, you don't believe me, do you? I know what you're
thinking and you're wrong.'

'I didn't say anything, Molly.'

'You don't have to say anything, Janice! You think I'm drinking again.'

'I think your imagination is on overdrive. Call me back when you come to your…'

*

'…senses.'

On the outskirts of south Dublin, Janice had just been hung up on by Molly. The phone call she had just received was the most disturbing phone call of her life and she'd had some strange phone calls in her life. Janice sat there in her living room, staring at her phone, very preoccupied. She didn't have a good feeling about this. Molly was right — she did think her friend had fallen off the wagon, which Janice believed Molly had never really got on in the first place. But that was only half of Janice's fear. Her real angst was why Molly was even drinking in the first place. Somewhere over the last few days, and we're only talking days here, Molly had become mentally unhinged because, somehow, she'd found a way to get her Henry back. After all, let's face it, the boy was Henry. Whatever was going on down there in the middle of nowhere, Molly had just mixed herself the perfect intoxicating cocktail. Janice thought about the three girls in that musty, dim, old house and sensed a flutter of repugnant panic. That was no place for children. Why hadn't she insisted more when she had the chance? Nobody else had seen the house. She should've stepped in and put Molly right, but she didn't. It was the kind of house that feeds and feeds on broken people.

*

She didn't regret hanging up on Janice. It was deserved. Janice just proved to her that she didn't really know her at all. She looked at the time on her phone screen and panicked. The time was much later than she realised, and she raced off to collect the girls from school.

As they were belting up to drive back from school, the school secretary, Gerry McAuliffe, passed by, discreetly saluting Molly before getting into his claptrap of a car. Looked like he could do with those book royalties. And then she remembered she'd been about to call him before noticing her nocturnal video. She'd forgot everything after witnessing that wondrously hair-raising piece of footage. She was dying to tell him about her new business venture. That reminded her she needed to speak to Prendergast first.

She pulled up next to his car. Through her window, she called, 'How 'bout that coffee?' Molly couldn't see his smile because of the face mask, but she knew he'd smiled back in surprise. 'You mentioned that you know a bit about my house?'

'The farmhouse? Sure. But I know you're only using that as an excuse to have coffee,' he laughed.

She could see herself growing weary of Gerry and his innuendos. She liked a laugh, but not every second, Jesus, c'mon. 'I want to know more about the history of the place. You could give me that and I

271

could give you some new evidence that has come to light,' she said tantalisingly.

'Did something go bump in the night?'

Molly had almost forgotten the kids were sitting right next to her. She cringed and lip-synched a *fuck*. 'Several things went bump in the night.' She winked at Gerry at the wrong time. Oh, God, oh no! He was going to misconstrue her series of unfortunate events. She tried to right it by discreetly indicating that her kids weren't aware of anything, except Mina, who seemed extra interested in this confusing exchange. Molly shook her head on a discreet, subliminal level, then flashed thunderous eyes at Gerry.

Judging by the school secretary's reaction, she wasn't sure if he'd noticed anything that had just gone down in this complex exchange of body language.

'Are you still insisting on fifty-fifty royalties?'

Since they'd last spoken, Molly had come up with her haunted house ghost tour. But it's always good to have several irons in the fire and the hotter the better. 'I think it's fair, Gerry. You're at home, snug as a bug in a rug, while I'm chasing, well.'

'What are you talking about, Mom?'

'Oh, it's nothing, Cora,' said Molly into her rearview mirror. 'I'll explain later.' She turned back to Gerry. 'So, my place?'

Gerry's reaction was hilarious. 'To the farmhouse, you mean? For coffee?'

'Um, yes.'

Gerry gave it some thought. 'Do you mind if we

meet somewhere else? How about Wilma's in town? I happen to have a day off tomorrow. We could meet up this evening. Do you know Wilma's?'

'Unfortunately, yes.'

Gerry was on the point of asking what the problem was, but Molly headed him off at the pass.'Long story.' But she also wanted to prove to Wilma that she didn't faze easily. 'Okay, good idea! You've got a date. Six sharp, 'kay?'

'A date?'

She corrected him with a laugh. 'Not that kind of date! Six sharp!'

'OMG, Mom,' commented Mina. 'That's all I have to say.'

The rest of the afternoon was filled with actual normality for the Greene family...until six o'clock came around when the farmhouse took on a life of its own, as it does every evening at the same time. That familiar sense of happiness filled Molly; a natural high. With this came the sickly sweet odour of overly ripe citrus that came and went. In a dreamy flurry of pleasure, Molly grabbed Louie from his cage and waltzed around the kitchen to the haunting 'Gramaphone' with the bird in her arms. At that moment, Emma thundered into the kitchen. She stopped and screwed up her face as she tried to make sense of what she was seeing: her mom waltzing around the kitchen with the cockatoo. Molly, full of love, then picked Emma up and circled the kitchen, holding onto bird and daughter tight in her arms. She held them, especially Emma, as if she were about to lose her. The fear and love in her were almost too much to bear as they spun slowly, Emma's floppy legs dangling at Molly's knees…

The mother twirled around the kitchen with her youngest daughter, she waltzed into an unexpected pocket of cold air, like an icy draught around her legs. It was here in the kitchen with them. Molly's heart began to pump a little harder in her chest. Emma stiffened in her arms, sensing some change in the kitchen, looked around before resting her chin on her mom's shoulder. Molly fought the urge to call Cora or Mina; she could just about hear them laughing upstairs. As they lazily twirled, a chilly softness latched onto her left leg, hitching a ride. The squatter wanted to dance as well. Tears came to Molly's eyes as a memory came flooding back: Mike doing the same with Henry. Her son would hop onto Mike's foot and cling onto his leg, father dragging son around the room, while Henry slid off with laughter. Molly laughed through the tears.

'What, Mom?'

'Just remembered something.'

'What?'

'I've forgotten.'

'Silly Mommy.'

'Yeah, silly Mommy.'

But it wasn't the memory that caused her to stall, but something else…something else which she'd considered once or twice already over the last few days but had pushed it right the fuck down into her subconscious, never to raise its weary head again. Her pulse thumped in her temples, but she kept dancing. *Keep on dancin'...isn't that what Mike used to say when things got tough? Just keep on dancin'.* How many moms in their mid-forties get to say they've danced a waltz with a cockatoo, a little girl, and a ghost?

'I'm cold, Mommy.'

Molly hugged Emma even tighter and kept on dancin'.

For a hallucinatory second, as she swirled around the worn flagstones, the cockatoo's stony expression turned into her dead husband Mike's smiling face, but Mike's nose was out of joint, having grown a hooked beak where his nose should be...but then there was some other flitting figment...it came between the image of her dead husband with the facial features of a cockatoo and the vision of dropping her child onto the stone floor...

Molly yelped and flinched!

She dropped Emma, such was the shock of seeing the nightmarish sight. The bird was collateral damage, both flopping to the floor. Louie flailed on the shiny smooth surface before finding his wings and launching himself up and across the kitchen to alight on the cage roof. The bird stared at Molly and squawked distaste. Emma just sat there in shock, unsure of what had just happened. She was on the ground, looking up, and that's all she understood.

Molly apologised to her daughter, 'Oh, Jesus, I'm sorry, Emma!' But, peculiarly, the most upsetting was seeing how helpless Louie had been on the floor, slipping and sliding on the smooth tiles. Emma's bottom lip dropped and before she had time to bring the house down, Molly swiped her up and presented her with the last chocolate bonbon from her handbag. The chocolate wasn't cutting it until Molly told her daughter it was, '...the last one' and to 'keep it a secret from your sisters.' These mind games placated Emma.

But other mind games were going on in the farmhouse of a deeper and darker nature, and for the next few hours, all Molly Greene would have in her mind was a blank space where the real reason she had dropped her child resided. Her mind had blocked it out. Such was the heinous distress of having to accept what just happened...the real reason Emma landed on the floor.

Molly sat down at the kitchen table and held Emma in her arms while she scoffed on the world's last chocolate bonbon. In a way, it really was. Something had changed this evening and Molly was afraid. Is the tightly knit knot always meant to unravel in the end?

That Thursday night, Molly Greene lay in bed, gazing at the ceiling, which was just about visible in the moonlight filtering through the window. It had come to Molly just as she had been falling asleep. She remembered now why she had dropped her daughter and not the bird...only it wasn't her daughter that she had dropped when she'd been waltzing around the kitchen, high on life. Subliminally, there was one fleeting moment when she'd caught sight of the right-side profile of Emma's face resting on her shoulder. It was Emma's blonde hair done up in her normal raggedy ponytail, but the face, or what she could see of it, wasn't Emma's. She recognised the creepy young-old face that had been peeping out at her from the shadows: Peekaboo, Mommy. In that moment, Molly had the spirit of the child who walked alone in the farmhouse in her arms. She'd flinched and dropped the child. Unsavoury as it seemed at the time, Molly regretted how she had reacted, not that she had any control over how she had acted in the moment. In retrospect, Molly should've kept on dancin'. All he wanted was to be part of a family… part of her family. She found this immensely desolate. The child — what was once a child — probably didn't even know he was dead and didn't understand why he wasn't being loved like Emma, Cora, and Mina. She had warned him not to interfere with the children, but he had done it, anyway. He was jealous, Molly deduced.

This got her thinking about when Emma had given her that enthusiastic hug in the kitchen — when her daughter had tried to strangle her. What had been his message? There were two ways of looking at this. Firstly, he hated her and tried to choke her through her own daughter, thus driving a wedge between her and Emma. Or secondly, he was jealous and used Emma to choke her. The conclusion was the same in both situations: drive a wedge between her and

Emma. 'Why don't you love me, Mama? Can't you see me? You see the others. What's wrong with me? You can love me too, Mama!'

Just when Molly thought things couldn't get any stranger on that Thursday, the farmhouse had one more trick up its deep, substantial sleeve. One more test for Molly Greene; one more obstacle to be in the running for the first prize in this macabre experimental contest.

Molly, from her bed, heard scratching coming from the fireplace in her bedroom. She had never used the fireplace but found the idea very cosy and quaint.

Until the child who walked alone in the farmhouse, the squatter, oozed from the impossibly small flue opening…its lair, as Mrs Noonan had called the farmhouse. As the pungent scent of rotting citrus, mould, and cloves filled the bedroom, Molly was aware of her own breath fogging out in front of her. She had seen the scene a hundred times over in scary films and would've laughed at the cliché, but Jesus Christ in heaven, it was happening now in real time. Her heart hammered in her chest, so frantic she thought she was going to suffer a massive heart attack right there in her bed. As the presence seeped from the fireplace, it looked to Molly as if the farmhouse was giving birth to this scrunched and deformed creature, slipping from its bag of amniotic flue fluid. The squatter child stood, to her sick fascination, and opened its opaque eyes to stare through Molly, apparently unaware she was there in the bed, watching. She shrunk beneath the bedclothes as the ethereal child floated across the bedroom in eerie silence, then went to the window and gazed for something out there before turning and drifting back into the fireplace.

Molly had only seen him up close once or twice but there was something odd about his movements tonight, almost mechanical, as if he was going through the motions, on an eternal loop, seeking something…

She was cursing herself for not having filmed the thing when her daughter cried out. Molly uttered a yelp! It had nothing to do with the thing living in her chimney, but her daughter crying out, 'Mom?'… 'Mom?!'

Will this night ever end? Molly asked herself as she climbed out of bed and went to her four-year-old's bedroom, keeping a cautious eye on the fireplace behind her.

Emma was sitting up in bed.

'Mommy's here, honey.'

'I want to go to your bed.'

Molly laughed hysterically. She was so relieved. This house was going to be the death of her. She scooped Emma up into her arms and went back to her bedroom, stalling at the doorway, before slipping into bed. It was such a precious moment to feel the warmth of her baby next to her. Emma fell asleep the moment her head hit the pillow. The deep, satisfying breathing of her daughter cast its slumbering spell over Molly.

It was the cold draught that had woken Molly. Judging by the dim, silvery light coming through her bedroom window, it was early morning, too early to get up. The vague outline of Emma curled up next to her brought a smile to her face, and she found herself thinking about that morning when the pregnancy test told her she was pregnant, which came as a surprise to both Mike and Molly. There were mixed emotions, and Molly was more worried about her work schedule than anything else. Mike had always said he wanted three kids, liking the energy of a trio. Boy or girl, Mike wasn't fussy, just as long as the child was healthy. But the pregnancy test hadn't told them Molly was expecting twins.

She leaned over to put her arm around Emma, the remaining half of her defunct twins, and flinched when she felt the unnatural coldness emanating from the child's body. A sickening nausea crept around her heart as her own personal nightmare swallowed her whole. 'Emma?'

The child didn't answer.

She screeched, 'Emma?!'

'Whaaat? You woke me up, mom…'

Emma answered but, for once in her life, Molly wished she hadn't…wished she hadn't because Emma's reply had come from her own bedroom down the hallway.

Molly eased over on the bed, tensed up into a fluttering ball of anxiety, unable to bring herself to look at the curled-up thing next to her in the bed. Despite the situation, Molly did not feel fear, but shocked confusion, disbelief, and she felt oddly maternal. Her hands rose to her agape mouth…

'Mom?' called Mina from upstairs. 'What's wrong?'

Wide-eyed, Molly Greene stared at the figure lying next to her, unsure of what to say or do next. 'Nothing.' Realising she spoke in a whisper, she repeated herself a little louder, 'Nothing, go back to sleep, everyone. Bad dream, that's all.' Injecting a falsely happy tone: 'Everything is just fine.' She was expecting Emma to say something else, at least question why she had woken in a different bed than the one she'd fallen asleep in. Molly was asking the same thing, for Christ's sake. The silence indicated Emma hadn't realised where she was, or didn't care, and had, thankfully, fallen back to sleep.

Molly pulled herself up into a sitting position, back against the wall, wrapped her arms tight around her shins, and watched the foetal shape by her side. Its stillness was disconcerting, no reassuring sign of the steady rise and fall of a sleeping child.

She sat there for another half an hour. The initial disbelief she had felt dissipated and, in its place, came that hollow and homesick pity for the child that had walked alone in the house.

Molly loosened as sleep hijacked her. She slipped down under the covers and gave in to sleep. The last thing she felt was the cold little torso creep up next to her and hugging her in a cold-blooded embrace. The world needed to know about this. Maybe this symbiotic relationship could work: 'You scratch my back and I'll scratch yours,' she whispered. It was time to sit the girls down and have a meaningful little chat.

19.

M Molly was alone in her bed when she opened her eyes on Friday morning. As on other occasions at the farmhouse, she had awoken with the sense that she'd dreamt everything that had gone down the night before. But last night's escapades were too vivid and too many to be just any old dream. She looked at the empty space on her left. To any other average middle-aged woman, last night would've been a nightmare in a nightmare and that average middle-aged woman would now be on the road to somewhere, anywhere, just as long as it was far from the farmhouse. But not Molly Greene because Molly was from a broken family, as Richard Prendergast kindly put it. She could relate to the child that walks alone at the farmhouse and the eternal and internal desperation it must feel…as she feels for having lost her own son. And this is where the line blurs and things get existential. No matter how much she would deny it, she was constantly reminded of her son, Henry, whenever she was in the phantasm's presence. She'd been trying to deny making these macabre connections, but how could she not? Having slept in the same bed as the spirit, she had taken it to a new level and, some might say, crossed that blurry line. Somewhere along the way, she had adopted the spirit of a lost child. What she couldn't deny was how she felt lonely not having the spirit lying next to her, finding comfort and solace in her presence. She'd been hoping to see it in the daylight, almost like a lover who had absconded during the night, though not quite.

It was time to call the girls for school. She wanted to laugh and cry all at once with the normality and absurdity of it all. She was living a double life, even a triple life, when she wasn't sure if she was asleep or awake.

Breakfast and morning chaos passed off without incident. Maybe it was too early to count her chickens, but Molly perceived the girls were coming around to their new life and were 'settling in'. They were chirpier this morning and went off to school with an extra spring in their step.

When Molly Greene went to pick up the girls after school that Friday afternoon, she was surprised to see an extra girl coming out of school with Mina.

Mina proudly introduced her to her mom. 'This is Christine.'

'Oh,' Molly's smile faltered, 'nice to meet you.' They politely bumped elbows, but as they piled their schoolbags into the boot of the BMW, Molly asked discreetly, 'Is this the same Christine whose mom berated me over the phone?'

'Yeah, her mom told her it was okay to stay over as long as she checks in with her a few times.'

'Really?' Molly smiled. 'That's good news.' She wondered why she had allowed her daughter to stay at the house of terror. Still, she was happy that she had done so. This will help Mina settle in and Mina's happiness will rub off on Cora. She thought about mentioning that it might be a good idea to give her a heads-up in the future, just to have enough food and set up an extra bed, but she'd only sound like a nagging parent who needed something to argue about. 'One thing,' she said, 'I got a date this evening.'

Mina almost fell over. 'A what?'

Molly giggled. 'Okay, so maybe *date* isn't the right word. I've got a meeting with Gerry.'

'The school secretary?'

'Yep.'

Mina rolled her eyes. 'Good luck with that one.'

'Purely business.'

'Does *he* know that?'

Molly hadn't considered that. 'He will if he doesn't know already. We're going to discuss a book he's working on.'

Mina wasn't convinced. 'Hmm.'

'It's based on the farmhouse, but he's going to write it as a scary novel, supernatural horror.'

Mina stopped what she was doing and looked at her mom. 'Oh, yeah?'

'It's regarding what we spoke about.'

Mina grew grave. 'Have you spoken to Cora yet?'

'Not yet,' Molly said with a hint of regret. 'I've been thinking about that. I've got big plans, Mina. I think we should—'

'Okay, mom, I'll leave it in your capable hands…'

'—have a family meeting tomorrow evening,' Molly finished, but Mina had already hopped next to Christine and Emma into the car. She had been on the point of telling Mina about her grand plan that would save them all but the giggles in the back of the BMW put that to rest. She'd wait until tomorrow evening and include it in her manifesto regarding the secret child they shared their house with and how this child would secure their future.

The Greenes went to the local supermarket to stock up on provisions. For the first time since they'd moved to Old Castle, Molly felt they were a functioning family as they laughed and zoomed their way up and down the aisles. Since when had it become fun to do the shopping? Her life had become so simple. What she'd taken for granted before was now a joyous event. Emma sat in the shopping cart, laughing her head off while Molly and the girls lobbed jars and packets into her cart. Christine joined them. The family got one or two caustic stares from other shoppers, but that didn't worry Molly. It probably roiled the locals to see the town pariahs had joyfully recruited one of their own — Christine — into their demonic ranks. It felt so good to fill up their shopping cart, but she was keenly aware of her diminishing funds. *Keep on dancin'*, she imagined she heard Mike say from inside the deep freezer.

Mina and Christine stayed in Mina's bedroom the rest of Friday afternoon. Molly could hear them laughing and giggling and it brought joy to her heart. Just before 6pm she informed the girls she needed to go out for an hour and that she was taking Cora and Emma with her. She didn't get into details in front of

Christine; she didn't want anyone knowing her business in Old Castle, not for now at least. There would come a day when everyone would know about her business. For the time being, she was keeping it under wraps. She had thought about cancelling Gerry, but Mina and Christine were more than old enough to look after the house for an hour, but what she wondered was whether the house would look after them.

Wilma bestowed Molly, Gerry, and the two girls with her famous Wilma Welcome the moment they stepped inside the door of the restaurant in the town square. All business, she led them to a prominent table by the window, looking out at the town square and the Norman castle. It was a little trick Wilma had to entice punters from outside, giving the impression her eatery was full of happy diners. Tonight, Wilma's was empty…almost.

Wilma's famous grin dropped from her jolly face when she realised it was Molly behind the face mask. Molly noticed how she glanced around surreptitiously to see if any of her virtually non-existent customers had seen Molly enter. *Thank Christ for face masks,* she thought. Now the hostess had the dilemma of having the Greene woman on full display like a goddamn hooker in Amsterdam's Red Light District.

'Gerry, how are you this evening?' Wilma asked with an accusatory tone, fishing for the reason why he was here in her establishment with Molly Greene, of all people. What next? Flying pigs?

'I'm well, Wilma.' Gerry asked Molly and the girls what they would like, and Molly told Wilma, through Gerry, she wanted a 'Glass of…um, coffee. Coffee will be fine.' She'd almost said it out of habit.

'Won't that keep you awake tonight?' asked Gerry.

She smiled wearily. 'If only…'

Molly and Gerry exchanged a momentary glance. 'And,' Gerry went on with their order, 'can you bring two slices of the wonderful Wilma strawberry cheesecake for the girls. I'll have a cuppa tea…and bring on another slice of that cheesecake. Molly, cheesecake?'

Molly declined graciously.

Cora and Emma grinned like a couple of Cheshire cats. Cheesecake of any flavour was their favourite.

Molly thanked Gerry. 'It'll keep them occupied while we talk. Sorry, I come with baggage. I don't have a babysitter.'

'Don't be silly.'

'Um,' Wilma interrupted, 'maybe you'd prefer a more discreet table?' She gestured to a table in the furthest corner of the eatery and also the most distant from the window. Gerry flashed a why-would-she-do-that look at Molly when there was already someone sitting at the table. 'But there's someone—'

'Yes, why?' Molly interrupted, gearing up to make a scene. 'What's wrong with this table?' Molly moved the table. 'Sure, it's a little rocky, but I can shove a napkin under one of the legs.' She laughed dryly. 'Rocky tables go with the territory in this type of place. It's the gold standard.' Molly smiled and sniffed defiance. It was nice to have a little sweet revenge.

Wilma threw Molly a look of disgust before trundling off for their order.

Both Molly and Gerry shared a nervous giggle.

Only seconds later, a waitress with dreads set down the food and drink, void of nicety. Molly could only see the upper half of her face, but she had a strong feeling the waitress was Wilma's daughter judging by the similar features.

'So,' Gerry finally asked with a hopeful face, 'you've been living there for a week or something, right?'

'Wait a sec…' Molly knew what was coming next. She asked the waitress if it was okay for the girls to move to the table next to them. The waitress flashed an unenthusiastic nod. Molly flashed her a sarcastic thumbs up. 'Fab!' Then turned to the girls. 'You want your own table like grown-ups?'

Cora jumped, 'Sure!'

The girls took their cheesecake to the table to the right of theirs and sat down, proud to be on their own like adults. They munched contentedly on their dessert and chatted between themselves.

Meanwhile, Gerry was waiting with great anticipation. 'Have you seen or heard anything you can't explain?'

Molly drank from her mug of coffee. 'I slagged off her furniture, but she does make a good mug of coffee.'

'Molly, the farmhouse?'

She leaned over and whispered, 'Gerry, something lives in the farmhouse with us.'

Gerry got up and sat down again with uncontainable excitement.

'It's true,' she said quietly. 'He's got like something sticking out of his head…like feathers or something.'

'Jesus!' Gerry's eyes were out on stalks.

Molly nodded. 'I didn't want to tell you this, but it doesn't have a normal mouth either….'

Gerry frowned. 'Christ, no?'

Molly shook her head. 'It's got a beak.'

'A what?'

'A beak,' she repeated in a low voice. 'And his name is Louie.'

Gerry sat back with a puzzled expression.

Molly couldn't hold in the laughter any longer. 'Louie's a cockatoo!'

'Molly! Oh my God, don't do that! You should've seen the monster I just conjured up in my head just now!' It took a few seconds for Gerry to see the funny side, already on tenterhooks. 'As you know, I'm working on a novel based on the house and the family who first built it. It was going to be a real non-fiction book on the place but, y'know, the locals wouldn't be best pleased. I've done quite a lot of research into the house and the family. I've forgotten most of it though. It's been a while since I decided to write fiction instead, but based on the farmhouse.'

'Okay, let's get serious.' Molly cast a furtive glimpse over at the counter area where Wilma was hovering. 'I can't believe I'm even saying this. I never believed in any of this supernatural stuff, but the place is haunted. Very haunted.'

Gerry fell back in his chair this time. 'Haunted by a cockatoo?'

Molly shook her head. 'It's a lot of things, but a cockatoo isn't one of them. You know how I know when he's around? The smell…'

'The smell?'

'Mouldy citrus and cloves.'

Gerry was shaking his head in disbelief. 'Did you just make that up?'

'A little specific, don't you think?'

'Molly, in the nineteenth century, children carried around fruits and spices to mask the musky smell of their own body odour. Children used to take citrus fruit spiked with cloves — we have roll-on deodorant these days. You said, "he". You mean *he* as in Louie?'

Molly paused. 'It's a boy,' she confirmed. 'A lost boy. And, y'know what, Gerry? As long as he doesn't bother us, we won't bother him. I believe we can all coexist in the farmhouse.'

Molly could see Gerry McAuliffe was growing more alarmed by the second. Something was bugging him.

'And,' Molly ignoring Gerry's reaction, 'he always appears after six in the evening.' Molly then relayed everything to Gerry like she had done with Janice. As she went down through the list of encounters, Gerry's facial expressions grew from mild curiosity to flesh-prickling horror. Molly's list went on and on and she mentioned the video footage. Now and again, she paused to drink her coffee and check on the girls. She concluded by saying, 'And that's just the half of it, but you get the picture… Now, how 'bout those royalties?'

'Molly, I'm, well, I don't know what to say. Yes, you've given me more than enough material, but that's not my concern. You need to get out of that place,' was Gerry's take on things. 'How can you be so flippant?'

Molly was surprised by Gerry's reaction. 'I thought you loved this stuff? I thought you wanted material for your book. *Real* material, not just rumours and gossip?'

Gerry was visibly shaking as he gulped his tea.

'Gerry, there's nothing bad in that house. It's a child.'

'Molly,' asked Gerry, 'have you lost your senses? How could you even consider staying there after what you've just told me? To be honest with you, I was taking everything with a pinch of salt, but…' He looked about the restaurant in disbelief. 'I'm going to write this book and use everything that you gave me, but let's take the money and run.'

'I'm not running anywhere, Gerry. The cold hand of death once tapped my shoulder. I don't frighten easily.'

Molly noticed Wilma busying herself around the tables, cleaning tables which didn't need to be cleaned. Anything to eavesdrop. Molly gave her a peevish look before she shuffled off behind the counter. She turned to Gerry. 'You've let me down. You were the one person in this godforsaken town I thought I could trust.'

'You can trust me. That's why I'm telling you to get the fuck out of that place, Molly.'

For a moment, Molly thought she sensed optimism in Gerry's eyes, as if she was going to come around to his way of thinking. She'd show him. 'Guys, finish your cheesecake. We're going home.' She realised their plates had been cleaned long ago.

Gerry pleaded, 'I'm going to write this book and you will get fifty per cent of the royalties.'

'Keep your royalties, Gerry. This is just a book to you, but I'm living this book.' She stalled as something else dawned on her — it was something Mina had said. 'You got me here under false pretences, didn't you? But you got more than you bargained for. Thought you could kill two birds with one stone? I'm not a stone, Gerry — stones have feelings.' Having bestowed these words of wisdom, Molly went to vacate Wilma's, admonishing herself for not having listened to her fifteen-year-old daughter.

Gerry placed his hand on Molly's arm. 'Wait, please. I want you to listen to what I have to say.'

Molly looked at her watch. 'I've got to get back to the house. Mina is with her friend and I don't want them to be alone for too long.'

'What I have to say will just take a second.'

'Get it out of your system.'

'I think you're in over your head. I think you don't

know what you're dealing with.'

'Gerry, it's a boy! A lost kid looking for a mother.'

Gerry looked at her with a did-you-really-just-say-that expression on his face. The school secretary fell back in his chair on hearing this declaration. 'Have you heard what you just said? I heard it and it gives me the chills. Perhaps you are the scariest thing at the farmhouse." Something about the way Molly spoke prickled every hair on his body. She gave him the chills. It was ironic, but the sharpest jolt of fear he had this evening was from Molly herself: she was the scariest thing at the farmhouse. 'Have you heard what you just said?'

'Gerry, the maternal instinct knows — mothers know, Gerry. A child needs a mother, no matter where that child comes from.'

'This isn't an orphan from some godforsaken country, Molly. This thing comes from the other *side*, not the other side of the world, Molly. There's a difference. It's not a boy. Boys play football in the park…make funny videos on TikTok with their mom's phones. What they don't do is make videos of themselves creeping across ceilings upside down!' Gerry checked himself from getting any angrier. He left it at that.

But tonight, whilst going over his old notes for his proposed book, one family member of the original Prendergast clan would pique his interest.

At this juncture, Wilma looked over at them with great interest.

Gerry struggled to keep his voice low. 'Sleeping

with a ghost boy who just wants a mommy? That's creepy, Molly.'

Molly got up to leave. 'Let's forget this ever happened.' She called Cora and Emma, who were now living out their own little fantasy in the corner of Wilma's, playing with another boy. Cora pleaded for just five more minutes. 'We're playing Statues!' From the corner of her mouth, Cora added with an embarrassed smile, 'He's taking it very seriously!'

Molly saw they'd made a friend. Kids need friends, especially in a town like Old Castle. 'Five minutes, got it? No haggling for another five when I tell you we have to go.'

The girls were happy and got back to their game of Statues.

Gerry seemed pleased to have found a five-minute reprieve. He looked eager to talk some more.

'So, we've got five minutes,' Molly curtly told Gerry. 'What should we talk about? The weather?'

Gerry shook his head disapprovingly. 'I can't talk about the weather with the same woman who has just told me that she wants to be a ghost's mother. Call me crazy…'

'Stop being such a drama queen. He's merely looking for a mother figure. Put yourself in his position.'

*

Gerry was finding this more and more troubling. He barely knew Molly Greene, but there was something seriously fucked up about the woman sitting across the table from him. He'd assumed she was a little out there, the independent type, single mom with three daughters who can conquer anything, but she was talking like a woman not dealing with a full deck right now. 'You're asking me to see from a ghost's point of view?' Why was Molly Greene, a woman who seemed so rational and normal, so completely besotted with a spirit? And then, as he sat there, he questioned whether the house had some kind of hold over her, or rather, the squatter had. What if it had latched onto her? What if it was looking at him right now through Molly's green eyes? It was there, like a subliminal message: he could see it, but couldn't read it. Gerry shivered and sat back, putting some distance between them.

*

An awkward silence festered until Molly declared, 'I've wasted enough of my time here. 'Girls, let's go. Say bye to your friend.' She turned to Gerry. 'See you at school.'

With this comment, it was clear Molly wasn't into having any further meetings. Gerry had let her down on two levels: firstly, he had used the book as an excuse to meet her. She had already suspected he had more in mind than swop ghost stories, and she didn't really hold it against him. A little love makes the world go around, after all. But that brought her to his second failing: Gerry wasn't a believer, and it was that which hurt her, just when Molly thought she'd found one sympathiser in the whole town. All he was interested in doing was penning a cheesy horror without ever knowing the truth. All Gerry wanted to do was cash in on gossip and rumours. But Molly was living this cheesy horror in real-time with stereo surround sound.

They parted company.

*

Gerry sat there, pondering this coffee meeting he would never forget. Wilma's was almost empty, save for the boy sitting at the corner table who he'd seen when he'd come in. He was still sitting there, motionless, staring this way, apparently still playing Statutes even though Cora and Emma had already left. He looked as lonely as Gerry felt.

Gerry McAuliffe left Wilma's. As he walked back to his town square flat just across the street, something began to dawn on him.

*

That night, Molly ordered four security cameras from Amazon. The cameras only recorded when they sensed movement. This was the deciding factor for Molly. She didn't have time to trawl through hours of blank footage and she could view the cameras from an app on her MacBook and her phone. She thought about her meeting with Gerry McAuliffe and was a little saddened it hadn't worked out.

20.

Later that evening, Gerry McAuliffe couldn't stop thinking about his unusual meeting with Molly Greene. She seemed such a normal person, but…

He broke his blank gaze from the goggle box and did a rudimentary Google search on Molly Greene, Dublin. The search engine returned a handful of Molly Greenes but no sign of his Molly. He then added a keyword: Michelin — she'd mentioned she used to own a Michelin-star restaurant up in the capital before Covid 19 came along and closed so many restaurants across the country. Google churned out several links on Molly. Yes, the keyword had worked, but 'Michelin' was but only a side note in her sad life.

'Aw, Jesus.' Now Gerry understood why Molly had wanted to divert the conversation from her past. To his sadness and worry, Molly Greene's Michelin star restaurant wasn't her only claim-to-fame: a car accident had taken the lives of her husband and son.

'Christ…'

He had been tempted to ask if there was a man in her life, especially as he had intentions of possibly being that man. But a son? Good God, he would've never guessed. As he sat in his living room, thinking about the farmhouse just a few kilometres away, he got the chills imagining Molly and the girls living out in that gloomy old place. In a strange way, the Greenes were meant for the farmhouse with a darker past; two darkness's coexisting. This was making regrettable sense. As he re-read the headlines…

Michelin star restauranteur, Molly Greene, loses up to half her family in a tragic car accident.

…Gerry began to doubt every word that had come from Molly's mouth. Accidents like that have a profound effect on the ones they leave behind, sometimes festering for months, years, before manifesting. Gerry believed Molly Greene had a deep trauma, a mental scar, left fragile and broken after the accident. There was no boy ghost in the farmhouse, but the ghost of a memory of a boy, brought to life by the never-ending torrent of innuendos surrounding the farmhouse. Gerry felt profound pity for the woman with whom he had been speaking just an hour ago. Should he feel deceived or cheated in any way? No, Molly Greene was a victim of circumstances. She's just a mom wishing to have her son back, and the form that took didn't bother her. Molly Greene was living more inside her head than outside it. That was all very well, but that didn't explain why Molly's daughters had also confirmed, according to Molly, that they had seen and heard odd movements and sounds, especially Mina. Molly had told Gerry she was just waiting for the right moment to verify what the girls had already felt in the house. He couldn't understand this on any level.

Riddle: What kind of fifteen-year-old is happy to share their house with a ghost?

Answer: A fifteen-year-old with a hole in her life

where her younger brother should be…and throw a convincing mom into the mix.

Then again, he was taking Molly's word for it; he hadn't spoken to the girls to hear their side of the story. Everything he knew had come through Molly, and that was the root of the problem right there. The more the school secretary thought about it, the more troubling this became. Finding the spirit of a child living in the house with them had been just a matter of time.

But then Gerry McAuliffe recalled something Molly had said…he remembered because it just stuck out of the conversation, a lot like the ears she mentioned, funnily enough. She commented on the spirit's ears being larger than normal. This was worryingly specific. And it went against everything that pointed to the ghost in the house being no more than the memory of her son. It had been bugging him during their fiery coffee meeting, and only now did Gerry realise it.

He got up from the sofa, so fast his head reeled, and went down the hallway to his little office. There, he rifled through his notes from his proposed novel and came across the black and white image of the boy which mesmerised now as much as it had done the first time he'd seen the sickly, forlorn, achromatic face of the adrift child. And those ears — they had given him so much hardship and strife during his childhood. The child had been ostracised because of his ears, both at home and in the schoolyard. His own mother shunned him. Still, no excuse for murder; less excuse for multiple murders — serial killer at nine years of age? His ears had been but only the trigger for the demon inside him. That's what had been nagging him. That pitiful, deranged face had been looking at him while Molly told her story at Wilma's, trying to get his attention and…

Gerry suddenly grew pale and wan.

He sat back and looked around his little office in horror…horror…HORROR! It had been looking at him!

A spine-tingling chill ran down his back. Not because he'd been trying to place this face in his subconscious, but because his subconscious was trying to tell him the face was right there with them at Wilma's. It had been watching them from the darkest corner of Wilma's, sitting there in silence. 'Jesus Christ…' It was true. He hadn't seen the child entering the eating establishment, and they were seated right next to the door, yet it was there, statuesque, staring at them. And there's something else. Wilma had gestured they sit at the table because she hadn't seen the child or whatever had been sitting there. Oh, Lord in Heaven, Molly's children had been playing with it! What game had Cora mentioned they were playing? Statues! Cora had said the child was taking the game very seriously. Gerry had found it amusing at the time, but not now. The boy was taking the game very seriously because it wasn't really there. There was something there, but not what the girls thought. They had been playing with a ghost, trapped between two worlds, there but not there, a hologram.

301

Gerry held his head in his hands as he remembered seeing the 'child' sitting on its own, and Gerry recalled how he'd thought it was odd that a boy would be sitting there on his own. He'd looked out of place. It was the eyes that had first caught his attention: a dead fish-eyed stare, expressionless yet bursting with expression.

Gerry left his office and went to the window overlooking the town square. He had a bird's eye view of Wilma's across the street from his second-floor flat. The restaurant was empty now, not a soul.

'Fuck,' he muttered, 'it followed her, there and back.' Then, with even more disbelief, 'She was telling the truth all along…'

*

While Gerry McAuliffe was reading the disturbing headlines in an online newspaper and before he made his even more disturbing realisation, the Greenes and Christine were about to sit down for a Friday night pizza dinner. Molly had got back to the farmhouse around quarter past seven, relieved the house was as she had left it. She pulled a couple of frozen pizzas they'd bought earlier from the freezer.

As they chatted and ate the uninspiring pizza, footsteps, out of nowhere, skipped across the ceiling above them.

A silence loomed around the table. Slack-jawed, everyone gawped at each other before focusing on Emma. The footfalls above their heads were those of a child, yet the four-year-old was sitting in her chair with a giant slice of pizza in her hand and an expression of mild amusement. The footsteps might've belonged to an older child, so then everyone looked in Cora's direction, but Cora was sitting there with a dumb look and a slice of pizza hanging from her teeth.

Christine uttered, 'If Emma and Cora are sitting here, then who…'

The footsteps skittered across from the other side of the ceiling directly above the fridge where Mina had first seen that crouching black mass.

Molly cringed and silently cursed the boy's poor sense of timing. She had planned to tell her girls the truth in her own time, the girls being Cora, but now it was too late and they will label her a liar, which was apt. And to make matters worse, Mina's new friend, Christine, her only anchor in Old Castle, was witnessing this at the same time.

'Mom?' Cora asked through a mouthful of pizza.

'Shush, everyone,' Molly hushed, 'keep calm. I've got this under control.'

The girls looked at one another, immobilised with fear. Molly's attempts to appear as if nothing had just happened was more eerily terrifying than the phantom footsteps.

'It's here, isn't it?'

Monosyllabic Cora turned to her sister with a dumbfounded expression. 'Mina?'

Mina and her mom exchanged telling glances. But it was Mina who spoke first. 'Cora, it's okay. Mom was going to tell you today, but our plans changed,' gesturing to her left at terror-struck Christine. 'There is something living in the house with us. It wasn't fully vacant when we moved in.'

In shock, Cora turned to her mom for some perspective, guidance, anything…

'I was waiting for the right moment to tell you and this is not it. I'm sorry it happened like this. I want you to know that he is just a little curious child.'

This time it was Christine's turn to speak. 'Him?'

'It's a little lost boy looking for attention, like you all did when you were young. Try to act normal around him and everything will be fine.'

Cora blinked, as if that might wake her from a vivid nightmare, but the nightmares in the farmhouse happened while awake.

Sweet music notes floated down to them from overhead. Somebody was up there playing one of the kalimbas Molly had jokingly bought in Old Castle's only redundant souvenir shop on that first day.

Molly thought about her friend Janice and how far away she seemed just then.

When Molly took her gaze from the ceiling back at Cora, she was surprised to see tears rolling down her daughter's face, a ball of pizza stuffed in her agape mouth. 'It's okay, Cora, it's okay. Believe me. I've seen and heard the child and he's just like any of you,' she smiled in reassurance. *More or less the same… except for the old face that sometimes lurks inside its youthful face.*

*

Mina wasn't sure what was scarier: the haunting *plink plink* of the kalimba coming from upstairs or her mom's reaction to all of this. She already knew she was sharing the house with something else, but there was something about her mom she couldn't understand.

*

'Mina, I want to go home…' Christine had grown very pale. 'I'm going to call my mom.' She spoke in a trance.

Meanwhile, above them, the random notes began to form a faintly audible tune…

Molly had a situation on her hands. She needed to reel it in before it got out of hand. 'I'm going up there.' Molly got up from the table, but the girls protested. Mina telling her to 'sit the fuck back down, *Mooom!*'

Meanwhile, the metal blades of the kalimba played melodic notes with Mina remarking in the chaos of the moment, 'I know that music,' Molly realised it wasn't just a random tune but the music she'd been listening to every evening: Eugen Doga's 'Gramophone' note for note. 'We won't bother it and it won't bother us.'

'Jesus Christ, mom!' Mina erupted. 'This isn't a wasp that's just flown into the kitchen!'

Molly felt a crazy giggle-bubble deep inside her.

Christine had her eyes shut, rocking back and forth, muttering sweet nothings to herself. 'I'm just stuck, that's all. None of this is happening. It'll all be over when I open my eyes. Stuck…Stuck…Stuck…'

Emma, not aware of what was going on, continued to eat the others' pizza — if in doubt, eat pizza.

'We can all live in harmony here at the farmhouse.' Molly considered Cora and Mina 'That's what I wanted to tell you. I know it's not the best moment… But better late than never.'

Cora chided, 'I prefer never…'

'I want my Mommy. Where's Mommy?' Sense of reasoning shutdown, Christine spoke as if she were on happy drugs.

'Then call her!' Molly answered back. 'Call the queen of Old Castle to come and collect you, Christine. She will come with her demolition paperwork, no doubt, and raze us all to the ground!'

'She doesn't know I'm here.'

This stopped Molly in her tracks. 'Mina, what did she just say?'

This was news to Mina as well. She turned to Christine. 'What did you just say?'

'I didn't tell Mom I was coming. Do you honestly think my mom would've let me come to the farmhouse? I wanted to see or hear the squatter for myself.' She looked around, utterly bewildered. 'I guess I should be careful what I wish for.' Christine looked about her as if she wasn't taking any of this in.

'There's something here in this house, yes,' Molly affirmed, 'but that's where the rumours stop being true, Christine. Don't think for a second it is any danger to any of us.' Molly was sick and tired of having to defend herself. 'Do you think I would put any of you in danger? It's the spirit of a little boy who is trapped in this house.'

306

What was becoming more alarming was Molly's acceptance of this surreal horror with an almost proud tone in her voice.

Christine was on the speakerphone to her mom. 'Mom?'

'Jesus, Christine!' Her mom boomed. 'Where the fuck are you?! Do you realise what you've put me through? Answer your phone! I spend the whole day telling you to put it away and the one minute I ask you to use it, you won't!'

Molly nodded. 'Yes! For once in my life, I agree with your mom, Christine.'

Christine then informed her mom she was at the farmhouse, then reality kicked in and Christine blubbered like a baby. 'I want to go home, mom! There's something happening.'

Between the crying and fretting, the ghostly *plinkity-plink* of the African thumb piano continued upstairs… And now Louie was getting in on the action, adding his choice words to the disarray.

'Ten minutes, Christine! 'Kay, sweetie? I'm not, repeat not, going down there. Get one of those freaks to drop you up to the road gate.'

Molly felt a streak of giddiness come through her. 'But she hasn't finished her pizza! It's barbecue!'

Christine's mom hung up.

'Oh, surprise, surprise, your mom hung up, Christine. She's a hanger-upper. Does that even exist?'

'Mooom!' screamed Mina. *'Get a grip!'*

Everyone, including the cockatoo, froze as Cora let

307

out a curdling scream. 'Everyone, shut the fuck up!' She implored with her mom. 'Please, make all of this okay!'

Her innocence and desperate honesty cut a hole in Molly's heart.

'My stuff's up in your bedroom!' Christine exclaimed, sounding as if Mina's bedroom wasn't at the top of the house but at the top of Mount Everest. 'I'm not going up there, Mina.'

'I'll get your stuff.' Ignoring the pleas not to go up there, Molly left the table. In the hallway, someone grabbed her, and she almost let out a scream as she turned to see Cora hugging her. 'I don't want to go up!' She whispered frantically.

'But nobody asked you to go up, Cora.'

'But I don't want to be left down here either! I'm scared.'

Molly saw this as an opportunity. 'Come with me and you'll see.' She took her daughter's hand and had to tug Cora a little before she would climb the stairs with her. They ascended the stairs, with every step, drawing closer to the phantom kalimba player. Halfway up the stairs, the familiar decayed citrus and cloves rose in her nostrils.

'Do you smell that?'

Cora nodded.

'Well, that's our little friend telling us he's here.'

Cora gawped at the strange delight on her mom's face.

They checked all the rooms, but it was Molly's room that felt different; a static charge clung in the air and Molly didn't have to ask her daughter if she felt the same thing because she could see it in her face. They heard the musical notes again, but now it came from further away. And the familiar tune had been replaced by random notes.

Bug-eyed, Cora pointed to the fireplace. The out-of-note chiming was coming from inside the chimney hearth. They both stuck their heads by the fireplace and listened to the disturbing chimney-chiming coming from somewhere deep inside the farmhouse.

'You see?' Molly whispered. 'It lives in there.'

*

Cora stuck her head into the hearth and gazed into the black grille at the back of the old fireplace and peered down into a tarry black hole. She shuddered with fear, imagining a boy living down there, in that dark and lonely place. But, right now, it wasn't the lost child living in the chimney that scared her; it was her mom acting all…weird.

And *weird* is the exact word she would use at school over the coming days when Christine's revelation spread through the school like wildfire. Cora would say in the schoolyard, surrounded by fearful children, she didn't feel intimidated by the ghost living in the fireplace, but by her mom who was acting…weird.

*

From downstairs, Mina called, 'Mom, say something?'

'Fine, hun,' Molly called back. 'I'll get Christine's things.'

309

'She just called. Christine's mom is at the road gate. She's not coming down. She wants you to drive Christine up to the road.'

'Christ on a cracker,' Molly muttered. 'These medieval people are really pissing me off. If I ever get—' Molly froze as an icy caress wrapped around her ankle. With the snake-like stroke, Molly heard giggling. The child was under her bed. 'Peekaboo, Mommy!' More giggling, petering into a haggard cackle…

The blood drained from Cora's face. 'Mom…'

Molly was sure her daughter was going to faint. 'Are you okay?'

'I'm dizzy. I don't feel okay.'

'Mama, why won't you play with me?'

'Mom, it's talking. I prefer if it didn't talk.'

Mina yelled from downstairs, 'C'mon, let's go! Christine's mom is waiting!'

'Oh, fuck Christine's mom!' snapped Molly, frightening Cora. The pale scrawny arm protruding from beneath Molly's bed, hand gripped on her mom's ankle, was the most disturbing of all, yet Molly seemed oddly unfazed by it.

'Are they for real?' Molly boomed. 'They just heard a kalimba — a *kalimbaaaaa!* — playing up here on its own and all they're concerned with is not having to delay Christine's mom? Jesus Christ and all the saints! Where did the world go wrong?!'

Headlights streaked across Molly's bedroom wall, accompanied by frantic horn blowing. Sweet Lord, she was down here in their front yard. Christine's

310

mom was here!

'Let me go!' Molly commanded. 'Do you see my other children hanging off my ankles?'

Cora's eyes widened as she saw how the hand loosened and retreated beneath the bed. She dropped to her knees and made the mistake of looking under there. Her breath was taken from her when two unblinking pallid eyes stared back at her from the darkness…and with those eyes came a mischievous giggle.

Cora screamed, not finding anything to laugh about.

'Cora, Cora,' Molly grabbed her daughter's shoulders, 'don't forget this is a child who has been on his own for longer than you or I could ever fathom, sweetie.' She laughed to herself. 'He's just a little excited that someone is finally seeing him and listening to him.'

Halfway through Molly's soothing words, which were anything but soothing, screaming erupted from the front yard below. Molly opened her bedroom window and popped her head out to see Christine's mom yelling at Mina. 'Bitch!' barked Molly. 'Who does she think she is? I'm going to fuckin'…' Rage inside her rendered Molly speechless. She bolted downstairs. Cora, traumatised, followed at her heels. Somewhere between upstairs and downstairs, Molly wondered how she would play this. She thought about pleading with Christine not to mention what had happened, but at the end of the day, Molly Greene was a businesswoman, and this was a stroke of good luck. Word of mouth was the best kind of publicity for her crazy new business venture. It was pure and clear as mountain dew. Cora and Mina would be her soldiers on the ground to help spread the good word. She kind of hated herself just then for using her kids, but she was doing this for all of them…for all the Greenes.

As Christine made a hasty retreat, Molly called, 'You're welcome any time.'

The Greene family stood there in the front porch watching the spectacle unfold.

'Why did you make me come down here?' Christine's mom screamed through her window at Christine, who sprinted across the front yard to the idling car. 'I told you to meet me at the road gate, *Christinnne*!' She flung open the passenger door. 'I had to go knocking on Prendergast's front door to let me through, and he's another nut job!'

Christine stumbled halfway across the front yard and fell to her hands and knees. She yelped when she hit the ground.

'Jeeesus, Christine! Get off the ground! Why did you fall?'

Christine yelped when she hit the ground, but got back on her feet just as fast, and jumped into the car, flashing a sheepish look over her shoulder.

Christine's mom targeted Molly for her next tirade. 'How dare you corrupt my child! I told you my daughter was not to come anywhere near this house and you brought her here, anyway!'

Mina screamed back, 'Christine told my mom and

I that she had asked you for permission to come here and you said yes. Your daughter lied to you! My mom had nothing to do with this. How dare you!'

'You stay away from Christine!' she screamed back.

The Greenes were left standing in the front door as Christine's car revved and screeched away, leaving nothing but the acrid smell of burning rubber in the air. They followed the headlights up the lane, out of the dale, and onto the main road above where Christine's mom easily broke the speed limit.

They were speechless for a moment before Molly turned to Mina. 'Thanks for backing me up. Her mom's a real psych—'

Mina erupted in her mom's face, *'What's going on?!'*

This started Cora off, untethered bawling as events of the evening caught up with her, just as worried about her mom as whatever else was in the house with them. Where was it now? Under her bed? In the fireplace?

Show over, Emma was already back inside gobbling down Christine's barbecue pizza.

'Okay,' Molly conceded, 'it's time we talked.' She led the girls to the kitchen table which seemed as good a place as any to hold the extraordinary family meeting. 'Now,' Molly cleared her throat, 'I really didn't want you to find out, especially you, Cora.'

Defiantly, Cora asked, 'Why?'

Mina answered for her mom. 'Cora, you know what you're like. The shower curtain freaks you out.'

'It's what's *behind* the shower curtain, Mina.'

'Please, girls, listen. Firstly, I said nothing because I was waiting to see what would happen. Call it morbid curiosity. Everybody in this town is right and wrong. Yes, there is something in the house, but it is not harmful or dangerous in any way. It is a boy. I think this child doesn't know he has passed on and all he's looking for is a little attention like any other child.'

'Mom, it's a ghost.'

'Yes, Mina, but think…Casper.'

'Mom,' Cora pointed out, 'you've finally flipped!'

'For once, I'm with sis on this one. Cora, I'm going back to Dublin. Coming?'

Cora looked about then down at her feet to see if she was wearing shoes for the 240 kilometre walk back to the capital.

Molly intervened. 'Nobody is going anywhere until you hear me out, and then we'll make a decision. Give me that courtesy and I will do you the courtesy of listening.' She paused. 'I want you to take what I'm about to say to you very seriously. My initial plan was to tell you about the young boy who has been living in this house long before us. But, um, now that the cat is out of the bag,' she said with an air of an apology, 'I want to propose an idea — a business plan.'

Mina barked, 'Are you for real?'

'This better be good,' Cora blubbered.

21.

'Just hear me out,' Molly pleaded. 'Let me say my piece, then I'll let you say yours. I didn't want to say anything, but I guess you're old enough. The woman who promised me a job here in Old Castle reneged on her promise.'

'Why?'

'Because I'm not good for her business, Mina. But that was a sign, you see? There's no work here in Old Castle, but there is a free house that is ours if we're willing to put in the hard work.'

'Hard work?' Mina asked. 'Mom, we're not talking about reforming a house here. There's a fucking ghost living in this house!'

'*Languaaage,*' Molly chimed. 'Now, where was I? We need money to keep afloat. We cannot wait for this pandemic to pass. Beggars can't be choosers. We're practically broke.' *And broken…* 'Even if we wanted to move back to Dublin, we couldn't. I've done the maths and unless we slept on Janice's floor.…'

Cora opined, 'Janice wouldn't mind.'

The honesty in Cora's face hurt Molly. 'Um, yes, she would. Maybe one or two nights, but imagine all of us in her little flat with nowhere to go? It would be like getting stuck in a lift with Emma.'

Mina and Cora flinched at that prospect.

'There's nothing to fear. Guys, this is the coolest thing that will ever happen to you in your lives; friends… boyfriends…all of that will come and go, but few people have the pleasure of saying their house is haunted.'

'Pleasure?' Judging by Cora's face, *pleasure* would be the last word she would have chosen to summarise this situation.

'Can you just trust me on this?'

'Mom,' answered Mina, 'we trust you, but it's the thing living in this house with us that we don't trust.'

'Okay, I'm just going to come out and say it: I want to open a haunted house attraction with a genuine ghost. We are taking it to the next level. That's my business plan.'

Cora and Mina looked at each other as if they'd both thought they mistakenly heard the same thing come from their mom's lips.

Molly clarified, 'Nothing cheesy, the real deal.' She concluded by quoting from the bible, 'If you build it, they will come.'

'I prefer Janice's floor.'

'But Mina…' started Molly.

Just then, the kitchen door swung closed by itself.

'A draught,' Molly explained in a nonchalant manner. The situation had become so absurd in the farmhouse, nobody questioned Molly's ludicrous explanation. 'I want to do this for us. We're going to make money, girls. Millions of people across this planet would do anything to see a real ghost. Everyone loves a good ghost story.'

'Everyone loves a good ghost story because it's just a story,' Cora commented.

'True, Clever Cora, but you're going to be famous.

Imagine all your followers on TokTik and Instantgram. You'll be the cool kids.' She was stretching now, and she knew it.

'TikTok and Instagram maybe?'

'Exactly,' she agreed with Mina. 'You're going to be, um, influencers, is that what they call them?' Molly was surprised to see a change in their demeanour. 'You're going to be the voice of the voiceless.' She mulled that over and thought it could be a catchy slogan. After sharing a sneaky glance, their faces brightened up simultaneously. Could it be that Molly's secondhand car sales techniques worked?

Mina wondered, 'Maybe it would be kind of cool?'

Mina's onboard! That means Cora will jump onboard too!

'Maybe…' Cora wasn't giving too much away. She turned to her mom. 'What would we have to do?' Mina was in and Cora knew it.

'Okay, brace yourselves. Here comes my plan of action. As already mentioned, I want to open the farmhouse as a haunted house tour. We will charge groups of people to take tours of the house. That's where I come in: I will be the tour guide, guiding the people through the house, spicing it up with real experiences as we go. Yeah, the icing on the cake would be if the squatter, the boy, would make an appearance. He seems to be more active after six in the evening, so we should plan our tours for that time. He wasn't afraid to play music here tonight and half of Old Castle already knows by now. I'm sure your lying friend, Christine, has already texted dozens of

317

her BFFs and those BFFs will text their BFFs and so on. It has gone viral already, faster than Covid 19.'

Mina's face lit up. 'Now I understand why you didn't beg Christine or psycho mom from hell to say anything. You want them to spread the word.' She couldn't help but laugh at the situation. 'Brilliant.'

'There's no such thing as bad publicity.' Molly winked. 'So, can I count on you guys?'

Cora held back her answer until her older sister answered. 'Mina?'

Mina shrugged. 'I suppose there's no harm in trying and I kind of like the idea of being an influencer. But,' drawing serious, 'I'm going to hold you to that promise, mom. If anything goes wrong, we quit this place without ever looking back.'

Cora, wise beyond her years, inquired, 'What could go wrong?'

Molly wasn't sure if Cora was asking what could go wrong, as in if this went ugly, how ugly would it get? Or just confirming in her lovable ironic way that nothing would go wrong. For the sake of argument and more empty promises, she went with the latter. 'It's a win-win for everyone.'

But it isn't quite everyone, is it?

Mina asked, 'Can't we just be normal?'

'Mina, we are a living experiment. Or better said, we are the guinea pigs.'

From somewhere came Emma's voice. 'I want a guinea pig!'

Cora's eyes lit up. 'An experiment?'

Wiley Mina wasn't falling for it. 'Mom's using

that word to convince you, Cora. Just like she told us that this would be an adventure moving down here. Remember that? This is not an experiment and I'm no guinea pig.'

Oh, how wrong you are, Mina. We're all its squealing little guinea pigs…

Cora looked about her. 'Well, you promised us an adventure, and this is an adventure.'

Molly nodded and smiled. 'Yes, it is, honey.'

'Aagh! I can't even believe we're having this conversation. It's crazy! I need someone else here to tell you how mental all of this sounds! What kind of family are we? Haven't we been through enough? Come to think of it,' Mina was already regretting saying it, but she was on a roll, 'why do we never speak about Henry or Dad?

An uncomfortable silence lulled in the kitchen.

Molly heaved a deep sigh. 'I guess we've just begun.' It almost sounded like an old love song she once knew. Molly had always promised herself she wouldn't cry in front of her children during those agonising hours, days, weeks, months after the accident. It was a sign of weakness and Molly Greene wanted to be that pillar of strength her children would come to lean on. But now she crumbled as something swam up from the deep well of pain and murky sorrow, where all her bottled tears had lain stagnant, and bit her with its needle teeth. She began to cry in front of her children. She hid her face in her hands and bawled the once stagnant stream of tears. *Is this really happening? Nobody said anything about crying…*

Mina did what came naturally to her and held her mom while Cora sidled up next to both. Emma, always looking for the opportunity for a group hug, jumped in and issued an, 'Hooray!'

Molly sniffled laughter through her tears. She wanted to tell her girls she was grieving for something that had happened far too long ago. They would understand why their mom wanted to save the child that walked alone in this farmhouse. Mina and Cora would see their mom wanted to make up for the past of losing their infant brother. But her girls didn't know everything as they held their sobbing mom, who wept for the lies that had been festering inside her for the last couple of years. If they had known that all of them (except Mina and Molly) were in the Volvo that Valentine's night because their mom had been too drunk to drive, would they be so quick to her side? Especially Cora and Emma, who had been in the accident and were lucky to be alive. Molly Greene should be in her grave now — the same grave where she would take her secret. Instead, Mike and Henry were in the ground. They say truth can be a bitter pill to swallow, but lies can be even more of a bitter pill and will fester in the belly. Molly wailed, bringing herself to the point of gagging, as she flushed the demons from her system, these fiendish angels who had haunted her more than anything this possessed house could ever raise.

The moment passed and Molly composed herself. Instead of explaining, she drew up in silence. She hoped her daughters had seen enough and let Lady Intuition whisper to them, telling them their mom was trying to make up for the past, though they would never know how deep it cut.

'I understand, Mom,' said Mina.

Cora shared her sister's opinion. 'Count us in.'

Molly looked up at them from her chair with bloodshot eyes. 'You really mean that?'

For a moment, and they weren't sure why, the sisters paused and shared a cautious glance.

The girls nodded and left the kitchen.

Molly was so relieved. She glanced at the bottle of wine on the counter and longed for just a simple glass of wine, that's all. Surely she deserved it? Her new business plan deserved a toast. She fought the urge and took a slug of the girls' orange juice from the fridge instead. It wasn't the same. As she sipped the bland orange juice, Molly experienced a twinge of guilt for putting her daughters through this. Have they not been through enough in their lives? But she was adamant this was going to pay off; this was for all of them. She toasted to herself and thin air. 'To the haunted house tours…where you are the voice of the voiceless.' She repeated her potential slogan. Louie added a squawk at the end, which took away from the power of her slogan. 'Hmm, might work as a pirate jingle,' Molly suggested. 'Voice of the voiceless? Hmm, maybe a little corny? A little too presidential campaign, perhaps?'

Molly's involvement in cringy haunted house slogans caused her to miss the faint trace of sickly sweet over-ripe citrus come wafting through the kitchen.

Nodding off as that Friday night became early Saturday morning, Molly heard movement in the bedroom. She detected the approach from the soft creak of floorboards. There was no need to turn around; Molly had a pretty good idea what was standing in the middle of her bedroom. No matter how many times this occurred, Molly Greene was convinced she would never be at ease with the presence in the house. Yes, she had got used to him, but what she would never get used to was the phantasm's creeping and lurking about the house, going about his business.

'Mommy?'

Molly clenched on hearing the whisper.

'Mommy, are you awake?'

'Emma?'

Molly reached for her phone on the bedside locker and tapped on the light icon. The mother-of-three was never so relieved to see her sleepy youngest daughter standing there in the doorway with tousled hair and looking as cute as a button in her carousel motif PJ.s.

'Can I sleep with you?'

So elated, Molly had no words just then. She opened her duvet and Emma skipped across the bedroom, then hopped into the bed. Molly held onto her as if it was their last night together. After all, Emma was the other half of Henry's twin. Holding Emma tight enough, Molly often thought she was reaching out to Henry through her. Nonsense, of course. But sometimes, just sometimes…

Her eyes flashed open. A heady odour of mould percolated through the bedroom. Molly's skin bristled in gooseflesh. They weren't alone in the room.

Emma, having sensed something even through the layers of sleep, woke and sat up.

Molly felt that familiar pulse of fear. She followed her four-year-old's line of vision to the corner of the room. Something was crawling over there. A Mexican wave of static electricity zinged through Molly. She was frozen, paraplegic in that very moment. As her eyes adjusted to the light in the bedroom, she could see the smoky apparition of a child sitting on its haunches by the fireplace. He was watching them in the bed. She could make out his silhouette and a vague pale face. He was so still he could have been a frozen glitch on a computer screen.

'Do you want to join us?'

Emma shrunk under the bedclothes. 'Mommy?'

Molly whispered, 'It's okay, sweetie. He's lost. We're only helping him. If you were lost, you would want someone to find you too, wouldn't you, Em?'

Even though Emma was only four years old, Molly could see the child's instinct was telling her something wasn't quite right with the situation, which was confusing her because her mom was assuring her everything was okay.

The child looked different tonight, twisted and humpbacked. He shuffled into life, and shambled across the bedroom in his staggering gait. Again, Molly was struck with the impression he wasn't thinking for himself but being manipulated by a foreign source. He gazed with his milky cataract eyes at Molly in bed, and she was sure she saw toothless, diseased gums. It was as if the child was slowly dying from a terminal illness. He stopped at the bottom of the bed, opaque eyes twitching back and forth between Molly and her youngest daughter, who had hidden her face.

'Don't be shy.' Molly beckoned him. 'We are your family. You're not lost anymore.' She patted the bed. The thing that had come from Molly's fireplace slipped into Molly's bed, filling the bed clothes with an icy waft of mould and citrus and something unidentifiable. Emma couldn't stand the unnerving feeling of being next to it, so Molly pulled her across her midriff and placed her to her left, while her other child slithered to her right. Molly closed her eyes and smiled into the darkness.

22.

Molly Greene would've loved to have a sleep-in that Saturday morning, but single moms rarely have such simple pleasures. And there was nothing simple about it now because Emma was full-on demanding pancakes 'with chocolate syrup.' Molly's lost son had left during the night and Emma had woken with apparently no recollection of their nocturnal bedroom visitor. Last night she felt they'd reached the next stage of rehabilitation for the lonesome soul in the fireplace.

Molly checked her phone on the bedside locker and was surprised and not surprised to see Gerry McAuliffe had left three missed calls and a final voice message. She listened to it.

'Molly, this is Gerry. I need you to call me when you can. I have some info on the house. It only dawned on me after our meeting. You will find this very interesting…and hopefully an eye-opener.' She listened again before deciding Gerry McAuliffe could simmer for a while. It was clear what he was up to. Was Gerry attractive? Maybe in an off-beat way, his rich voice perhaps, but that secret ingredient, not even known to Molly, wasn't there. Maybe he had valid information on the farmhouse, maybe he didn't. Molly didn't care anymore.

'Mom, pancakes?'

'Okay, okay.'

That Saturday afternoon, a messenger called Molly

to tell her he was up at the road gate with the cameras she'd ordered on Amazon. Molly drove up there to meet him and sign for the cameras. The skinhead suggested Molly should have better access to her house. When Molly asked why, the messenger told her, '…the guy in the bungalow with the attitude problem refused to open the gate. "Nobody's allowed down to the farmhouse without permission," is what he told me. What are you hiding down there?' He cackled and lit a cigarette. Molly apologised and made a mental note to speak to Prendergast at a more opportune moment. For now, she was determined to get her cameras installed and working. She wondered if she should ask for Prendergast's permission to install the cameras, but she hastily decided to forego that because this was all part of the 'make the house your home' deal.

Following the instructions, which were well explained for a change, Molly placed the four Bluetooth security cameras at strategic locations around the house: the first in her bedroom in the wall above the window with a view of her bed and the fireplace. The second camera was placed on the second floor with a view of the landing and the stairs leading off to the right. Molly set up the third camera in the kitchen, screwed into the wall just above the message board. But when it came to the fourth camera, Molly admitted she had bought one camera too many, so set up that fourth camera in the front porch with a view of the front yard. Why? For security, of course.

*

While their mum was busy screwing cameras into the walls, Cora had been looking through her mineral collection, studying the crystals up close under her magnifying glass. Every time Cora studied one of her minerals really up close in the magnifying glass, she was looking at a different planet from the view of a rocket ship passing overhead. It was a whole new world right there, in just a couple of centimetres.

It was this unseen world that bugged her. Putting her tools and minerals aside, Cora left her bedroom. At the end of the hallway to her right, she saw her mom attaching a camera high on the wall while talking to herself…or maybe she was talking to the child hiding in the fireplace. It was difficult to tell. She went upstairs to Mina's door and knocked.

'Yeah?' Mina called.

'Can we talk?'

'What about?'

'Mina, can I just come in a minute?'

'Okay.'

Cora found Mina sitting on the bay window, looking out across the front yard and beyond. It wasn't like Mina to be just sitting there without a gadget in her hand. 'What are you looking at?'

'You mean, what am I looking for? Prendergast is out there again.'

Cora joined her sister in the bay window. 'See?' Mina pointed to the far corner of the front yard, where it met the copse of trees. 'I've seen him there twice already today. He comes out from behind the trees and just stands there. He comes down from his place through the field, so he's not seen on the lane. I've seen him come down by the hedge that separates the lane from the field.'

'Creepy.'

In a fit, Mina opened the window and shouted, 'Stop stalking or I'll call the police!'

Prendergast stood there defiantly before turning and disappearing into the woods.

Mina promised her sister she really would call the police.

Cora said, 'I don't think Prendergast is our problem.'

Her sister's answer surprised her. 'What do you mean?'

'I mean our problem is closer to home.'

Mina gazed out through her bay window, wondering what could be closer to home than this?

'It's mom'

Mina didn't answer because what her sister said didn't surprise her. She was wondering why they hadn't spoken about any of this. She had just sort of gone along with it. 'Yeah, mom.'

Cora went on to tell her sister what she'd seen in her mom's bedroom, under the bed. 'Mina, I don't know if it's really a boy like mom says it is.'

Mina looked at her with tears in her eyes.

'The scariest thing was the look on mom's face.'

Mina watched Cora's eyes grow wide and petrified as she remembered and felt the recoiling horror of seeing a stranger in her mom's face.

'She smiled in a really weird way,' Cora said quietly. 'It wasn't her, but it was her, Mina.' She stopped and blinked, something Cora did when she was trying to remember. 'There's something else.'

'Yeah?'

'It was something Mrs Noonan said to me. I kind of forgot it, but it has been bugging me lately. You know that time she interrogated me in front of the class?'

Mina nodded.

'Well, she said something about smoke coming from the chimney. "The day you see smoke coming from those chimneys is the same day you run" …or something like that.'

A horrible sense of foreboding filled Mina. She gazed out through the window, scanned the valley, and up to the Gatehouse's roof and chimney just visible through the treetops. In pensive silence, she took her phone from her back pocket and called the number she should've already called.

*

That Saturday night had been the quietest night at the farmhouse. At least Molly's sleep hadn't been interrupted. Though that didn't necessarily mean the night had been without its complications.

23.

Molly Greene rose at 6.30 on Sunday morning. The night had passed without incident, or so she thought. She had work to do this morning and needed to think in silence before the girls came down and made any kind of productive contemplation a fantasy. If she knew her girls like she thought she knew them, Molly had roughly one hour before Emma came thundering down the stairs, and probably two hours before Cora joined her sister, and only God knew when Mina would decide to show her dopey face.

The cockatoo greeted Molly with his usual "Allo! 'Allo! 'Allo!' And added a, 'Peekaboo, Mommy!' for a little variety. Molly asked Louie to keep his voice down. She needed this hour of dawn tranquillity.

She prepared herself a hot, strong mug of coffee and sat down at the kitchen table. The goal was to come up with some kind of plan for her haunted house attraction tours. She opened a blank Notes page on her MacBook and was about to bullet point some ideas when she remembered the cameras she'd installed. Considering the wonderful sleep she'd had last night, she didn't expect to see much. She minimised her Notes page and clicked the app on her home screen and was surprised to see three of the four cameras had captured movement. A little disconcerting was one of them being from the camera she placed outside on the front porch. Probably a cat or some animal that had wandered in too far from the surrounding woods, not that there were any birds or animals in the trees around the farmhouse. The camera in her bedroom and on the landing by the top of the stairs had also captured movement.

Molly clicked on her bedroom camera first — Camera 1. She was taken aback to see the camera had captured 19 seconds of footage. Growing more exhilarated and a little uneasy by the second, Molly clicked on the recorded material and went to take a gulp of coffee as it loaded…the mug reached her lips, but Molly forgot to open her mouth as she watched a black mass swirl from the fireplace like sooty smoke, pool on the bedroom floor, and gather itself into the form of a little human silhouette. Just like the time before, it hovered to the window and looked out into the night. Then, with unnatural speed which gave Molly a sickening feeling in her stomach, the black shadow person — he — disappeared through the wall next to the open door at exactly 3:04am according to the time logged on Camera 1. The creepiest element to all of this was that it moved with such stealth Molly could hear her deep sleep breathing in the background throughout the clip. Maybe if she had known she was watching a comedy, she might have chuckled to herself on seeing the spirit disappear through the wall next to the open door. But right now, this was anything but a comedy.

She took a moment to process what she'd just witnessed and swilled down a large reassuring gulp of her warm beverage, never so grateful for something so normal as hot coffee. It was beginning to look as if her cameras were going to pay for themselves. This footage was gold, and she knew it. These nineteen seconds of footage guaranteed queues at her door!

Zinging with electricity, Molly Greene screeched a little yelp of joy, jumped up, and jigged around the kitchen table. Louie, the cockatoo, showed his appreciation by fanning his yellow headpiece. She had the evidence to prove to the world that her house was haunted and she had the evidence to prove to the local do-gooders that the presence wasn't malicious in any way, but the trapped soul of a child living an eternal loop: comes from the fireplace *(sorry, Mrs. Noonan, I mean lair)* ...looks out her bedroom window for some obscure reason...then goes for a nocturnal walkabout around the farmhouse. Where's the harm in that? Yes, he occasionally slipped into bed beside her and called her Mommy or Mama. But again, where's the danger in that? It's a beautiful symbiosis, if anything. Not for everyone, granted, but a miraculous union between the living and the dead. The cherry on the cake: She was making up for past misgivings.

Molly went to the kitchen window above the sink and peered out at her backyard to gain some perspective on what she'd just seen on her screen, just making sure it was still the same foggy Sunday morning she'd got up to just a few minutes ago.

Drawing a deep breath, Molly sat back down to click on the landing camera — Camera 2 — to view the recording. This clip was even shorter, only six seconds. At 3:05am the same apparition appeared in the hallway as it came from the opposite side of

Molly's bedroom wall it had just come through. The view was grainy as the second-floor landing was in more darkness than her bedroom had been. It had floated towards the camera and passed below the lens. Out of curiosity, Molly had googled different types of hauntings. On the one hand, it seemed to be a residual haunting with a specific behavioural pattern that Molly had witnessed on two different occasions. Like a recording, the squatter played the same events over and over again, oblivious to any audience. But that didn't explain the other occurrences. The rest of the ghostly behaviour fell under the category of an intelligent haunting. Molly had accumulated several experiences to support this. There were two other categories of haunting were poltergeist and demonic. Thankfully, she didn't have to go there, not yet, at least.

The lens on Camera 2 captured a brilliant view of his face, semi-translucent in the darkness, but (and this gave Molly the chills) there was something not right with the face of the child as it drew closer to the camera. Molly's jaw dropped as she slowed down the replay speed. She scrutinised the screen and recoiled back in horror to see when the ghostly presence aged as it proceeded along the landing towards the camera. From the freshness of youth to the twisted features of a small, crooked old man with something wicked in his distorted face to something else entirely. It was this phase, the third phase, which shook her. Immediate prickles formed on her flesh as she watched how his eyes and how they rolled back in their sockets while it loomed closer to the camera placed high in the alcove at the top of the staircase. Thos eyes changed from the beady eyes of childhood…to the sickly and opaque of the elderly… to no more than black cracked gaps in his hideous face, made even creepier by his crouching shambling gait. She watched the convulsive workings of his face with hypnotic fascination.

By the time the apparition turned left at the top of the staircase and disappeared, the face had become something mouldy and deformed. Molly could swear a snout began to protrude from his face before it or he turned stage right and off-camera. In that stretch of landing, it had aged from a child of four or five to an old man nearing death and then, well, Molly didn't have words to describe the final phase, except a flitting notion that phase three was a level no living mortal should have to see. Molly felt a dart of raw repulsion when she realised she'd been lying in bed next to that. In what phase had it cuddled up to her? Oh, dear Jesus, she shuddered to think.

Molly's phone vibrated, startling her out of her enthralled state. It was Gerry McAuliffe on the other end of the line. 'Christ, take a hint.' Briefly questioning how far men were behind women in Darwin's theory of evolution, Molly set her eyes back on her MacBook screen. 'Fuck,' she uttered as she gazed at the screen. A six-second nightmare was captured in that camera lens. If Mina or Cora, no matter how brave or open-minded they took themselves for, happened to ever come across this footage, they would run screaming from the farmhouse. And they'd be right; any normal human being, child or adult, would run screaming. Molly Greene, herself a broken soul, felt the repulsion like any normal adult would, but the abnormality was the deep melancholy she felt for him. Why? Molly had experienced death in life and now she was experiencing life in death. Somewhere along the way, the two had become confused and fused. In a nightmarish, endearing way, Molly Greene was coming full circle. Life and death were a natural thing, only she'd just seen it revved up into six seconds.

Having gathered her wits, Molly clicked on Camera 4's findings. If the previous two clips had given Molly the shivers, then the third piece of footage gave her cause for concern. She pressed play and was instantly greeted by the camera's view of her front yard at night, though not in complete darkness as the front light illuminated the yard. Someone was standing in the yard, just beyond the reach of the front porch light, staring at the house. It wasn't the fact that a stranger was standing in her front yard that scared her; it was the fact that she knew the stranger standing in the yard. She recognised that distinctive ankle-length black raincoat. He had been wearing the same coat the night they had turned up at his door.

'Prendergast, what the f…?'

That notion put the fear of God in Molly, which shadowed anything else caught on the cameras. What was he doing out there? Mina had told her she'd seen

Prendergast spying on the house from the lane, but Molly hadn't paid much attention to her because Mina had a propensity for exaggeration and imagination with it. Not for the first time, Molly thought about the road gate. When she'd moved in, she kind of liked the idea of having a dragon at the gate. She felt protected from the outside. But now she wanted to be protected from the inside. Come to think of it, hadn't Janice mentioned something about that on the fateful day when Molly met the house and the house, and its occupant met Molly and her beautiful family? Probably. Had Molly listened? No.

For the first time since she'd moved to the farmhouse, Molly felt vulnerable. It was what was outside the house rather than what was inside it that posed the threat.

'That's it, no more stalking.' She'd call him and nip this in the bud. He couldn't come and go as he pleased just because they both lived behind the same goddamn gate. But it wasn't only that. Prendergast was waiting for something, but what?

But for now, Molly had other things on her mind, like creating a YouTube channel and some other social media channels where her footage would speak for itself…and more importantly, speak for her. She didn't know much about social media, but the girls could give her a hand if she needed guidance. Her restaurant was only used to take bookings and not promotions. The key to her success would require an online presence. That was key right now. She clicked on the YouTube app. Before she knew it, Molly was a

YouTube Creator, filling in the card to tell the world about the squatter boy living with her and her family.

Hi, my name is Molly Greene, mom-of-three. I live in a HAUNTED 200-year-old farmhouse. This is the real thing, guys, not some cheesy smoke n' mirrors attraction park prop. My family and I are being haunted by the ghost of an inquisitive young boy looking for a little love in a cold and sterile world…

The ghost's black-eyed dissolving face sailed by her mind's eye…

…who loves to come out and play when the sun goes down. He's known as The Squatter. I can guarantee you will see and hear ghostly phenomena. Check out my YouTube Channel here where I'll be uploading actual footage. I'm opening the farmhouse to the public for ghost tours on the…

'Shit, wait…' Molly looked at her phone calendar to decide on the all-important grand opening date. She wasn't even sure if anyone would turn up. The inauguration would be on Valentine's night, one week from now — a bitter-sweet night for Molly, and she did everything in her power to stop the welling tears. She was coming full circle, indeed. It felt right to Molly. She wasn't sure if one week was too far away or too soon, but it would give her time to form an even stronger bond with the spirit of the farmhouse.

She typed:

Valentine's Night, 14th February!

She added a red heart followed by a menacing skull and crossbones for a little spice.

As she clicked on her MacBook's keyboard, Molly experienced a moment of insecurity. Was she was doing the right thing? She needed a good old-fashioned heart-to-heart with her friend, Janice. Though she already knew what Janice would say. She'd neglected her friend over the last couple of days, hadn't answered any of her calls or texts. Life had been overlooked in her pursuit of the afterlife.

Instead of thinking, Molly started doing. She took her phone and wrote Janice a text:

Love you, Jan. Thanks for always being there…

She paused before pressing Send, but now it was all about carpe diem.

She re-read her letter of introduction on her YouTube channel. It was missing one important detail: her address. She was about to type her address when, on second thoughts, maybe it was best-left blank for now. Uninvited guests were undesirable — she had enough of those. Well, they weren't all uninvited…

Complete Address provided in two weeks from

now before tours commence. Suffice to say that the house is located in a secluded area in the southwest of the country.

Molly giggled to herself as she added…

Gimme a like and smash that subscribe button for the latest spooky content!

She'd heard that closing line enough times on her girls' YouTube stuff. Molly read over everything. The tone seemed a tad light-hearted, playful, even tawdry? This was serious shit, not Disneyland. But she was aware most people were naturally afraid of anything related to contact from the other side, so best to keep a cheery spin on things. A yearning crept into her mind to let the world know in her letter of introduction how her husband and son had been taken in a car accident, but that could come across as looking for a sympathy vote. And, more importantly, knowing Molly's tragic past might cast some doubt on the validity of her claims.

She needed to put an admission fee. The round figure of twenty euros sounded liked a good idea, and returning 50 percent of the admission fee if no activity presented itself would be a good addition, if a little risqué. She fleetingly pondered whether she should refund all the money, but that was a fool's game. After all, people would be traipsing in and out of her house, taking up her time and space. That counted for something. She wasn't going to lose money on this venture. No, fifty percent was fair, she thought. The key to this was presenting her evidence, showing ghost hunters that there is something in the house and not just one big hoax. And she would make it clear before punters crossed her threshold that there were no guarantees (but 10 euros in her pocket was guaranteed). It was piling the pressure onto her, but she was showing the world she had nothing to hide. She might have another look at those prices once it was rolling.

20€ admission fee. 50% will be returned if no phenomena is witnessed or experienced.

How about pegging on another 50 euro if her child played 'Old McDonald had a Farm' on the kalimba? That thought caused her to break down in peals of laughter.

Molly then transferred all the media she had on her phone and from the cameras to her channel… everything except the clip showing the child transforming into something ugly. Molly quickly learned to edit this on free software she downloaded to her MacBook. She then uploaded the edited version to her YouTube channel, showing brief footage of the squatter in its child form floating along the landing. Why didn't she upload the original version? Because what she witnessed would stop a lot of people from coming. But everyone loves a friendly ghost. Maybe Molly should market her child as Casper-like figure?

She decided to forget she had ever seen the child's dark side. Every child hides things from their parents. It was natural; that's what kids do.

After a hearty fry-up breakfast, the Greenes went for a Sunday stroll around the eight acres of land surrounding the farmhouse. As they walked, Molly reflected on how her life had changed so much in such little time. Now and again, she would cast a glance over her shoulder. Who was she expecting to see? She wasn't sure, but she couldn't lose that ominous feeling of being watched.

Cora said in passing, 'How come there are no birds around here? There are billions of trees, but I haven't seen one bird.'

As they returned home (and yes, the house was becoming their home), sleet began to fall, coating everything in a light white blanket of slush. This jogged Molly's memory. Cora had found footprints in the snow on their first outing of the countryside around the farmhouse. She'd dismissed the tracks while Mina insisted the footprints belonged to their favourite neighbour, Richard Prendergast. Mina had been right, not that Molly would ever admit it to her girls…or herself: Richard Prendergast was stalking them and had been shadowing them since the first moment they moved into the infamous farmhouse.

When the Greenes got back to the farmhouse around midday, the girls went about their business while Molly made an Italian lunch, though she could never remember its name. Once, maybe twice, she

341

sneaked a peek at that eternal bottle of wine on the counter. It was a sin to see wine of that calibre collecting dust. Was that a good or a bad sign? She wasn't sure. A thought from her old life popped into view about how she loved a tipple, or two or three, while cooking a Sunday roast, waltzing music playing in the background.

Lunch simmered while Molly checked her YouTube channel to see if her videos had any views yet.

'Jesus Christ Almighty and all the saints…' Molly sat back in her chair. The phone videos had notched up over 50,000 views each and her surveillance camera footage had garnered over 200,000 views and climbing…climbing… Not only that, but she'd gained an incredible 23,757 new subscribers and 21,569 likes and 1330 dislikes. Molly couldn't believe the rising numbers as she stared disbelievingly at her MacBook screen. Just from the thumbs up and thumbs down alone, Molly guessed she was winning, but not without her enemies. She began to flick through the hundreds of commenters, mainly supportive, commented on her bravery more than anything else, which was a little disconcerting. But there was also a fair share of wet blankets, haters, even online bully-trolls or whatever they call them nowadays, choosing to target Molly's children as their line of protest. Some of the comments were quite hateful, labelling Molly: '…an abusive mother…' for having her children '…in that poisoned environment.' Or simply: 'You're f'n crazy,' which Molly happened to agree with, although she knew they meant not-in-a-good-way crazy, as in disturbed. Molly wasn't fazed. She'd been expecting this and was mentally ready for such a backlash. Nothing…*nothing*…was going to get between her and her dream house. Not only was this a free house, but it was also the house that would secure college fees for her daughters.

But what irritated Molly Greene was those trolls declaring: 'Hoax!' to every video. This was something Molly hadn't foreseen. Getting defensive, she fought back, responding feverishly to all those comments insisting her videos were 'fake' and 'photoshopped' until her fingers knotted into numb claws. 'Bastards!' she yelled at her screen. 'How dare you insult my child!'

'Mom!' Mina called from somewhere upstairs. 'Are you okay?'

Oops, maybe a tad too enthusiastic with her protest. 'Yes! Dandy, Mina, just dandy.'

'Okay.' Another second or two went by before Mina howled: 'Moooom!'

Constantly on standby these days, Molly screamed back, 'What's wrong?' Her daughter could yell anything back right now and Molly would just take it on board and deal with it.

That's the frame of mind Molly Greene was in during those final days at the farmhouse; on edge… waiting for something to happen…increasingly unsure what was real and what wasn't…alienation from her children and herself…happy and in love…

Mina appeared in the kitchen with a shocked

expression. 'Mom, we're blowing up!!'

'Jesus! What?' Molly scanned the kitchen for the explosion. 'Where??'

'Online! We're going viral, Mooom!'

'Christ, Mina! Don't do that to me! Viral? The whole world has gone viral.'

'Christ, mom, I'm not talking about Covid! You created a YouTube channel? Why didn't you tell us?'

'Forgot.' Molly had and hadn't forgotten. 'No big deal.'

'No big deal? My friends in Dublin — oh, they're talking to me again, by the way — just sent me this on Instagram.' Mina played the videos of their own farmhouse and them sleeping.

It was only looking at the video from this perspective that Molly considered it to be a real invasion of privacy for her children. 'Um…' That horrible sinking feeling was fluttering inside her as Molly realised the video showing her sleeping daughters was, perhaps, crossing the line, when Mina interrupted…

'We can monetise this!' Mina interrupted Molly's train of concerns.

'What?' *So, this isn't about the world watching my sleeping daughters?* In Molly's innocence, she assumed YouTube content creators were creating content out of pure interest and enjoyment. She never realised they were being *paid* to do it.

'We can generate revenue each time someone watches one of your — our — videos.'

Oh, talk about a turn-up for the books. She was

chuffed on hearing how her daughter had changed to "our" instead of "your". But Molly didn't really grasp what Mina was talking about. 'I don't get what you mean about monetising?'

'We need to set up Instagram and TikTok accounts, so we have multiple income streams. I can do that for you. We'll upload the same stuff across the three platforms — a triangle of victory, Mom!'

'Wow, Mina, I am impressed with your business acumen.'

Mina smiled with a proud grin. 'Y'know, I think I want to study marketing at college.'

On any other day, Molly would've smiled a rictus grin while contemplating her dwindling finances and the college fees, but it was starting to look like the Greene clan had a bright future. The trick was to not look too far into that future.

A single powerful knock resounded around the kitchen and Molly and Mina turned to the kitchen doorway, or rather the door itself. Molly had heard that single knock before and it unsettled her then, as it did now. It's not that her child was looking for attention, but it was how he went about it, always creeping up on them. The first knock had caught them by surprise and left them with gormless expressions, trying to figure out what had just happened. But, already on her nerves, Mina winced, dropped her phone, and screamed on the second louder knock. The kitchen door opened and shoved back to the kitchen wall. The two knocks had come from the wrong side of the door, behind it, somewhere in the few inches

345

between the door and the wall.

'Relax,' Molly told Mina, 'he's looking for our attention, that's all.'

'You keep saying that.'

Molly's eerie smile came about her face, the same one noticed by Cora when the child, or whatever it wanted to be seen as, took a hold of her mom's leg from under her bed. Anyone in their right mind wouldn't be here. What was happening?

Cora and Emma came to the kitchen. 'What was that bang?' Cora asked.

Molly sized up the situation. 'Girls, I think it's time I formally introduced you to our squatter — your soul brother. This evening, we are all going to sit down and summon the entity.'

Mina asked with incredulity, '"Summon the entity?" I think you've been watching too many seances on YouTube.'

'Mom, do you think it likes it when you call it a squatter?'

Molly was a little taken aback by Cora's question. 'Well, honey, that's what he is.' And rather innocently, she reamed off what she'd read as the definition of squatter in the dictionary. 'A squatter is a person who unlawfully occupies an uninhabited building or unused land.'

Cora scowled. 'It has always lived here, Mom. It was here before we were. So, aren't we the squatters?'

Molly thought about that and flushed crimson as it dawned on her that her 10-year-old was right. *From the mouths of babes,* thought Molly. 'Anyway, it's all just a technicality,' she brushed it off. 'If we're going to be sharing a house together, we need to meet the child who walks alone at this farmhouse. He wants to be part of this family and we should formally introduce him into our circle.' Molly looked out the window at the encroaching twilight. 'Family meeting, six o'clock sharp.'

Even though the girls had agreed to go along with their mom's absurd business scheme, her behaviour was worrying. If asked, they wouldn't be able to pinpoint the moment when they had begun to see a change in their mom. It had just kind of happened.

'Now, in the meantime, please tidy your bedrooms.'

The girls went off and got on with their own chores, trying to hold on to any semblance of normality while the situation was anything but normal.

Molly decided it was high time she called Prendergast. She called his number, but he didn't answer…or wouldn't answer.

Normality, as the Greene family knew it, ceased forever when the wall clock in the kitchen chimed six electronic bells…

24.

'Spirit, come!' Molly summoned the presence in the house. 'Come, child. Join us.'

At a 6.01 that Sunday evening, the Greene family (technically, not all of them present yet) sat down together in the playroom for an extraordinary family meeting that was about to change their lives forever. Not once did the matriarch sense she was using her children. They sat on the old Chesterfield, Molly in the middle while Cora and Mina sitting tensed and upright on either side of her. Emma sat in the beanbag with Creepy Baby. It was the most awkward family meeting of the century.

Molly asked for silence. Of course, the moment she asked for this, Emma began to snicker, which set off Cora, and even Mina was finding it hard to keep a straight face despite circumstances. The sombre occasion broke down into a wild giggle-fest…that dissipated when something woke upstairs. A muffled shuffling came from the ceiling above their heads.

Emma freaked and flailed around in the beanbag before pulling herself out of it and running to her mom. She squeezed Creepy Baby in her arms.

Meanwhile, Cora was admonishing herself for not having realised she was sharing her house with a ghost. 'I thought I was observant,' she said to nobody and everybody.

'You are,' Molly assured her. 'Ever get that feeling you see something from the corner of your eyes? It isn't just your imagination, Cora.'

Cora stiffened, sombre and chilled. She looked at Mina, who was shaking her head in disbelief.

'Or heard something, but you dismissed it?' Molly went on.

Cora clammed up in dread of what they were about to witness. Mina could see this and discreetly gestured to her mom to tone it down a little. Cora was very sensitive, and Molly knew this more than anyone, but for some reason, she seemed to have forgotten everything in her quest for the fourth child in the house. Mina's eyes stayed on her mom, studying her, studying her like she was trying to figure out who this woman sitting next to her was…

A keen silence came down around them, as if the whole house had suddenly tensed up and was holding its tired old breath. On cue, the whole family, even Emma, started and turned towards the doorway leading to the hallway. For Molly, the most terrifying was the expression on her children's faces. Emma giggled nervously, cracking in the tense moment, but she sobered again when she saw the bug-eyed panic etched in her sisters' faces.

'Mom?' whimpered Cora. 'What's happening?'

'Relaaax,' Molly whispered. 'Don't forget that he's been living with us since we got here. We were just too busy to notice him.'

The stairs creaked as, one by one, the child who walked alone descended each step. On any other evening, the squeaks on the stairs could be dismissed as the house settling for the evening, but the creaks were too pronounced and furtively deliberate.

Mina was beginning to panic. 'It's coming.' She struggled to keep her breathing under control. Molly put an arm around her and reassured her everything was going to be just fine. 'Don't bother him and he won't bother us, remember that.'

By default, Cora said, 'The wasp.'

Molly nodded, impressed her daughter had been listening.

'I can't do this! I can't do this!' whined Mina. In the freezing heat of the moment, hairline fractures appeared in her tough facade. 'Mom, what happens if we do bother it?'

'We get stung.' Cora's chilling pearls of wisdom weren't reassuring to anyone, especially Molly, who was doing her utmost to keep the brave side out. What if it did sting? She hadn't even thought about that in her hurry to get her children acquainted with their long-lost brother…

That familiar smell of antique mouldy citrus and cloves came wafting into the playroom, and with it, icy electricity that raised everyone's body hairs. A silent shadow figure came through the doorway, hovering around them, sending chills through them. At the same time, Louie began to squawk in the kitchen. They huddled up to each other as the shadow, without its owner, came right up behind Molly. The children gawped in morbid fascination as their mom's blonde hair was lifted from the nape of her neck, then magically cascaded down, almost like in a TV advert but with no hands to play with the lustrous, wavy hair.

Molly couldn't move. From a distance, yet right next to them, they all clearly heard, 'Mama? Mama?'

Molly turned to the vision of the child. 'These are my daughters. This is Mina.' Then gesturing to her right, 'Emma, and that's Cora.'

Someone's phone rang, which sounded strangely absurd in the moment. The ringing was coming from Mina's pocket. She slipped the phone from her jeans when her mom instantaneously boomed at her, 'Don't you dare ruin this moment! You can call your little buddies any other time, but not now, Mina, not now. Now is us time.'

Mina just had time to see who the caller was before putting the phone back in her pocket and letting it ring out or suffer her mom's wrath.

Cora whispered, 'I'm dizzy.'

Mina squeezed her nose as the overpowering stench of rotten citrus clung thick in the air; the aroma of mould thick enough to clog in their throats.

Cora looked ghastly pale. 'The room's spinning… I'm going to be sick.'

Molly, numb with emotion on many levels, also felt that same light-headed nausea. With difficulty, she explained in hushed tones, 'This queasy feeling and dizziness is a common side effect of being in proximity to a spirit drawing on the energy of the living to manifest. Immortals are at their strongest when in the vicinity of mortals.'

Not for the first time, Cora and Mina stared at their mom, wondering what this mom had done with their real mom.

Mina froze when she felt the soft strokes of the child preen her hair. She whispered, 'O.M.F.G, this is so creeeeepy! It's touching my hair' from the corner of her mouth. Her phone kept ringing. She let out a cry when her hair was tugged, pulling her head backwards so far, she caught a glimpse of the back wall behind her. 'Ow, my neck!'

'No!' snapped Molly. 'Behave!' She spoke to the spirit like she would a misbehaving dog. 'Don't worry, Mina. It's been many years since it was around people and he has forgotten how to behave.'

These creepy almighty words coming from her own mom's lips frightened the living daylights out of Mina and she said as much.

The black swirling mass left Mina and spiralled towards Cora who went numb as it came sniffing around her.

Cora came in with, 'I'm cold, Mom.'

'Me too. It comes with the territory, Cora. Let him get to know you.' Again, she spoke as if the thing with them was a dog or something.

The presence seemed to grow in size, looming large and dwarfing Cora on the sofa. It grew a snout and opened its jaws in Cora's face. She flinched as she got a mouthful of stench. Her hand slapped her mouth, then she gagged, wretched, and spewed a string of vomit that she tried to catch in her hands.

'Boy, no nonsense! Keep calm, everyone, keep calm. Cora, wipe your face.'

Mina saw this as a chance. She slipped her phone out of her pocket and saw the missed call and the text, which she read while her mom looked on at the apparition with unhealthy glee.

I'm at the road gate, but Prendergast won't let me through! He knows me! We met that first day we came to see the house.

Mina sighed with relief, ecstatic Janice was just a minute or two away, but a world away at the same time. She couldn't understand what was happening. Why wasn't *Bendergast* letting Janice through the gate?

The monster (and it was useless calling it anything else now) turned on little Emma just as Molly was speaking and levitated the screaming child ten feet into the air.

Molly commanded, 'Stop playing with her! Put her down.'

The child was launched through the air and landed in a sitting position in the beanbag, still holding onto Creepy Baby with a look of stupefaction on her face.

Molly swore and jumped to the child, sweeping her up in her arms to hug her. She turned on him. 'This is NOT how we treat our own!'

The metamorphosing shadow mutated into a boy, blurred and translucent. It was difficult to focus on the child even here, beside them. It looked as if he had been photoshopped. The entity didn't look at them but through them, as if gazing at them through frosted glass. He was seeing them from another dimension. The inquisitive, stony-faced child wraith sniffed at the Greene family, individually looking them over, but seemed most taken with Emma. It was the first time Molly got a good look at the child who walked alone at the farmhouse. The ethereal creature had enormous ears, out of proportion with his head, yet the apparition was merely a puny waif.

The phantom extended his pale hand and tried to hold Emma's free hand, but Emma flinched on contact. The child spirit recoiled as if he had just been burnt.

'Stay calm,' whispered Molly, her breath fogging out in front of her now. 'Stay calm for the love of Christ.' Molly was reassuring herself more than her children. 'The worst thing you can do now is agitate him.'

Mina screamed, 'Stop this! It's mental! What's wrong with us!?'

A round of gasps filled the playroom when the spirit child slinked itself between Mina and Molly, to hug Molly's midriff, wedging Mina out. The icy embrace had a numbing effect from her waist down. The last time Molly felt anything close to this was when she'd had the epidural for Cora's caesarean birth. Cora, such a sensitive soul, had been defiant about touching down in this cold, harsh world, and who could blame her?

Mina began to sob, not because it was hugging her mom, but how it had shunted her aside to get to her mom.

Seeing Mina break down set Cora off. Warm, salty tears streaked down their hot cheeks as they bawled in silence, looking as if they didn't want to draw attention to themselves.

In a fit of blind rage, Mina took her phone from her pocket and called Janice's number.

'Who are you calling?'

'What do you care? This is all about you, Mom! You don't care how we feel!'

'Don't make me ask you again!' warned Molly.

'Janice! I'm calling Janice!'

'Who?' Molly screwed up her face in confusion, recognising the name from a different lifetime. 'Why do you want her?'

'I miss her...'

Molly was suspicious. 'You can call her later. Have a little respect for our guest. Mina, take a selfie,' she suggested.

'A selfie with the ghost?'

'Can you do it? I don't have my phone...I'm filming this.' Molly gestured to the single wall shelf. The girls hadn't seen their mother's phone filming them.

Later, looking back over what she captured, the footage would remind Molly of an entire family, yes, all four of them, who had fallen over the barrier into a silverback gorilla's zoo enclosure. It was just seconds before the enormous and curious primate came sniffing around them.

Cursing Janice for not picking up, Mina hung up and raised her phone in front of all of them, including the apparition. Shaking so badly, she had to steady her right hand with her left. They all fit into her camera lens, but her phone wouldn't focus on the squatter sitting between them. Seeing her little sister Emma's terrified grin for the selfie broke her heart.

'This is going to get our social media the attention it deserves…viral, that's where we're going, girls. We'll call it Selfie with a Ghost.'

The others didn't know whether to laugh or cry.

'Say shriek!' joked Molly, flashing a tepid smile for the picture.

Mina took the picture and glanced at the photo, which captured an overexposed hazy mass, or rather mess, sitting next to the Greenes, all with fearful grins. Strangely, it was Molly who looked the most terror-stricken of all of them. It was as if Mina caught a glimpse of her real mom in the selfie.

Then, just as quickly as it had materialised, it left their side, glided through the playroom door and down the hallway, then turned into the living room. The Greenes followed the spirit and watched it recede down into the belly of the stone fireplace. A wave of depression came rolling in as the child floated away…

They stood there in dumb silence. Five minutes went by before Cora took the initiative to speak. 'Even though I'm terrified and this feels all wrong, I'm never going to forget this moment. I just know it.'

Stunned, Mina, and even Molly, nodded in unison. Mina had even forgot about Janice as the enormity of what they'd all just witnessed consumed her.

'None of us are going to forget this beautifully disturbing…life-changing moment,' Molly attested, 'when we shared a connection with a being from the other side.'

Molly Greene's daughters would hold on to this through the dark days ahead, remembering what had been, and wondering where it had all gone wrong. No, they knew where everything had begun to unravel — it was the moment they had moved into the farmhouse.

Mina picked up her phone and saw Janice hadn't returned her call. She looked at the selfie a little closer. 'Fucking hell!'

'Mina, language.'

'The selfie.'

They looked at the image on Mina's phone.

He was sitting between them, like a member of the family. The child's face was distorted, motion blur distortion. But on closer inspection, the child's face was horrifically scarred, burnt, a boy tragically disfigured.

Cora whined, 'What happened to his face?' Mina and Molly were taken aback when they saw tears come to Cora's eyes. Her lip jittered. 'I feel sorry for him. He looks sad.'

The fact that the ghost graduated from 'it' to 'him' didn't go amiss on Molly. It came as a surprise to know it was Cora who was trying to make the ghost more identifiable by giving it a gender.

'He looks like the weedy kid who is bullied in the schoolyard…' observed Mina.

Cora nodded. Mina was right. The child — what was left of the child — had a face that was a magnet for bullies. 'And those ears don't help him.' Yet, they had all witnessed how it grew in stature and played with Emma as she would play with Creepy Baby.

Molly had zoned out. She wasn't listening anymore. Her mind was in a bedroom that looked too much like her own, but with very different decoration. A woman in period costume, perhaps Victorian, and roughly her own age, entered the bedroom and locked the door behind her. Without notice, she launched herself towards the bed, at Molly, and propelled a merciless beating on the one whose eyes Molly was looking through. Molly wasn't privy to the identity of the person receiving the blows, but it was as if she was receiving the terrifying beating and, in an odd way, felt she needed to feel the pain of those punches. The hatred in the woman's bulging eyes drilled through her as she trounced the mystery camera person. The picture in her mind's eye was silent, and that made the spectacle even worse. As with her daughters before her, Molly could do nothing but look on in horror as she was beaten senseless through the eye of the beholder…

Molly's phone rang, sounding weird and comforting all at once. Molly wasn't in the mood to entertain just now, but felt she had to answer — it was Janice, after all. 'Hi Janice.'

Janice didn't answer. Molly only heard laboured panting on the other end of the line. She could also hear a man yelling in the background and Janice screaming back.

'Janice?'

358

'Molly, call off your goon!'

'What are you talking about?'

'I was parked up at the front gate, but this creep wouldn't let me go through the gate, so I climbed over the gate, but he headed me off at the pass as they say in the Westerns and he's hunting me off his land. Please come and let me through. Mina told me you have a key for the gate.'

Molly looked across at Mina. 'Oh, she told you that, did she? Mina's been a busy little girl, hasn't she?' Throwing thunderous stares at her daughter now. 'Why are you here, Jan?'

'Mina told me she's worried about you.'

'Jan, let's be honest. You only came down to Old Castle to check up on the girls. Take my word for it: they're fine. We've just had a beautiful family experience here at the house. We're in the middle of something unbelievably complex — an experiment — and we need our time and space to complete it.'

'I don't know what you're talking about.'

'Exactly, so please, go home. I'll call you if we need a babysitter.'

'But, Molly, I—'

Molly hung up and confronted her eldest daughter. 'What have you been saying to Janice?'

'Nothing.'

'Bullshit, Mina. Spill the beans!'

'I just told her we — Cora and I — are worried about you.'

Molly turned her angry gaze on Cora. 'Is this true?'

Cora nodded in that meek way of hers. 'We don't like the farmhouse. There's something horrible here, but you see something else.'

'I see a lonely child looking for a suitable family. That's what's horrible. If ever there was a family, then it's us — the broken Greenes.'

Mina and Cora looked confused.

'Mom,' Mina ventured, 'you think you can save the lost child in this house to make up for Henry. Just admit it. Your confused brain has come up with this motive. You've made connections where there aren't any.'

Molly squinted at her eldest daughter as if she'd just grown a second head. 'How dare you! Can a woman not just act out of kindness without thinking of herself? I'm trying to do something very special here, girls. You don't see it now, but you will when you're older and you're going to thank me for being part of the experiment where you were once a guinea pig.' Molly Greene found herself staring at Emma, waiting for her daughter to tell her she wanted a guinea pig, but Emma just looked at her in a way that unnerved her.

Cora added, 'Okay, so maybe Mina's wrong, but you're still not yourself lately. We don't feel safe here, mom. I was puking a few minutes ago and you didn't care. What's it going to take for you to see whatever's in this house isn't one of us?'

Mina added. 'It wants something, but I'm not sure what that is. It acts differently around us, the girls, I mean. You saw it with your own two eyes in the

360

playroom, how it pulled on my hair, flung Emma across the room, and…'

'And opened its jaws in my face!' finished Cora. 'And it had real bad breath!'

'It was growing a snout, mom!' Mina protested. 'The child you so lovingly speak of was growing a full-on wolf—'

Molly snapped, 'Gimme your phone.'

'What?'

'You heard me, Mina. Hand it over.'

'Why?'

'I don't trust you.'

Mina didn't budge.

'Hand over the phone before we really have an issue in this house.'

As Mina handed over her phone to her mom, she looked at it as if she'd just signed her life away.

Molly tramped to the kitchen.

The girls didn't know what that sudden commotion coming from the kitchen was, making a God almighty racket. Yes, it was the screaming whirr of a blender, but whatever had been thrown into the appliance didn't sound like anything the girls had ever heard before. Mina sprinted into the kitchen. Horror, more intense than when she saw the squatter for the first time, grew on her face. She pushed her mom aside to see her phone revolving into a thousand tiny pieces.

'What have you done, you bitch?' Mina screamed, her head in her hands. 'That was my phone! I hate you!'

Molly gestured to her ears. 'I can't hear you, sweetie.' Then she pointed to the blender with a 'Tut, tut,' as if the blender had made the executive decision of allowing its blades to chew down on Mina's phone. She switched off the blender and poured the contents into the bin. 'Ah, doesn't that feel better, hmm?' Molly breathed a long sigh of relief.

'No, it doesn't!' Mina yelled back.

Cora stood there in amazed silence. Emma looked to Creepy Baby for guidance.

Molly shoved the rubbish bin back under the sink. 'Mina, you don't need it. You only think you need it. Life will be much more fulfilling if you're not a slave to this. This is, excuse me, was nothing more than a pair of handcuffs.'

'I…hate…you!' Mina bawled before running upstairs.

Molly considered her other two children standing there, mouths agape. She winked. 'She'll thank me in the future.'

25.

That Sunday night, when the girls finally went off to sleep, Molly went to bed. She lay there, awake, staring at the ceiling, wondering if she was doing the right thing. Had she crossed the line? She was putting her girls through a lot, first the move, and now this. But what was this, exactly? The whole thing was as surreal as finding her little Henry's toys in hidden corners during the days and weeks after he had left them, a dagger to the heart every time.

As she stared at the ceiling, a growing black mass appeared in the blank spot where she was gazing. At first, she thought it was an optical illusion of the light coming from the hallway, but it spread larger across the ceiling until the whole ceiling was a black stain opening out above her. It was another silent film, so clear Molly was expecting the credits to roll on that ebony background. She was back in the same bedroom as before — the same room where she was lying in bed right now — staring up at the ceiling like some twisted version of the IMAX theatre with stereo surround silence, which made her viewing a more horrific experience. The same woman, dressed in period costume (only it wasn't a costume), was standing by the open fireplace where a log fire was burning. Molly thought the image looked cosy and homey. But on second glance, she noticed the fire poker resting in the flames. The woman took the poker from the fireplace and turned on Molly. Whoever she was viewing this through backed up on the bed. The crazed woman bore down on her, reached out, and grabbed at the camera person's hand, and by extension, her hand. Molly instinctively grabbed her own hand in defence, only she saw a child's hand on her bedroom ceiling where her own hand should be.

It was then when she put two and two together: she was seeing what her spirit child had seen and felt before he met his untimely demise. Old buildings store energy, but this was taking it to the next level. On her bedroom ceiling, Molly watched in absolute horror as the wicked woman shoved the red-hot poker onto Molly's palm. She watched her little hand writhe, jerk, sizzle, and smoke in blinding, blistering pain her tears would never quench.

The giant mouldy screen on Molly's bedroom ceiling began to twirl and swirl in on itself. A black vortex emitting an overpowering stench of decay and mould dripped from the roof like a hellish stalactite. Molly's pitiful sobs cut to a sudden gagging halt in her throat as her child oozed from the ceiling, descending through the whirlwind of blight. She had to remind herself he was harmless, as he stood there in the middle of the bedroom, next to her bed, looking through her, motionless, just like the first time she'd seen him standing still on the stairs, so statuesque, she had mistaken his head for a piece of the stairway. In hindsight, how could she have mistaken his head with those ears?

Unsure if she was dreaming or temporarily insane, she glanced through her window just to make sure the world was still outside. The gently swaying treetops of the spruce trees in the darkness were a comfort, anything to stabilise her. She thought about Janice fleetingly, but Janice should have gone back to where she came from. There was nothing for her old friend here…

It was a comfort knowing Prendergast wasn't letting anyone down here who might hinder her good work. He knew Janice would try to get her to leave, but he had Molly's best interest at heart. He wanted her to succeed; her dear neighbour wanted her to win first prize in this macabre contest.

Prendergast or Janice were somewhere out there, but not here in the front yard. Who was here, though, were her Mike and Henry. They were floating there, wide smiles on their pale faces, waving in at Molly. She didn't fall back in horror and shock. She waved back as if she'd been expecting them. Their glazed, unblinking gazes looked right through her. Molly's skin crawled, seeing how both shared that same lifelessness that infected both of them after she left Dublin. They have travelled through the valley of darkness and it had left its mark.

Mike tapped on the window and pointed into the bedroom. 'He's a good boy!' he called. 'You can trust him, Molls. The girls are going to turn you against him, Molls. He's just a kid who got lost somewhere along the way. He means well, but he's been in a dark place for far too long. You better watch your eldest child — our eldest child — because she's trouble, Molls. She's going to get you put in a place where there are no chimneys, Mollsy. They're jealous of your love for the boy.'

For a second, Molly Greene thought Mike had been referring to their son, Henry, but then she realised he was speaking about her other adopted child. By default, Molly never trusted anyone who uses the word 'trust'. He didn't sound like Mike. There was something wrong. Back at the house in Dublin, Molly would hear his voice but never see Mike utter any words. Through the glass, she could see her dead husband's lips move and the words leave his mouth, but the voice wasn't Mike's, and it wasn't hers either. Yes, it sounded like her husband, but there was something off in his cadence of speech. Something was making Mike move, and it dubbed his voice, but there's a guttural croak Molly didn't recognise, coupled with that rictus grin pulling his face into nightmarish proportions. And Mollsy? That wasn't Molly or Molls, but something in between, just like what she was seeing now.

Henry spoke, breaking Molly's heart. 'I love you, Mommy!' But his voice was wrong, too. Molly never forgot her child's sweet melodic voice; Henry sang when he spoke. This was the same voice that spoke for Mike. Now, even the audible words weren't synchronised with Henry's moving lips, coming in a fraction of a second later than his lip movements.

'We still love you, Mommy!'

We?

'Sometimes he comes to visit us and tells us all about my mommy and my sisters. But he says that my

366

sisters are bad and don't want my friend in our family just because he's…different.'

This version of Henry spoke about her and the girls as if he wasn't even aware he was talking to his mom. Molly had the sneaking suspicion if she asked him his sisters' names right now, he wouldn't know. 'Henry? Mike? Is that really you?' Desperation told her it really was them. 'Oh, Jesus, Oh, Christ, I'm sorry…so, so sorry. I live with the guilt every day.' Molly wailed. 'I…I…suffer…I suffer every single minute of every single day. Why didn't I just —'

'Shush, don't suffer, Molls. We didn't suffer. We didn't have time to suffer. Oh, Molly,' croaked Mike, 'I never stopped loving you, even when the Volvo's engine came through the dashboard…'

'We love Mama,' said Henry, who clearly didn't know Molly was his…Mama. Molly's skin bristled. It wasn't the first time she'd heard Mama at the farmhouse.

'Trust him…' gurgled Mike, 'he's a good boy,' as they vanished into the night.

Once the curtain came down on this stellar piece of theatre, the child spirit came to life and skittered across the room towards her bed with movements far too erratic to be an actual child. She couldn't deny the repulsion she felt. It wasn't a child anymore, but had once been, and it's this last part she had to keep reminding herself. Standing there at the end of the bed, his dead eyes considered her. 'Mama?'

Molly's skin crawled on hearing the child-shadow whisper in the night; always the same word: 'Mama' and she thought she'd never get used to it, no matter how many times this perversion of nature called her that.

'Do you love me now, Mama?'

Its string of words paralysed Molly, not only for what had been asked of her, but because the words spoken came from the same voice as Henry and Mike. It was a child's voice, but a disconcerting rasp came to the top of every second syllable. The spirit, she was sure, had put on that little piece of mental theatre to convince her. There had been nobody at her bedroom window. She knew that, of course, but maybe—

The wraith laughed a high-pitched giggle which was endearing and creepy as fuck. Molly shrunk down into her bed and pulled the blankets up on herself. From her new angle, the hallway wall lamp shone through the child's disfigured face, horrifically burnt. Yes, she was sure of that now. The child had been disfigured by some form of hot object. The compassion, confusion, and sorrow gnawed at her insides. One minute she loved him, the next minute she found him repulsive in all his living dead glory.

'I love you Mama…do you love me, Mama?'

There was no room for doubt now. The thing had imprinted on Molly like a newly hatched duckling imprinting on the first moving object.

'Yes, I do.'

Before she had time to correct herself, the ghost, wanting to be the child it once was, moved and gestured as it thought a child should move and gesture. It broke into motion, loomed up on her, and bent down to kiss Molly on the forehead. If asked, the best way she could describe was rubbing an ice cube to her forehead while having a fever. And where that failed to impress, she would tell the truth of the matter, which was that Molly had wet the bed for the first time in over four decades…

With the icy kiss came a jarring cocktail of bittersweet emotions. Molly's bed almost became her death bed as it sat next to her, still and silent, no deep reassuring breathing her children gave as they slept the sleep of angels. That infinite silence terrified Molly Greene.

'They always leave in the end, Mama.'

Molly thought she'd heard the lingering words in her sleep: soft, subtle, and scary. What had it meant? She felt intense pity for the spectre, caught between life and death, unable to go back or forward. It sent a chill through her to imagine that he, it, the squatter, would be here long after she was dead, long after her children were dead. Yes, Molly was the squatter.

She turned to see the nightmarish face of the child. 'I'm not going to leave you. You are part of this family now. We love you. We are your family.'

The spirit moved closer to her. A wave of coldness moved along her left side.

Molly peered up at the tiny green flashing light of the recording camera. She felt a little ashamed for cashing in on the spirit of the child. *You scratch my back and I'll scratch yours. The farmhouse is free, but it comes with a price. Yes, the small print of Prendergast's contract was pretty accurate.*

Just then, Molly was sure she heard a menacing growl come from the fireplace, which didn't make any sense, not that anything made any sense in this house anymore because she was lying in bed with the manifestation. Now was one of a few moments when Molly Greene suspected there were two entities in this house, not one. It would back up what she had seen down in the kitchen when their child spirit had been whispering to something or someone else in the darkness, and again when her own daughter had heard various voices coming from the chimney hearth. Molly had heard a whole conversation coming from the grille at the back of her fireplace.

For no apparent reason, he left her bed, then crossed the bedroom in his sickening way of moving, and squeezed itself into the fireplace…the same fireplace where a poker had once been left in the hot coals to mark the child in its former self. The child had been abused in his own house by his own mother. Why? Was it any wonder the child wasn't at rest?

As Molly Greene succumbed to sleep, she wondered what the child had done to deserve such cruelty at the hands of his own mama.

26.

The following Monday morning, the girls got ready for school in some vague semblance of normality. In place of the daily chaos of a school morning, a tense quietness prevailed as Molly, Mina, and Cora went about their business in a subdued manner. The meeting last night had shaken all of them, their heads still reeling. Molly had woken up feeling like a stranger in her own bedroom — a squatter, as Cora had kindly pointed out. She had been so confident falling asleep last night, but on this Monday morning, in the cold light of day, she wasn't so sure she could explain anything anymore. The girls were on edge as they made their sandwiches for break and little to no playful banter and screaming matches filled the kitchen. Molly, too, felt the tension in the air. But it was clear to everyone they were alone for now. When the spirit was gone, it really was gone, somewhere far off inside the chimney flue.

Everything was running with relative normality until they arrived at the gate at the top of the lane on their way to school. Molly got out of the BMW to unlock the gate, and she noticed now where the gate had been dented along the middle bars where Mina had crashed into it. Also, there was a car parked up to the side of the gate. She was stunned to see the car looked a lot like Janice's car. For a second, she thought it might be just the same vehicle, but how many sky-blue Volkswagen Beetles are on the road these days? The Dublin registration plate confirmed her worst suspicions. It was Janice.

Mina asked through her window. 'Is that Janice's car?' She opened her door to get out and have a closer look.

'Stay in the car.' Molly warned. She looked inside the Beetle and found Janice asleep in the back seat. Just as she was about to turn and tiptoe away, she heard the door click open behind her.

'Molly?'

She cringed. Molly wanted nothing more than to get into her car and drive away, but she just couldn't bring herself to do it. Doing the right thing, she turned around to face her best friend. 'Don't tell me you slept here all night?'

'I knew it was the only way I was going to get to see you and the girls.'

'You're crazy.'

'Wow, that's rich.' She cast a wave at the girls sitting in the car. 'Can I just say hello to them?'

Molly hesitated. 'On one condition: you do nothing or say nothing to jeopardise what we're doing here. This place is so much more, Jan. We have found something here that's going to make everything right. I just need a few more days.'

'I've seen your videos. I subscribed to your channel.' She chuckled.

Molly smiled back, adding, 'Smash that like button.'

The women shared their last laugh together.

'Are you sure you can handle what's going on in that house? It's terrifying, Moll.'

'Terrifying for the uninitiated, Jan. What we're doing in that house is going to change how the world thinks. Oh, before you ask, I haven't touched a drop of alcohol. Because that's what you're thinking, right? I'm not making up any of this, Janice. You have seen my YouTube channel for yourself. What you see is what you get. I need a drink just to stay sober.'

*

Her friend's words gave Janice the creeps. 'Molly, I'm going to say this only once: you have nothing to prove.' Janice turned away and walked up to the BMW, where she flashed Mina a look of apology. 'I tried,' she lip-synched. Mina nodded back and smiled her recognition. Janice leaned in and hugged Mina in the front seat. 'She blended my phone,' Mina whispered in that brief hug through the window. Janice met her eyes. In that infinitesimal moment, Janice hoped the 15-year-old could read her to understand what her eyes were trying to say.

'Did you really sleep in your car last night?' Cora asked with a bemused smile.

Janice nodded.

'Why?'

'I was too cheap to pay for a hotel.'

Cora giggled.

'Hi Jan!' Emma called out from her car seat with a big smile. This went right to the core of Janice's being, opening a well of emotion. 'Hi, Emma! How's Creepy Baby doing?'

The four-year-old held up her rubber baby for

Janice to see.

'Ah, there she is! She looks really happy, Em!' Janice asked the girls how their new school was, determined to speak of neutral matters. Right now, she wanted to grab the girls, pack them into her car, drive the fuck away and never look into her rear-view mirror. She could feel the oppression here, even here on the side of the road. The children weren't themselves; drawn and pallid, bags under their eyes. Whatever was in that house with them was sucking the life force from them while it grew. Maybe she'd been watching too many horror films just lately, but that's how she felt.

'So, how is everything?'

Cora answered, 'Getting there. Now that we are becoming influencers, maybe we'll be a lot cooler.'

Mina added, 'Mom's viewing statistics on her YouTube videos is crazy. We're going to be the cool kids.'

Janice smiled but was crying inside. This wasn't right. The YouTube channel was the only good thing in their lives…for all the wrong reasons. And of course, they loved it because they're kids! The Internet was everything for kids these days — Instagram, YouTube. Kids are somebodies, not nobodies, when they have a popular social media channel. It's what validated kids nowadays, not the fact that they finished the *Lord of the Rings* trilogy. It saddened Janice to think that Mina and Cora were grasping onto whatever good came out of this situation. It wasn't right. These were three splendid girls and Janice would not let this happen, not without a fight and not on her watch.

Janice told the girls it was great to see them and that she was happy they were getting on with their lives. She lied, not because Molly was standing next to her with a strange look in her eyes, but because she felt helpless pity for the girls who were doing anything but getting on with their lives.

Considering Molly for a moment, Janice was going to make one last-ditch effort to convince her friend that the house wasn't good for her or her family. But those glazed eyes told her Molly was very far away and couldn't hear her and wouldn't if she could. Janice got into her car and drove off.

Molly wanted to knock on Prendergast's door and ask why he wouldn't let Janice pass through the gate last night. But she was in a hurry now to get to school. Besides, he had done her a favour.

A greeting party of biting stares was waiting for the Greenes at the school gates. Molly refused to be intimidated and held her head high in defiance. It's about time someone cashed in on this phenomenon. The fools in this town had been covering up the farmhouse when they should have been pocketing the proceeds from punters who want to see a ghost. Molly knew it was only a matter of time before a whole ghastly industry was going to build up around the squatter and the farmhouse; Wilma would convert her lacklustre restaurant into a souvenir shop selling tacky battery-operated merchandise with 'Made in

PRC' written on them, while the real horror remained very real out at the farmhouse.

Molly was and wasn't surprised to see Gerry coming across the schoolyard towards her as she waved her kids off to an encore of caustic glares.

*

Inside the main hallway of the school, Mina was hanging her jacket on her peg when something fell from her right pocket onto the ground. It was a small, dated flip phone, silver in colour, and about the same size as a Matchbox toy. She picked it up, wondering if it had fallen from someone else's coat pocket as she hung up her own. It was wrapped in a charger and cable. She unravelled the cable and flipped it open. A scribbled note fell out.

Mina, use this phone if you need help. Keep it hidden at all times. Janice

Mina couldn't fathom it. When had Janice…oh, wait, she'd slipped her the phone this morning when she'd leaned through the car window to give her a hug. Oh my God, how Mina loved Janice just then, more than her own Mom. Janice had known her Mom was going to take the phone after contacting her. Good 'ole Jan! Not just a pretty face.

*

Very conscious of the onlookers, Gerry asked in a hushed voice, 'Why haven't you answered any of my calls or texts?'

'Good morning, Gerry. How are you? And, yes,

I've been busy.'

'Is it true?'

'Is what true? If you're referring to our ground-breaking ghostly evidence, then, yes, it's true.' Her face became quite serious. 'Gerry, I'm going to milk this for every cent. I'm going to open the house to ghost tours, but the irony now is that I won't need to, with the revenue I can earn from my YouTube channel. I must ask Mina to give me a hand with that.' She laughed. 'I am an utter dinosaur when it comes to the Inter…net. Mina says we can open an account on TokTik and Instantgram.' More hilarious laughter followed.

Gerry McAuliffe was convinced Molly Greene was on the edge of a nervous breakdown. She was pale. Her eyes darted uneasily above the line of her face mask. Either that or she was on something.

'We have a happy little symbiosis going on at the farmhouse. I'm going to put this town on the map, Gerry. Old Castle will prosper, mark my words. This dirty little secret has been kept hidden for too long. When are you and the rest of the locals going to get it? The farmhouse is my home and I'm going nowhere. If anyone is going anywhere, then it's—'

'I know about the child in the house.'

This stopped Molly. 'What?'

'We need to talk.'

'Tell me here.'

Gerry looked around. 'It's complicated. Coffee later?'

Molly raised her eyebrows.

'No, it's nothing like that.' The hint of a smile crossed his face beneath his mask, which helped to hide his embarrassment. 'Although, I will admit that, well, you know…a beautiful woman comes to town… she's living with a ghost, blah, blah, blah…'

They laughed it off, though it felt a little awkward.

Gerry placed a hand on her arm and saw she was suddenly taken aback. 'I'm afraid for you and the girls, Molly.' The hopelessness in his eyes and voice was unmistakable. 'You don't know what you've got yourself into.'

'I beg to differ.'

'Some details have come to light since we last spoke.'

Molly appeared intrigued. 'Which are?'

Gerry and Molly realised hovering parents, helicopter moms and dads with nothing else to do with their time, were listening in on their conversation.

'Why don't you come around this evening?' Molly suggested.

Gerry shook his head. 'No, that's not going to happen; that's not an option.'

'Be brave,' challenged Molly. 'You'll see I'm right and you'll be able to tell the local villagers they were wrong about the squatter.'

Gerry McAuliffe wanted to tell Molly about the photograph he had found and the information on the big-eared wicked waif of a child who once lived at the farmhouse, but this wasn't the time or the place. 'Look, it's not what it seems. It's deeper…'

378

'Deeper?'

Gerry nodded.

'Gerry, I've seen this boy you're telling me about. I've seen the life the child had. He showed me in my bedroom ceiling.'

'Jesus Christ, Molly.'

'I saw the abuse and torture.'

Gerry stilled himself as fear crept up from his toes to his head.

'He was abused by his mother, Gerry. Tortured. Scarred for life with a fire poker. I think she did something very bad to him, Gerry.'

Gerry considered her for a moment. 'Molly, I didn't mention anything about a boy.'

'What do you mean?'

'You've been going on about this child as if I had mentioned him. I didn't open my mouth, but I *was* thinking about him. I came across that same child in my notes on the house after we had coffee. The big-eared boy who was abused, just like you told me.'

Now it was Molly's turn to fall silent. Had she just read Gerry's mind? WTF? He hadn't even spoken about the victimised child. 'Now, you're scaring me, Molly.' Gerry McAuliffe walked away, looking once over his shoulder at Molly.

*

She was about to call after him when her phone buzzed. 'Hello?'

A woman's voice asked, 'Hi, am I speaking to Molly Greene?'

'Yes?'

'Hi Molly, I'm calling on behalf of RTE in Dublin.'

'RTE?' repeated Molly. What would the national public service broadcaster want with Molly?

'The news department, to be more precise,' said the woman.

'Oh?'

'I'm a researcher for RTE, Molly, and we've been made aware of your, um, paranormal experiences in the house where you're living now. Would I be right in saying that?'

Molly clammed up. 'Well…'

'We were wondering if you would be interested in giving us an interview for the six o'clock news on TV? Maybe we could do a little tour of the house and whatever else you think might be interesting for our viewers?'

Molly stalled. 'Um, yeah, I'm not sure if we're up for that.' Nationwide exposure was just what she needed for her new business. But Molly was baulking. She was scared because this was real, no longer existing inside her head where everything else had been happening.

'According to our sources, you're opening your house to the public…ghost tours? Do you realise that we get on average of five hundred thousand viewers for the Six One News? That's a lot of eyeballs. If you're any good at maths, you'll count a million eyeballs.' She laughed.

'Can I get back to you? I need some time to think.'

'Sure thing,' said the researcher and gave Molly

her number. 'Don't take too long to come to a decision,' she gently warned Molly. 'The news is a fickle business. Nobody wants yesterday's news, and everybody wants tomorrow's news.'

Molly assured the woman she would let her know. She just needed time to think, not that there was any thinking to do. This was a golden opportunity, being handed right to her here, and she would forever kick herself if she passed on it.

She got into her car and headed home sweet home.

On the drive back to the farmhouse, Molly had a change of heart and called the researcher back. 'Hi, this is Molly Greene. Let's do this before I change my mind.'

The researcher was delighted Molly had come to her senses and asked if tomorrow morning would be okay to do the interview. It would be pre-recorded for that evening's 6pm news.

'How about we do it live tomorrow evening, some time around six?' Molly countered. 'He normally comes out to play at six o'clock. The star of the show will be a no-show if you come earlier.'

'I need to make some calls. I'll get back to you.' She hung up.

Five minutes later, Molly's BMW pulled up at the road gate. She fetched the key Prendergast had given her and was opening the padlocked gate when she saw the kitchen curtain move. Prendergast was still avoiding her for some reason. She needed to speak to him anyway about her ghost tours and the TV interview and everything else that would come after to put her on the rich list and provide a loving family for her misplaced child.

She was reaching for the brass knocker of the front door when her phone vibrated in her coat pocket.

'Yes?'

The RTE researcher was back on the other end of the line. Not wanting Prendergast to know her business and already knowing that he liked to sneak about for no apparent purpose, Molly took herself to her car, sat in, and turned on the engine.

The researcher agreed to do a live interview on the 6pm news, '...but this evening. We can get our gear together and be down there before six.'

'Oh, okay.' Molly thought she'd have a full day to mentally prepare herself and time to chicken out if needed.

The researcher picked up on the doubt creeping in. 'I know it's short notice, but we have other commitments for the rest of the week. We'd like to pounce while this is a trending topic. Some live ghostly activity would be the icing on the cake,' she half laughed.

Molly's intuition was telling her this researcher didn't believe a word of what she was saying. She was just going along with it. It was a harmless novelty story, and everyone could do with one of those in the present climate. 'You won't be let down,' Molly promised, firmly in the driving seat again. 'I'll rattle my beautiful boy's cage and, hopefully, he'll be in the mood to communicate. He might even give you an icy kiss...' This time it was Molly's turn to laugh, but there was an uncomfortable hiatus of silence on the line before the researcher thanked Molly and told her a team of three (reporter, cameraman, and sound engineer) would be down around 5.30pm.

As Molly hung up, she swore she saw the kitchen curtain of the Gatehouse fall back into place.

'Right, that's it.' It was high time Molly Greene spoke her mind.

*

In a small office, on the opposite side of the country, the RTE researcher's skin crawled as she hung up the phone. Molly Greene seemed like such a rational woman, yet she spoke about a ghost — a ghost! — as if it was the most normal thing in the world. She had been pleasantly surprised until that icy kiss line. Those chilling words prompted the researcher to do a quick background check on Molly Greene. Just like Gerry McAuliffe before her, she learned about Molly's success with her Michelin restaurant that closed its doors due to the pandemic. But she was more taken with Molly's pre-Michelin life. Her tragic past led the researcher to feel great pity for the woman she'd just spoken to and she hoped, for all their sakes, that there really was a ghost in the farmhouse. A cold clammy sweat broke on her forehead, making her think she'd made a terrible mistake in agreeing to do this interview, live or otherwise. Her last wish was to make a mentally unstable woman the laughingstock of the country; this was a serious news department with serious current affairs.

383

Molly slammed the car door behind her and trotted to the Gatehouse where she swung off the brass knocker. Prendergast didn't answer. Molly peeped through the letterbox. She had a clear view of the hallway. The family pictures she'd seen that first night hadn't been rehung and, from this angle, she could see the outline of the doorway halfway up the hallway on the left beneath the wallpaper.

'Yoo-hoo!' she called. 'I know you're in there. I've seen you twice at the curtain, Richard.' Molly spoke to him like he was a little child playing hide-and-seek. 'Oh, by the way, I also saw you spying on us the other night from the front yard…and my daughter saw you. Creepy. I don't care if you're Lord Shiva or the landlord, it's called stalking. If you have something to say, please say it to my face. I don't bite…not yet. Can you please come to the door? I have a question.'

The moment she said it, the door swung open, yet nobody had come down the hallway. 'Jesus Christ! You scared me.'

He'd been standing just inside the door, to the side of the letterbox, out of view, less than six inches from her lips as she'd called him Lord Shiva.

'Yes, Molly? How can I help you?' Prendergast's bloodshot eyes shifted as he tried to focus on his front yard and the road gate beyond. Molly was certain she noted a slur in his voice. She didn't get any whiff of alcohol from him, yet he looked a tad under the weather.

'Would you like to come in or would you prefer to

speak to me through the letterbox?'

'The letterbox will be fine, thanks.'

'You sure you won't have a coffee?' Prendergast was clearly under the influence. 'I need one.'

Molly now had a lot of questions. 'Okay, maybe a quick one. I have to get back to the farmhouse as soon as possible and tidy up. I have an interview this evening.'

'An interview?' That word sobered him up some.

Molly nodded. 'For the six o'clock news tonight,' she told him as she stepped inside. Prendergast walked off in silence to the kitchen, where he prepared the coffee.

Molly hung her coat on the coat perch, then enabled her location on her phone, just in case the police would need it to find her, God forbid.

But Google Maps wouldn't cover where Molly was going because Google didn't exist where Molly was going.

'Okay, it's like this: I know you're spying on us. You have been seen around the farmhouse on more than one occasion. You're watching us and you're watching the house. Why? I have no idea, but I think it's time you filled me in. I know there's a reason why you control the road gate outside, and I know there's a reason why it's the only gate. I think you are bound to this place. None of this is just coincidence. You are the guardian at the gate, and I want to know why.'

Prendergast brought her a mug of coffee. 'Molly, there is a lot more going on here with me than what you see. But you don't have to concern yourself about my plight — my curse. All you have to do is concern yourself with the house and what is inside the house. I believe it has chosen you. If it hadn't, we would all know by now,' he told her in menacing tones.

'I know you were married and had a son. What happened?'

Prendergast gazed out his window at somewhere far off. 'It was a very difficult time,' he began. 'They're not with me any longer.'

This wasn't how Molly thought it was going to go. 'I don't like to talk about myself, but I just wanted you to know I have been through my own family tragedy. So, you have someone to talk to if you ever feel the need. Despite our differences, I believe we have some experiences in common.'

He handed Molly her coffee. 'I don't know where they are.'

'Sorry?' Molly wasn't ready for this existential conversation so early in the morning and with someone she didn't really like all that much. 'It's not as if you can simply pack your bag and go to wherever they are.'

'I would if I could.'

'Me too. But I'm afraid I won't be able to get a passport for where my son and husband are.'

Prendergast seemed intrigued by this. 'I could get a passport, but I don't know where they are. My wife and son are alive, Molly.'

She was confused. 'I thought they were dead. Sorry to be so blunt…the passport thing.'

'Figuratively, yes, they are dead to me. My wife

left me, and she took our son with her. I have no idea where they are. She broke all contact.'

Now everything was making sense. 'So, you didn't kill them?'

Prendergast got a hearty laugh out of this. 'Okay, so which of the locals have you been speaking to?'

'Just word on the street.'

'I don't know if I prefer to be in your situation or mine.'

'How could you even say that?' Molly asked.

'Because I know my son is out there somewhere. It's agonising knowing this, wondering if he'll ever come through my door. No offence intended, but you know where you stand, and you don't wait in eternal hope.'

'Why did they leave?'

'We used to live at the farmhouse, but my wife couldn't handle it. It latched onto her and haunted her every waking moment.'

Molly was trying to understand this revelation. 'What do you mean "latched"?'

'It became possessive and followed her…'

'You mean it can leave the farmhouse?'

Prendergast nodded and sighed. 'That's when we moved here to get away, but not far enough, unfortunately. That's when Catriona then decided she needed to go further, and she took Abraham with her. They're at an undisclosed location. That's what having a family curse will get you.'

'Why did you take down all your family pictures?'

For the first time, Prendergast looked vulnerable.

'Seeing you and your daughters here that night woke up old pain, anger, and sadness.' His eyes filled with tears. 'If they decide to walk back into my life, I'll be here with open arms. But until then, I suffer every day from this curse I'm stuck with. I cannot stand back any longer and feed the farmhouse broken people… broken lives.' Prendergast's eyes rolled. He struggled to focus.

'Are you okay?'

'No. No, I'm not.'

'Wallpapering over your son's bedroom? I assume it's your son's bedroom. I know there's a door in the hallway. My daughters found it when we were here for dinner.'

'I need to forget, Molly, before I'm driven to madness. My mistake was moving an unbroken family into the farmhouse — my family. The presence prefers broken families in which it can slip into and belong.'

Molly interjected, 'Hence, the experiment, forever your little guinea pigs. The house is going to be mine. I'm going to win the first prize.'

'And I would like nothing more than this, Molly, believe me. The house has gone through many broken families because they had nothing to lose, just like you and your family. Nothing to lose because you have already lost so much.' He held her in his off-putting dead stare. 'Carnage will continue until it finds its mother. Sometimes, I wonder if the child will ever find his mother.'

And so, it had come to this: the real reason Molly

Greene was chosen to move into the farmhouse. She just happened to be a broken mother who showed some wonderful potential of being the surrogate mother. Whether she would stay was yet to be determined.'I am willing to be his mother — he knows that. We will all live together in my first prize house and I will make shitloads of money off the presence in the house. He'll scratch my back and I'll scratch his. Sorry to be blunt. To be honest, I think you missed a trick there, Richard.'

Prendergast half chuckled. 'You are the first prize in this contest, Molly, not the house.'

Molly felt claustrophobic. She didn't want to know what he meant, but he was going to tell her. He didn't seem to be his cool, calm, and collected self. 'You are here to take a problem off my hands. I want my wife and son back. If I can satiate the ghost with a loving, broken family then I might be able to *unbreak* mine. You are the first prize in this contest.'

'So, you're using us.'

'As you're using me.'

He had a point.

Prendergast went on with a warning. 'I have come to detest that thing with every bone of my body. It has broken me and my family, not only mine but generations of Prendergasts. This is the price we're paying for a sad atrocity that happened over two centuries ago. But have a little compassion for a tormented soul, Molly. This isn't a circus. You have to understand the phantom is looking for a family; it doesn't want to be a freak show attraction.'

'That's the deal,' Molly shut him down. 'I need money and I'm going to use what I have to make it. I'm providing a loving home and family for him and, in return, he will help me. It's called a symbiotic relationship.'

'Are you the victim or the host?'

Prendergast didn't give Molly a chance to answer as he excused himself. He abruptly left her to stew on her own thoughts. A couple of minutes later, he returned, rolling down his left shirt sleeve. Molly noticed this but made nothing of it.

'Have you asked it how it feels?' he asked.

For a second, Molly thought he was joking. 'No.'

'Hmm.'

Molly answered in cold, clipped tones, 'Sometimes, in life, there's no room for feelings. We must do things from time to time for the good of the family. At the end of the day, Richard, we are all scratching someone else's back.' She made to leave. 'Thank you. This has been very enlightening.' Too enlightening for Molly's taste, but perhaps it was fitting that it was to be the last time she would see Prendergast alive.

27.

It was time to get back to the farmhouse to get everything ready for the evening show and what a show it would be. As she drove down the lane, she remembered another question — possibly the biggest question — what 'sad atrocity' had Prendergast been talking about.

Molly had viewed a few ghost hunting videos on YouTube and learnt all about trigger objects which were objects that would trigger a physical response from the spirit, not that she needed them because this spirit wasn't shy. She went upstairs and searched Cora's and Emma's bedrooms, locating a small red ball and a Barbie doll. Molly had thought about using Creepy Baby as a trigger object, but that would only trigger Emma. Back in the living room, Molly placed the trigger objects by the stone fireplace. She placed Emma's Barbie doll on one side of the open fireplace and the ball on the other side. She sat back on the sofa and stared at her trigger objects so hard she was sure Barbie winked back at her.

Her phone startled her. Thinking it might be the TV news crew, she ran to grab her phone from the kitchen table. 'Christ, again?' It was Gerry McAuliffe. Just to get it over with, Molly answered. 'Hi Gerry. I'm a little busy right—'

'Molly, I know who the ghost child is. I wanted you to get this before you go ahead with his idiotic news interview — saw it advertised on your channels.

It might come back to haunt you.'

'Idiotic? Gerry, I'm doing it for our future.'

In time, Gerry McAuliffe would recall this line and appreciate the sick irony.

'Do you know how much it costs to send a child to university? Oh, sorry, I forgot you don't have children.'

'Could you not find a normal job?'

'I came down here on the promise of a job which turned out to be a big fat lie! You know why? Because a small-minded, irrational, backward virus infects toxic Old Castle…as if Covid wasn't enough, Jesus! I had everything invested in my restaurant, Gerry, until the pandemic closed me down. *Hellooo?* as Mina says. What's a gal s'posed to do? I'm officially on the poverty line.' A crack appeared in her bravado. She stifled a whimper on hearing herself tell the ugly truth. And without giving it a second thought, Molly Greene made a determined beeline for Prendergast's priceless bottle of wine on the counter and uncorked it. She didn't need an invitation, no sir. She was celebrating…celebrating the fight that was life and winning that fight and fuck the begrudgers! Cheers! Chin-chin! Salud! Barnacles off the hull!

On the other end of the line, Molly knew Gerry McAuliffe heard the uncorking *Pop!* of a wine bottle, then a pause before hearing the clink of a glass as Molly toasted her bottle of wine. 'Molly?' he asked.

'I'm here…' She toasted her bottle of wine and took a deep satisfying gulp of the red. Oh my God, Jesus, what had Molly been waiting for? Waiting for the cows to come home? It was simply divine. 'Where was I? Oh yes, I have three mouths to feed… four if you include mine. If you haven't understood by now, Gerry, I need the money fast.'

'The child is evil.'

'Oh, please, enough with the horror movie clichés, Gerry. The child is harmless. All he needs is a loving mother…a surrogate mama. We can all turn ourselves around, Gerry. It's never too late to start again.'

She drained off her glass of wine in five uncompromising slugs. It was so satisfying to feel the warmth of the alcohol heat her neck and chest as it flowed downwards.

'They called him the big-eared midget.'

Molly froze. She could see the outline of the silhouette's big ears as Gerry spoke. It was him. She poured herself another glass of wine.

'The novel I'm working on was going to be non-fiction about the boy and the house. I think I already mentioned that. I did quite a lot of research, so I dug up my old notes.'

'You're not going to change my mind, Gerry. What can you tell me that I don't know already?'

'I can tell you what he was like when he was alive.'

Molly remained silent. She sipped while casting furtive glances around the kitchen.

'He was the youngest son of Lord and Lady Prendergast,' Gerry started, 'worth a fortune, only he was never going to get any of the Prendergast fortune because it was destined for his older sister, Erin, who went on to take over the business. The eldest child was James, but he had a fondness for the drink. He was a party animal and, if rumours are to be believed, was a member of the Hellfire Club in Dublin. His biggest love in his youthful years was knocking seven colours of shit out of his younger brother who was the runt of the family, born with a disease contracted from his mother. Some sources said syphilis, but they tried to keep that under wraps. He was bullied at school because of his oddness and his ears didn't help.'

Molly blocked the spontaneous bout of laughter. She thought she was going to burst out with a real good one, wine-spraying quality. It was the way Gerry had said it. Her nerves were shot.

'His siblings ostracised him because he was different. Fearing what the public might think of her freakish son, Lady Prendergast disowned her child, shunned him, kept him locked up in one of the bedrooms of the farmhouse. Many people, workers on the farm, would see the child prisoner standing for hours at his bedroom window looking out.'

As Molly drank her well-deserved wine, the hair stood along the nape of her neck. She understood now why her lost child gravitated towards her bedroom window after coming from the fireplace, then stared blankly out at the nothingness of night. It haunted her as it still haunted him. 'Jesus Christ,' Molly heard herself say.

'Lady Prendergast was ashamed of her son's malformation. She treated him like a freak of nature;

a diseased thing that good folk shouldn't have to see. Of course, now with the advent of science, we know the child had suffered from Macrotia, which is a medical condition in which the ears are abnormally large.'

A single tear fell from Molly's right eye and *plinked* into her glass of wine. Now, she guessed she was beginning to understand what Prendergast's sad atrocity was.

'The Prendergast family let the young boy out for an hour every evening from six to seven when the place was quiet, in that hour between the farmworkers going home and the lavish Prendergast dinner parties that began around seven. Someone would always lock away the child in time before their high-powered guests arrived.'

Molly shook her head in dumbstruck amazement. Each evening at the farmhouse she had experienced that enormous sense of freedom and elation as the clock struck six electronic chimes. She looked up at the clock on the wall. She was feeling what he had felt.

'And this is where things get a little dark. During these hours of freedom in the evenings, the child would spend his time trapping birds and killing them, then leave them in a shoebox by his parents' bed for them to find. Like a cat might bring home a gory gift for its owner. That graduated into killing the family dog — a Saint Bernard, Molly, not one of those rat-poodle things.'

Molly assumed he was referring to the size of a

dog and how much more difficult it would be to slay a Saint Bernard than a 'rat-poodle'.

'And get this: the child was a gifted musician and artist; highly creative and talented. It was the one thing he excelled at. Could pick up any instrument and play it by ear alone.'

'The child was an artist?'

'It is said that the child carved every inch of his bedroom walls with illustrations. But nobody knows what those drawings consist of.'

Molly looked up at the ceiling, towards where her bedroom was located. She recalled the day Emma had drawn Louie on the chalkboard, all strange and out of character. It was endearing to think the child spirit had been living out one of his first loves by using her daughter. It was also frankly terrifying. And what about that chalk drawing of the farmhouse with the whole family, all of them, and the snowman? Molly recalled the evening they all heard sweet plucking notes of the kalimba upstairs while they ate pizza with Christine. That had been the real start of all of this, Molly felt. She gulped her wine and made a silent toast to the squatter — she wasn't sure if it was her or him anymore.

'That graduated with attacking small children.'

Gerry McAuliffe's words rocked her out of her semi-drunken daze.

'He would slip out through the window and come into Old Castle, which was a village back in those days…'

It's still a village…

'…And lure little kids away from their parents with sweets, then beat them with whatever he could find. Lord Prendergast had one of his workers seal the child's window. Some accounts say Lady Prendergast wanted her husband to block up his window, but Lord Prendergast didn't have the heart to do it. Instead, she beat her son and tortured him. It's reported she used a hot poker on the child to expel his demons, but she failed in spectacular fashion, only succeeding in stirring from its slumber whatever demon that lay dormant inside the child.'

Molly, back in her bedroom two centuries ago, looked up at the insane woman, Lady Prendergast, with crazed eyes and a red-hot poker in her hand.

'Lord and Lady Prendergast were convinced the child was possessed, which wasn't unusual in those days. Nowadays, with the advent of science, the white coats would say the child was mentally ill, cognitive damage because of whatever illness he was born with. What do I know? But what is unusual is what the child said to police when they asked him why he had burnt his victims' eyelids and plucked out their eyes before he killed them.'

Molly winced. 'Jesus, what?'

'Oh, yeah. I forgot. The child sneaked out one night and murdered two children, a four-year-old boy and a three-year-old girl. At nine years of age, the child was already becoming a serial killer.'

A rocking wave of dizziness washed down over Molly. She wasn't sure if it was the shock of hearing about her child or the wine taking effect. Just to be sure, she took another slug of wine. By now, she'd gulped down half the bottle. 'What did he say? To the police?'

'Are you sitting down?'

'Yes.'

'He said he did it so the children in the next life wouldn't have to see what he sees in this life. It was a mercy killing.'

Molly's skin crept. She gaped around sheepishly. More wine…

'The police didn't believe him. Their official report was the child didn't want to be identified, so he took their sight first, which doesn't make any sense because he killed them, anyway. The child went on terrorise the children of Old Castle. Too young to be put behind bars, his parents institutionalised him, which only further segregated him. By the time he was eleven years old, he'd lured another four young children away to their deaths, battered, stabbed… whatever he could get his hands on became a killing tool. He was the youngest ever recorded serial killer and his record stands to this day. I'm convinced you're sharing your house with the spirit of this child, so you'll understand me when I tell you that you don't know what you're dealing with.'

Molly was sceptical. 'How could a nine-year-old boy become so hateful and twisted? It just doesn't make sense, Gerry.' Maybe a few more tipples might shed some light on this darkest of darkness as she floated further and further out to sea.

'The criminal justice system failed Lord and Lady

398

Prendergast, just like it failed their wayward son. Having more power than the local law, Lady Prendergast took matters into her own hands, so ashamed of the child who brought a stain on the Prendergast name. The youngest of the Prendergasts disappeared off the face of the planet. Rumours say his mother put him out of his misery, but that's never been proven. They did not find him or his remains. But contemporaries at the time believe the child never left the house…never left his bedroom.'

Jesus, Molly had a ghastly feeling she knew where the child's remains were. Of course! Why hadn't she thought about it sooner? It was obvious they had murdered the child and burnt his body, limb by limb, in the fireplace while his deranged mom stoked the fire. It all made horrible sense.

'The child was a monster, Molly. All of this started because of his big ears. I think the nicknames and bullying triggered something already in him, snowballing when his mother turned on him. A vicious circle. Lots of kids are bullied, but most of them get on with their lives and even become successful people because it made them tougher. Molly, he was a bad egg from the beginning. The one person I feel sorry for in all of this is Lord Prendergast. These problems with his younger son and wife left him a broken man. I can't say I blame him for what he did to end the misery.'

Just then, light on the breeze, Molly heard the melodic words come in very faintly: a broken man with a broken family for a broken house…

'Oh, I almost forgot another thing. He said something else to the police, which mystified them. Want to know what that was?'

Molly took another heavenly sip of the red stuff. 'You're going to tell me anyway, Gerry with a G.' She was heading towards the heady shores of Drunklandia now.

'He told them someone else had told him to do it. Today we would call that schizophrenia?'

'I guess we'll never know,' answered Molly.

'I think we have a pretty good idea when the kid's telling the police someone in the fireplace is telling him to do it.'

Molly dropped her glass of priceless Spanish wine.

On the other end of the line, Gerry McAuliffe heard the crash of glass followed by Molly Greene swearing profusely. 'Molly, are you okay? What was that crash? It sounded like breaking glass. More swearing came down the line into his ear.

A minute went by before Molly picked up again. 'Sorry, dropped a glass.'

Hearing what Gerry said had winded her. She struggled to find her breath. Molly grabbed another glass and poured the rest of the bottle to steady her nerves. She had heard a deep and disturbing voice coming from the fireplace while her wandering child had lain next to her in bed. Whatever was in the fireplace had called her son home. For a hair-prickling moment, she considered if his real mom was down there somewhere in the tar-caked, sooty chimney pipes, tormenting her son in death as she had in life. But that didn't make sense. Or did it? 'What did he do?'

'Who?'

'You said something like you can't blame Lord Prendergast for what he did.'

Gerry spoke, but a volley of footsteps above her interrupted his words.

'What? Sorry, I didn't get that?' She gazed at the ceiling. The footfalls had come from somewhere to the right of the light shade.

'Lord Prendergast had her committed,' Gerry repeated. 'But get this: had her committed in the very same bedroom where she had kept her son a prisoner and, very likely, ended his sad life. He wanted her to be tormented every day for the rest of her existence, a constant reminder of what she had done to the one who needed help the most. Old Prendergast knew the truth. And just like their son, Lady Prendergast stopped coming out of the bedroom one morning. Nobody wanted to say anything, but smoke billowed from the chimneys the whole night through. C o i n c i d e n t a l l y , on the same night Lady Prendergast vanished. Between you, me, and the four walls, I think Lord Prendergast cracked. My opinion is that old Prendergast sent his wife where she had sent their son to live forever in Purgatory. That's just my theory.'

'We've been talking about this child for the last… I don't know how long,' Molly finally asked, 'Did he have a name?'

'Henry.'

28.

Molly was speechless.

'Are you there?'

'Not sure anymore.'

'Molly, what's w—'

Molly hung up. She heard the voice again, an indistinct whisper coming from the hallway. 'Mama, look what I found.'

Molly got to her feet, head reeling from the effect of the wine, and followed the voice of reason. She stood in the hallway, listening out. She was sure she heard a sough of breath coming from her left. How far away? Impossible to tell. Molly walked down the hallway and stopped at the basement door.

She hated going down there. Then again, she'd never been down there. Prendergast had spoken about it to her the day they arrived, but one look down the rickety stairs at the peeling walls evaporating into darkness, and the waft of sewer pipes was enough for Molly. She'd locked it and hidden the key for fear one of the children might go down there and get hurt. But now she was listening to gentle scratching coming from inside the basement door. For some reason, Molly wasn't afraid. The alcohol had numbed her senses. She was in control, by God. She fetched the basement key from the mug with the broken handle high on the kitchen side shelf. That was a brilliant hiding place for it, and she put it in there the first day they'd arrived, out of sight and out of mind. Molly got back to the basement door. As she stood there looking at the white paint, she thought she'd only imagined hearing the scratching. She turned and walked back towards the kitchen when the scraping stopped her, then she turned on her heels. There was scratching coming from inside the locked basement door.

That strangely distant voice from inside again said: 'Look, Mama!' It could've come from next to her. Molly, in her altered state of being, didn't question what was inside the basement door or why it was even there. She stuck the key into the lock and turned it. The door clicked and Molly opened it back quickly, trying to stave off that niggling fear flittering inside her.

A sweet, cloying voice sounded from the darkness below. 'It's all for you…'

'What is?' the mother of three asked, flicking the switch, but the dusty lightbulb had blown years ago. She slipped her phone from her pocket and switched on the flashlight app. She descended the creaking wooden steps which creaked and heaved under her weight and worthy of the finest horror film cliché, but it was real, and Molly was living this.

As she descended into the gloom, Molly was aware of how no footsteps appeared on the dusty steps, except her own.

The sugared voice called out again once Molly hit the bottom step. Molly heard, 'Peekaboo, Mama!' She swung her light ahead of her and saw a huddled black figure ducking to the right into a smaller room leading off the main chamber. Screaming fear seized Molly, not allowing her to take one more step forward. She was vulnerable and knew it. When casting a glance over her shoulder, she was thankful for the light of the hallway streaming down the wooden stairs. If the door should simply close shut now, she thought her heart would give out. It was already galloping in her chest and temples.

Unsure what to do, she decided to call Prendergast. She needed some clarification fast. He hadn't told her anything about the basement, except that he kept it closed. Why? He hadn't told her, and she or Janice hadn't bothered to ask. She tried calling but panicked when she saw she had no Wi-Fi signal. Of course, she didn't.

The basement door began to swing on its hinges, agonisingly slow, as if taunting her. Nobody knew she was down here. If anything should happen to her, she'd never…

No, that's not an option right now.

Molly bolted for the wooden steps, hair standing on end, decay and rot thick in her nostrils. The stench of sewer pipes was thick in the subterranean chamber but there was something else beyond the sewerage system, something rotting, ropey, and sick. Molly leapt higher on the stairs, screaming, and waiting for something to grab her ankles. She stumbled, fell, then dragged herself upwards on the heels of her hands.

She fumbled for the door handle, while anticipating something to appear at the bottom of the stairs…but nothing came into the beam of light cast from her phone. Terrorised, unable to turn around to find the door handle, she kept her flashlight on the steps below her while her right hand blindly searched for the door handle above her.

Within seconds, she knew there was something wrong, very wrong. She focused her light on the door, where the handle should be, but there was nothing there. Nothing but a strange blank gap existed where the handle should be. Molly whimpered with fright. She rubbed and scratched at her eyes, thinking she was seeing things…or not seeing things. The door with peeling white paint looked as if it had never had a handle or lock.

'Mama…' came that monotone infantile voice. 'Mama.'

Molly's flesh crept.

'It's only me. Don't be afraid, Mama. Look, see what someone's left for you.'

Molly tip-toed down a few steps, just enough to get a good view of the back of the basement where she thought the voice was coming from. She swung her phone and aimed. Standing against the peeling paint of the back wall was a small bobbing shadow figure, its opaque beady eyes reflecting in her phone's light beam. It couldn't have been a shadow. It was the squatter, but not in his fully formed self. He shuffled off behind the corner, moving as a crab would. Molly had a flashback just then, catching crabs with her bare hands in the rock pools of the black rocks on Ballybunion beach.

Braving the elements, she followed the being. She turned right into the small open room where the child had vanished, her heart in her mouth…

Molly was stunned to find a small cellar of dusty wine bottles. She was alone down here. The squatter was gone. The atmosphere had changed, a profound sad emptiness in its wake. That unidentifiable, malodorous stink had also left the basement.

She browsed the dusty wine bottles, perhaps 40 or 50, lying on their sides and gathering years of dust. Molly cleared the settled particles from some of the labels and saw the collection of wine was from Spain. Oh, how she had a soft spot for mouth-watering Spanish wine. She was beginning to think Prendergast had taken that bottle from this collection. Molly wondered why he hadn't told her about this amazing stash hidden beneath the house. Had she told him she had a problem around alcohol or joked uncomfortably that it had a problem with her? She couldn't remember. But what she could remember was what Prendergast had said when he handed her the very vintage (antique?) wine that first official day at the farmhouse: 'Compliments of the house…'

Molly browsed the shelves. She stopped when her hand brushed against something hanging from the end of them. Molly shone her phone on a grubby corkscrew hanging from a nail hammered into the shelf. If this wasn't a sign, then she didn't know what was. Her judgement already fuzzy, Molly lifted the corkscrew from the nail and walked along the selection of vintage wine and picked a bottle dated 1898 from Toledo, the old capital of Spain. She'd once visited the City of Three Cultures with Mike before they were married. The old memories chased her hazy brain while Molly took the bottle of wine from the shelf and uncorked it. The delicious fruity aroma rose in her nostrils, a welcomed change from the foetid stench of old sewers. Without a wine glass, Molly chugged unceremoniously from the bottle of what had to be priceless wine, a century and a quarter old, and tasted absurdly delicious. Bottle in hand, Molly made her way to the bottom of the stairs and could see, even from here, the door remained shut and without a door handle. But for some reason she couldn't fathom, it felt right to be down here now. Her son — her living-dead son, Henry — had shown her the way.

'Tut-tut, oh, Henry. Are you here? I know you can hear me. I want you to know you don't need to do these things to make me love you. I do love you, Henry. I always have. You are a victim of life, but you won't be in death. That is a promise. I was…' Molly took a drunken slug of the expensive wine, '…meant to be here. I wouldn't have found you if it hadn't been for the pandemic. To Covid!' Molly toasted the musty air with a swing and swig from her wine bottle.

She thought about what Gerry McAuliffe had told her. 'Henry, sometimes we rub people up the wrong way. We all make mistakes.' In her drunken, altered state of mind, Molly Greene justified everything, and this was meant to be. 'At the end of the day, Henry, we are both victims and we have both sent people to Heaven…we are THE match made in Heaven, Henry! Let's have a cellar-bration!' Molly slugged and guzzled the 123-year-old bottle of strong alcohol. 'But you already know that because it was me who sent you to Heaven, Henry…Heavenly Henry, it even rhymes…slips right off the tuh-tongue,' slurred Molly, 'just like this wine, Henny-Henny. Remember when I used you to call you that? Peekaboo…' Tears came to Molly's eyes. 'That was your first word, oh, my good Jesus…' She snorted a drunken chuckle and drained the last dregs of wine.

As she laid the empty bottle on the floor next to her, a horrible realisation rose to the surface of her maudlin state of being. Even though she was quite drunk by now, her senses were numbed, yet her whole body bristled as that strange delirious idea took hold of her. She looked about the cold, gloomy basement cellar. Had she been shown the way here or lured here? That was the million-dollar question. Why would Henry lead her to the one place that wasn't good for her? 'Well, fuck that for a game of soldiers,' stated Molly. 'This is Disneyland right now…the wine, not the basement. Henny-Henny does have my buh-est interests at heart, right?' She giggled drunkenly. 'You even took the duh-door handle away so I could enjoy myself, didn't you? Hmm? And nobody…nobody will disturb me because there's no handle on the door.' She drew her head back in laughter. 'You're such a clever-clogs, Henny-Henny…'

Molly got to her feet and went to her open bar. Just as she was about to order another priceless bottle of Spanish wine from a dusty, dickie-bowed waiter who lived down here. Her flashlight went out. The alcohol flowing through her veins had taken the slicing edge off reality. Molly Greene giggled to herself in the pitch darkness. The alcohol had given her Dutch courage because she was surrounded by the warmth of loved ones her sozzled brain had concocted. But in the cold light of darkness, it was only Molly standing in that subterranean place of decay and secrets. What Molly had surrounding her were mental versions of herself, agreeing with everything she said and thought.

But it wasn't just Molly down here now…

Her harmless drunken laugh graduated into a nervous gulp in her throat when her phone battery died. Molly was sure she had charged her phone to full capacity before they set off for school this morning, which seemed very far away now. That earthy yet unearthly smell wafted around the basement. Molly chilled with unexplained terror.

Within the silence of darkness came a rustling somewhere outside in the main chamber. At first,

409

Molly thought it might be a rodent of some description. But as it grew closer, it graduated from a shuffling rustle to pronounced dragging and alternating footsteps: footfall…drag…footfall. There was someone coming her way, dragging one leg. What sent Molly over the abyss was the ragged death-rattle wheezing breaths that accompanied the one-legged visitor.

'Hello?' Her trembling voice sounded utterly alien to her. 'Can I help you with anything?' How absurd could this get? Molly spoke as if she was a shop assistant asking a customer if they needed help. Who else was going to be down here? 'Henny-Henny, is that you?' She reached out into the darkness. She knew damn well it wasn't Henry, whoever Henry was, yet she had to say something to placate herself, to stave off the madness of the situa—

'Molls?'

Molly ran cold, dropping her phone. She whimpered like she was a four-year-old child again. 'Mike?'

A gurgling voice answered back from the darkness. 'What are you doing down here, Molls? You're not going to find happiness down here.'

Molly felt a panic attack come on. She inhaled a deep breath, kept it in for a second, then let it out slowly.

'Whatever are you doing down here in the dark?'

'I…I…followed Henry…'

'Henry? Is he down here too?'

There was a pause just then.

'Why don't you switch on the light, Molls?'

'I don't have a light. The battery just died on my phone.' It was now Molly recalled how manifesting spirits drain energy from wherever they can get it. 'Mike, is that you?'

More rasping breaths' …Switch on the light and see, Molls.'

'But there's no light…the bulb is blown. I already —'

'Give me your hand…'

Molly whined and sniffled. The wheezing gasps were just inches from her face. 'Fuck, fuck…'

'Come on, Molls. Give me your hand…Take my hand, baby…'

Molly cried to herself, afraid for her life to hold her hand out into the darkness. Suddenly, the basement was filled with a gagging croon, a broken hum. On cue, Molly's bladder opened when Eugen Doga's 'Gramophone' waltzing cracked hum filled the underground chamber. Was this even a basement anymore? It was Mike, she was sure of it. Stretching her hand into the darkness, she flinched as something cold and slithery slipped in between her fingers. A hand, cold and oily. Molly could've been holding hands with an octopus. The fishy hand pulled hers a little towards the wall and it came as a surprise when her fingers brushed over a light switch.

'There you go, Molls. Now, let's shed some light

411

on the situation, shall we?'

Molly, drunk on the notion she was about to be reunited with Mike once again, didn't hesitate to flick the switch…and then wished she never had…

Mike was standing in front of her, beneath the swinging lightbulb. His left leg was facing the wrong way and was longer than the right. The whole left side of his body was mangled, rib cage caved in, and Molly feared the pointy objects at strategic points along the left side of his bloodied tracksuit top were protruding rib splinters. Mike's face was perfect, and it was this that broke Molly's heart and brought her to her knees. Mike's right side was as perfect as the Valentine's night he sat into the Volvo to go fetch their daughter in the rain. But his left side had received the Volvo's engine when it came through the dashboard. He reached out his left bloodied hand and extended his fingers. Molly noticed the digits weren't in their right positions, pointing off at odd angles. Mike croaked, 'One last dance, Molls?'

She was numb.

'For old times' sake?'

Hot tears streaming down her cheeks, face contorted in gut-wrenching pain and sorrow, Molly took the dislocated fingers in hers and joined her husband for one last waltz. But Mike couldn't dance anymore; his coordination gone as his left knee softly crunched and buckled. Yet she held him close, supporting him, as he hummed the raspy waltz in her ear. Mike was a bag of bones in her arms as they slowly revolved. She could feel bones in her husband's body where there shouldn't be any and sickening hollows where there should be. Mike was in his altered state because his wife had been too drunk to drive and collect Mina that Valentine's night. Here she was, waltzing with her mangled, living-dead husband around a wine cellar ballroom. Poetic justice? Sick irony? Who was responsible for this twisted joke? Henry? It was Henry who had led her here, after all. But in her cocktail of confusion, Molly Greene couldn't tell the Henrys apart anymore and it didn't seem to matter. It's the thought that counts.

Mike's gently cracked lilt came to a stop and so did their eternal waltz. For a short second, Molly looked into Mike's eyes; his left eye was nothing more than an empty socket, but deep inside the glazed right one, her real Mike was there, buried deep inside.

'Till death do us part,' he whispered, struggling to catch his breath, and led her to the steps. 'Till we meet again,' he said, gesturing Molly up the stairs to the door without a handle. Molly could see the vague outline of the steps and climbed them shakily, realising she was drunker than she'd thought. As she approached the door, she saw the door handle, like it always had been there.

Molly opened the door and felt a rush of fresh air and relief as daylight streamed in on top of her. She looked down into the chasm beneath the hallway floor. Mike sank and morphed into something squatting and dark, like a big old overcoat, before

413

crawling off into the darkness in twitching movements that left Molly cold. What had been the purpose of this ghoulish one-act play? Molly Greene could think of many reasons, but the one reason coming to the fore was a gentle reminder of what she had done.

*

An hour later, Molly collected the other children from school. She wasn't sure about Cora, but the very minute Mina sat into the car, she saw her mom's bloodshot eyes and flushed face. Her hair was a mess, and she was acting all weird. The smell of stale alcohol filled the car. It was tense. The only communication that went on was between Mina's and Cora's scared and vulnerable glances. They shared a secret. Mina had met Cora in the schoolyard and had told her how the brilliant Janice had slipped her a second phone when she'd hugged her that morning. It could only be used in an emergency and it would be their lifeline out of there.

29.

At 5.30pm, Molly received a call. It was the news reporter asking Molly to be let through the gate. Molly told the woman to knock on the neighbour's door and he would give her access. The news reporter responded by saying Molly she had done just that, but there had been no answer. 'No sign of life' were her exact words.

Molly told her to sit tight. She cursed Prendergast to kingdom come, simultaneously telling Mina and Cora to watch Emma for a second. She drove up the lane to meet the Six One News satellite truck and greeted them with a wide grin from behind the steel gate. If the news crew had known Molly, they would've seen she was a little tipsy, on her merry way. A news reporter calling herself Sheila greeted her and she would be conducting the interview with the cameraman whose name Molly didn't catch. A third individual waved from the back of the satellite truck and Sheila explained that Liam would be '… commandeering the dials and buttons during the interview. Liam is our sound engineer' Adding with a smirk, 'Liam is also more than happy to stay in the truck, being of a squeamish nature.'

Molly saluted everyone and cast a glance at the Gatehouse to see if she'd catch Prendergast at one of the windows. Not seeing any movement, she took note of his vintage Jag. Molly's phone vibrated. She slipped it from her jeans pocket and saw Gerry McAuliffe was calling. 'Not now, Gerry,' she told her screen as she hung up. Molly politely apologised and swiftly led the TV crew down the lane to the farmhouse. Once there, she led Sheila and the cameraman into the living room.

'This is where the encounter will take place,' Molly told them. The 'encounter' even caught Mina's and Cora's attention. Their mom had rehearsed this and had come up with a sinister word, figuring *encounter* sounded ominous.

'Spooky!' uttered the cameraman as he set up his camera while the reporter looked over her notes. The reporter then suggested they conduct a quick interview with Molly, so she gathered up the children and introduced them to the team. Each of the girls was wearing their finest clothes they could find in their wardrobe and were scrubbed clean beyond recognition. Molly took them to the sofa in the living room and the four of them sat down, looking stiff and too perfect, like dolls lined up in a dollhouse.

As the clock in the kitchen struck six electronic chimes, the reporter looked at herself in her phone, sniffed and cleared her throat several times. As the chimes counted down six bells, she made the comment that the arrival of 'the ghost' coincided with the opening of the Six One News, which was spooky.

Before any of them knew what was happening, the Greenes were being interviewed on live national TV and online. The reporter asked some rudimentary questions about the property. She asked Molly and the girls to recount an experience they had at the house. Molly saw this as an ideal opportunity to speak about the most hair-raising experiences, going so far as to speak about sleeping in bed with 'the squatter'. Not once, in the opening section of the interview did Molly mention her son or anything remotely similar. She referred to the presence in the house as the squatter, just like the rest of Old Castle. It had a good ring to it. Molly constantly reminded the reporter and everyone else tuned in that the spirit in the house was a lost soul with good intentions.

*

The reporter then asked Mina to relay an experience. She tried to follow her mom's directions for the interview, not wanting to wreck the moment. Mina spoke about the evening she was on a live call with her friends in Dublin when they saw something in the background behind Mina and how it had gathered in a black swirling mass by the fridge. After she relate her story and before the reporter turned to her sister, Mina had an overpowering urge to scream into the camera: 'Save us for fuck's sake! This isn't mom!' But she chickened out and was also aware she had the emergency phone in her pocket right now.

*

Then it was Cora's turn. She told of the night she and her mom saw the spirit of the child waving from behind the living room curtain. They had rehearsed these accounts earlier that evening and Molly had nicely warned Cora not to mention how she had lied about the identity of the waving child to protect her… when she was actually buying time. Emma didn't want to sit still and was being awkward during the interview, sticking her tongue out at the camera, oblivious to the hundreds of thousands of smiles she had generated around the country and abroad — a brief light-hearted moment choked out all too soon.

'Now, Molly is going to give us a tour of the house,' the news reporter said to the camera. She was about to say something else when she fell silent as happiness overcame her, undiluted and flowing through her. She smiled at the camera, creating much-dreaded dead air, ironically. The cameraman waved frantically behind the camera to snap her out of her apparent trance when he, too, became still.

Molly, quite aware they were experiencing a sudden feeling of happiness that she knew so well, beamed uncomfortably. Should she speak to the camera or the temporarily hijacked news reporter? 'Don't worry, um, when my ch… the squatter appears, anyone in its presence is consumed by an overwhelming sensation of happiness, almost a feeling of transcending. I became aware of the pattern a few nights after moving in…always at six o'clock and lasts for a minute or two. This phenomenon means the squatter has awoken upstairs where it resides in my bedroom fireplace.'

*

By now, smiles across the country had begun to falter. Molly Greene's seemingly normal response was profound. Text messages were being sent back and forth across the country and around the globe, telling friends and loved ones to tune in to the Six One News FAST.

Molly could see the dismay grow in the reporter's face. The cameraman was looking fidgety. Right now, she imagined what scared them even more was how the children seemed so fine with it. She was proud of her girls…

Suddenly, the atmosphere changed in the room.

'Do you feel that?' asked Molly.

The news reporter, Sheila, looked about the living room with darting eyes. 'Yes, and I can't explain what it is, but I do feel something.' This was the point in the infamous interview where Sheila realised this was no joke and the fear was evident in her face.

The cameraman was indicating to Sheila they had a problem. The news reporter apologised to the studio and the viewers at home. She turned to the cameraman, live on air. 'What's the issue, Liam?'

Everyone in the farmhouse, at home, and in the news studio clearly heard the cameraman telling the reporter the battery pack in his camera had just died. He assured her he had a fully charged battery before the interview. Thankfully, he had a backup, but would need a few seconds to run to the truck for it.

The news reporter laughed it off. 'This is live TV, folks.'

Molly interjected, 'This is another side-effect of a haunting. The spirit will drain any energy it can to manifest and let us know when it's with us.'

The cameraman made a dash for the satellite truck to get another battery pack, gesturing to the news reporter to buy him time.

Molly asked the reporter, 'Do you smell that?'

The reporter sniffed at the air and a peculiar look came about her. 'I smell dampness…mould.'

Molly smiled, her eyes twinkling. 'Anything else?'

'Fruit? Oranges? Spices, maybe?'

Molly suggested cloves, and the reporter agreed wholeheartedly.

The cameraman slipped back in behind the camera and discreetly changed the battery packs before the camera died completely.

'Shush, listen.' Molly indicated for everyone to be quiet.

A heavy stillness fell in the living room as the Greenes and the TV news crew listened to something shuffling on the ceiling above them. The reporter and cameraman exchanged fearful glances as a child's footsteps walked across the ceiling and…

'Here it comes,' Molly whispered, infectious relish and delight etched in her face.

*

The stairs creaked ever so slightly. It could have been just the wood expanding, but they began to hear a pattern as the squatter's steps trod on each step. Sheila, the news reporter, stood poised next to the sofa where the Greenes sat, with her microphone held to her lips but unable to speak. Suspended in disbelief as she was about to come face-to-face with an entity from the other side.

This would be the live event of her career. This was about to change their lives forever. Nothing, nothing, would ever be the same after this evening.

The reporter mumbled something inaudible to the cameraman who panned the camera around from the sofa. There, standing in the doorway, was the dark, vaporous silhouette of a child, so statuesque it appeared to be a cardboard cutout. As the camera rolled, the entity became animate and glided into the room in that insect-like staggered manner, making it more difficult to believe this thing was ever human. The moment the squatter moved, it became a blur in the camera lens.

Sheila, for the first time in her life, had lost the gift of the gab and stood there in dumb, stunned silence. They had come down here thinking they would find a cheesy seance affair, or worse still, a mentally unhinged woman who couldn't accept her son's death. Sheila had spoken to the news researcher, who had first contacted Molly before coming down to Old Castle. She also shared the researcher's fear after reading about Molly's tragic past. But what they were witnessing — what the country, and the whole world was witnessing — proved them both wrong. Molly was a very sane woman living happily in an insane house. How could this be happening?

The reporter whispered, 'I'm dizzy…'

'Me too…' Viewers around the country heard the cameraman mutter. 'The room's spinning…'

At the same time, the camera went in and out of focus, unable to centre on the dark mist.

'I feel nauseous.' Sheila was sensing she was deathly pale.

Molly assured her, 'The nausea will pass. The

421

squatter is pulling energy from wherever it can.'

The wraith drifted to the sofa and came to a dead stop, motionless, paused by an unseen hand.

'Mom, I'm cold,' said Emma.

*

The camera had been going in and out of focus, unable to centre on the dark mist. Behind the scenes, the reporter and cameraman indicated they were queasy. Now the camera began to pick up their breaths, icily puffing out in front of them. Viewers around the country had been wondering if the phantasm was nothing more than an elaborate camera trick. Little by little, as their horror grew, people realised this was the real deal. Finally, irrefutable evidence of a ghost. But coming to the fore was the growing distress, not because of the haunted house, but because of the children living there in that toxic atmosphere. Already, complaints were beginning to filter into RTE broadcasting headquarters in Dublin, expressing fear for the children.

The anomaly approached the camera. The camera's lens widened as the thing materialised the closer it came. Now, it was no longer the dark human mass but clear and translucent, like looking at one's reflection in a car windscreen. The world watched the reporter rubbed her eyes as she tried to focus on the wraith in the same room as them. By now, Sheila had apparently forgot how to be a news reporter. It was as if she was a young child again, mesmerised, with a gormless, open-mouthed expression, as if she'd just been stunned by a blunt object to the head. Across the

422

nation, and those watching online around the globe, saw for the first time an actual real-life ghost, a phantasm, a living dead. These few minutes of TV news were changing lives on a profound level.

This 6pm news bulletin would become the point where B.C. and A.D. meet. Children watching would remember for the rest of their lives the night the ghostly child — the squatter — came on the telly.

*

The spectre turned from the camera and went back to Emma, Cora, and Mina, who were now sitting on the floor with the trigger toys Molly had strategically placed earlier, reminiscent of a Victorian seance. The Barbie doll levitated into the air, held by the effervescent child spectre. The squatter played with its hair, then turned to Molly and began to stroke her locks. Molly froze, but tried to keep a smile for the camera. She had been in this situation many times before, but it always caught her by surprise. It was like posing for a picture with her head between the open jaws of a bull alligator, waiting — *Hurry on for fuck's sake!* — for the person behind the camera to say, 'Say, cheese!'

What came next Molly figured would melt hearts in good and bad ways across the globe as the cameras' sensitive microphone picked up the faint words: 'Mama?' as if spoken from a different room through a hollow tin can.

Molly beamed on hearing this while, inside her head, she heard the cash register go off with a resounding Ka-Ching! Jackpot! There's the money shot right there!

Forgetting her microphone was on, oblivious to the fact she was even holding a microphone, Sheila let out a heartfelt, 'Jesus fucking Christ…' live on air. But it didn't really matter anymore. She could've told her viewers that she didn't give two flying fucks about her viewer ratings and it wouldn't have made a blind bit of difference to the overall outcome of this fiasco.

'Yes, Henny-Henny…'

Both Mina and Cora looked overwhelmed on hearing the squatter, the child who walked alone at the farmhouse, call their mom, 'Mama'. 'That's not Henry. Why did she call him Henny-Henny?' whispered Cora to Mina.

The cameraman picked up on this and swung the camera on Cora. 'This isn't Henry, Mom.' The ten-year-old was no longer aware of the camera in her face. This had become personal.

Everyone in the living room could hear whispering coming from the entity, only there were voices, that of a child and that of an old man, or was it an old woman?

'Mom?' Mina asked. 'What's wrong with it?'

The cameraman panned in on Mina's face, perhaps sensing it was clear to everyone the Greene children were experiencing something new.

'I don't know, darling,' Molly answered. 'But did you know there was a cellar of wine below our feet we knew nothing about? Henry, I mean the squatter, showed me earlier. I brought up a few bottles and left them in the kitchen. Wait…' Molly got up from the sofa and disappeared and returned, humming Eugen Doga's 'Gramophone' with an uncorked bottle of wine and three glasses. She offered a glass of wine to the cameraman and the news reporter. Both kindly declined while Sheila indicated they were in the middle of a live interview for the 6pm news.

'Suit yourselves,' replied Molly, sitting back on the sofa between her children and messily pouring herself a large glass of wine.

Sensing something wasn't going according to plan, Mina stood up and told the TV crew. 'Let's stop this. Please, leave. I don't think Mom is feeling very well…'

'Cora!' Molly bawled. 'Every show needs a dancing monkey!' She'd forgotten her own children's names by now. No, she hadn't forgot their names, but she couldn't remember which was which.

*

A ten-minute drive away, school secretary Gerry McAuliffe was sitting with his mom at the dining table, having dinner while watching the Greene's interview on the 6pm news. The live interview had begun with playful mystery, but he lost his appetite on seeing how things descended into chaos and the distress it was causing Molly's two eldest daughters, lacerated by their pleading gazes. He fell back in his chair when the spirit of the child appeared in the doorway of the living room. It was a seminal moment in many ways. The scariest element of the interview, by far, was that Molly had come unhinged.

425

Throwing his fork and knife onto his plate, he marched down the hallway, protesting, 'I told her this was a bad idea! Why can't people just take some advice?'

'The best advice is to take advice,' said his elderly mom to herself as her son grabbed his car key and coat before storming out of the flat. 'Gerry? What about your chicken pie?'

*

'Mom! What's wrong with you?! What're you—'

Mina spasmed as a short guttural growl came from the ethereal child, sending everyone's hair standing on end. The sound was somewhere between a pig's snort and a toad's croak.

Sheila let out a spontaneous shriek and apologised to everyone in the same breath while the cameraman emitted a harmonious 'Fuck!' that graced the ears of the nation and beyond. But this was only the beginning. When this piece of historic live TV had finished filming, just a few would recall a melodic 'Fuck'.

Limb by limb, the child who walked alone at the farmhouse popped Barbie's limbs from her body. First, the left arm…then the right.

Emma began to bawl, seeing her Barbie dismembered.

The left leg was dislocated and jerked free, followed by the right. Finally, her glamorous head was popped free of her torso. All six pieces were thrown on the floor by the fireplace.

'Oops!' Sheila uttered in a sanguine tone.

'Naughty!' Finding some reassurance by forcing herself to believe the child spirit can also behave like any other spoilt child. She slapped the back of her hand, 'Tut, tut!' and grimaced for the camera's benefit.

This sudden change in character worried Molly. It was becoming one of those interviews with the family grizzly bear that suddenly turns on his owners after 25 loving years of trying to humanise an animal which needs to be out hunting salmon in a secluded mountain river — *Helloooo!*

'Is this part of the show?' the cameraman asked in a voice too high pitched to be considered his normal voice.

Molly snapped back, 'This isn't a show! This is my son we're talking about here. Jesus Christ, don't you think Henny-Henny's been through enough? Hmm? Don't you think we've all suffered for our sins?' She boomed in one breath.

And so it began: Molly Greene's metamorphosis on live TV. Go big or go home; Molly chose big. She had wanted the biggest audience and now she was going to get it.

The squatter twitched and spasmed, then crawled across the room in that crab-like manner, stopping behind the sofa where it stroked Molly's hair.

'You see?' she said to everyone. 'He's a harmless child, looking for Mama, looking for a little love in a world gone wrong…isn't that right, Henry?'

'Mom, Henry's dead,' Mina said, low and serious. 'He died in the car accident.'

Molly huffed a chuckle as she purred to the strokes of the wraith. 'Yes and no, sweetie. Henry is with us.' She cast a furtive glance at the camera. 'And I'll talk to you about this later. This is neither the time nor the place, and you bloody well know that. Have you tried to superglue your phone back together, hmm?'

On cue, Mina pulled a small flip phone from her pocket and called a number on fast dial. Molly scowled and was about to let go with one all merciful, keening scream when Cora screamed even louder:

'This isn't Henry! Henry was a little boy who played with his toy cars!' She frantically searched the air as she cast her memory back to happier days. 'Remember the train set he had? How he used to put his plastic soldiers into the trailers and watch them going around in circles?'

During Cora's outburst, a series of hard knocks came at the front door, adding to the growing disarray.

'Really?!' snapped Molly. She turned to Sheila. 'Can you ask the woodpecker to please go away? We're in the middle of a live news interview here.' Turning back to Cora, she said, 'Sorry, Mina, I am listening to you, darling. Go ahead…' It was as if Cora hadn't said anything of significance.

'I'm Cora! Mina's over there!'

Molly's ghost child turned on Emma and snapped Creepy Baby from her grasp. The living child almost suffered a heart attack right there when her comfort object, her Lovey, was taken from her. In the hands of the crooked, dire phantasm, Creepy Baby didn't look so creepy anymore. Its head and limbs were yanked free of its body. Emma witnessed this and bawled so hard her mouth was just an open O in her face. She turned blue before she found her breath and *screeeeamed!*

Molly saw the news reporter was still standing there with that idiotic expression on her face while someone pounded on the front door. 'Answer the door and tell whatever inbred yokel's who is out there to go jump in a lake!' She turned on her daughter. This time, she didn't bother asking for the phone. She bore down on Mina, wrenched the phone from her hand, and smashed it off the wall.

*

Gerry was relieved when the front door opened.

'Hi, you'll have to come back another time. We're in the middle of a live interview for the Six One News.'

He knew who was speaking to him as he had just seen her from the TV in his dining room. 'Yes, I know… My name's Gerry McAuliffe. Molly knows me. Please, cut the interview. I don't think she's in her right mind. There's something not right about her. This interview should've never gone ahead.'

For a moment, Gerry was sure Sheila, the news reporter, was going to try and stop him as he brushed by her. But when he did, she ran in the opposite direction away from the house, screaming into the night and skidding to a stop at the satellite truck, hammering to be let in.

Gerry sprinted down the hallway to the living

room. He would later say he lost consciousness as he stood there, stunned and horrified, when he entered the living room.

*

A five-minute walk up the lane from the farmhouse, Richard Prendergast was sitting in his living room, watching the horror unfold on the Six One News. Should he have done more to stop it? He didn't have any right to interfere in the contest…the experiment. That was the only way of knowing if the mother was right for the house. For once, he thought this was going to be it, after 200 years of searching, a search which had come down from one generation to the next. The Prendergasts had finally found what they were looking for as the U2 song went. The farmhouse wasn't the real prize of this contest; the farmhouse was the judge. Just as Molly wasn't a contestant, but first prize in this never-ending unearthly contest. She'd got one thing right though: she was the guinea pig in this experiment, as they all were, until that elusive all-round, broken 'mother' was found. Jesus, no matter what he tried, Prendergast just couldn't get rid of the farmhouse. It kept coming back to him like a dirty penny with its dirtier secrets. If only the child, for want of a better word, wasn't so possessive, they could all live in harmony…if only.

He watched the true nature of the beast reveal itself on live TV, and Richard Prendergast decided he couldn't do this anymore. It had taken everything belonging to him, including his conscience. He

430

should've felt something now, watching that poor misguided woman and her innocent children become part of the farmhouse. It was time to do what he should've done after he offered up his wife and child as bait. There's a certain comfort in knowing what's gone is gone, but what's half-gone is pure agony. Maybe, someday, they would walk back in to his life, but it would be too late by then. Maybe he'd meet them in the next life…maybe.

Prendergast switched off the TV and the hysterical screams coming from it. As he left the living room for the last time, he wondered why the television channel hadn't gone to an impromptu ad break or intermission or something to save its viewers from the harrowing yet horribly fascinating live images.

In his bedroom, he pulled out the family pictures he'd piled up at the bottom of his wardrobe. He then went down the hallway to his defunct surgery and took a syringe from the same valise young Cora Greene had seen when he'd treated her bird bite. There was a moment there when he thought everything would turn out okay as he helped the child. He'd felt proud and good about himself for the first time in a long time. And maybe, just maybe, he and Molly might've become something more than neighbours. He was wrong. His heart and soul, especially his soul, knew a nip from a cockatoo would be the last of this little girl's worries. He had put a Band-Aid on a gunshot wound and he'd known all along.

Prendergast took a vial of methadone from his

431

doctor's bag, which was his drug of choice when it came to self-administering anaesthesia.

Pictures in his left hand, dripping syringe in his right, Richard Prendergast switched off the light, left his little surgery office, and closed the door behind him. He walked seven steps down the hallway and made a hard right straight through the wall, or rather, tore through the wallpaper that concealed his son's bedroom. There, he sat on his son's bed and peered out the window towards the horizon, in the direction of the farmhouse, and waited for it to appear…legend said it would happen this way.

The double beam of headlights streaking across his son's bedroom wall caught his wavering attention. He got to his feet and stared through his son's window. The satellite truck he'd seen earlier through the curtain came fishtailing up the lane from the farmhouse at high speed. The truck roared past the Gatehouse in top gear and Prendergast squeezed his eyes shut just before the smashing of steel and iron filled the night. The satellite truck crashed through the road gate and kept going east.

Prendergast sat back down on his son's bed.

Five minutes of silence went by (silence at the Gatehouse but not at the farmhouse). The peace and tranquillity were almost soothing considering what was happening at the bottom of the lane right now…

And then he saw it, rising high against the blood twilight sky. That first puff of snow-white smoke came from one of the farmhouse chimneys, just as legend said it would. A thick bubbling column of snow-white smoke plumed for the heavens. Under any other circumstances, Prendergast would've liked the sight of smoke coming from the farmhouse chimney. Nice to have someone living there again. Putting some life into the house…but not this kind of life.

Satisfied it was finally over, for now, Prendergast laid down on his son's bed and spread the framed photographs of his family around himself before injecting 300 milligrams of methadone into his arm to kill his pain indefinitely. In a way, he was proud. He had managed to find a suitable mother for the farmhouse while two centuries of ancestors had failed to placate the place.

Molly Greene had won first prize. The house had chosen. The farmhouse belonged to her, and she belonged to the farmhouse. It was a joint first prize.

30.

The squatter turned and crawled straight up the wall by the fireplace.

Molly was howling heinous laughter by now, not knowing why or caring. Her eldest daughters stood back in shocked numbness, wondering where all of this had gone wrong while Emma screamed as she tried to put Creepy Baby back together.

The ghost of the child crawled across the ceiling, while calling, 'Peekaboo, Mama! Peekaboo, Mama!' It was an oddly ineffectual voice, as if it had been pre-recorded and sounded too calm and monotone for the context they were now in. The child grappled with the light shade, pulling something from inside it.

'That's mine!' Emma pointed upwards. 'He took it!'

Melodic notes came from the upside-down nightmare on the ceiling as it played Eugen Doga's 'Gramophone' on the kalimba: *plink…plink…plinkity plink…plink-plink-plink…* while the overhead light shade swung, throwing flittering shadows on the onlookers below.

'I know that tune,' commented the unnamed man behind the camera, like the ghost playing the African thumb piano wasn't any big deal.

Molly rejoiced, 'It's Eugen Doga's *Gramophone!* Oh, Henry, you're playing Mommy's and Daddy's old waltz. You remembered our lovely dances around the kitchen! God, I've missed you!' Molly's eyes sparkled in the dancing light. 'But now that I have you back, hopefully, we can make up for lost time, hmm? What do you say we all go for a walk in the woods later? How about that?' She excitedly added, 'Maybe we could get lost, Henny-Henny! Wouldn't that be fun?'

But it was Molly Greene who was lost in her own Forest of Chimera, treading further and further into the darkness where the sun doesn't shine.

'We can catch birds if you like. I know you like that…a little birdie told me!' Through the mists of time, Molly remembered something someone had once said about a bird in a shoebox.

The thing on the ceiling, which didn't look like a child anymore, but a folded crooked child with a muzzle for a snout, turned to look down at Molly through its beady dead peepers. It began to rock back and forth, slowly at first, then growing more excited, reminding Gerry McAuliffe of the kids with Down syndrome he used to volunteer with at the community centre at the weekends. This was a nightmare on a whole new level, he thought, gazing upwards, fully sure he was going to puke. But the rocking got faster and faster until it was a head-banging blur before breaking from its disturbing rocking and skittered across the ceiling, and exiting through the top of the doorway frame.

A confusing moment of silence ensued before a single screeching squawk screamed in the kitchen.

'Louie!' bawled Cora.

The squatter returned a second later, moving across the ceiling with Louie's limp body in its grasp.

435

It crouched and began to pluck the cockatoo, showering everyone in wintery snow-white plumes that cascaded downwards.

'How romantic!' Molly declared.

The manifestation then cast the flaccid, bald body of the cockatoo aside. The poor thing landed with a splat on the mantlepiece. Cora ran to save what was left of the bird.

Mina tried to cover her little sister's eyes, but Emma wouldn't allow it. She pulled the tartan blanket draped over the back of the sofa over herself, curled up into a ball, and rocked herself into an involuntary sleep. Emma slipped under the blanket with Mina. She hid under the blanket, next to her sister, in the comfort of darkness. Sweet music and terrifying raucous screams were all around them. Their senses must have gone into overload. The squatter crawled down to Molly with a single tail feather in its grasp, then stuck it in her hair behind her ear. Molly, in response, howled a stereotypical bullshit Native Indian howl and laughed heinously. The squatter retook its position on the ceiling and continued to play the waltz, note for note, upside-down, in some hellish solo concerto. The thing crossed back over the ceiling, descended the wall by the doorway, not missing a note. As it approached, the malign odour of centuries of decay filled their nostrils. That overly sweet citrus perfume wasn't there anymore, nor the spicy touch of cloves.

It came to the blanket hiding the girls and raised it, inch by inch, just enough to hand the instrument to petrified Mina. Cora kept her hands over her face to shut out anything she might see. Mina looked up at it in repulsion.

'Take it, Mina,' Molly ordered. 'Henry wants you to take it.'

Mina didn't want to take the instrument.

'Don't be rude, dear. These nice people have come down here for a show and that's what we're going to give them. Now, take the goddamn *kalimbo, kalibimbo* or whatever it's called!'

Mina took the thumb piano from the spirit. 'What does it want me to do with this? I can't even—' Mina plucked the bars and looked at her mom in amazement as she began to play Eugen Doga's waltz, pitch-perfect. 'Mom!' She giggled with dumb amazement. 'Since when can I play the kalimba?'

Molly answered back, 'Since now, sweetie! I always knew you had it in you!'

*

Viewers around the country and further afield watched the horror…the miracle before their eyes while others remained suspicious. It seemed like this Molly Greene would do anything to get a little free advertising for her haunted house tours.

*

'Mom?' Mina asked in confusion. 'What's happening?' Her fingers became a bloodied blur as the blades ate into her flesh. 'Mom!' She screamed. 'I can't stop!' Mina's fingers moved faster and faster on the blades. An odd expression came over her as the germ of panic manifested. Her stupefied smile

437

faltered while her fingers plucked faster and faster, now with preternatural speed, without even looking at the instrument…faster and faster…A darkly demonic, feral face replaced Mina's face before she became Mina again. It all happened as fast as a subliminal message.

Cora screamed a despairing sharp wail, ripping her vocal cords.

Mina began to drool. Saliva dripped from the corner of her mouth onto her manic fingers, spinning spittle in all directions. Her fingers knotted, but there was nothing she could do. She glanced over at her mom waving an imaginary baton.

Gerry McAuliffe came to and jumped in, trying to grab the bloodied instrument from Mina screaming through her tears. *'Make it stop! Make it stooop!'* The camera was on her. They were still on live transmission. She tried not to look hysterical, which made it even worse. What the fuck was the cameraman still filming this debacle for, anyway?

Gerry brayed, 'Switch off that camera! You've already got your story!'

But the cameraman just looked at Gerry with a stupefied grin before falling backward from the camera, which was still rolling. Sheila and Liam, the sound engineer, had left him behind; the cameraman remained loyal to his viewers, documenting the terror that would forever link him with the Musicians of the RMS Titanic as they played 'Nearer, My God, to Thee'.

'By Jiminy!' Molly rejoiced. 'Everyone's doing a runner!' She exclaimed in a spontaneous British accent, which was hilarious…for Molly, at least.

Mina's fingers had cramped and turned to gnarled, useless talons. Some prodigious strength working through the fifteen-year-old kept a hold of the instrument and there was nothing the school secretary could do to prise it away from her steely grasp. In the mêleé, Gerry McAuliffe happened to look across at Molly sitting on the sofa with a wide, satisfied smile on her face, chugging from a bottle of wine, as a second apparition stood behind her, playing with her hair. It had a feminine shape with the face of sin. It was so tall; its head touched the ceiling.

'I mean,' Molly uttered, 'when does a widow stop becoming a widow? What's the official line on this? Even the word sounds sinister. Will she always be a widow even if she never remarries? Hello, I'd like to introduce myself. My name is Widow Greene. Apologies in advance, but that's creepy as fuck. I'm in my forties for the love of Christ!'

Gerry fell backwards, hit his head on the stone fireplace, and knocked himself out cold. Meanwhile, Molly rabbited on about the perks of being a single mom in 2021.

The girls recoiled in horror as the hellish contortion spasmed across the living room to the fireplace and crawled up into the chimney stack. A ruckus came from inside the chimney breast, sounding like there were rats up there. They listened to it scramble up through the chimney to the second floor, where it came out in Molly's bedroom. Heavy footsteps, the first time they'd ever heard these adult steps, boomed across the ceiling. Halfway across, those footfalls became the sound of thudding hooves. There was an animal up there, trotting around, *clippity-clop*. Then the dragging sounds came from inside the chimney again, before…

Mina and Cora screamed in perfect unison!

…an upside-down pallid face peered out from the chimney at them and growled once. Mina thought of Santa Claus, but this was Santa with a c-l-a-w-s.

In her dreamy haze, Molly Greene heard this growl and recognised it. She'd heard the same single guttural snarl coming from her bedroom fireplace on a different night.

The moment they heard the growl, the 'child' waddled across the ceiling and retreated into the fireplace to join the other entity, who appeared to cower sheepishly. It crouched where any other house would have a pile of burning logs.

The Greenes, including Molly, heard the freakish muffled croak of 'Peekaboo, Mama,' coming from the fireplace in front of them. It was no longer the voice of innocence, but demonic and hateful, yet still trying to hide behind the guise of childhood innocence. It barked, grunted, and hissed in their faces. The stench was sickening.

'Henny-Henny? Is that you? What are you doing in the chimney, dear? Tut-tut! You'll have a long wait for Santa. It's still only…' Molly couldn't remember they were in the month of February; let alone which year it was.

She approached the fireplace and bent down to look up the black tunnel of the chimney…

*

There is a brief fraction of time when life passes before the eyes of one destined for death. Scientists believe it is the body's defence system, the brain flashing out a strobing one last fighting hurrah, before curtains.

The three Greene girls saw the sudden horror in their mom's face — or what was once their mom's face — as she looked upwards at whatever was looking down at her. She just had time to scream before being pulled upward, kicking and flailing. It was as if Molly Greene had realised, all too late, she'd just become first prize.

*

As she was dragged up through the chimney pipe, with the smell of death and old soot clogging her nostrils, Molly realised her life had been an illusion since she lost her boy. She'd been living a lie, lying to herself and everyone else. This was payback and if she had to be a mother to a demon child in purgatory, then so be it. In this otherworldly horror, Molly somehow felt at home here in this musky miasma. She was strangely at ease as the third presence in this house, a male of enormous and frightening stature, yanked her up through the chimney by her shoulders.

*

The girls, muted into shock, listened to their mom's screams go up inside the chimney flue. One of

441

her shoes fell into the fireplace, followed by the other.

Then, almost as if they were seeing things, a spark fizzed and crackled before a silent tendril of smoke rose from the floor of the fireplace next to Molly's shoes. Before anybody knew what was happening, that single curling smoke tendril became a bubbling, winding mass of thick, ropey white smoke, billowing out into the living room and filling every nook and cranny of the farmhouse, consuming it as it went. The Greene girls scattered, blindly grappling for anything that seemed familiar, their hair-raising screams the only way they could find each other through the smoke without a fire. They reunited and dropped to the floor where they huddled close while white plumes engulfed them like the force of a fire extinguisher with a deafening whoosh!

It was Cora who heard the sirens first. Then they all saw the wondrous swirl of blue lights coming through the fog of smoke, filtering in from the front yard.

'Girls? Girls!' came Janice's voice. 'Are you in there?'

The End

PS…

If you enjoyed this novel, I'd appreciate it if you could take a minute of your time to leave a rating/review on Amazon/Goodreads or anywhere you think matters. This will help me greatly and encourage others to take a chance on a nobody like me ;)

Regards, Jon.

Keep up to date with Jonathan Dunne at his author page at Goodreads http://bit.ly/2Om32xO

Hi, I'm Jonathan - Jon to you. Once from the leafy greens of Limerick, Ireland, I now live in the medieval city of Toledo, Spain, a town steeped in legends and ghost stories. I normally can be found at the local cemetery. But for god's sake, don't sneak up on me, as I'm of a nervous disposition. I have a BA in Literature. I'm a member of the Horror Writer's Association (HWA). I am the author of horror novels *The Squatter* and *Billy's Experiment*. New horrors *Crazy Daisy* and *Hotel Miramar* coming 2023!

Printed in Great Britain
by Amazon

20155728R00257